Kidnapped by the Pirate

Also by Keira Andrews

Contemporary

Honeymoon for One
Beyond the Sea
Ends of the Earth
Arctic Fire
The Chimera Affair

Holiday

The Christmas Deal
The Christmas Leap
The Christmas Veto
Only One Bed
Merry Cherry Christmas
Santa Daddy
In Case of Emergency
Eight Nights in December
If Only in My Dreams
Where the Lovelight Gleams
Gay Romance Holiday Collection
Lumberjack Under the Tree (free read!)

Sports

Kiss and Cry
Reading the Signs
Cold War
The Next Competitor
Love Match
Synchronicity (free read!)

Gay Amish Romance Series

A Forbidden Rumspringa

A Clean Break
A Way Home
A Very English Christmas

Valor Duology

Valor on the Move
Test of Valor
Complete Valor Duology

Lifeguards of Barking Beach

Flash Rip
Swept Away (free read!)

Historical

Kidnapped by the Pirate
Semper Fi
The Station
Voyageurs (free read!)

Paranormal

Kick at the Darkness Trilogy

Kick at the Darkness
Fight the Tide

Taste of Midnight (free read!)

Fantasy

Barbarian Duet

Wed to the Barbarian
The Barbarian's Vow

Kidnapped by the Pirate

by Keira Andrews

Author's Note

I'm so grateful to Alicia, Anara, Becky, Mary, Leta Blake, Davina Jamison, and Robert Winter for their help writing this novel. Many thanks as well to speech language pathologist Elizabeth J. for her invaluable assistance.

While I always strive for accuracy—historical and otherwise—in my books, sometimes creative license is employed. As I'm sure you know, Primrose Isle is entirely fictional.

Dedication

I grew up reading bodice-rippers in the '80s, and this book is my loving homage to those deliciously tropey tales of pirates, virgins, and swashbuckling on the high seas.

Chapter One

1710

IF PIRATES WERE to be the bloody, savage end of Nathaniel Bainbridge, he wished they'd get on with it.

The windswept deck was damp beneath his bare feet, prompting thoughts of the dewy grass of home. What he wouldn't give for the freedom to run across the fields of Hollington Estate, wind rushing in his ears over the steady thump of his heart, the world falling away in his wake.

Instead he was confined by an endless, restless sea taunting him with its wildness. In England, he'd heard countless tales of villainous pirates and their dastardly deeds. People spoke as if the ocean teemed with the brigands, but the voyage had been mile after mile of...*nothing*.

Nathaniel shook his head at his foolishness. Not that he actually wanted pirates to attack their ship and massacre them. If only he could *move*, he would keep boredom at bay.

He gripped the railing, longing for dirt beneath his nails, scratches on his palms from tree bark as he climbed and explored, wonderfully aching muscles from hours in the lake. If he could only run a simple mile. Hardly any distance at all, but trapped on the ship, that much clear land would be a marvel.

He wiped sea spray from his eyes. If only the ability to run and jump and swim was worth anything at all in his world instead of being childish folly he was supposed to have outgrown. Men did not climb trees or swim for hours, and certainly they didn't *run* for the sheer pleasure of it the way he had at Hollington.

Of course, the estate wasn't theirs anymore, sold off to pay debts, so even if he made his way back to Kent one day, he would never return to those rolling hills. Its verdant trees and round, tranquil lake would now be home to another family.

No, for the foreseeable future, home would be Primrose Isle, a new colony his father desperately wanted to see flourish. Walter Bainbridge had found his fortunes in England not the least bit fortunate, and as a governor in the New World had the thing he loved most dearly: power.

Nathaniel's future bride waited there. Elizabeth Davenport stood to inherit quite a fortune, and for the colony—and Walter—to thrive, alliances had to be made. So Nathaniel would do the only useful thing he could and marry.

He brushed a fresh spray of briny seawater from his face as he stared out at the endless night, keeping a firm hold on the rail. His untucked shirt flapped in the breeze, the lower fastenings on his breeches unbuckled under his knees.

In the dark, there was no one to comment on his state of undress, and he supposed the crew didn't care a whit anyway. His trimmed hair curled at the ends in the dampness, and he tucked a lock behind his ear. It had been his little act of rebellion to cut it much shorter than most gentlemen. He certainly wouldn't be wearing dreaded wigs, either, if he could help it.

Clouds conspired to hide the stars and razor-thin crescent of moon. He shivered in the late September night's chill; he really should have worn his hated shoes and jacket.

At least the wind was no longer the bitter cold of the mid-Atlantic as they neared the West Indies. He shifted back and forth on his feet, lifting them like a racehorse stamping at the starting line.

The *Proud William* was fairly large, a merchant ship carrying a cargo of salt fish and forged metal tools to the colonies. But when he'd attempted even a light trot around the main deck, the crew had reacted with consternation at best, hostility at worst.

Running was his very favorite activity and the thing he excelled at most in life—much to his father's disgust. Swimming in the lake in summertime, cutting through the placid water with sure, even strokes, was a joy as well.

To be surrounded now by endless water but unable to dive in and soothe his cramped muscles was the worst torture. He'd asked the captain if he could at least climb the mast or sail rigging and had been flatly refused.

So he stood by the starboard rail and sometimes paced, careful to stay out of the crew's way. At least he had been told their progress was swift, and that after a month's voyage—thirty-one days and some thirteen hours since they left England, to be exact—they would reach the island in a fortnight if the wind held.

He was informed that some ships took several months to reach the colonies. Ships could leave London the same day and arrive weeks or more apart. Such was the way of the sea.

Staring out at the nothingness, he stopped his restless shifting and squinted. The weak sliver of moon had valiantly escaped the clouds for a moment, and Nathaniel thought he spotted a strange kind of movement. The night took on shape before becoming uniform once more.

Perhaps it had been a great ocean creature surfacing—a whale or giant squid, or some kind of mysterious monster.

He chuckled. Earlier that evening, Susanna had read aloud fables from one of the old leather-bound tomes they'd brought from home, and his imagination was clearly running wild.

She'd always been the far more indulgent of his two older sisters, and he knew she'd packed books he'd favor, although she certainly had a taste for adventurous tales rather than the sentimental stories ladies were supposed to read. They'd both enjoyed the diary of a naval captain who'd served on several ships of the line and described life aboard in vivid detail.

Although the cabin Nathaniel and Susanna shared was tiny, at least they had privacy. He really should rejoin her in their cabin to sleep and end another interminable day, but the walls closed in on him, and it felt like a prison. Susanna's thunderous snores didn't help matters, but he couldn't begrudge her anything.

For the hundredth time, he wondered what his life on Primrose Isle would be like. The colony was only a few years old, and there had been whispers of struggles with agriculture and trade, rumors of corruption and settlers packing up already.

He'd be forced to work for his father or at some other respectable job procured for him, like Susanna's husband, Bart. Handsome Bart was thirty and penniless, but of good breeding and an agreeable disposition. He and Susanna had insisted on each other, waiting several years until both their fathers gave in and agreed to the match.

Bart seemed happy enough to do Father's bidding, including leaving early for Primrose Isle some months ago, not knowing at the time Susanna was with child. When Walter Bainbridge made a demand, it was met. Sometimes Nathaniel marveled that a man he had rarely seen since childhood could loom so large.

Susanna and Bart had hated to be parted, but she was needed to oversee the packing up of the estate and auction of the more valuable items. Certainly it couldn't have been left to Nathaniel, who wouldn't have known where to begin given he'd spent as much time outside away from the ornate house as he could.

Nathaniel had considered refusing when he and Susanna were summoned. But what would he do? Where would he live? His marriage to Elizabeth had been agreed upon by their fathers, and should he fail in his duty, Walter would disown him. He'd have nothing, not even a roof over his head.

Bile rose in his throat. No, that would not do. So onward to Primrose Isle he went, to marry as his father saw fit. All he knew of Elizabeth Davenport was that she'd lived with her wealthy family for some years in Jamaica before her father joined forces with Walter to establish a shipping company on Primrose.

Well, he also knew her writing was unfailingly neat, and from Susanna's recounting of the letter, that Elizabeth enjoyed needlework and greatly looked forward to sharing her life with him.

He'd received her letter just before leaving England and had burned it in the grate in his room. At least the voyage was a worthy excuse for not responding. And as much as he'd wished to stay in England, he couldn't allow dear Susanna to sail the perilous Atlantic alone.

Although with how smooth their journey had been, completely lacking in beasts of the deep or even a gale of note, he apparently hadn't needed to fret. Still, it was done.

He'd accepted years ago that he was feeble-minded, and although he knew he should be grateful for the opportunity to hold a position of at least some stature on the new colony, he dreaded the notion of truly being under his father's thumb once more.

It had been blissful having his father overseas for years. He supposed he should feel remorse for such churlish thoughts, but there was so much else to consume his stores of guilt.

So much else indeed.

He turned away from the rail, resigning himself to another long night in the swaying hammock. Susanna was of course sleeping in the cot in the only cabin their father could afford now that he'd squandered so much money.

The cry from above pierced the night, and Nathaniel jumped a mile.

"Sails!"

In the flurry of activity and shouts, he pressed himself to the ship's side as the crew emerged from the hull like ants. Nathaniel squinted into the darkness, turning to and fro and seeing nothing.

Then he spotted it—the hulk of a ship emerging from the night, not a single light flickering upon it, drawn to The *Proud William* like a moth to flame. With a sickening twist of his stomach, he realized he had indeed spotted a monster, and it was upon them.

He raced down to the cabin, bursting inside. Chestnut curls unpinned and tumbling over her shoulders, Susanna bolted up on the cot, her book thudding to the floor. One hand pressed to her round belly, she cried out, "What is it?"

"I think it's pirates." He could hardly believe the words as he uttered them. Had he wished them into existence by grumbling over boredom? Oh, what a fool he was.

The blood drained from Susanna's sweet, round face. "Pirates?"

"I don't know what else it could be." He threw open a trunk and dug for his sheathed dagger, cursing himself for not raising the alarm sooner. His mind raced, thoughts jumbled as he grasped the hilt of the weapon and tossed the leather scabbard aside.

The thunder of the crew's footsteps shook the ceiling, dust motes shaking loose and shouts filling the air. Susanna looked down at her nightgown, despairing.

"There's no time for petticoats or any of that nonsense." She threw her flowing green gown over her head, her voice muffled by it. "My God, it really is pirates, isn't it? Oh, I think I'm stuck."

Nathaniel helped tug the material down over her swollen belly. She emerged from the folds of soft fabric and peered up at the ceiling, as if she could see through the hull. Footsteps scuffled and thumps reverberated, tense voices shouting commands too distant to make out clearly.

Susanna whispered, "No gunshots. Must be too many. The crew isn't fighting them. Help me pin this shut." She had stopped wearing her corset, adopting what was apparently a new French style while she was with child.

After he'd pinned the material enough that the robe-like gown would stay put, drawing a prick of blood from his fingertip in his haste, Nathaniel yanked on his stockings and refastened his breeches below his knees before jamming his feet into his buckled shoes. He wouldn't face these brigands in a state of undress.

He tucked the dagger into the back of his trousers and whipped on his sleeveless waistcoat, fingers clumsy on the buttons. But there was no time for his cravat or jacket. Raised voices already echoed down the corridor. He spun about, belatedly hoping to find something to bar the door.

Susanna had apparently had the same thought. "The trunks aren't heavy enough. Besides, it will only anger them. It's no use."

"Get behind me." He urged her to the back of the cabin, which was barely wider than the breadth of one's outstretched arms.

"Be sure to mind your tongue," she said. "You know how thoughts can sometimes go right from your head and out your mouth without pausing for assessment."

He huffed. "What exactly do you think I'm going to say to *pirates?*"

"Shh!" She slapped his shoulder. They waited, listening.

More pounding footsteps, and shouts that possessed an undeniably feral quality. The hair on Nathaniel's body stood on end, his mouth going dry. Perhaps the pirates would pass them by. Perhaps they'd plunder the cargo and be done with it. Perhaps—

The door burst open, almost flying off its hinges, and Nathaniel barely held in his yelp. His heart drummed so loudly he was certain the two invaders could hear. One of them brushed matted hair from his eyes. They both wore ripped and stained trousers as baggy as their shirts, and their boots were worn out.

The long-haired man's beady gaze raked them up and down,

and he asked his squat companion, "You ever fuck a bitch with pup?"

Nathaniel's stomach swooped. *How do they know?* Susanna was hidden behind him. He lifted his chin, forcing strength to his words. "You shan't lay so much as one filthy finger on my sister."

Ignoring him, the squat man leered, baring snaggled, yellow teeth. He answered his friend's question. "Good and juicy, I tell you."

Behind him, Susanna dug her fingers into Nathaniel's shoulder. Heart in his throat, he yanked the dagger from the waist of his breeches, brandishing it toward the pirates. "Stay back!"

The two blinked at Nathaniel, then each other, before bursting into raucous laughter. The long-haired man said, "Oh no, we're done for, Deeks!"

Heavy footfalls sounded in the corridor, brazen and commanding. Spines snapping straight, the pirates stepped aside as a man filled the doorway, shoulders almost brushing the frame. He was tall enough to duck slightly as he entered, and his sharp gaze swept the cabin, which had never seemed quite so small.

He wore black from head to gold-tipped toes—open-collared shirt, trousers tucked into knee-high boots, and a long leather coat that flared out behind him. A pistol was tucked into his wide belt, and a cutlass winked from his hip. Gold gleamed on the belt buckle, matching the small square earring in his left ear, rings on his fingers, and the tips of those black boots.

The ends of a red sash dangled over his hip, the only splash of color aside from the gold. He had to be twice Nathaniel's age, his face weather-worn, a scar jagging across his left temple. His dark hair was cut fairly close to his head, a surprise since Nathaniel had expected all pirates to have long, unruly hair like the animals they were.

His trimmed beard shadowed his strong jaw. In the low light, the color of his narrowed eyes was impossible to ascertain, but

Nathaniel imagined they must be as black as the pirate's soul.

He might have been the very devil himself.

Nathaniel's palm sweated around the handle of the dagger, and he hated the tremors in his outstretched arm. His throat was painfully dry, and he croaked, "We—we don't have anything of value. No gold or jewels worth your effort."

Susanna added, "Even my wedding ring is plated."

Tully, one of the *Proud William*'s young crew, had entered the cabin. The man—the pirate captain, undoubtedly—glanced to him. Tully nodded. "'Tis true. Only clothin' and trinkets in their trunks." He sniffed dismissively, tossing his reddish hair. "Nothin' hidden anywhere in here we could find since we left London."

Nathaniel had thought better of the crew, but saw now how naïve he'd been. It must have been Tully who had informed the pirates that Susanna was with child. "What a coward you are, Tully."

He snorted. "As soon as I got a good look at the flag, I knew we were done for. Everyone knows the Sea Hawk will gut you from stem to stern once you're in his talons. I ain't dying for cargo I don't give a fuck about and a captain who treats us like garbage."

"Your destination is Primrose Isle?" The pirate—this Sea Hawk—demanded, his tone low and calm.

"Yes," Nathaniel answered. "It's a new colony."

Tully nodded. "Her husband's there. We're to drop them off with their father. The old man's the guvnor or some such thing."

At this, the Sea Hawk seemed to jolt, but a moment later the ripple had vanished and he was still again, fearsome and dispassionate. Nathaniel thought he must have imagined the hiccup.

Yet a gleam entered the captain's devilish eyes, and dread slithered through Nathaniel. The Sea Hawk loomed nearer and demanded, in the same deliberate but undeniable manner, "Your name, boy."

Heart hammering, all he could manage was, "Uh…"

"This one's called Bainbridge," Tully offered.

"Bainbridge," the captain repeated, barely a whisper now. "As in Walter Bainbridge?"

Fingers going numb around the dagger, Nathaniel nodded. He'd have bruises where Susanna clung to him, her sharp exhalations ghosting over the nape of his neck. There was no sense denying it. "Our father."

"You're the son Walter Bainbridge killed his wife to achieve?" The captain's focus sent chills down Nathaniel's spine.

He couldn't hide his wince, and had to nod. His mother had never even held him before the rest of her lifeblood drained away. Susanna had been but six, spying through the keyhole, and she'd confessed it all after Nathaniel's endless badgering when he was a lad.

Strange how he could experience the aching, hollow absence of a touch he'd never had, even after eighteen years.

The captain's eyes glinted. Good God, the man was enormous. Nathaniel was tall enough, five feet and seven inches or so, but this monster towered well over six feet. It was all Nathaniel could do to hold his ground and not stagger back against Susanna. The tip of his blade quivered mere inches from the villain's black heart.

The Sea Hawk gazed down at them as though they were prey he was most eager to consume. "Your father is a liar. Corrupt. An evildoer in silk stockings and a curled wig."

Nathaniel swallowed hard, hand shaking. Could he lunge and push the dagger into this vile man's heart? Not that he had much love for his father, but who was a *pirate* to talk of evildoers?

The Sea Hawk's eyes glowed with hatred. "Your father cheated me. He was tasked with justice, with fairness. Instead he conspired to steal from me. He branded me a pirate when I was a privateer."

"Aren't they the same thing?" Nathaniel blurted. As the Sea Hawk's nostrils flared, Susanna dug her nails into Nathaniel's shoulder.

"No, they fucking are not," the pirate gritted out. "Privateers are licensed. Legal. Privateers follow rules. Laws. Just as your father was supposed to as a judge in the Court of Admiralty in Jamaica. Your father tried to strip me and my men of everything we'd worked and suffered for. We escaped him, but in the years that have followed, he has never paid the price."

Dread consumed Nathaniel. His father's greed and avarice would once again bring suffering. If not for Walter's mounting debts, Nathaniel and Susanna would still be safe at home, waiting until she had her babe before making the journey. Hollington wouldn't have had to be sold at all, and now they faced God knew what at the mercy of pirates.

Oh Lord. Please spare Susanna and her child!

Bile rose in his throat at the thought of any harm coming to his sister, terror clammy on his skin. Sweat slipped down Nathaniel's spine. "I..." He racked his brain for something—anything—to say, some means of escape. His dagger shook, and he licked his dry lips. "I'm sorry." He had to *fix* this.

A slow, ghastly smile curled the devil's lips. "You will be."

Chapter Two

HAWK IGNORED THE boy's trembling dagger, nodding to his men. "Relay these orders to Mr. Snell: Confiscate any cargo worth taking. Leave the ship and crew unharmed and with enough food and water to survive. The lady shall continue to Primrose Isle. Unmolested."

As the men scurried out, followed by the redheaded sailor who had happily given up all the *Proud William*'s secrets, he gazed down at Walter Bainbridge's precious son. "Your journey will be delayed."

"De—delayed?" Bainbridge asked. He was smooth-faced and slim, long-legged with ordinary brown eyes. His short, light-brown hair curled, damp with sweat. He'd missed a button on his dark waistcoat, and it hung askew above his white shirt and tan breeches.

His black, square-toed shoes were surprisingly scuffed, white stockings bunched at one ankle. Red splotches flushed his pale cheeks. He had surely been untroubled by hard work a day in his life.

Utterly unremarkable aside from his parentage.

"You're coming with us."

The woman cried out. Hawk almost laughed as Bainbridge screwed up his courage and lunged. With a simple twist and squeeze, Hawk liberated him of the dagger, which was constructed of fine steel in a simple wooden handle.

"Don't hurt yourself, boy. Your father won't pay for a carcass." He spied the dagger's sheath on the floor and held out an imperious hand for it. Bainbridge bent and reluctantly handed it to him. Hawk tucked the weapon into his belt.

"Pay?" Bainbridge's daughter sputtered. "But he hardly has any money!"

Hawk assessed her. Modestly expensive gown, yet paste jewels. He took a step forward, and they jerked back as one. He asked, "And how did that come to pass?" He likely knew most of the story, but perhaps Bainbridge's children could impart new information.

She inched around to stand by her brother's side, clutching his hand. "The family fortune went to his elder brother. He's squandered everything else on his dream for Primrose Isle. He managed to win the governorship, but if not for the Crown's money to establish the new colony, he barely has a thing."

Bloody son of a bitch couldn't even spend my prize wisely after he stole it. The Spanish galleon had been laden with spices, gold, and tons of uncoined silver. Hawk still cringed when he remembered how proud he'd been to appear at the Court of Admiralty with his hard-won plunder those years ago. Ready to give England her share in accordance with regulations, doing his part in the war with Spain. What a fool he'd been.

He pretended to mull it over. "In that case, I'll offer him the fairness he denied me."

The siblings exhaled, shoulders slumping in relief. The girl said, "Thank you, sir. Whatever it was our father did, I swear—"

"I'll give him a month to gather the funds before our arrival. A hundred thousand pounds."

As one, their jaws dropped. The boy sputtered. "It's too much!"

Possibly, but an arrogant man who valued his heir would find a way. Bainbridge's pride would demand it. Besides, Hawk hadn't waited years for revenge to go easy on the swine now.

Ignoring their dismay, he announced, "Around about the night of the next dark moon, we will arrive at Primrose Isle and announce ourselves. Your father will personally row out a skiff into the harbor. Alone. He will meet my ship. I will exchange his son for the ransom. Simple."

Bainbridge's children locked gazes, hopelessness passing between them, tears slipping down the girl's cheeks. Hawk understood their dread. Their terror. Remembering his own after being unfairly sentenced by their father, he reveled in their misery.

She cried, "Sir, have pity! My poor brother has committed no sin."

"Pity? Your father created me: the Sea Hawk. And I have become the monster he bore and so very much more." Hawk added, "And your brother will only be the first to suffer if Bainbridge doesn't comply. Tell your father that his precious Primrose Isle will bleed and burn unless he meets my demands."

She opened her mouth to speak again, but Hawk tired of her calls for mercy and cut her off with, "No treachery, and your brother lives. But if Bainbridge plots against me..." He kept his voice low. A calm utterance was sometimes more menacing than a shout. He peered intently at the son, who had wrapped an arm around his sister's shaking shoulders.

"If your father defies me, this boy dies. Painfully. *Slowly.* I will gut him like a fish, slice him into pieces, and deliver them to your father one by one."

He had been so very patient in his revenge, and this was his moment. He grasped hold of it with both hands, giving no quarter.

She gasped, slapping a hand over her mouth. Bainbridge the younger's chest rose and fell rapidly, but he kept his chin up.

His sister's eyes overflowed with more tears. "Please, I beg you.

Let my brother come with me. He's to be married! We're starting a new life! He's never harmed another creature. He's kind and good."

Hawk sighed to himself. *Enough of this.* He curled his tongue into his cheek and gave her a leering appraisal. "If you prefer to take your brother's place—"

"No!" the boy shouted. Bainbridge's eyes burned with a fierceness he had lacked before now. "I'll do whatever you ask. Just don't harm my sister."

Hawk's lips curled up. If he were a tender-hearted type, he'd almost be touched. As it was, well…

Breathing hard, Bainbridge yanked his sister into a hug. "I'll be all right. I love you, Susie."

She clung to him. "Don't go. Don't let him take you."

Wishing he could roll his eyes, Hawk hauled Bainbridge from the cabin, dragging him out by the scruff of his neck. He didn't fight, apparently surrendering to his fate for his sister's sake, or perhaps having used up his shred of bravery.

The girl would have been no use—if Hawk recalled correctly, Walter Bainbridge had two daughters. But, rumor was, it had been a son to carry on his name that he'd obsessed over and valued above the health of his own wife. And now here was that very son, in Hawk's grasp.

Why the Fates had blessed this night so roundly, he'd never know, but he wouldn't question it. Not every wind blew such good luck into his sails. Here was his opportunity for revenge at last.

Would the snake be able to raise the money? Perhaps. Most likely, given his connections. But at the very least, Hawk held Bainbridge's precious legacy in his grip. Oh, what he would give to see the old man's face when he heard the news.

Hawk laughed out loud, his delight echoing off the water all around. He shoved the boy toward Snell at the rail. "Behold our prize, Mr. Quartermaster. Walter Bainbridge's precious son."

Snell was a hair taller than Bainbridge and quite a bit thicker, solid muscle beneath the extra layers that had come with age as he passed fifty years. His silver-wreathed fingers gripped Bainbridge's arm ruthlessly.

Dark eyes meeting Hawk's beneath his thinning mess of fair hair, Snell laughed, wide-mouthed, earrings glinting in the torchlight. Snell's black shirt gaped at the neck, revealing an anchor tattoo just below his throat. He had five or six tattoos hammered into his flesh. Hawk was content with one.

After confirming his orders with Snell, Hawk passed on the ransom demand to the merchant captain, a salty old seaman who merely shrugged and nodded, the boy's life clearly of no concern. Bainbridge watched the exchange with obvious dismay.

For his part, Snell eyed young Bainbridge with nothing more than a raised brow on his craggy face. "Come on, then. Over you go."

The boy blinked at the long wooden plank connecting the merchant ship to *The Damned Manta*. He glanced over his shoulder toward the stairs belowdecks, where his sister's sobs echoed. His body flexed, as though to run, or take flight.

"Now, now, none of that," Hawk said, smirking. "Where would you even escape to?" A darkness in him fed on the Bainbridge boy's terror. "Unless you plan to be shark food, there's only one place for you to go now."

He turned his gaze to the shadowy hulk of his ship, its sleek sails temporarily furled, the crew following his orders to the letter. It had been his home for years, yet he grew restless.

This was it. This was bloody well it.

Revenge would finally be his. Up until tonight, Hawk's luck had been running out. He'd felt it. Either he'd meet his fate at the bottom of the sea, run through on a blade, or at the end of a hangman's noose. Now, here the Bainbridge boy stood, like a living, breathing chance at regaining at least some of what he'd lost.

Perhaps even a chance at a new life. It was foolishness, but... *Maybe.*

"Up you get." Snell pushed the prisoner to the plank. "Captain Hawk isn't a patient man, I warn you. Nor am I."

Breathing hard, Bainbridge climbed up, legs visibly trembling. He looked over at the *Manta*, then back at Hawk.

Then down at the waves.

"Don't even think about some noble sacrifice," Hawk snarled, vaulting up behind him. "Or we'll take your sister after all. She won't be so pretty when we're done with her." He grabbed the boy by the nape again. "Move."

After his boots hit the familiar deck, he marched the prisoner to the stern and stood surveying the crew, still holding Bainbridge fast. When the plank was raised and hooks released from the *Proud William*, Hawk shouted orders to set sail. In the gray hint of dawn, they caught the wind.

Even weighted with the pilfered cargo, *The Damned Manta* was the faster ship. Hawk remained astern regardless, watching to be sure the merchant vessel didn't make any attempt at following. Stranger things had happened.

Bainbridge shivered beside him, fists clenched and lips pressed tight, watching the *Proud William* grow smaller in their wake.

Some pirates favored warships, but Hawk preferred the agility of a sloop, its forty-six men a lean crew compared to some ships. Fewer men to share prizes with. Fewer men to cause trouble.

Hawk's mind whirled. For most of his years, he'd dreamed of a life on the waves, but he'd never wanted piracy. Walter Bainbridge had given him no choice. There was no possibility of restoring his tarnished honor, but with his share of the ransom, perhaps he could escape the brutality.

Maybe he could find...somewhere. A quiet stretch of island,

beyond England's reach. A place to fish and raise a few animals, enough to live comfortably. To know peace on his own terms. He'd be alone, but he was long accustomed to that.

A distant pang twinged, dull after all this time. Years ago, he'd imagined finding a mate, a man to share his life with. Even to love. Such absurdity.

Unbidden, a memory of blond hair and impish blue eyes flared before returning to the dark morass of the past. He'd had love for a brief moment before it was ripped away. Ah, the folly of youth.

Yet here I am dreaming of a peaceful life. Folly indeed.

Hawk centered his mind on the task at hand, peering into the distance. They were well away, so he hauled the boy belowdecks to his cabin, ignoring his yelp.

There was just enough murky light through the stern windows to see without bothering with the tinderbox. His desk sat at the rear, bed built into the wall opposite it, on the other side of the cabin's open space. In that space, Hawk crossed his arms and eyed his captive up and down. "Boy—"

"I'm eighteen years." Bainbridge puffed up his narrow chest. "I'm a man."

Hawk had to laugh, a sharp exhalation. "Are you now?" At one and forty, Hawk could barely remember being so damned young. "Listen, *boy*. Here's how it will be."

"My name is—"

"Unimportant," Hawk barked. He'd surely heard the name when he'd looked into Bainbridge's history, but it didn't matter now. In fact, it was easier this way. "You are merely cargo. My treasure, my prize, my plum. That is all you are until your father pays what I'm owed. I would put you in the hold, but the men would be tempted to have at you, and your father wouldn't want what was left. Do you understand... Plum?" It was all the name the prisoner needed aside from his accursed surname.

Not waiting for an answer, Hawk opened a trunk by the starboard hull and dug out a scratchy wool blanket he rarely used, tossing it. It hit Bainbridge in the chest and pooled at his feet. Hawk nodded to the corner by the windows. "Sleep there."

Bainbridge snatched the blanket from the floor and straightened unsteadily.

"For the next month while your father gathers funds, you will not be leaving this cabin, so food and water will be brought to you. You'll have use of a bucket that will be emptied regularly so your filth doesn't stink up my cabin. Don't speak to any of the crew. Don't speak to me, unless spoken to. Nod if you understand."

"Not leaving this cabin?" Plum blurted, horror written plain on his boyish face.

"Clearly you do *not* understand." Hawk took a stride forward, gratified when the boy jerked back.

"It's… It's just—please. I won't be any trouble." His breath came quickly, chest heaving. "Can't I go up to the deck at times? To stretch my legs?"

"Be grateful I'm not chaining you to the bed." Hawk raked his gaze down and back up his prisoner, instilling fear with a leering snarl. "Naked."

Plum's light-brown eyes widened, darting to the mattress. Hawk turned on his heel and fetched the key from his desk. Now that they'd settled that, he'd—

"I could work! Up on deck. Help the crew with…whatever it is they do."

Disbelieving, Hawk straightened to his full height and whirled, making sure—yes, his coat flared behind him. He hadn't garnered the Sea Hawk's fearsome reputation in only four years without some dramatics. Yet incredibly, Bainbridge *kept talking*.

"I'd be happy to work." His eyes implored, fingers twisting in the blanket. "I'd do anything you say."

Clearly fucking not, as the command to shut his damn mouth had already been tossed aside. Hawk sneered. "Work? *You?* Tell me, have you worked a single day in your delicate little life?"

Cheeks red, the boy stared at his scuffed shoes in answer.

"You will stay in this cabin, and you will only speak when spoken to. But I'm not wholly cruel." He waved his arm magnanimously at the bookshelf. "Read all you like."

Bainbridge looked at the volumes with a strange sort of despair bordering on disdain, his shoulders slumping even lower.

Fury sparked, and iron dug into his palm as Hawk gripped the key. "Is my library not to your liking, *my lord?*"

"No, no. I'm sure it's excellent," Plum answered meekly, backing up a step.

"Most men on this ship can't even sign their names. It took me years to learn. Years of bettering myself word by word. You're a privileged little piece of shit, and you will sit down, shut up, and pray your snake of a father pays the money he owes. Or you'll be the one who pays. You and your sister. Her babe."

In truth, Hawk would never harm an innocent woman or child—or permit his crew to do so—but Bainbridge didn't have to know that. "Am I understood? *Plum?*"

Head down, he whispered, "Yes."

Hawk crossed to the door in two long strides. He slammed it behind him, put the key in the lock, and—

Nothing.

Iron grated as the stubborn lock refused to turn. Hawk jiggled it for a few moments. Of all the times for the lock to seize up, it had to be when he was terrifying a prisoner. *For fuck's sake.* Jaw clenched, he threw open the door again. Plum still stood where he'd left him, clutching the blanket.

Tugging his arm roughly, Hawk dragged him out of the cabin, hollering, "Mr. Cooper! Fix the lock. You have ten minutes." He smiled humorlessly at Bainbridge. "It seems you have a momentary reprieve. It will be the last."

Chapter Three

NONE TOO GENTLY, Captain Hawk tugged him along to the ladder to the main deck. Nathaniel glimpsed the crew's quarters at the bow of the ship, a cramped space, dark and stinking of sweat and mildew and heaven knew what else.

A cook was toiling over a stove, men stowing their hammocks as the sun rose and pulling out long tables for eating. Then Nathaniel was roughly pushed up the ladder.

On deck, he inhaled the cool, fresh air gratefully, the sun blinding where it peeked just over the horizon. He soaked in all the sights and smells around him, the threat of a month alone in the pirate captain's cabin filling him with dread that threatened to undo him.

The confinement of a ship was awful enough. To be trapped in that one room? His stomach curdled.

He gazed about, heart lurching as he spotted sails in the distance. Was it the *Proud William*? Must have been, since no one paid it any mind. Nathaniel watched glumly as it shrank to a speck.

But Susanna was safe, and that was what mattered. He hated that she would be alone for the rest of her journey, especially in her delicate state. Guilt pricked, even though he knew there was not a thing he could do.

He glared at the captain, who at least had released Nathaniel from his vile grasp. The rising sun showed the pirate's eyes to be a surprisingly vibrant blue tinged with gray. The little square gold earring gleamed.

The quartermaster, a Mr. Snell according to the captain's gruff greeting, approached. "Captain, the men want to eat some of the salt fish we took. Shall it be given to Cook?"

"Aye."

Nathaniel's stomach grumbled at the thought of food, but he'd starve before asking Captain Hawk—no, simply *Hawk*, because he didn't deserve any title of prestige or honor. As Hawk and Mr. Snell walked some feet away, conferring in tones so low he couldn't overhear, Nathaniel examined his prison.

The Damned Manta was a single-masted sloop that had likely once been a merchant vessel. Thick coils of rope crowded the ship. If there had originally been an aft deck near the stern, Nathaniel suspected it had been removed to add more guns. He counted fourteen around the top deck, which was about sixty feet from bow to stern and flat the whole way across.

From a distance, the sloop would appear lower in the water. It would also make for good running, and Nathaniel's feet itched to race from bow to stern, around the ship's massive wheel, and back again.

He wasn't sure how many pirates toiled aboard, but guessed forty-five or fifty men. They seemed to be a piecemeal lot, men of all colors, ages, and sizes, some with long hair, some short; some with cleaner faces and others with ratty beards.

Many wore loose pants, but some were form-fitting. Tattoos and piercings decorated bare skin. One man in a leather vest had dark ink so thick on his arms that Nathaniel at first thought he was wearing a shirt.

High above, a lookout perched on the yard, holding onto the mast. The pirate black still fluttered against the sky, this flag emblazoned with a white bird of prey, wings spread wide, beak cruel. A sea hawk, he presumed.

As he watched, men yanked on the ropes to lower the flag, keeping it out of sight to lure in the ship's next victims. He lowered his gaze from the sails and rigging. Hawk and Snell now seemed to be talking about him, eyeing him in such a way that the hair on Nathaniel's arms stood on end.

Unable to bear their scrutiny, he turned to look out at the waves, skin crawling. Wind rushed in his ears, and he wasn't sure whether or not to be grateful he couldn't make out their words.

The truth was, he had a terrible suspicion Hawk was quite overestimating Nathaniel's worth to his father. It was accurate Walter had wanted a son with a fervor bordering on obsession, or so Nathaniel had always been told. Nathaniel's uncle—his father's elder brother—had not only inherited the family fortune, estate, and title of baronet, but had sired three strapping, intelligent sons.

Walter had resented them all bitterly, and had been determined to achieve a son of his own, an emblem of his manhood. Margaret, Nathaniel's mother, had first provided Walter with the Hollington estate. Then a daughter, Jane, who lived in Kent with her husband, a naval officer often at sea, and their four children.

Next came Susanna—another disappointment for Walter. So again and again he got Margaret with child, despite the physician's warnings that the first two had almost killed her.

Nathaniel wasn't sure how many babes had been lost before she'd managed to birth him. Walter had finally acquired his prize, and though he'd sincerely mourned his wife by all accounts, Nathaniel suspected Walter's greater sorrow was Nathaniel's utter failure to be the son he'd desired so fervently.

To say he had been a disappointment quite understated the matter. For a moment he allowed himself the childish yearning for the mother he'd never known. She'd given her life for his, and he was certain the trade had not been worthy. How he would have let her down too. A half-wit and a sinner.

"Time's up," Hawk announced, tearing him from his wayward thoughts. Then those blue eyes narrowed. "What do you look so guilty about?"

"N-nothing."

With one powerful stride, Hawk closed the distance between them, and the rail jammed into Nathaniel's back. Hawk leaned in, towering over him.

"Whatever heroic ideas you have in your head, get rid of them. If you attempt any kind of attack on me or my men, or you wish to fling yourself over the side in some misguided notion of noble sacrifice, we will hunt down that merchant ship and see your sister and her child suffer. Oh, how they will suffer. Do I make myself clear, or do you require specifics?"

Nathaniel shook his head, desperate to back away farther from Hawk's mocking sneer. He was caught painfully with no retreat at hand, the man's body an unmovable wall, his will impenetrable.

Hawk was right—to go overboard would be suicide, and Nathaniel didn't have a prayer of overpowering a single man on the ship, let alone fifty of them. He was trapped.

"Any other questions?"

"Who did you steal this ship from?" The words flitted through his mind and somehow rasped right out of his mouth. Nathaniel snapped his jaw shut, blood rushing in his ears.

Hawk straightened up as if offended. He growled, "This is *my* ship. I earned her fair and square in a wager. It was your father who tried to steal her from me."

"I don't understand. Why?"

He gritted out, "Not that it fucking matters what you understand, but after years of toil, I finally had my own ship. I considered carrying merchant cargo, but I wanted to do more for my country despite—"

Nathaniel waited a few moments, watching the way Hawk's jaw clenched. "Despite what?"

"Nothing," he spat. "I was bestowed my letter of marque, permitting me to raid enemy ships. I was a proud partner of the Crown, battling the Spanish grip on the West Indies. I followed the rules and shared my winnings. I was respectable. Legitimate."

"Then how did you fall so far as to become *this*?"

Hawk's large hand clamped around Nathaniel's throat, metal rings digging in painfully, cutting off his air. He leaned low again. "Keep a civil tongue in your head, boy, or I will cut it out and feed it to you. Yes?"

Nathaniel nodded desperately, horror clawing at him, lungs already burning. He stamped his feet, wanting to kick and free himself somehow. Hawk's grip loosened, but didn't release. At least it was enough that Nathaniel could breathe again. Barely.

Face hard, Hawk still leaned in close. "That day seven years ago at the Court of Admiralty, when I presented my Spanish galleon loaded with treasure, your father announced that the Spanish captain had claimed cruel treatment, in direct contravention to regulations. I knew it to be a lie since the man had stayed in my cabin, utterly unharmed. I saw to it that no prisoner was ever harmed on my ship."

"Perhaps the Spanish captain was the liar?" Nathaniel scraped the words out. Truthfully, it sounded exactly like something his father would do. Anything to further his own selfish desires.

"Of course the captain could not say, as he had suddenly died the night before in the court's custody. But my letter of marque was invalidated, and in a heartbeat, I was declared a pirate. My ship and men would be seized as well."

He tightened his fingers on Nathaniel's neck. "Your father and his cronies damned me and my crew to the gallows without a second thought. They took that galleon for themselves, sending little of the treasure to England's coffers from what I heard later. Your father is a greedy liar. You're probably just like him."

Nathaniel struggled for air, his hands coming up to grip

Hawk's wrist, skittering fear clawing. *Surely he won't kill me yet!*

Blessedly, Hawk loosened his fingers. The rail dug into Nathaniel's back, and he cursed his father.

Damn him and his insatiable greed.

Nathaniel had heard stories of the New World's rampant corruption, and a Spanish treasure ship would certainly have been a tempting prize. Once again, he loomed large over Nathaniel's life even in his absence.

Nathaniel gazed up at Hawk's grim expression and the bitter twist of his full lips. Walter could wait—he must deal with the villain who currently clutched him in his talons, the scent of sweat and seawater filling Nathaniel's nose.

Hawk continued, "Your father and his conspirators underestimated my men—Mr. Snell and many of this crew. They overpowered the force sent to arrest them and rescued me from my cell. We reclaimed *The Manta*, but that was a name for a lawful ship. Since we'd been branded pirates, I thought a change was in order. She's *The Damned Manta* now." He tightened his hold on Nathaniel's throat. "And I give no assurances on the well-being of prisoners."

With that, he pushed Nathaniel back belowdecks and toward his cabin, where a jittery crew member stood with a metal tool in hand. "Lock's fixed, Cap'n." He handed over the iron key.

Nathaniel found himself sprawled on his face as Hawk shoved him inside, narrowly missing the edge of the desk. He pushed up to sitting, hating how he cowered, yet tempted to crawl under the desk as Hawk towered over him. The thought of being choked again was unbearable.

The pirate sneered, then turned and stripped off his long coat, hanging it on a hook. His dark, open-necked shirt billowed slightly at the sleeves. As well as his sword and pistol, Nathaniel glimpsed the handles of two daggers tucked into Hawk's belt, one of them Nathaniel's own.

His head spun with the rush of shame. What a failure he was. He hadn't even managed to scratch the fiend with his blade before it was snatched away as if from a naughty child. What would Mr. Chisholm think?

That I'm a failure in everything, not only my studies.

He blinked as the door shut, the key scraped in the lock, and Hawk was gone without another word. Thank the Lord for small mercies. The less he had to suffer the brute's presence, the better.

Still on the floor, Nathaniel surveyed his cell. Sunlight warmed the air through the square windowpanes across the stern. On the port side, bookcases were built into the hull, thick books and rolled nautical charts tucked away neatly. He didn't bother going closer to see any of the titles.

To starboard, there were built-in drawers and a large chest on the floor from which Hawk had plucked the blanket. Nathaniel could hardly bear to touch it and kicked it into the corner.

He sat there and pulled his knees to his chest, thoughts tumbling through his mind willy-nilly. *Could* he have done more with the dagger? Mr. Chisholm's face filled his mind, and a pang of longing chimed through Nathaniel. His tutor had always seemed so capable, so strong and intelligent.

Nathaniel closed his eyes and conjured Mr. Chisholm's square jaw, his green eyes, and blond hair pulled back in a queue. The width of his shoulders and the way his coat had hugged his broad chest.

Mr. Chisholm winked. "It's a dangerous world over in the colonies. On land and at sea."

Nathaniel gingerly examined the gleaming metal in his hand, turning the smooth wood handle between his fingers. "You're giving me this?" His heart thumped almost painfully.

"I know most tutors would bestow a book or some such thing, but I fear it would be rather wasted on you. Don't you agree?"

He did indeed. Nathaniel longed to throw his arms around him and press his lips to the strip of bare skin above Mr. Chisholm's cravat. Since he was a boy he'd dreamt of it, knowing his tutor was a good, decent man, not a sinner like Nathaniel. Admiring him for it whilst despairing of it.

After he shook Mr. Chisholm's hand like a gentleman, he watched him, heart in throat, as Mr. Chisholm rode to the end of the drive, around the bend, and was gone forever.

Fighting a rush of tears, Nathaniel opened his eyes. He was still sitting on the floor of the pirate king's cabin. It was truly happening. He'd been kidnapped. It wasn't some nightmare that would soak his nightshirt with sweat but leave him unscathed.

His tutor had tried to shield him from the world as best he could, but there was no preparation for this. Nathaniel missed him desperately, aching for his reassuring presence, his kind, thoughtful answers and advice.

They hadn't the money to buy Nathaniel's way into Cambridge or Oxford, and Mr. Chisholm had warned Walter that he simply "did not possess the aptitude" for academics or law, his generous way of saying Nathaniel was too stupid.

Even the church wasn't an option, since reading was too important a requirement. Not that Nathaniel had a whit of desire to be a clergyman. He'd considered the navy, but Walter had insisted Nathaniel would marry Elizabeth first.

His studies had been a struggle for as long as he could remember. While Susanna was well pleased to while away hour upon hour reading, Nathaniel had always longed to be outside—to run and climb and swim. To *move*.

Words on a page didn't unfold and flow for him the way they seemed to for others. When Susanna read aloud to him, she didn't stumble or become confused. The words streamed out like water, with meaning and inflection. Nathaniel understood everything he heard, but when ink was put to paper, words confounded him.

When they were children, she'd helped him memorize words,

explaining what they meant and teaching him better than any tutor, even dear Mr. Chisholm. She'd be a wonderful mother, patient and kind, with a mischievous streak he hoped would remain all her days.

Once, as a lad, Nathaniel had confessed to his tutor that he envied the servants and their physical tasks. Mr. Chisholm had given him an uncharacteristically stern look and said, *"Spoken like a boy of privilege who will never serve."*

He was right, and shame still pricked Nathaniel that he was so discontent with his lot in life when many others had it very much the worse. He just wished he didn't feel so...*wrong*. In so many ways.

Mr. Chisholm had then softened and ruefully said the stork had delivered him to the wrong house before drilling him on his pathetic Latin conjugation again, a useless endeavor if ever there was one.

He laughed humorlessly to himself now. *The stork*. By the time Mr. Chisholm had determined Nathaniel old enough to be informed of the true manner of how babes were born, Susanna had already told him in great detail. He still wasn't sure how she'd learned, since prim Jane had never been one to gossip.

Susanna. Was she all right? He was powerless to comfort her, and despair welled up again, along with a wave of loneliness that would have laid him low if he hadn't already been huddled on the floor. He closed his eyes again, memories filling his mind.

When he'd questioned the stork theory, Susanna had whispered that they could watch when the stud horse came to impregnate their new mare, and that would explain everything.

On that rainy, gray day, they'd squirreled themselves away around the corner of the barn, flat on their tummies, coats soaked through, taking turns with Father's ornamental—yet entirely functional—spyglass. In the paddock, the mare had whinnied and run this way and that, before finally being cornered and mounted.

"That's what Father did to Mother?" Nathaniel had whispered in horror.

Susanna had huffed. "No, that's only how animals do it. Women lie on their backs. But otherwise it's the same."

Watching the stallion have its way, Nathaniel's blood had stirred in ways he couldn't comprehend. When he'd eventually begun waking with wet sheets, and his prick stiffened seemingly with a life of its own, he'd often take himself in hand, the image of that stallion filling his mind time and time again.

Coat black as pitch, hind legs thick and powerful as it mastered the quivering mare.

Its cock when it cornered her had hung impossibly huge and thick, and Nathaniel had imagined how that hot, iron flesh must feel inside. When he'd heard from one of his older cousins what sodomy meant, it had stirred something deep and unsettling in him.

While his friends from neighboring estates fantasized about lifting a lady's skirts or touching her creamy, delicate breasts, Nathaniel had remained unmoved by women's charms. Not only was he feeble-minded, he was a deviant to boot.

He wanted cock—hard and thick and unrelenting. At times just rain or mud and a brisk wind could conjure vivid memories of that stallion on that spring day. Living in England, it had rather been a hazard.

He cringed at the thought of dooming an unfortunate girl to a life with not only a dunce who could barely read two words before stumbling, but a sinner with unnatural defects. He knew he should strive to overcome his nature, but any attempts had left him despairing of the hopelessness.

Perhaps it would be better for poor Elizabeth Davenport and him alike if the scurrilous pirates were his doom. His sinful desires to rut with men, to be consumed by them, had only grown stronger the more he tried to quell them. There had been several times when he'd desperately wanted to confide in Susanna, but he had feared her rejection too much.

Nathaniel blinked at the cabin. He'd opened his eyes at some point, and he was still there. If only he could wake on the *Proud William* with Susanna's snores rumbling. His throat tightened painfully. God, would he ever see her again?

He couldn't just sit there. He had to try and do something. Anything! With one eye on the door, Nathaniel tiptoed, the floor creaking. He wagered the pirate wouldn't be back for some time.

He stopped to unbuckle his shoes and roll off his woolen stockings, which he tossed into the corner where he'd been told to stay. He spread his toes on the worn planks in relief.

Peeking in drawers, he found dark clothing—trousers and shirts. Some pale linen underthings. No stockings or waistcoats, for what use would a pirate have for those? Nathaniel couldn't deny a moment of jealousy at the freedom. He unbuttoned his own hated waistcoat and tossed it in the corner as well.

He wasn't even sure what he was looking for. Did he imagine he would stumble upon a weapon and then…what? Best not only the pirate captain, but the entire crew? Still, he searched.

The chest only held more linens and odds and ends. The dark desk dominated much of the cabin, facing the door, which was tucked off to the side near the port hull. The bed was built into the wall adjacent to the door.

Red velvet drapes were tied back with yellow tassels on either side of the bed, the colors faded from the sun. Judging by the dust clinging to the velvet, the drapes hadn't been closed or shaken out in some time.

The bed linens were wrinkled, though surprisingly white. Nathaniel glared at his scratchy, musty blanket. Listening for footsteps in the corridor, he examined the wide, dark-wood desk.

It had a tinge of red in the grain and was well constructed, wood extending on the front and sides all the way to the floor, making it a singularly solid piece of furniture.

The carved chair was of an almost-black wood. The high back was carved in the form of a winged bird—a hawk, naturally—looming over serpents. The neck of one was captured in the hawk's beak, talons tearing into the thing, its fangs useless as it struggled.

The chair certainly made a statement.

The seat cushion was again red velvet, well-used. The top of the desk was neat. A nautical chart had rolled in on itself, and the thick captain's log sat closed, ink and quill nearby. A curling silver candelabra with melted-down candles sat off to the side, a few drops of wax having dripped onto the desk and dried there.

There was no guest chair on the other side of the desk, perhaps indicating that the pirate didn't entertain much consultation. The desk of course contained drawers. Bottles of rum and port were stashed in a lower one.

As Nathaniel edged out the top drawer, he heard a thud and voices outside the door. Heart in his throat, fresh panic popping in his veins, he dove for the corner, curling against the wall atop the horrible blanket, eyes locked on the door, waiting for the key to scrape in the lock.

Yet it didn't, and as minutes passed, no one entered. *The Damned Manta* sailed on, hull creaking, rocking gently as it cut through the waves. Would the merchant ship reach Primrose Isle when its captain had predicted? And would his father care enough to attempt to save Nathaniel?

Would the last days of his life be spent locked away in this room, either alone or with a monster for company? He wasn't sure which was worse as he lifted his fingers to his tender throat, which throbbed after Hawk's rough treatment.

He imagined Susanna's slender hand tucked into the crook of his arm as they strolled the decks of the *Proud William* in the afternoon. Could hear the lilt of her sunny voice reading him story after story.

Useless tears pricking his eyes, he bowed his head and prayed she and her babe were unharmed on their journey to Primrose Isle. If only their father hadn't set them all on this course to the New World. Nathaniel pushed away his fear in favor of resentment.

Father had spent a ridiculous sum importing primroses and other flowers from England to the island. According to Susanna's husband, he'd been furious when they hadn't taken root, the tropical plants running roughshod over them, choking them with flowering vines and bright bursts of blooms.

The island had previously been uninhabited, and Nathaniel secretly hoped it would remain untamed for years to come. Yet he knew no matter how unyielding the vegetation, if England was determined to overrun it, she would, without concern as to how many suffered and were enslaved in the process.

Some years ago, during one of Walter's visits home from Jamaica, Nathaniel had argued with him at breakfast about paying fair wages for labor in the colonies. If the law said a person could not be a slave in England, how was it right in the New World?

He could still envision Father's red-faced fury at these "radical" ideas, spittle flying from his lips as he'd demanded to know if Nathaniel had learned them from his tutor.

Protecting Mr. Chisholm, Nathaniel said he'd seen a Quaker pamphlet on a trip to London. *"And how did you read it, you simpleton?"* Nathaniel had insisted a neighbor boy relayed it to him. Truthfully, there *had* been a Quaker publication, but Mr. Chisholm had read it to him.

Perhaps Nathaniel could argue for fairness on Primrose Isle. Not that he would be much good at it with his dim wits. Still, he would try—if he survived. He curled in the corner of his prison, where he'd remain for the next, what? Four weeks, the devil had said. And if Walter refused to pay…

No, Nathaniel couldn't dwell on it. All he could do was hope this wouldn't be his bloody end. He touched his tender throat again, remembering the crush of Hawk's powerful hand. He had to withstand his captivity, and he'd drive himself utterly mad if he didn't push aside his fear.

Nathaniel was powerless over everything but his own mind, and if he could just keep himself occupied, he'd survive this. He glanced around his prison, heart sinking. Of course, keeping occupied was easier said than done when he couldn't move.

Even after being *kidnapped by pirates,* restless boredom would apparently be his companion once more. The captain's cabin was surely the largest on the sloop, but trapped inside it, Nathaniel would go mad in a matter of days.

Chapter Four

THE BOATSWAIN'S WHISTLE for all hands on deck cut through the air, and the men gathered. Standing at the helm, Snell at his side, Hawk surveyed them silently, waiting for the shuffling and jostling to cease. Waiting until he had their undivided attention.

He still carried all his weapons, including the dagger confiscated from the prisoner. His lower back protested at the extra weight on his belt, and he cursed himself for not locking it all away safely before returning up top.

He made sure his voice carried across the deck. "By now, you are all aware of the unexpected treasure we've captured. My brothers, this windfall will reap us a reward greater than we could have dreamed when we spotted that merchant ship. Our new mission is to ransom Walter Bainbridge's son."

"For 'ow much?" a voice called.

"One hundred…" Hawk paused for dramatic effect. "*Thousand* pounds."

The men looked at each other, murmuring and smiling, visions of their share of the bounty dancing in their heads. Yet one, Deeks, asked, "Shouldn't we have taken a vote?"

Hawk sighed internally. Yes, they should have, and he hadn't even paused to consider it, his vision narrowed on the dual prize of revenge against Bainbridge and the possibility of a peaceful retirement from the sea. But he also wanted to leave the crew in good stead, with enough money that they could live well unless they squandered it, which some surely would. That was out of his hands.

He nodded. "Yes. Forgive me, my brothers. I was swept up in my excitement over our future riches. By all means, of course we will vote. Your choices are these: Continue to sail without a plan, hoping we stumble upon a prize. Perhaps some tobacco or sugar we can trade in Nassau for enough coin to spend a few days drinking and whoring before we set out to do it all again. And again. And again."

He waited, letting that option sink in. "Or, we ransom lying, cheating Walter Bainbridge's only son for a hundred thousand pounds." Or however much Bainbridge could raise, but the men didn't need to know that.

Hawk had set the bar high for the men's sake as well, and hopefully the ransom would come close so they could share a generous bounty. More than they could ever expect to win unless they miraculously stumbled upon a ship with treasure in its hold.

"For the next month, we relax. We don't fight over scraps with other ships flying the black. We don't risk death battling said ships. We stay out of the trading channels. Then we simply deliver this one piece of cargo and become richer than we thought possible with one haul."

He let that sink in as well. Then, "Mr. Snell, the vote, if you please?"

Doing an admirable job of not smirking, Snell cleared his throat. "We all know the captain is a man of his word. While most privateer captains take up to fourteen shares of a prize, Captain Hawk only ever claimed two, the same he does now. A fair share for the work he does guiding us. Protecting us. Mr. Walker, you made how much doing backbreaking work at a rich man's estate in Boston?"

Walker answered, "Twelve stinking pound a year."

Snell gazed over the men. "Twelve pounds. A *year*. There are forty-six of us on this ship. Captain will get two shares; one and a half for me. Part will go into the fund for the injured, and so on. But when all is said and done, it will be two thousand pounds for each of you. I know we all dream of striking Spanish gold in the next ship on the horizon. While this may not be millions, it is not a prize to be underestimated. All in favor?"

Hands went up with a raucous cheer. Hawk grinned. "That's the spirit of *The Damned Manta*!" He waited a few moments before raising his hands and quieting the men. "The boy will remain in my cabin. Untouched. Unharmed. Some of you will tend to him when needed—food, water, emptying the pot if I am otherwise engaged. Do not speak to him or allow him to ensnare you. Some of you will remember his father or have heard the tales of his treachery. Walter Bainbridge is a snake in the grass, and his son is surely just as slippery and deceitful."

The men nodded, murmuring in agreement.

"Don't be taken in by his innocent countenance. He's a spoiled, lazy brat who's had everything handed to him without a minute's work, without a moment's hardship."

More agreement. Then, "What 'appens if the old man don't pay?"

Hawk identified the man speaking. Red hair, scrawny, a perpetual scowl, rapacious hunger coiled in his long limbs. It was the sailor who had just joined them from the *Proud William*.

Already speaking so boldly could signal trouble, but Hawk would give him the benefit of the doubt. Hawk knew how miserable those merchant ships could be, just like the navy—working oneself to the bone for next to nothing.

"Ah, our new brother. Your name?" Hawk asked.

"Tully." He glanced around as if daring anyone to contradict him.

"A valid question. I'm confident Bainbridge will pay the ransom."

Another man spoke up. "I thought Primrose Isle was failing. Ain't supposed to be any money there, not enough food, more and more people pulling up stakes and going to the Carolinas or Jamaica. Thought that was why we've never bothered with the place."

"Absolutely true. But Bainbridge is a venal, greedy man. We've heard as well that he lives in a grand house on the colony; that he thrives while his people struggle. He grasps for power, and what message would it send to the rest of the New World if he allowed pirates to murder his only son? If he displayed such weakness, such vulnerability?"

The men murmured, nodding to each other. Hawk continued. "He cannot permit it. His pride will not. If he doesn't possess the funds, he will acquire them one way or another, or his reputation would suffer a devastating blow. No matter the truth, he cannot *appear* weak. Of that I am certain. I am also certain we will have a battle on our hands once we make the exchange."

Hawk grinned wolfishly. "But *The Damned Manta* never runs from a fight when our prize is so valuable. Who's with me?"

The men cheered, raising their fists. One shouted, "Revenge'll be fucking sweet!"

Hawk couldn't agree more. "Now we sail for Nassau to trade the rest of the cargo."

More cheers, and Hawk didn't tell them the stop in Nassau would be far, far briefer than they'd like. It was too great a risk to anchor there for long. If word got out of their ransom, they'd be fighting off other pirates.

No, better to keep moving, staying out of the shipping channels, sailing close enough to Primrose Isle, but not too close.

The men went back to work, excitement fueling their steps, and Hawk turned to survey the sea behind them, the ship's wake fanning out. Snell rejoined him after a time, asking, "Spot anything we don't?"

Hawk laughed softly. "Afraid my eyesight's not what it once was."

"My everything's not what it once was." Snell ran a hand over his thinning blond hair and patted his thick stomach.

They stood in companionable silence, and Hawk scanned the horizon. It was true his vision wasn't quite as sharp as it had been decades before when he'd earned his nickname, but he still kept a keen watch.

As a lad, he'd quickly become known as the best lookout on the ship he'd served. *"Eyes like a hawk up there!"* He credited his boyhood on Cornwall cliffs, watching the sea, pining for her embrace.

Careful what you wish for.

Sometimes Hawk missed the peace of the lookout, high above the bustle and chatter. It was a good crew, a hardworking crew, but if they'd just *shut up* sometimes… He shook his head. "I'm getting too old for this."

Snell snorted. "If you're too old, I'm fucking ancient."

"Well, I wasn't going to say it in quite those words, but…"

"All right, all right." Snell's smile faded. "Walter fucking Bainbridge. That piece of shit. I suppose it was inevitable that our path would cross his again." He was silent for some time, but Hawk knew Snell had more to say, so he waited.

Finally Snell continued, gaze on the horizon. "I've wondered why we've avoided Bainbridge after what he did. Because of him, we almost swung. Many men would have paid him a visit to settle accounts long before now. But not you."

"At first, it wasn't worth the risk. We had to make a living. Establish ourselves under the black."

"Aye. Create the Sea Hawk's reputation."

"Mmm. When Bainbridge became governor of that new colony, I thought about paying him a visit. Fantasized."

He gripped the rail, conjuring the vision of his hands around Walter Bainbridge's throat, the whoreson's skin violently red, eyes bulging, tongue lolling as Hawk choked the life from him. Or perhaps he'd run him through on his sword, or tie him up and—

"Yet we've stayed away. Why?"

Taking a long breath, Hawk banished the images of Bainbridge's demise. "I expected you to ask long before this."

Snell cut him a glance and smirked. "You think I haven't learned that you'll do a thing when you're good and ready, and not a moment before?"

Hawk had to smile. "Fair point. The last thing I wanted was to make a martyr of the man. That's what would have happened if we'd stormed into the new colony and strung him up. It would be another mark against the evil pirates, and he our innocent victim. They'd probably erect a fucking statue in his image. No. I couldn't abide it. I knew the time would come for revenge, and that I'd recognize it. Sure enough. Here we are."

"And in the meantime, we hear Bainbridge has lost the confidence of the Crown in his mishandling of affairs on Primrose Isle. That we took his son at all will be another blow."

"Yes. Rumor has it his time in power will end soon. I imagine the future of the colony itself is in question. England doesn't want to send good money after bad."

"Why the fuck would they? Not with such prosperity elsewhere in the New World."

Hawk's blood stirred at the promise of finally having his revenge. "Bainbridge will be desperate to preserve what he can of his reputation and not appear weakened. The money is the least he owes us after destroying our livelihood with a stroke of his quill. And when I kill him now, few will mourn and no one will canonize him."

"That whoreson underestimated us before. Not likely to do it again. Not sure if that's a good thing or bad."

"Neither am I. We must take care."

"Will the son be any trouble?"

Hawk shook his head dismissively. "He's a nothing little man. Sniveling coward like his father." To be fair, Bainbridge seemed willing to do anything to protect his sister, but that was a low bar in assessing a man's worth. "He won't be a problem."

Snell whistled softly. "Just think if we can pull this off."

Hawk spread his hands wide over the railing, watching sunlight gleam on the waves, unfamiliar hopefulness flowing through him. "Perhaps it will be the Sea Hawk's final operation."

"Pardon?" Half-laughing, Snell stared at him with brow furrowed. "What nonsense is this?"

Resisting the urge to shift from foot to foot under the scrutiny, Hawk kept his gaze on the sea. "With this ransom, I would leave you and the men in good stead. You could be captain when I'm gone."

Snell snorted. "I'm a damn good quartermaster because I know how to keep the men happy enough to stay in line. Captains must plan battles and the like, be mysterious and forbidding. Not my area of expertise. Besides, you won't be going anywhere."

His stomach twisted. "I won't?"

"I've seen this before. This restlessness. It'll pass. You'd never be able to leave when it comes down to it. I mean, what the fuck would you do with yourself?"

He shrugged, cheeks hot. "Fish. Farm a little. No more fighting."

Snell laughed heartily. "You'd be bored in a day! The grass may seem greener and all that, but can you really fathom such a life?" He clapped Hawk's shoulder, smile fading. "Besides, the sea doesn't give up her servants so easily. You know there's only one way out for us. So we should enjoy ourselves in the meantime."

A sickening sensation washed through Hawk, his limbs

weighted with it, a cannonball in his gut. He croaked, "Aye."

Snell sighed. "After these loggerheads get their act together." He shouted behind him, "Peters, are you fucking deaf? What did I just tell you this morning?"

Hawk smiled obligingly as Snell gave him another clap on the shoulder and went about his business. Gazing out into the vast nothing, Hawk still couldn't help but imagine what could lie beyond.

A little house, a hearth and warm tea in the mornings, an honest day's work ahead of him. A full night's sleep in a proper bed, ground that wasn't forever shifting beneath him.

Perhaps even a man to warm that bed, to live by his side in comfort.

He laughed harshly to himself. Nonsense indeed. Men who lived by the sword didn't enjoy peaceful retirements. He didn't deserve it, and regardless, Snell was surely right—it wouldn't suit him in the least.

A life at sea was what he'd craved as long as he could remember, so why would he want to give it up? Especially now that he was a pirate captain with more power than he'd ever imagined.

Yet Hawk couldn't quite banish the fantasy completely, tucking it away in the corner of his mind since he was apparently intent on tormenting himself despite his better judgment.

He took the wheel for a time. The day passed slowly, and several times he had to stop himself from returning to his cabin to see how his prisoner fared. The longer he left little Plum alone, the sooner the boy would be cowed completely. Hawk ate his evening meal with the men of the second dog watch as the sun went down.

The young man stationed outside Hawk's cabin snapped to attention as he approached. Hawk asked, "Did he try to bargain with you?"

"No, sir. Barely looked up from the floor."

Hawk held out his hand for the key. "Very good, Mr. Porter.

Be sure to keep your guard up around him in the days to come. Dismissed."

Following his own advice, Hawk turned the key swiftly and entered his cabin braced for attack. None came. Arms around knees, Plum huddled in his corner, where the starboard side of the hull met the stern. Hawk could just glimpse his head over the desk.

Hawk swaggered around as if he didn't have a care in the world, remaining alert, hand resting casually on his sword hilt. Plum kept his gaze on his feet, which were now bare. At least he had the good sense to do away with shoes and stockings.

After a day of full sunshine, Hawk longed to tug off his stifling boots. But not yet. He surveyed the bowl of food on the floor, which appeared untouched. So fucking much for good sense.

"Eat."

No reply.

Hawk growled, "Have you gone deaf?" Plum mumbled something, and Hawk demanded, "Look at me."

Plum's head snapped up. "I said I'm not hungry!"

"Is that so? And what makes you think I give a fuck whether or not you're hungry? You will eat when I tell you to. Do I have to hold your nose and shove that stew down your throat?"

The boy was full of shit—of course he was hungry. He'd drained most of his cup of water, at least. But this brainless rebellion had to be crushed. Hawk stepped closer, spreading his legs slightly, looming over his prisoner. "Do I have to chain you naked to the bed after all?"

Adam's apple bobbing, Plum's gaze darted to the bulge of Hawk's cock in his trousers, his breath catching. Was it simply fear, or something else as well?

A spark in the air like flint on stone tightened Hawk's bollocks. Hmm. Could it be Bainbridge just might *enjoy* being ravished?

But no, Plum's lip curled with disgust. "You're repellent. A filthy animal."

"Keep fighting me, and you'll find out just how filthy I am."

Plum shuddered. "You know Father won't pay if you hurt me, you monster."

Hawk took his time, looking him over as if he were a piece of meat. He lifted his lips in a leering smile. "There are plenty of things I can do to you that won't leave a mark."

"You blame my father for branding you a pirate, but clearly your heart was already black."

Hawk lowered his voice another octave. "I'll make you like it. Just imagine how much you'll hate yourself after that."

Bainbridge had no response but to reach for his bowl and shove a spoonful of stew into his mouth. He chewed angrily, but Hawk let him have his impotent rage.

Plum was one of English society's puppets, so of course he was horrified by the thought of men fucking. He lived a buttoned-up, pathetic little life of obedience to his father. This excursion on a pirate ship would probably be the one burst of excitement in his entire existence.

Might as well give him a show, then.

Slowly, carelessly, Hawk strode around the cabin, disrobing bit by bit. He took off his belt and tucked away his weapons, including the boy's dagger, in a chest and locked it.

He considered commanding Plum to pull off his boots. Hawk would sit on the side of the bed with his trousers unlaced and shirt off, legs spread as far as he could, making his captive kneel.

The thought coiled desire in his belly, a low, hot pulse. Must have been the lingering thrill of the hunt and capture that stirred him. Tormenting Bainbridge's son was one thing, but Hawk had to keep his lust in check. It wasn't typically a problem. He could go months with only his own hand, and happily.

Yet there was something intoxicating about Plum and his little acts of defiance. Many men would have pissed themselves and wept. Hawk had seen it enough over the years.

Still, he'd already given the boy too much time. Although it was fun to toy with him…

Hawk stripped off his shirt and unlaced his trousers, peeling them and his drawers down his legs although he still wore his boots. He was quite sure he had Bainbridge's attention as he bent over bare-arsed and pulled his feet free, resisting the urge to sigh in relief as he stretched his toes and kicked his trousers away.

Naked, he walked slowly around his desk, passing within a few feet of the prisoner, Bainbridge's gaze surely following, hot on his skin. Hawk opened the top drawer and pulled off his rings one by one, hiding his vexation when one of them caught stubbornly on his scarred knuckle.

He liked the gold earring—he forgot about it most of the time and was occasionally surprised by it in the hand mirror when he shaved and shaped his short beard. But the rings he found cumbersome, and they only came out when Captain Hawk was in his full regalia.

After dousing the lamp, Hawk stretched out on his mattress naked, wincing at the stiffness in his back. He commanded, "Behave. Or remember how your sister will suffer. Yes?"

"Yes," came the reply, brimming with resentment.

Despite his resolution to ignore his prisoner, Hawk smiled to himself.

Chapter Five

"*I*'LL MAKE YOU *like it. Just imagine how much you'll hate yourself after that.*"

Even with the break of day, the words still echoed in Nathaniel's head as if hissed by the devil himself. There was no need to imagine a thing—he despised his weakness in not being able to rid himself of traitorous desires.

He'd pretended to be asleep when Hawk roused in the darkness. There had been a few moments of silence when he'd been sure he was being watched, and he could understand deer freezing in place under a predator's scrutiny.

Even after the key had scraped in the lock and he was sure he was alone, Nathaniel had stayed curled under the horrible blanket, sleeping fitfully again.

Now the sun was in the sky, and he wasn't sure what time it was. There had been no delivery of food and water, but perhaps that would only be once a day. He would have to ration his water or risk sipping from Hawk's bottles of alcohol, a dangerous proposition if he was discovered. Nathaniel had never been much for drink, but was tempted to dull his senses.

Good Lord, it had only been a *day*. He'd never survive a month without going mad. And perhaps he wouldn't survive at all. If his father didn't pay…

He wanted to scream. There was no way of foreseeing the

future, so he must focus on the present and force away the worry lest he go mad.

He kicked off the blanket, sweating, his breeches straining with a morning erection. A turgid state that only grew more pronounced as images of the pirate captain stripping off his clothes ran riot through Nathaniel's head.

I can't even control my feeble mind.

He'd tried not to look. He truly had. Yet he'd glimpsed the tanned, muscular flesh, the dark ink of a tattoo painting the pirate's sternum depicting—what else?—a sea hawk with wings spread wide.

The villain had dropped his drawers and trousers to his ankles, *then* bent to remove his boots, the pale, firm globes of his arse facing Nathaniel.

Nathaniel wondered anew how the long scars had come to be over the pirate's buttocks, fingers of faded pink that were undoubtedly blood red when inflicted. He couldn't imagine Hawk bending to anyone's will; being overpowered, subjugated.

Yet clearly he had, since there was little doubt the scars came from a punishment. Curious. How had he suffered those scars and when? Nathaniel thought men who were lashed took it on their backs, not lower.

That line of reasoning of course made him think of *lower*, and the pirate's cock and balls hanging thick between his legs.

"I'll make you like it."

The memory of Hawk's growl, his accent that carried perhaps a lingering hint of the West Country, sent flames of desire licking through Nathaniel. He spoke with the profanity of the sea, yet also like a learned man.

Nathaniel wondered how he had come to be not merely a pirate when branded it, but the formidable Sea Hawk. Tall and broad, scarred and weatherworn, dark hair dusted over thick muscles. Fearsome and bold, wholly *male* in the primal way of a horse or a beast of the jungle.

He groaned, giving in and unfastening his breeches, breath hitching as he wrapped his palm around his shaft. He admitted the truth that the devil wouldn't have to put in much effort at all to make him like it.

Spitting in his palm, he jerked himself, attempting without success to focus solely on the physical sensation.

Does he really fuck other men? Would he make me suck his massive prick? Make me bend over and take it?

Moaning, Nathaniel spread his knees, feet flat on the wooden planks. He'd used his own fingers in the past, but what would it be like to have another man's cock inside him? Not just *any* man's—the pirate blackguard's? It would be huge as it split him open...

When Mr. Chisholm had taught him to wrestle so he could turn the tables on his vexing older cousins, it had somehow still been a gentlemanly pursuit. Nathaniel had loved the press of their bodies and feverishly dreamed of more while pleasuring himself in the privacy of his chambers.

But when he tried to conjure Mr. Chisholm now—his blond hair, green eyes starting to wrinkle in the corners as he passed thirty years—there was only darkness: the pirate king in his black raiding costume shining with gold, as bold and proud as the stallion that day in the paddock.

Nathaniel shouldn't want *that*. He should want a good, kind man who would be gentle. Not a monster. Yet as he touched himself, he reached up with his left hand, fingers skimming the sore bruises Hawk had left on his throat. He remembered the big, powerful hand choking him, as if it could have snapped his neck like a twig, and he moaned again.

He skimmed his fingers over his face, which stubbornly refused to grow much hair. Other hand flying on his cock, he thought of the beard around Hawk's mouth and how rough it would feel against his skin, in complete opposition to ladies' creamy, tender cheeks.

Images ran rampant of Hawk bending him over the rail of the ship, mounting him, mastering him—

Nathaniel cupped his hand over the end of his prick as he came, thudding his head back on the floor as he shuddered with each pulse, the hot pleasure scorching him, leaving him raw.

Leaving him empty and bitterly ashamed.

Gut churning, he searched for something on which to wipe his seed. Then he was caught in a nightmare as heavy footsteps approached and the key turned in the door.

Desperately wiping his hand on the cursed blanket, Nathaniel barely got his breeches fastened and his shirt tugged down, springing to his feet as the door opened.

And of course it wasn't some crew member, but the devil himself. Hawk froze in the entryway, eyes narrowing. He kicked the door shut. "What the fuck are you up to?"

Nathaniel backed into the corner. "N-nothing."

Hawk's fierce gaze swept around the cabin, then returned to Nathaniel. "The hell you say." He stormed over. "What have you got there?"

Too late, Nathaniel realized he'd instinctively thrust his sticky hand behind his back when Hawk entered the cabin. Now Hawk wrenched his arm out, Nathaniel wincing through the bolt of pain. He hadn't been able to wipe all the evidence away, and he cringed.

With a derisive laugh, Hawk peered down at Nathaniel's sticky fingers, his grasp cruel. "Thought you'd *spend* your time wisely, hmm?"

"There isn't anything else to do!" Nathaniel straightened his shoulders and lifted his head, snatching back his hand, surprised when Hawk released it. "I... Well, why shouldn't I?"

"Why indeed. Dreaming of tupping your pretty little betrothed?"

Nathaniel sputtered. "What? Who?"

A dark eyebrow arched. "Your sister said you were to be married."

"Oh. Yes." He cleared his throat and lifted his chin. "Don't you dare speak of her."

Hawk crowded him against the wall, all heat and muscle, and a sconce dug into Nathaniel's neck. "You dare tell me what to do? No. Not in my cabin. Not on my ship. Not ever. Understood?"

He managed a nod, cursing how his flushed body tightened again at Hawk's proximity. Then Hawk turned and took a seat at the desk. He unrolled a nautical chart and opened his log, picking up the quill and dipping it in ink. For minutes, the quill scratched over paper, and Nathaniel stood against the wall, unsure what to do.

Finally he sank back to the floor, and Hawk didn't blink, ignoring him completely. When a man came with water and rations for Nathaniel, Hawk never so much as glanced up.

Nathaniel determined he would wait until Hawk left again before eating. He hugged his knees to his chest and kept his eyes on the floorboards. Waiting. And waiting.

And waiting.

He broke down and had a sip of the tepid water, watching Hawk from the corner of his eye. Nothing. It was as if he wasn't even there, and somehow that made Nathaniel feel lower and more despairing than he had with Hawk's hand around his neck.

Why should he want the attention of the villain who might kill him? No, of course he didn't.

After a time, the quartermaster arrived. He stopped short when he spotted Nathaniel, as if he'd forgotten they'd taken a prisoner. Hawk asked him a question and continued to ignore Nathaniel's presence.

Mr. Snell eventually did too as he spoke of navigation concerns and dark clouds in the distance. Yet every so often, his eyes darted back to Nathaniel and he shifted from foot to foot where he leaned on the front of the desk, Hawk still sitting behind it.

When Snell left and Hawk went back to writing in his log as if he were alone, Nathaniel's mind wandered, settling on the issue of his future wife. He knew the duties of a husband and would do what he must. Perhaps he and Elizabeth could be dear friends, and having children to dote on wouldn't be unpleasant, not at all. He'd always liked little ones well enough.

"Dreaming of tupping your pretty little betrothed?"

He didn't even know what Elizabeth looked like. She was nothing more than a notion, a vague idea of full skirts and flowery perfume, of a lady. Not that it mattered—no matter how fair her face, it wouldn't change his unnatural inclinations. Squeezing his sticky hand, he shuddered, shame pooling in his belly.

So many times, he'd wanted to ask Mr. Chisholm what made some men abominations, but had never dared. Instinct had told him he'd never be able to ask without giving himself away.

Although Mr. Chisholm had never shown any indication, sometimes Nathaniel had wondered if he suspected the truth. But suspecting and *knowing* were two quite different things.

Why had he been born thus? Was he being punished for killing his mother so he could live? For he *had* killed her, as much as the pirate accused Nathaniel's father.

It had been Nathaniel who'd torn her open and stolen her last breath. He'd grown into half a man, his brain faulty. Unable to read, his desires unnatural.

Wrong.

Nathaniel realized Hawk's quill had gone quiet. In the silence he dared a peek, watching as Hawk blew on his freshly inked log so it wouldn't smear. Did the pirate have a wife somewhere? A mistress? Or perhaps he simply visited the whorehouses Nathaniel was told sprouted like weeds in the West Indies.

"I'll make you like it."

He couldn't banish the words from his head, and he mulled over the implications again. Could it really be that the pirate king shared Nathaniel's inclinations?

Of course men at sea found release where they must, at least according to Nathaniel's cousins, who allegedly had it on good authority. They'd all shuddered at the thought of it, while Nathaniel had bit his tongue so hard he drew blood in an effort not to demand more details.

Hawk would probably only take pleasure in tormenting Nathaniel; controlling him—punishing him. Nathaniel had never to his knowledge met another man who truly shared his sin, who would *choose* a man over a woman rather than simply indulging in unnatural couplings due to circumstance. Another who craved not only a man's touch, but kisses and smiles as well, companionship such as a wife would bring.

Not that it was the kind of thing spoken about at dinners and garden parties.

Apparently reading over his words, Hawk absently rolled up the flowing sleeves on his black shirt, cuffing them at the elbow. His tanned skin was scattered with dark hair, forearms thick with ropy muscles.

Yet without the flaring black coat, Nathaniel noticed Hawk wasn't quite as huge as he'd first thought. Still a good head taller than him, but not quite the *giant* he'd seemed.

Another scar slashed across the back of Hawk's right hand, which rested by the logbook, his left dipping the delicate quill into the pot of ink with precision. Writing with one's left hand was reputedly the mark of the devil, so Nathaniel supposed he shouldn't be surprised.

It was madness to think he was really there. On a *pirate ship*. That he wouldn't wake up swaying in the awful hammock, pretending to still sleep while Susanna used the pot. Spending another long, boring day on the merchant ship, where he couldn't run or swim or climb.

"Eat." Hawk didn't look at him, eyes still on the page.

"I'm—" Nathaniel stopped the lie. He *was* hungry. There was no sense in denying it or weakening himself by refusing his rations. He ate a spoonful of sloppy fish stew as bells tolled, choking down too-soft potatoes and then biting painfully into a thin, rock-hard biscuit as Hawk left the cabin, turning the key in his wake.

Nathaniel thought of Primrose Isle, his father and a proper young lady named Elizabeth, a new life waiting on a new colony. A new life that would ensnare him even more thoroughly than he already was. Then he laughed out loud as he thought that being a monster's captive on a pirate ship and ending his life here was perhaps preferable.

Madness indeed.

Chapter Six

"WILL I BE permitted to cleanse myself at any point in the next month?"

Hawk didn't look up from the chart he was examining. "Yes, let me ring for the servants. We'll have the tub filled with perfectly heated water in no time. Scented with lavender—or would you prefer jasmine?"

Bainbridge huffed from the corner. "It's been a week down here." His voice adopted a hopeful lilt. "Perhaps I could take a swim if we're dropping anchor close to shore? For a few minutes? That's all I ask. It isn't much."

Hawk tutted with false sympathy. "'Truly I was born to be an example of misfortune, and a target at which the arrows of adversary are aimed.'" He glanced at Plum, who regarded him blankly. "Surely you've read *Don Quixote*."

"Of course!" Plum insisted, too quickly, looking away, cheeks flushing.

Odd. "While I know you believe you have suffered the slings and arrows of outrageous fortune, I assure you it could be worse. Much worse."

"I have been kidnapped by pirates. If that is not outrageous fortune, I don't know what is."

He had a point, and Hawk controlled a huff that threatened to become laughter. "Your lot could be far worse than the desire for a bath and apparent boredom even though I've offered you dozens of books to pass your time. Of course you could always amuse yourself in other, more *physical* ways."

He didn't have to look over to know Plum was blushing furiously. The taunt had the intended effect, and there was silence as minutes went by. The unintended consequence was that images of Plum pleasuring himself intruded into Hawk's mind—bow lips parted with soft cries, cock straining, losing himself to a few minutes of abandon, of freedom.

The boy had a restless spirit Hawk hadn't expected in the least from Walter Bainbridge's son. Although he was whining for a bath, Hawk had a feeling it was more about getting back up on deck with freedom to move. He was a coiled spring, despairing at his containment, fidgeting endlessly. Hawk had expected a much more indolent creature.

Sure enough, Plum said, "If I could only go on deck the next time it rains. How I miss the rain. I used to go out exploring in it for hours. But even just for a few minutes—"

"Whatever ploy you have concocted, abandon it."

"It's no ploy! It's been cloudy for days, and it has to rain soon. I only want to breathe some fresh air and be cleansed."

The stern windows in Hawk's cabin were closed to the chilled wind, and if the brat couldn't be bothered to open them from time to time, to hell with him. Clearly he was lazy after all. "No."

"If I'm so useless, why don't you let me up there? What could I possibly do to a ship full of pirates?"

"Aside from get in the fucking way?"

"I said I'd help. I'm sure I could learn."

Hawk laughed sharply. "You probably don't even know how to tie a simple hitch in the line."

"I could learn," he repeated. "I bet I can."

Hawk's simmering annoyance flared. "A bet? All right, have it your way. Let's put you to the test. You'll have one demonstration, and one chance to tie it yourself."

Plum nodded, leaping to his feet eagerly. "If I win, I get to spend the days up on deck. I won't try to escape or harm anyone."

"As if you could. And no. If you win… If you win, you'll be permitted a bucket of water and sliver of soap."

Lips pressed together, the boy nodded. "Deal." He bounced on his toes. "Let's go."

Hawk went back to the chart, picking up his divider, the cool brass warming in his hand as he measured the shoreline of an island west of Nassau. "We'll go when I say we do."

As he continued working, Plum shifted back and forth, then paced across the cabin. Minutes ticked by, and Hawk could have stopped, but he walked to the bookcase and pulled out another chart before settling back behind his desk, enjoying the increasingly agitated nature of Plum's steps.

Finally, Hawk noted, "I'm sure you're used to having everything you want with the snap of your fingers. Sadly, you'll find only disappointment aboard this ship."

Plum laughed bitterly. "I've never had anything I've truly wanted. I never shall."

"Oh, and what poor, thwarted desires have you suffered? Pray tell." Plum snapped his mouth shut, and Hawk added, "If you'd like to learn of true hardship, we liberated a slaver ship last spring. Some of the men chose to stay with us. I'm sure they'd have much to say on the subject."

Face flushing, his shoulders slumped. "Yes. I'm sure they would. You're right."

Taken aback by the capitulation, Hawk blinked at Plum for a few moments. Then he tossed down the divider and rounded his desk. "All right, let's put you to the test." He grabbed Plum's arm and shoved him out of the cabin and up the ladder to the main deck.

The crew looked askance, and Snell approached, asking,

"What's this about?"

Hawk pushed Bainbridge to his knees. "I've made a little bet with our prisoner. He thinks he can bend the line as well as any man aboard." The crew laughed uproariously, and Plum's shoulder was tight with tension where Hawk held him fast.

Hawk could imagine how red his cheeks were. "What do you say? Shall we let these delicate hands prove their mettle in return for a bucket of water?"

Amid the cheers and laughter, a voice called, "Thought wagering weren't allowed on ship." It was Tully. He'd been of service when they'd boarded the merchant ship, and he wasn't wrong now, but as some of the men grumbled, Hawk wished Tully would shut his big mouth before Hawk was forced to shut it for him.

Snell answered, "This is true. But seeing as we're killing time waiting for our prize, perhaps we can make an exception this once." He glanced at Hawk. "Provided the men can make their own side wagers."

"Of course. Just this once." Snell always knew how to keep the peace amongst the men, which made him an excellent quartermaster. The brat would fail in no time, so the wagers wouldn't spin out of control.

"All right," Hawk called. "Let's start with a simple half hitch. Mr. Lee, will you demonstrate? Then the boy gets one chance."

While the men murmured amongst themselves, placing bets, Plum looked up over his shoulder. "And how many knots do I have to master before I win?"

Hawk gave him a wolfish grin. "As many as I say." He knocked Plum in the back with a sharp tap of his knee. "All right then, prove us wrong. Bend the line."

And then...*he did.*

Each knot and hitch Lee demonstrated, Plum mastered in one go. Figure eight, reef, even sheepshank. Hawk came around and watched the concentration on Plum's face, pink tongue sometimes darting out between his lips, gaze focused in on Lee's hands, ignoring the growing murmur of the crew, who called out suggestions to Lee to stump the prisoner.

Somehow none did. The coarse rope reddened Plum's fingers and palms, but he didn't hesitate as he mimicked Lee's movements, watching keenly, sweat gathering on his brow even in the day's chill.

Despite himself, admiration began to grow in Hawk. Plum was unbowed, unintimidated. Some of the crew started cheering for him, and wagers flew fast and furious.

Finally, his attempt at a back splice unraveled, and Hawk called an end to it. "Do we think he's earned his prize?" The "Ayes" were almost unanimous.

Then Plum grinned up at him.

And for an insane moment, Hawk wanted to *smile back*. For fuck's sake, clearly his brain was addled from too many days of peaceful routine aboard ship instead of stalking the seas for prey.

Fortunately, he schooled himself in time and hauled Plum to his feet, hurrying him back down to the cabin. One of the men brought the bucket of seawater, and Hawk sliced off a sliver of soap.

Back behind his desk, he couldn't force his gaze away as Plum stripped off his shirt, revealing surprisingly firm, lean muscles. Plum realized he was being watched, and his hands stuttered on the waist of his breeches.

Hawk almost turned his head, feeling strangely guilty, before reminding himself he was a God-damned pirate and this was his prisoner, to whom he owed no courtesy or shred of privacy.

He turned his chair to face Plum's corner and leaned back. Still in his breeches, Plum blinked at him. He glanced down at himself, then back at Hawk. Clearly he was unnerved, but there was something else—a hum vibrating through the room, a low tug between them. Hawk recognized something in this boy that flared his nostrils and stirred his blood.

Legs spread in his chair, boots planted on the floor, Hawk took him in. "Where did the spoiled son of Walter Bainbridge learn to bend a ship's line?"

"I never have until today. I'm just good at using my hands."

Better than good, and quicker than many men Hawk had sailed with. Perhaps there was more to the younger Bainbridge than met the eye. *Not that it matters, since he is nothing more than a means to an end.*

Yet Hawk found himself asking, "Is that so? Hmm. More muscles than I expected. You're small, but strong. Would've thought you much…softer."

"I… I always…"

He raised an eyebrow. "Do go on."

"I always loved the outdoors. Climbing trees, running, swimming. And there's wrestling. My tutor taught me." He flushed scarlet all the way down to his chest, shifting guiltily.

"Did he now?" Hawk smiled slowly, wickedly. He lowered his voice to a conspiratorial pitch. "Did your tutor also bugger you senseless?" The thought that another man might have unlocked that treasure was strangely disappointing.

Plum's eyes popped wide, and a gasp escaped his bow lips. "No! He was a good man. Not like—" He swallowed hard, apparently thinking better of what he was going to say. "No. I've never… I would never! My tutor wasn't like that. He was kind and proper."

"Ah. Kind and proper men are scarce. How fortunate for you. A shame your luck has run out."

Plum licked his lips, his gaze dropping from Hawk's face down to the bulge between his spread legs, and he shuddered, unmistakable hunger in his eyes.

Ah yes. There it is.

Hawk's instincts were correct—he knew it in his bones. The question was why he should care in the slightest. What did it matter that they shared common desires? Plenty of men did.

Over the years since that initial bloom of excitement and tenderness, Hawk hadn't given it much thought beyond finding the odd anonymous man for release.

It had been so different with him. *John.*

Irrepressible smile, blond hair falling over his blue eyes, rebellious and beautiful. They'd been so innocent, so fucking naïve, believing they could have anything good and pure in the belly of that frigate. That they could have happiness despite their low circumstances, their virtual imprisonment.

Perhaps it was Plum's clear innocence that tugged at him. Sodomy was strictly forbidden in the Royal Navy, and Hawk's fumblings with John had happened only in shadow. But as a privateer and now a pirate, it was hardly unusual. Men fucked as they pleased, jaded and far from the giddiness of youthful discovery.

He hadn't thought on John for years, and it was weak and foolish to do so now. But even as he banished John's specter, he couldn't take his eyes off his captive. As Plum's nipples went hard, his cock now unmistakably swelling in his breeches, Hawk fought his own excitement, his bollocks tightening.

He wanted to sully that innocence. Steal it. Bask in it. He fought the urge to draw Plum between his thighs so he could suck Plum's nipples, one and then the other, so he could hear his gasps of pleasure.

Instead he asked, "Have you truly never fornicated with a man?"

"Of course I haven't!" Plum whirled away, dropping to his knees and splashing water over himself from the bucket, his voice ragged. "That would be unnatural. A sin." He shook his head violently. "It's disgusting. Shameful. No decent man would entertain such a notion. You're a fiend."

Ah yes. And there that *is.* It was foolish to be disappointed, but it settled heavily into Hawk's limbs. Ridiculousness, especially since he might be killing Plum in a few weeks.

He shifted his chair back to face his desk, distinctly uncomfortable, stomach unsettled. He pulled his log near, running his fingers along the sturdy spine and over the worn leather cover.

It had always given him a measure of comfort to record the ship's activities in his logbook. Report the weather and make notes on anything of interest. As if the writing of it somehow gave weight to his meaningless life.

He dipped his quill and inked a fresh page with: *Prisoner is typical gentleman; hypocrite who denies himself pleasure for England's false sense of morality.*

Then he barked, "You have a minute to wash. Starting now. Do not waste it with sermonizing."

From the corner of his eye, he caught the pale swathes of flesh as Plum stripped off his breeches, splashed water over his skin, and lathered the soap. Hawk shouldn't have wanted to turn his head and look properly, just as he shouldn't have been surprised Walter Bainbridge's son insisted on nonsense about shame and sin.

Why had he thought even for a moment that there might be more to him? That there was any common ground between them? Of course Plum was just as false as his father.

"Time's up. Bucket by the door."

Hawk fixed his gaze on the logbook and dipped his quill. He'd had to hide his inclination to favor his left hand for years after his father had caned him for it. He supposed it was one of the benefits of being a pirate—everyone already thought you possessed by the devil.

Although he bent his head to the log, he found his eyes following Plum's progress. Water dripped down naked flesh, his tight, round buttocks flexing as he bent.

When Plum turned, Hawk jerked his gaze back down at the page to find dots of ink all over it. Swearing, he ripped it out and started anew.

Chapter Seven

S HOUTS.

Indistinct and urgent, they echoed overhead, rousing Nathaniel from an unpleasant, fitful sleep in his corner atop the awful blanket. The sun was high in the sky. The stern windows acted as a magnifying glass so that sweat slicked Nathaniel's skin and dampened his hair into a mess of curls.

There were no drapes, and all he could do was huddle in his corner as the temperature rose. They must be well and truly sailing in the West Indies now, for this day was hotter than any other on the journey.

Bolting up as thuds echoed, he rubbed his eyes and listened, breath lodged in his throat. Yes, more shouts, growing in urgency now, and the ship seemed to be changing course. He hurried to the stern windows, peering through the squares of glass framed in wood, seeing nothing but the unbroken horizon.

He waited there as minutes ticked by, footsteps pounding above and orders being shouted, none clear enough for him to make out in his prison cell. Despite the flurry of activity, time passed without anything else actually happening. Then there was a strange calm that stretched out, where the thud of Nathaniel's heart was too loud in his ears.

More time passed. Perhaps it had been nothing at all. A change of course, and now back to the regular routine, water slapping the hull, the ship creaking.

Yet there was something in the air—a palpable sense of expectation. He waited. Perhaps they'd spotted another merchant ship in the distance to plunder. Or perhaps—

There! In the corner of his field of vision through the windows, it was indeed another ship. Three masts, bigger than their sloop. Nathaniel's heart raced. Was it a Royal Navy ship? Or a Spanish man-of-war? He squinted, forehead to the hot window, wondering if Hawk had another spyglass tucked away in his desk.

Whatever it was, it seemed to be following, full sails arching in the wind.

He knelt on the narrow window seat and lifted his hands around his eyes to cut the glare, trying to make out the vessel's origin, praying to see the Union Jack fluttering in the sky. It was no use, the ship still too far away.

More time passed, the ship steadily gaining on them. Nathaniel's damp skin squeaked on the glass. The mystery vessel came about another few degrees, and there was its flag, snapping in the wind. His stomach dropped.

Black.

It was solid, no white or red embellishments, simply a blunt declaration of intent. But why would pirates attack each other? He supposed for the same reasons they attacked any ship, and it was foolish to expect any kind of loyalty amongst thieves. Pirates surely made rivals of one another.

The ship disappeared from view, and Nathaniel waited. *The Damned Manta* didn't seem to be attempting to outrun it now. Perhaps the captains knew each other and were friends, and now that they were close enough to make a certain identification—

Nathaniel flew off the window seat as the blast rocked the ship, air slamming from his lungs as he crashed flat on his back. Then another blast, and another. Another, another. Wood splintered, the *boom* of each cannon rattling his teeth, his ears ringing, heart about to burst from his chest.

He scrambled into the enclosure under the massive desk, tucking the chair back in after him as if that would help, curling into a ball, grateful the wood on three sides reached the floor, giving him an effective hiding place.

The humid, cloying air in his enclosure was even harder to breathe, and terror seized his lungs. If these other pirates won, what would become of him? Would they want him as a ransom, or simply slit his throat or toss him over the side? Or worse?

He gripped his knees tighter, making himself small, hoping to be as forgotten as the cobwebs that strung across the underside of the desk. What if they kept him? Passed him around, or tortured him, or God knew what pirates were capable of.

As much as he hated being Hawk's prisoner, and as much as he hated the idea of living on Primrose Isle with a stranger for a wife, doing his father's bidding, either prospect seemed preferable to this horrifying unknown that had exploded upon him.

He huddled tighter into a ball, whispering a prayer, the continued blasts wreaking havoc on his nerves. Screams tore the air, ragged and despairing, the song of dying men.

The ship shuddered and groaned, its own cannons returning fire. On and on it went, jolting and rolling, the air made of thunder. He plugged his ears and only knew he was screaming by the hoarseness of his throat.

At any moment, Nathaniel was certain *The Damned Manta* would disintegrate in the roar of gunfire, sending him plummeting to the bottom of the sea, the desk his coffin.

Abruptly, the guns went silent. More shouting up top, and the other ship's cannons fired again but seemed to miss their target with mighty splashes. Were they moving? He wasn't certain. Then there were no more cannon blasts at all.

Had they surrendered? Were they to be boarded? He strained, listening, but he couldn't make sense of it. Sweat drenched him now, and he swiped it from his eyes, his shirt and breeches clinging to his skin as he waited, barely breathing, afraid he might piss himself.

Nathaniel wasn't sure how long he remained huddled under the oven of the desk before the key turned in the lock of the cabin door. He pressed his lips together, frozen. *Oh Lord. Please. Please save me. I promise I'll be a better man.*

The door opened.

Whoever it was didn't say a word. Nathaniel would be invisible to them beneath the solid desk. Yet there was a little chunk of wood missing at the bottom, a gouge that had perhaps been ripped away in some unknown battle, or was simply due to a clumsy job moving the desk.

Heart booming in his ears, Nathaniel inched down to peek through. He'd never thought it possible to be so very relieved to spot those gold-tipped boots, but he exhaled in a rush as Hawk thundered, "Where the fuck are you?"

Nathaniel hadn't intended to anger him, and now he stayed motionless, terrified any movement or response would be his last. The door slammed shut, and Hawk's boots thudded on the planks. Yet it didn't sound like his usual confident stride, and then there was a burst of noise—a venomous curse and a mighty bang.

It startled Nathaniel from his hidey-hole, and he shoved the chair aside, crawling out and coming almost face-to-face with Hawk, who had tripped onto his hands and knees. Blood splattered across his face, and he grimaced, teeth bared. He wore his coat, which must have been terribly warm although it was unbuttoned.

Nathaniel could only open and close his mouth like a helpless fish on a hook, waiting for Hawk to explode to his feet and perhaps run Nathaniel through with his blade, which still hung from his belt.

Then realization dawned: he couldn't. Was he—yes, he was

injured. The mighty pirate king had been brought low, not because he was about to haul Nathaniel out from under the desk, but because he'd *fallen.*

And he didn't appear able to get back up.

"I… Are you…?" Nathaniel crawled closer, dangerously within reach. Hawk only seethed in response, a savage, guttural groan. Nathaniel looked to the closed door. "Should I call for help?"

"*No!*" The notion seemed to infuriate Hawk so much that rage fueled him back to his feet, where he leaned heavily against the desk.

Nathaniel couldn't spot exactly where Hawk was hurt until he came around to stand before him. The coat fell open, and Nathaniel could see the hunk of wood lodged in his right thigh. Sucking in a breath, he inched closer. "You need the surgeon."

Tendons in his neck bulging, Hawk shook his head. "The men need him more."

"Are we safe now?"

"Took out her main mast. She'll be licking her wounds for a while. Serves them right for trying to take us on. Fucking One-Eyed Alfred and the *Javelin.* He attacks anyone and everyone without provocation, no matter the risk. Madman."

"It looked like quite a big ship."

Grimacing, Hawk said, "Aye, but bigger isn't always better. Those hulking ships are not as…" He waved his hand in the air as if searching for a word.

"Agile?"

"Yes, you fancy little fuck. Not as *agile.*" He pushed off the desk. "Stay out of my way while—" He stumbled and would have crashed to the floor if Nathaniel hadn't darted forward to catch him, almost toppling with the weight as he jammed his left shoulder under Hawk's right. Hawk insisted, "I don't need hel—"

"Oh for goodness' sake, you clearly do." Nathaniel took a step, bearing as much of Hawk's weight as he could, their sides pressed together as they crossed to the bed.

Hawk's harsh breathing was loud in Nathaniel's ears, and gunpowder, blood, and sweat filled his nose. At least the cabin was compact, and it was only several feet before he levered Hawk around and deposited him on the side of the mattress.

"I'm fine." Hawk winced, shuddering as he tried to shake off his coat. "Go back to your corner."

Perhaps he should have left the man to his own devices since he didn't deserve any assistance, and certainly not sympathy. Yet here he was, the mighty pirate king, grimacing and bleeding, crippled by injury like any number of sailors before him. He wasn't some fearless, untouchable god, rising unscathed above danger.

No, he was merely a *man*.

It should have satisfied Nathaniel to see him humbled. Should have made him triumphant. But it unsettled him in a way he couldn't understand, previously held truths splintered by cannon fire as surely as *The Damned Manta*'s hull.

If the Sea Hawk was vulnerable, what hope did Nathaniel have to survive in the brutality of the New World? Here Hawk was, bleeding, *hurting*, and Nathaniel wanted to make it stop.

He climbed onto the bed behind him and peeled the coat off, easing Hawk's arms free of the sleeves, the leather hot to the touch. Then he knelt at Hawk's feet and took hold of one of those ostentatious boots. He looked up with eyebrow raised.

Hawk watched him, his usual bland or mocking expression replaced by one of genuine bafflement, forehead creased and nose slightly wrinkling. But he lifted his foot, and Nathaniel gently tugged the boot free.

Then the other, which he did slowly since that was the injured leg. He leaned in close. The wood was two inches thick, jagged and splitting. It was lodged in Hawk's thigh, his tight black trousers torn where it impaled the muscle, a few inches sticking into the flesh. Hopefully it got some fat too.

Nathaniel shook his head. "You need the surgeon."

"I told you, my men need him more. Just pull it out."

"Do you have bandages, at least? Anything to clean the wound?"

Hawk nodded to the desk, and Nathaniel rifled around, finding a bottle of rum, clean bandages, and a tin of medical instruments. When he turned back, Hawk was removing his weapons, keeping them close at hand behind him on the mattress. He narrowed his gaze.

"If you even consider some scheme to arm yourself, I assure you it will be ill-fated."

Nathaniel shook his head. "How often must I remind you that I won't endanger my sister? I am at your mercy." He should let the wound fester and perhaps eventually kill Hawk, but couldn't bring himself not to lend assistance, imagining how dreadful the pain was.

Hawk tried to remove his trousers, fingers clumsy on the fastening, belt unbuckled. It seemed the tables had turned and that Hawk was at *Nathaniel's* mercy, at least for the moment.

Pulse skittering with a fresh pulse of odd excitement, Nathaniel knelt and batted the pirate's hands away, finishing the job. "Up."

Hawk *obeyed*, raising his hips so Nathaniel could ease down his trousers and drawers, taking special care over the chunk of wood, tearing the material to make it easier. Hawk clutched the side of the bed, fingers white.

Now the pirate was naked from the waist down, and Nathaniel was faced with a thick, meaty cock and bollocks nestled in a thatch of dark hair. Throat dry, he ripped his gaze away, focusing on the bloody wound instead.

He handed Hawk the rum. "Drink." Again, Hawk obeyed, and Nathaniel's skin prickled, his breath catching. This man might *kill* him, yet Nathaniel thrilled at being close to him, at helping him. Perhaps winning some measure of approval. It was lunacy.

He held Hawk's leg fast, hand over his knee. There was really nothing to do but get the wood out as gently as he could. He grasped the protuberance. "Relax your leg as best you can," he ordered. Hawk did as he was told.

Fortunately, the wood came free without much effort. Quite unfortunately, it left several slivers of varying sizes embedded in Hawk's flesh. Nathaniel glanced up to find blood smeared on Hawk's lower lip and realized he'd bitten through the skin.

"You can shout. I doubt the men will hear, given the racket up there." Footsteps clomped, and voices called out, a general commotion in the wake of battle.

"No need," Hawk gritted out.

Nathaniel rolled his eyes. "Yes, clearly all is well." He fished out a pair of tweezers from the tin. The thought occurred again that he should leave the shards behind, practically ensuring an infection. But if Hawk died, Nathaniel didn't know what the rest of the crew would do with him—or *to* him.

Better the devil I know.

With his left palm flat on Hawk's upper thigh, only inches from his groin, Nathaniel leaned over and went to work. Blood oozed from the wound, and he had to stop to soak it up.

Hawk's gaze weighed on him as Nathaniel teased out a thin piece of wood, and the parallels to the fable of the lion with a thorn in its paw weren't lost on him.

When Hawk spoke, it was to hoarsely bark, "Why the fuck is it so hot in here?"

"Because you somehow never thought to install drapes to keep out the sun?"

Hawk gave him a withering look. "The windows open to let in the breeze."

"Oh." Nathaniel blinked over at them, still not seeing how to shove them up.

"The ones on either side can be hooked open," Hawk muttered. "Just push them and make sure they latch."

Nathaniel crossed the cabin and did as instructed, sighing and breathing the fresh, cool air deeply. "That's so much better."

"Indeed. Are you almost done?"

Nathaniel got out a tinderbox and lit a lantern, then handed it to Hawk. "Hold it close." He poked around in the wound as gently as he could. Hawk's labored breathing grew harsh and the other sounds of the ship distant.

"Are those from the lines?" Hawk asked. At Nathaniel's frown, he added, "Your hands. Not as smooth as I would have expected, given your station."

"I climb trees." Hawk stared down at him, and Nathaniel shifted uneasily, that gaze prickling his skin much like slivers of wood. "I enjoy…using my body."

Hawk's lips twitched, gaze assessing—*teasing*. "Do you?"

Without warning, Nathaniel splashed rum into the wound, enjoying Hawk's indignant yelp. Then he quickly bandaged it, keeping his eyes off the pirate's devilish face and nether regions. "There. I think you'll live, but the surgeon would have a better idea."

Hawk thrust the lantern at him, any hints of teasing gone. "This is sufficient." He pushed to his feet and promptly almost fell flat on his face, the bandage red and soaked.

Nathaniel put the lantern on the floor and pushed Hawk back onto the bed, pulling up his feet and swinging his legs around. "For the love of God, just rest here a few minutes at least."

Perching on the side of the mattress, he pressed another bandage over the seeping wound. The sheets and floor were splattered red, and Nathaniel's shirt and breeches were splashed with blood as well.

Keeping his eyes away from Hawk's nudity, Nathaniel asked, "Were many men hurt?"

"Some."

"Killed?"

"Two, last I knew."

"Oh." Nathaniel remembered how quickly the other ship had come upon them, everything going from normal to high alert in a heartbeat. And just as quickly, a life could be snuffed out. "Did they have families?"

"Us."

"What would have happened if the other ship had gotten close enough to board?"

"We'd have a lot more dead men on our hands. On both sides."

He wondered how many men Hawk had killed over the years but didn't think it prudent to ask. At least Hawk finally surrendered, relaxing back against his pillow, gaze on the ceiling as Nathaniel kept pressure on the wound.

Hawk actually shut his eyes after a time, and Nathaniel's pulse fluttered at the intimacy of it. The pirate king made mortal, his stubborn blood seeping out between Nathaniel's fingers, though slower now.

Despite his best efforts, Nathaniel's gaze zeroed in on Hawk's soft, reddish prick, curving flat against his belly. His substantial balls were hairy and thick. It was impossible to ignore, and he had the brief luxury to look.

Filled with blood, Hawk's cock would be…impressive. Nathaniel wondered what it would feel like in his hand, if it would be hot to the touch. Would it be bitter, or salty like sweat on his tongue? Would his spendings taste different from Nathaniel's when he'd shamefully licked his own seed from his hand in the past?

He swallowed thickly. What would that cock feel like shoved

inside him? He wouldn't run from it the way the mare had tried to escape the stallion. No, before he died, Nathaniel wanted to experience a man's prick inside him, even just once. He was going to hell for his sinful desires regardless, so the journey might as well be worth it.

What if I die on this ship?

A bolt of panic caught his breath, and he had to steady his hand on Hawk's wound, fighting the urge to scramble away. He stared down at the pirate. *What if he kills me?*

Would this man truly gut him if Walter didn't pay? Perhaps if Nathaniel continued to help him—if he could ingratiate himself—Hawk would be unable to slay him or follow through on his threats against Susanna. Perhaps Nathaniel could save himself.

His gaze was drawn back to Hawk's prick, a low beat of *want* resounding. Perhaps he could save himself *and* fulfill his cravings. He'd always imagined he had plenty of time to explore his fantasies, to meet a man he could trust with his secret.

But even if he survived the trip to Primrose Isle and the ransom exchange, how soon would he have to marry Elizabeth Davenport? Growing up, he'd known he'd have to wed eventually, but perhaps not until he was thirty. Plenty of time.

Yet now the sands tumbled through the glass relentlessly. He'd told himself he'd only need it once—to be fucked the way he'd envisioned, to satisfy his curiosity and desire. And the itch, once scratched, would be manageable, and he could marry as required and be a faithful husband.

But the risks of finding a man to trust on the unknown Primrose Isle were great. He should have done it before he'd left England, but short of polling the servants on who would be willing, he hadn't had the opportunity.

He'd have greatly loved for Mr. Chisholm to share his desires, but the man was good and kind and devoted to his wife and young daughter. Nathaniel had known he'd be rejected. He hadn't been able to bear the sight of disappointment—and worse, disgust—in his tutor's eyes.

His own breathing was harsh in his ears. It was beyond sinful and improper to be stirred by Hawk's genitals, the man's blood all over, an open wound under Nathaniel's hand. Had it only been, what, not even an hour since Nathaniel had cowered under the desk, certain he'd be swallowed by the sea at any moment?

The fear had left a strange desire thrumming through him. Not mere desire for the male form—that he'd felt for ages. But a yearning to reach out and take hold of life while he still could.

He could feel Hawk's pulse through the wound, the steady drum of his defiant heart, and he wanted to touch it, taste it, revel in being alive.

At that very moment, another volley of cannonballs might be hurtling through the air, about to obliterate them. Nothing was assured, each breath its own little miracle.

He eyed Hawk, wondering what the reaction would be if he leaned over and took the pirate's cock between his lips. Surely most men wouldn't protest a wet, warm mouth around them, no matter whose it was.

One of the boys from a neighboring estate had been sucked by an admiral's daughter once, and he'd described it in such ribald detail Nathaniel had stiffened in his breeches and not known of whom he should be more jealous—his friend for being serviced, or the girl for being able to take a hot prick into her mouth.

"See anything you like?"

Nathaniel jerked his head up, ripping his gaze from Hawk's groin to find the pirate watching him. His mouth had gone dry, and he hoarsely replied, "What? No." He busied himself changing the bandage again. "This needs to be stitched. There's no way around it."

"Mmm. Time will tell."

He huffed. Why was the swine so stubborn? "I bet you it

does."

Hawk met his gaze then, blue eyes fathomless, but his lips twitching. "What will the prize be this time?"

Was it possible? Not only was the pirate king a mortal—bleeding and as vulnerable to injury as the rest of them—but he was entertaining a joke?

Heart picking up, Nathaniel pondered his answer. "The next time you go ashore, I accompany you. I get to run down the beach as fast as I can."

Hawk laughed sardonically. "Yes, I'm sure you'd love to run away."

"Not running to escape, simply for exercise. For the sake of it."

"That's it?" His forehead creased. "You want to…run?"

"It's been far too long since I had the opportunity."

Hawk shrugged carelessly. "It's a bet."

There was no way Hawk could think he'd win given the amount of blood already soaking the fresh bandage. Nathaniel simply nodded and accepted the unsaid thanks, his own blood rushing far too fast in the hush of the cabin.

Chapter Eight

SITTING ON THE side of the bed, Hawk hid a grimace as grizzled Mr. Pickering poked at his thigh. Graying hair flopping over his forehead, the surgeon nodded. "Stitches are healing up nicely already." He glanced at the corner of the cabin. "Thanks in no small part to young Mr. Bainbridge's ministrations."

Hawk grunted, and Pickering went about applying a fresh bandage. It was true Plum had been helpful, and Hawk was still puzzled as to why. Surely Plum had an ulterior motive.

Hawk needed to remain vigilant and not be moved by any acts of kindness, for kindness always carried a price. The prisoner only wished to worm into Hawk's good graces to save his own skin. Hawk had already made the silly bet, but that had to be the end of it.

Of course Plum had been right, and as soon as Snell had taken one look at the bloody mess in Hawk's cabin, he'd shouted for the surgeon and the needle and thread had come out.

But Hawk had to remember the boy was his prisoner. He was nothing more than a representative of money and revenge. Of the sea's justice. There was naught to be grateful for.

Still, it was impressive that he hadn't been at all squeamish about the blood. For having lived a life of luxury, he truly was surprisingly practical and adept at physical tasks. The weight of his hand against the wound had been reassuring, as was the touch of his knuckles to Hawk's forehead a few times in the night, following Pickering's orders to check for fever.

The last time, just before dawn, Hawk had pretended to remain asleep. The windows were still open, the cool breeze lovely on his skin, his sheet kicked aside. He'd heard the whisper of Plum's feet on the planks, the press of his fingers against his forehead, assessing for a few moments before lifting. He'd waited for the footsteps to retreat, but Plum had remained standing by the bed.

He'd witnessed the hunger when Plum had eyed his prick after he'd tended to the wound, and if not for the burning ache in his thigh, Hawk might have gotten hard under that eager gaze.

In the early morning, that gaze had returned, hot on his skin, and Hawk had allowed him to look. His balls had tingled, and he'd had to shift and stretch to send footsteps scurrying back to the corner.

Pickering finished the bandage and groaned as he straightened, arching his back. Hawk frowned. "You weren't injured yesterday, were you?" The surgeon's hair grayed more with each week, it seemed. He'd been forced into service on a pirate ship years back thanks to a bad wager and had discovered he liked it.

Pickering laughed. "No, it's simply old age. More aches and pains by the day, it seems."

Hawk knew the feeling, but kept that to himself as he pulled up a clean-but-rumpled pair of trousers, aware of Plum's gaze on him. Hawk had determinedly dressed—boots and all, ready for battle even if he was being treated as an invalid. He eyed his feet. The leather could do with a polish, and the gold tips had dulled. He should shine them now while he lazed around useless. He stood, the bed frame creaking.

Pickering was already upon him. "No, no, no. You will stay abed the rest of this day. You insisted on leading the funerals last night, walking up there as if you were unscathed when you were in agony. You can fool the men, but I know better. You lost more than your fair share of blood, and infection could kill you. So you will remain here and rest until at least tomorrow, and preferably the following days as well. The sun is shining, the wind is blowing, and we're nearing Nassau with nary a sail on the horizon. If that changes, you'll be informed. In the meantime, get some rest for fuck's sake. Or I'll hold you down and dose you."

Standing had sent a fresh burning throb through his thigh, and although out loud he grumbled, Hawk secretly was grateful to sit again. As captain, he should want to be surveying his kingdom, ensuring smooth operations.

But truthfully, his muscles were sore, a low headache that had seemingly been present for years pulsated, and of course the gash on his leg was impossible to ignore. The thought of being up top with all the men and their incessant *noise* was off-putting in the extreme. He still made a show of his displeasure, and Pickering resolutely ignored him before taking his leave.

He'd barely gone when there was a knock, and a young voice called out, "Rations."

"Wait," Hawk answered, shoving himself off the bed with a wince.

Plum piped up from the corner. "But the surgeon just said—"

"Shut up." Hobbling slightly, Hawk stood behind his desk. Sitting would probably be worse, so he opened his log and leaned heavily over it, hands on the scarred wood. He called, "Enter."

Their newest crew member, the redheaded Tully from the merchant ship, came in with fresh water and a bowl of salted meat and peas. He glanced around as if looking for something. All the blood had of course been cleaned.

His eyes narrowed at Plum, who wore one of Hawk's old shirts, too big on him by half, the sleeves rolled up and the collar loose almost to mid-chest, a scattering of light hair peeking out of the white linen. Plum's shirt had been ruined by blood, but his breeches only had a few stains that were invisible under the tails of the shirt.

Tully nodded toward Plum. "Got 'is food. Not sure why we's wastin' it."

Hawk gazed unseeingly at the log, fingers tightening on the desk. "I don't recall asking for your opinion."

"Well, here you go, Bainbridge, you bloody loiter-sack." Tully carelessly dropped the cup and bowl on the floor near Plum with a clatter. "Wonder how your bitch of a sister is. I was always real nice to her, and she never gave me the time of day. Stuck-up cunt. I hope your father don't pay and we get the chance to really stick it up her."

Plum was instantly on his feet, fists clenched. "Don't you dare even speak about my sister. No one's going to lay a finger on her while I still have breath."

"I'm sure it can be arranged that you don't no more."

Hawk banged the log shut and stood straight, ignoring the fiery throb in his leg. "Mr. Tully." He eyed him. Mangy red hair, freckles, yellowed teeth with at least one missing, skinny and hard, a feral little man with a beady gaze. "I'm not sure what you hope to gain with this display, but if it's to impress me, you've missed the mark. Leave, and tell Mr. Snell you are no longer permitted in my cabin."

After opening his mouth as if to argue, Tully apparently thought better of it and scuttled out. Plum took a few steps, as if he wanted to give chase. "I can protect myself against him."

Hawk snorted. "Good. That wasn't about you. Mr. Tully needs to learn to obey my orders."

He managed to make it back to the bed with even steps, swallowing a groan as he stretched out again, his boots undoubtedly sullying the linens. It was a luxury to have a true bed and not a hammock, to have soft sheets.

He should enjoy his rest, since it didn't come often, yet he found himself thinking too much of his prisoner. "Now eat, and if you say you're not hungry I'll shove that food down your gullet myself."

After a minute of silence, Plum said, "You should eat too. Or at least drink." He scratched at his face. There was little more than peach fuzz there, but he clearly wasn't used to it.

Hawk had a jug of water by the bed, and he sipped from a cup. "There. See how amenable I can be?"

It was Plum's turn to snort, and Hawk had to stop himself from smiling. Why on earth was he *smiling* at Walter fucking Bainbridge's son? The blood loss must have been severe indeed. He stretched back on his bed.

"How old were you when you first killed a man?"

Hawk blinked at the unexpected question. Plum poked at his food and added, "I'm just wondering who was the first?"

John. The answer came unbidden. Hawk hadn't fired the cannon, true, but he could still feel the grip of John's hands as they shoved him to safety. Could still taste the spray of John's blood. Shaking his head to banish the past, he said, "Fifteen."

"Oh. Was it awful?"

He simply answered, "Yes," before he could craft a more appropriate response. As a pirate captain, he should have laughed cruelly and proclaimed that he loved every moment of bloodshed.

Truthfully, he'd done what he must over the years, but he never enjoyed it. Constantly striving and hunting, his power over the men tenuous, watching over his shoulder with one hand on his cutlass, any control over the sea merely an illusion as well. Oh, for a life where he could just *be*.

But enough of this. If they were to be trapped in the cabin together for the time being, he had to forestall any more damn questions. Imperiously, he ordered, "Read me something. Shakespeare."

There was only silence from the corner, and when Hawk looked over, Plum sat frozen, a piece of dried meat between his fingers, his hand halfway to his mouth. "R—read?"

Was it Hawk's imagination, or had the color drained from Plum's face? "I'm bored. Surely you are too. Here is the solution." He narrowed his gaze. It would be an agreeable way to pass the day, yet Bainbridge was acting as if he'd been ordered to walk the plank.

Plum seemed to recover himself and shook his head. "I'm afraid I can't. I wasn't able to bring my spectacles when you kidnapped me." He shoved the meat in his mouth and chewed.

"There's a magnifying glass in the top drawer of the desk."

His throat worked as he swallowed. "Oh. I'm… I'm not sure it will really work the same."

Annoyance flared. "Try it."

Face pinched, Plum made his way to the desk, bare feet hesitant. He opened the drawer, then closed it. "I don't see it."

"Look. Harder. If I have to get out of bed and it's in there, I will not be pleased."

Sighing, Plum opened the drawer and promptly removed the glass. Why the devil was he so opposed to the idea? The longer he dragged his feet going to the bookshelves, the more Hawk's bafflement gave way to irritation. He declared, "I want *The Tempest.*"

Tilting his head to read the spines, Plum ran his fingers over them, the glass hanging unused in his right hand. Seconds ticked by, and he still hadn't picked out the book.

Was he being obstinate for the sake of it? For fuck's sake, now that Hawk had decided he *wanted* to relax, his prisoner was apparently determined to be difficult. "The blue one at the end."

Plum took the book back to his corner. Very, very slowly. Hawk inhaled deeply, fists clenching. Clearly he'd been too lax, or seeing him brought low by the injury had put ideas into Bainbridge's head as to just who the fuck was in charge here. Plum was his prisoner and needed to be reminded of it.

Hawk commanded, "Start reading. *Now.*"

Feet tucked under him, Plum opened the book, the old leather creaking. He held the glass, but didn't use it. "Uh…"

"I believe we begin on a ship at sea, do we not?" Then Hawk sneered. "You are *lettered,* aren't you?" He'd worked damn hard to learn to read and speak more or less like a gentleman, a struggle Walter Bainbridge's son could never understand. Hawk had wanted to pass the time pleasantly for both of them, and this bizarre rebellion was his thanks?

Plum's cheeks went even redder, and something flared in his eyes—embarrassment, fear, *shame.* He gripped the book so tightly his fingers were white. Hawk realized there was a tiny divot in his chin that was only visible from certain angles, not quite a cleft.

As Plum's jaw clenched, Hawk watched him, baffled, the rush of anger and frustration giving way to utter confusion. Did Bainbridge raise a son so lazy that he hadn't learned to *read?* No. Impossible.

The sheer misery etched on Plum's face tugged at Hawk, and for a moment of madness, he wished he could ease the mysterious pain. He crushed the impulse, his voice hard as stone. "Are you stupid?"

Instead of indignant denial, Bainbridge slammed the book shut and shouted, "Yes!"

Hawk blinked. He could only ask, "What?"

Plum clutched the book to his chest, eyes on the floor. "I'm a dullard. I can't read."

Ridiculous. Hawk laughed humorlessly. "What game do you think you're playing?" He tried to imagine what Plum would gain from this ruse and came up empty. "Do you think *I'm* stupid? Your station, the way you speak—of course you can read."

Face scarlet, Plum's chest rose and fell. "I'm telling you I can't.

I'm stupid."

Fury swept Hawk to his feet despite the howl of protest from his wound. "And I call you a liar. It's a peculiar lie, I'll grant you that. A simpleton wouldn't know the words you do. Wouldn't be able to use them properly, as you do. You've shown intelligence in how quickly you learned to bend the line, in tending to my leg. Why do you insist on this fiction?"

Plum slumped against the wall, and when he spoke, his voice was hoarse. "I barely read half as well as most children. A quarter. It's the truth. Susanna has read to me since I was small—read *for* me, covering up my insufficiency. Tutor after tutor failed to educate me. Then Mr. Chisholm came, and…" Looking down, he swallowed hard.

Yes, there was definitely something there, a vulnerability regarding the tutor. Hawk filed away the information, ignoring a spark of something that could *not* be jealousy, before prompting, "And what?"

"He was able to teach me more than anyone else had, but there was nothing to be done for the fact that I'm simply lacking. I don't have the capacity to read and learn the way other men do. The way ladies do. My sisters are far my intellectual superiors, but they had to marry and have children. Susanna would have excelled at Cambridge or Oxford. Alas." Still gripping the book, he cleared his throat. "Mr. Chisholm tried everything to teach me, but it was hopeless. He made sure to drill me in vocabulary. Made sure no one in society would ever know from a drawing room conversation. It was all he could do."

Hawk stood there in the face of Plum's defeat and found he hated it. He'd worked for days to cow him, but now Hawk was decidedly—most inconveniently—unsettled. "How can this be, when your mind is not diminished?"

Plum laughed, a harsh bite of sound. "I wish I knew. Here, I'll demonstrate."

Opening the book again, he struggled through the first part of the scene, his voice lacking any inflection, mixing up small words and stumbling over others, with names especially garbled. He didn't pause in the proper places, all the words streaming together in a slurry as if they held no meaning, as though he was reading a foreign language.

Hawk held up a hand. "Enough." He sat back heavily on the side of the bed, his stitches straining, fire in his thigh. He ignored it. "I believe you."

"Thank you," Plum muttered, head down, still holding the book to his chest like a shield.

"What does your father make of it?" He had a feeling he knew the answer. Not that he should care. *It's merely curiosity.*

Plum raised his head, expression grim. "As much as my father wanted me when I was an idea, the reality has been a marked disappointment. Susanna and my tutor did their best to shield me, but of course my father found out the truth. He was furious." He shuddered. "He insisted I wasn't applying myself. He…"

After a few moments, Hawk pressed, tension stringing tighter through him. "What did he do?"

Plum stared at his feet. "When I was ten, he rapped my knuckles with a ruler until I was able to read a verse from the Bible without stumbling, until I could say every word properly. After an hour of failure, he'd broken my hand. It swelled up terribly. Susanna and Jane were horrified. I think he was too, because he left me alone after that. He accepted I was a useless dunce. The truth is, he probably won't pay a penny to get me back." As soon as the words escaped, he jolted, eyes wide.

For a moment, Hawk couldn't quite catch a breath. Bainbridge would pay. He *must.* Before Hawk could respond, Plum added, "I didn't mean—no, you see, of course he'll pay the ransom. Everyone will know about it, and he'd never be able to abide seeming weak."

Acid roiled Hawk's stomach. If Bainbridge didn't pay and the men were denied their prize, it would be a bloody mess.

"And he always speaks highly of me outside the family, boasting of my fictitious accomplishments. He won't let me be killed by pirates. He does value me. In—in his own way."

"He'd better." Hawk's fervor for the ransom remained strong, while the urge to strangle Walter Bainbridge with his bare hands had intensified intolerably.

It was nonsense to be affronted for Plum's sake that Walter should treat him so poorly because of his difficulties reading. After how determined he'd been to father a son, Walter still wasn't satisfied, even though Plum was smart and capable and—

Enough. Hawk quelled the absurd urge to offer some reassurance. The boy was his prisoner! He was satisfactory. Nothing more, and nothing mattered but getting the money. Exacting revenge.

Hawk remained confident that Walter Bainbridge's pride would rule the day. "He will raise the ransom or face far too much ridicule and scrutiny from his peers in the New World."

Plum nodded eagerly. "Yes. He hates to be seen as lesser in any way. Even if I have to work myself to the bone to repay him, he'll find a way to raise the money. Susanna and her husband will see to it. Susie loves me truly and is impossible to resist when she sets her mind to something. She has always had a way with our father."

Hawk grumbled, "Your father had better pay." They sat in awkward silence as he cursed himself for engaging with his captive in the first place. Then he said, "I suppose I'll just have to read myself to pass the time."

Holding out his hand, Hawk waited for the book. Plum passed it over, then retreated to his corner. Hawk stretched back on the bed gingerly, his wound aching. He opened the book, its pages slightly yellowed and delicate, the binding beginning to come loose. Plum sat with his legs pulled in, his forehead resting on his knees.

"On a ship at sea: a tempestuous noise of thunder and lightning heard."

Plum raised his head, and Hawk noticed his eyes weren't really brown, but the color of warm honey. As Hawk read on, pitching his voice alternately lower and higher for the different characters, Plum listened avidly, a small smile curving his pretty lips.

Chapter Nine

GAZING OVER THE assembled men, Hawk stood tall, his wound only throbbing dully now, hardly anything at all. After three days in his cabin reading Shakespeare, Cervantes, and Marlowe aloud while Plum listened, seemingly content, it was time to resume his duties. He'd made the odd appearance up on deck so the men didn't suspect, and now his leg was fit enough that he barely limped.

"We're docking at Nassau." As a cheer rang up, he raised his hand. "Only for the day to trade our cargo and resupply. We are all strictly on duty. No drinking. No whoring." Now a grumble vibrated across the deck. "I assure you, I will provide you with all the rum you can drink tonight when we are back aboard and safely tucked away in a cove down the coast. Not just swill either—the finest in the West Indies."

A voice whined, "Can't we get the girls to come down to the docks, at least? We won't say nothin', we swear."

Hawk bit back a sigh. "You know damn well that those ladies are adept at ferreting out information that could be useful to sell to another crew."

More grumbling, and O'Connell, an Irishman rigger who'd proven himself sensible and brave, said, "The captain's right. No sense in risking our ransom for a few minutes of pleasure."

Another man piped up, "Speak for yourself! I last a damn sight longer."

There was laughter then, the current of resentment dissipating. Hawk gazed at them intently. "We need to stay sharp. No one is to breathe a word about our hostage to anyone. No exceptions. Not a drop of alcohol, and if you dare to darken Mrs. Atherton's door to visit her girls, you will lose your share of the ransom. Understood?"

Snell called out, "Aye, Captain," and the others joined in, some more reluctantly than others.

Hawk smiled. "It will be worth the short-term sacrifice in the end, I promise you. Let's keep our heads on and eyes on the prize!"

This roused a cheer, and he dismissed the men, turning to the bow. Snell joined him, saying, "That rum had better be exquisite, or they'll take a vote on a new captain."

Hawk chuckled at the joke, ignoring a slither of unease. He'd kept control by being firm yet fair, but many a pirate captain had been bested by mutiny. In another fortnight, they'd have their prize and see that the sacrifices had been worth it. "It will be Nassau's finest."

"So piss, then. But they'll guzzle it nonetheless." Snell squinted up at the sky. "Clouds coming in from the north. Better find a safe harbor tonight close to Nassau. Pearl Cove, perhaps?"

"Aye."

"Who will watch the prisoner while we go ashore?"

A strange pang of guilt squirmed in his gut. It would be torture for Plum to be so close and unable to get solid land under his feet. "I'll keep him locked in. Put...Grady on guard duty. He's trustworthy. Yes?"

"Yes. And you should relax. I can handle the trade. Perhaps you should find an arse to give a good fucking."

"Maybe I will." It had been ages and would do him good.

Some of the men on board had each other, and in Nassau, no

one gave a damn who fucked who. In the pirate world, men could be as good as married if they chose. Some even wore each other's rings and contracted together in matelotage.

"That's the spirit." Snell clapped him on the shoulder and left him in peace.

Hawk knew it likely mystified Snell and the others that he didn't bugger anyone on board. But he'd decided years ago that he'd rather his prick didn't fall off from some rotting disease and that his own hand was sufficient.

He'd been tempted at times to take up bold young men on offers of willing mouths or arses but had instituted a rule against ever screwing a crew member. It only bred competition and hostility. Better to hold himself removed. Untouchable.

It hadn't even been that difficult. The last time he'd experienced the fever of true desire, he'd been little more than a boy, spending nights in a hammock with John in the stinking, black belly of the *HMS Leaside*.

He allowed himself a moment to remember John's impish grin and cowlick of fair hair falling over his forehead, the breathless intensity with which they'd kissed and touched, each exploration new and thrilling, young enough that no one paid any mind to them sharing a hammock.

The memory gave way, as it always did, to flashes of cannon fire, Spaniards upon them in the dawn. It had been a bloody, hard-won battle to escape the man-of-war. Hawk could still hear the quartermaster's relief as he said, *"Could have been worse. Most of us are still here."*

Most.

John's head had nearly been taken clean off, his rosy-cheeked, dear face gone before Hawk could even understand what had happened—that John had propelled him out of harm's way.

His blood had still stained Hawk's face—his hands, his lips, his very heart—when they'd put John into the sea along with a dozen other men, each wrapped in cloth. The quartermaster had spoken John's name aloud before the splash, as if he were an offering to the sea gods. Perhaps he was.

Hawk had stood solemn with the others along the rail, the flag fluttering at half-mast. He'd watched the canvas entombing John bob for a few moments before sinking beneath the waves and forever into the deep.

When the last body was out of sight, the men had turned back to their tasks, bustling about and getting on with it, readying the ship and themselves to do it all again when called upon. Hawk had no path but to follow, unless he wanted to dive after John.

He'd been sorely tempted.

In the months following, Hawk had found the pain crippling and of absolutely no benefit to him. Nights had been the hardest, alone in his hammock without the sweet nuzzle of John's kisses, and he'd told himself, *never again.* Over the years, he'd fucked some men. But his lips never touched theirs, his hands never lingered over bared skin. He never held them close and slept as one.

It had been so very long now, John only a distant speck on the horizon in Hawk's wake. Why he crowded into Hawk's mind now was a mystery. He probably didn't even remember John's face correctly. Over the years, it had surely morphed and reshaped in his memory.

Yet he could still see the red crosses on the Spanish sails. With the metallic tang of John's blood in his mouth, Hawk had climbed the mast for his lookout duty and scanned the seas, eager for another battle. Wishing the Spaniards would pursue them once more so he could blow them to smithereens.

Perhaps it was that day his course was set to become a privateer, and now this, a lawless pirate.

Shaking his head, he ducked down the ladder. Plum waited in the cabin, limbs jittery with excitement as he asked, "Do you know how long the beach is? How far it extends? If I run—"

"You won't be running."

Plum smiled, a puff of laughter escaping with a flash of white teeth. "I told you, I don't mean to escape. I am resigned to my fate as your prisoner. You threatened my sister, and I'd never endanger Susanna or her babe. Never. I will return. Or you could run alongside? No, not with your leg. Another crewman could?"

Hawk could not allow himself to be swayed. "No. You'll stay on board." He strode to his desk and sat in his chair, taking up his quill.

Plum certainly wasn't laughing now. "But we made a bet. I won. I know you remember. Those stitches in your leg should prompt you."

"I remember. Nassau is not suitable. Far too many people. It's not possible."

"But you *promised!*"

Unbelievably, an *apology* formed on Hawk's tongue, and he barely bit it back. Why should he be sorry to break an oath to his hostage? He was a pirate, after all. Walter Bainbridge had seen to that.

Still, he found himself saying, "Too many people. We'll find an island soon enough. We need to make repairs thanks to that lunatic Alfred. Somewhere uninhabited. Big enough for you to have a run." There, he was being reasonable.

Plum shook his head, pacing, rolling his shirtsleeves past his elbows, displaying a hint of the firm, trim muscles hidden beneath the linen. "Can I at least go ashore? Get off this ship and stretch my legs?"

"You'll stay here."

"You're a liar," Plum spat, creamy cheeks flushing as he paced.

While Hawk had thought him quite plain upon first glance, now he found himself drawn to Plum's face. A few times whilst reading aloud, he'd lost his place in the text because he'd found himself watching Plum and the way he listened with his eyes closed, a dreamy smile tugging at his mouth.

A few freckles on his nose caught Hawk's eye, and then Plum's tongue darted out to lick his lips. "Why did I believe you even for a moment?" he demanded. "Why did I think better of you because you read to me and were kind about my deficiencies?"

Hawk tore his gaze away. "I don't know, since apparently I must remind you I'm a fucking pirate!" Plum's anger and hurt shouldn't have moved him. He shouldn't have wanted to live up to any expectations. Why the devil should he care? He had nothing to prove.

"Can I at least go up on deck?"

"No." He wanted to explain that there were too many risks; that if Plum were captured by another crew, he might be tortured or worse. *And I won't get my ransom. That's what's really important.* He sneered. "You'll survive."

He turned his attention to his tasks, going over the list of cargo to trade, and soon enough they were in Nassau. Voices rang out over the water, and Plum went to kneel by the open window, craning his neck. Hawk stood behind him, failing to keep his eyes off Plum's firm, round arse.

There was only a glimpse of palm trees and huts, people milling around where the beach curved. "If you shout…"

Grumbling, Plum sighed. "I won't."

Hawk grabbed his coat and left before he was compelled to make any more promises.

HEAD BUZZING PLEASANTLY, Hawk left the men to their merriment in the forecastle, closing a hatch behind him in the passageway. The music and boisterous shouts faded by the stern, and the lashing wind and rain reached his ears.

With a sigh, he climbed to the main deck, soaked to the skin in moments, his coat forgotten by the barrel of rum. He made his rounds, checking on the poor sods who'd drawn the night watch, promising them extra grog tomorrow. They were safely at anchor, but it was still miserable on deck.

Carrying a small sack, he returned below, finally approaching his cabin. He nodded to Grady. "Any trouble?"

"Not a peep, Captain."

"Dismissed. Go eat and have as much rum as you'd like."

Grinning, Grady passed him the key and hurried away. Hawk hesitated. It was foolish to still feel guilty—or to feel guilty whatsoever—but he hated not living up to a wager, no matter with whom it was made.

He'd stayed on deck while they left Nassau and made their way to the cove, then eaten and drank too much rum with the men, Snell watching him with a raised eyebrow. He couldn't avoid it anymore and twisted the key.

Plum was in his corner, curled on the blanket, either asleep or pretending to be. He'd lit one of the lanterns at some point, and it still flickered. Hawk was about to tiptoe inside when he caught himself and marched boldly, boots striking the floor. *It's my cabin, for fuck's sake.*

He dropped the sack on the floor by the corner. "There's fruit. Mango, orange, and…a plum."

Dropping any pretense, Plum sat up and opened the rough canvas. "Thank you." He pulled out the mango and held it in his hands, peering at it curiously, then poking at the skin.

"Here." Hawk took his dagger from his belt and handed it to him. Only once the brass handle was in Plum's grasp did he stop to question just what the fuck he was doing. *This is why I should keep to one cup of rum.*

But Plum only peeled the fruit before passing the weapon back. He took a tentative bite of the mango, then moaned. Juice dripped down his fingers, and his tongue darted out, licking them clean, as if he didn't want to waste a drop.

Hawk spun around and started tugging at his soaked clothes, commanding himself to ignore the coiling heat in his belly. He stripped them off and stretched out naked on the bed, determined to go to sleep.

It had been a long day, and he'd had to be on guard in Nassau—weighing every word, performing, wearing his cursedly hot coat, satisfied with the whispers that followed in his wake. *"There goes the Sea Hawk."*

Now he could exhale and relax. Well, he would if Plum stopped making such obscene noises. Each slurp and sigh of pleasure went straight to Hawk's prick.

To hell with it.

He took himself in hand, because why the devil shouldn't he? It was his cabin, and he didn't give a fuck what his prisoner thought. Even if a glance told him his prisoner was now transfixed, the rest of the fruit abandoned in his lap, eyes locked on Hawk's stiffening rod.

With his right hand tucked behind his head, Hawk spread his legs. He licked his palm with a long, slow stroke, then spit in it a few times. Lazily, he worked himself to full hardness, Plum's feverish gaze boring into his skin, setting him aflame.

He could only glimpse Plum's shadow from the corner of his eye in the low, guttering light of the lantern, but was certain he watched every pass of Hawk's hand over his shaft.

Get it done and go to sleep.

Yet he couldn't ignore Plum's curious hunger. Couldn't deny himself the thrill of it, even though he knew it was madness. He'd kept himself in check for so long.

More than that, it was forever since Hawk had been desired with such pure, raw honesty. Why shouldn't he have a taste of forbidden fruit? Just this once, if Plum wanted it.

Is it honesty, though? Or is he playing me like Mr. Cooper's fiddle? Trying to ensure his survival?

The merry tune Cooper currently played in the forecastle as the men caroused echoed faintly through the ship beyond the din of the storm. Hawk should close his eyes, jerk himself quickly to completion, and let the distant music be his lullaby.

Yet his craving would not be denied. Hawk would leave it up to Plum. Teasing back the hood from his cock, he asked, "Does it make your prick hard, to watch me?" For the space of too many heartbeats, each faster and faster, he was afraid there would be no reply.

Then, from the darkness, a breathy answer. "Yes."

Relief shouldn't have sweetened his veins, but it flowed. It was unwise to play these games with his prisoner—his bounty. But really, what better revenge than deflowering Bainbridge's son? What a blow to the snake's pride that would be.

And if it gave Hawk the opportunity to touch those trim muscles, to taste and explore… All the better. A slow smile lifted his lips. "Do you want a closer look?"

On tentative feet, Plum neared, wide eyes darting between Hawk's face and his cock. Bending up his left leg with his foot flat on the mattress, Hawk ignored the twinging from his stitches and rocked his hips, his body afire, in danger of being consumed by Plum's gaze alone—by the *longing* in it.

If it was false, Plum belonged on the London stage. His chest rose and fell rapidly, and he licked his lips before blurting, "I want… If I should die, first I want…" He seemed to be searching for the right words before croaking, "I don't want to die like this."

"Like what?" Hawk raked his gaze down Plum's body and up again. The shirt was hanging loosely, obscuring the tenting of his breeches, but Hawk was certain he was hard. Oh, he ached to see that swelling cock, to behold the evidence of Plum's desire.

Plum opened and closed his mouth with a snap, and Hawk

put him out of his scarlet-cheeked misery. "A virgin?"

Sighing, Plum nodded. "I've been too afraid."

Hawk's blood sang, a primal, possessive urge galloping through him. "Truly, no man ever bent you? No lady slipped her hand into your breeches behind the rosebushes, or whore plied her trade?"

"Never. I don't want a lady. Or a whore. Only a man. I don't know why, but it's always been like that for me."

His innocence was as intoxicating as the damn rum, and Hawk reached out his hand and crooked his finger.

Adam's apple bobbing, Plum took another step, still out of reach. "Is it... Would you rather have a woman? Or..." he whispered, eyes shining with unmistakable hope, "Are you like me? Unnatural?"

It was absurd to betray any truth, yet thinking of John earlier had stirred up the memories of how it had felt to know such fear and loneliness for the crime of one's own nature. He found himself nodding.

But his desire wasn't selfless—far from it. The urge to be the first to plunder that sweet, tight arse beat in Hawk like a war drum, and it was all he could do to keep himself in check.

Leaving his hard prick alone for the moment, lest he embarrass himself, he caressed his nipples instead, satisfied when Plum's gaze followed his fingers.

Hawk said, "I tried a woman once. Friction took its course. But it wasn't like this." He took hold of his shaft again, thumbing over the head. "Do you want me to show you? How it can be between two men?"

Jerking his head in a nod, Plum yanked off his clothing and tossed it aside bravely. His long, slim prick stood straight out from a nest of dark curls, bollocks heavy between his legs. Tension rippled through his lean muscles, and in the fading lamplight his flesh was golden, light-brown hair scattered thinly over his chest and body. His nipples were a dusky rose, peaked without being touched.

And oh, how Hawk wanted to touch.

Plum licked his lips. "What should I do?"

"Get the bottle of oil from the middle drawer of my desk. Then come here." Instead of creeping hesitantly, Plum rushed to the desk and then the bed, eyes raking Hawk up and down. Hawk put both hands behind his head and raised an eyebrow. "Well?"

With a sharp inhalation, Plum climbed up over him. They both shuddered as their naked flesh met, and Hawk took hold of Plum's hips, tempted to plunge right up into him but keeping himself in check.

"Like…like this?" Plum asked, straddling him, strung tight. Surely frightened, but pressing on, at the edge of the precipice and ready to leap. His muscles quivered, excitement lighting his honey eyes, and Hawk wondered if he looked similar when he ran.

"Is this right?" Plum gazed at Hawk with such openness, asking for guidance, trusting despite every reason he shouldn't. A little furrow appeared between Plum's brows. "Does it work like this? Or should I be on my hands and knees? Like…like an animal?"

And despite every fucking reason *he* shouldn't, Hawk found himself opening too, enticed by Plum's innocence. He smiled up at him, running soothing hands over his tense thighs. "It works in all sorts of ways."

Not since John had he had anyone so sweet. And as much as he would love to pummel Plum on his hands and knees, right then he'd rather ease him and sate his innocent craving. Reward that trust. They both wanted it, so why shouldn't they steal pleasure where they could?

He took Plum's hand and poured oil over his fingers, the scent of coconut sweet and cloying. "Open yourself for me."

Eagerly, Plum reached behind, then tensed, a gasp on his lips.

"You won't fit," he blurted.

Cock painfully hard, Hawk drew small circles on Plum's firm thighs with his fingertips, avidly watching the flex of Plum's muscles. "Slowly. Have you fucked yourself like this before?"

"Yes. But it will take too long to go slowly." Plum whimpered, eyes fluttering and mouth parting. "Just fuck me now. Do it."

"Patience." Aside from not wanting to tear him open, Hawk's blood roared watching him work, even though his hole and fingers were hidden from view. It made it more exciting that he couldn't see, the anticipation growing, every moan and sigh sending tinder sparks to his bollocks.

"Please, it's enough." Plum withdrew his slick hand and leaned onto Hawk's chest. His face creased as if he were pained. *"Please."*

Hawk oiled his own cock, then took hold of Plum's hips and guided him onto it, the head nudging that tight opening. "Is this what you desire?"

In answer, Plum closed his eyes and bravely sank down, taking in the whole head of Hawk's prick, his eyes watering as he gasped. "Oh!" A flush spread down his chest, and Hawk traced it with his fingertips, circling Plum's nipples, eliciting a shameless moan.

Inch by inch, Plum lowered himself, Hawk holding his hips steady again, easing some of his weight and biting back a groan. That tight, perfect heat enclosed him—embraced him, the pressure almost too good. He couldn't remember the last time fucking had been like this. Normally he barely looked at the other man, but with Plum, he was riveted.

He watched as emotions played over Plum's face—pain, wonder, exhilaration. Such a dauntless young man, boldly taking what he desired. The heat of him gripping Hawk was exquisite, and sweat beaded on Hawk's forehead as he struggled to keep control.

Had Hawk been so fearless his first time? It had been rushed and awkward and painful, though John had taken as much care as possible. Hawk was struck by the thought that he didn't want to hurt Plum, which was idiocy.

He might have to *kill* him.

His breath caught and muscles seized, and Plum opened his eyes, almost all the way impaled on Hawk's prick, trembling, a tear hovering on his lashes.

Hawk should roll him over onto his hands and knees and fuck him the way he would an anonymous man on the beach in Nassau in the dead of night. Instead he nearly reached up to wipe the tear away before it could run down Plum's red cheek.

Thankfully, Plum swiped at it first, gritting his teeth as he fully seated himself, not backing off. He looked down, then up at Hawk, an incredulous, giddy smile blooming over his face. "It fits," he breathed. "I have a cock inside me." He ran his palm over Hawk's chest, leaving sparks in his wake. "I've dreamed of this for so long."

His smile flickered, brow creasing as he breathed harder, and Hawk could practically see the dogs of shame giving chase in Plum's mind. Plum murmured, "I know I shouldn't. And with you, of all men. Yet..." He rolled his hips experimentally. "Lord, it feels so good." Taking a deep breath, he nodded. "I shall have this. I will not be denied."

Hawk found himself smiling, warm satisfaction flowing through him to be not only the first man to breach that un-touched arse, but the one to give Plum that which he'd craved and denied himself. It filled a need in Hawk so deep he hadn't known it existed.

He'd been patient, but he needed to touch. Plum's prick had flagged somewhat. Hawk poured a glug of oil into his palm and smoothed it over the shaft, gratified by the clench of Plum's arse, his long moan, and the way his cock responded almost immediate-ly, swelling back up.

Hawk stroked him and ran his right hand up and down Plum's side, then over his nipples, tweaking them, teasing.

"You've imagined this before? Being fucked by a man's cock?"

"Oh yes." His eyes were dark with lust, feverish and bold.

Hawk took Plum's hips and thrust up sharply. Plum threw his head back, arching like a bow, crying out, little sounds falling from his open lips, a desperate, heady song. It reverberated deeply through Hawk, and he dedicated himself to seeing Plum utterly go to pieces on his prick.

Trying to find just the right spot, Hawk experimented until he brushed the swollen nub perfectly, and Plum nearly snapped in half, whipping forward to lean over him.

"Oh God, that's... You're so deep."

Thighs flexing, he fucked himself, his tight arse like heaven. His hands lay flat on Hawk's chest, fingers digging in for purchase as he moved in a jerky rhythm, struggling to find that spot inside him on every stroke.

He panted so prettily, sandy hair damp and curling around his forehead, honey eyes bright with discovery and lust, little whines escaping his pink mouth: "*Oh, oh, yes.*"

The ten points of pressure from Plum's fingers might actually bruise, new dark spots amid the lines of his tattoo, but the hint of pain sent fire to Hawk's balls. Plum was wild and free on top of him, eyes shut as he fucked himself fiercely.

Hawk reached up to cup his cheek, needing to see his eyes again, swallowing his own gasp when Plum looked down at him with pure pleasure and reckless abandon, fearless as he took what he wanted.

Plum was supposed to be the prisoner, yet Hawk was ensnared, powerless to deny him anything, a fishing boat caught in a frigate's churning wake, swept up and only able to hold on.

"Oh, oh, I need..." Plum slammed down, wincing.

Hawk burned to give him that release. Plum's dripping cock was flushed a deep red, the hood pulled back. Hawk swiped a thumb over the head, then gave it a swift, commanding stroke from root to tip. On the third pass, Plum cried out, splashing Hawk's chest, his arse gripping so sweetly, eyes squeezed shut in ecstasy.

As Plum trembled, Hawk fucked up into his clinging heat with powerful thrusts, unable to contain himself a moment longer. Plum's eyes shot open, a cry on his lips as another spurt of cream splatted on Hawk's chest.

He clamped down, and that was all it took to unleash Hawk's release, wildfire sweeping from bow to stern and back again as he emptied himself, their eyes locked together. Hawk barely managed to clench his jaw and choke down his shout.

"God in heaven," Plum muttered, head dropping, his arms going slack where he still braced himself, fingers that had dug into Hawk's flesh relaxing.

"I'd say this is more the devil's arena," Hawk drawled, his attempt at a joke sounding hollow. Indeed, Plum ignored it. Hawk had to pry himself free and regain his senses, but he still held Plum's slim hips, tanned hands stark against that pale skin.

Hawk's prick had begun to soften, resting inside Plum's slick, well-used hole, where he'd been the first. Unlike his typical rushed encounters, he wasn't yet ready to withdraw, instead reaching out to trace the edges of Plum's swollen rim around him.

Chest rising and falling, Plum lifted his head. His glazed eyes met Hawk's, then lowered. He swallowed thickly, blinking as if he was coming back to himself after a fevered dream, and Hawk dreaded seeing guilt furrow that brow once more. Why should their desires be deemed unworthy? Because England said so? To hell with England.

Hawk lifted his thumb to press over the tiny divot in Plum's chin, wondering if he'd been born with it or acquired it on some adventure, perhaps running or climbing trees. Their skin was slick with sweat where they pressed together, and Hawk was struck by the urge to roll Plum under him and cover him from head to toe.

Plum swiped at his seed, only succeeding in making the mess worse, matting together the hair on Hawk's chest, tracing the edges of his tattoo. "I'm sorry." His fingers shook as he tried to clean it up.

"There's no shame in it." Hawk captured Plum's wrist and drew up his hand, sucking his fingers and the musky, tangy treat laced with the lingering mango juice as Plum watched with wide eyes.

"Nathaniel." His gaze snapped up to Hawk's as Hawk froze. Hoarsely, he added, "My name, it's—"

Hawk roughly lifted him off not only his cock, but then shoved him from the bed entirely, plopping him on his feet. He swayed, and Hawk held on a few moments longer before letting go. After all, it wouldn't do to have his prize tumble over and crack his skull.

Forcing a wide yawn, he leaned over and plucked Plum's linen drawers from where they'd been abandoned on the floor. With swift movements, he cleaned his prick and what he could of his chest, then tossed the sticky drawers at Plum, who was too dazed to catch them. The white cloth landed at his feet.

Although his heart thumped too quickly, Hawk kept his tone even. Disinterested. "There. Now you won't die a virgin."

He folded his hands behind his head and closed his eyes, willing his breathing back to normal. The ship's sway usually lulled him to sleep almost instantly on the nights he wasn't worrying over the men, or other ships, or weather, or cargo. Or being captured by the English. Or French. Or Spanish.

His limbs were loose, and he should have been able to drop off right away. There was no reason to wonder how Plum was feeling. Sure as hell no reason to *worry*. No reason to soothe him. Hawk had given him what he wanted.

He'd taken what he wanted too. It had been too long since he'd lost himself in a fuck, and now he had. He'd buggered Walter

Bainbridge's only son, adding another layer to his revenge.

That was the end of it.

Yet sleep was elusive as he listened to Plum retreat to the corner. Hawk cracked his eyes to watch him clean himself, the guttering lamp casting jerky shadows. Taking the bucket Hawk had once again allowed him, Plum splashed a bit of water on his soiled drawers, then reached behind himself, wincing.

Hawk imagined how skilled Plum would grow, his nature passionate and curious. Oh, the things Hawk could teach him…

Enough.

This had been a one-time indulgence. He'd marked Bainbridge's heir, and even if the snake never knew, Hawk would. Nathaniel would—

No. His name is only Plum. My bounty. My revenge. Nothing more.

Resolutely, he closed his eyes to Plum's creamy skin and spent, sweaty limbs. Soon the lamp extinguished, and all was darkness. Two words echoed in his mind.

Never again.

Chapter Ten

I'VE BEEN FUCKED.

Well, to be accurate, Nathaniel had largely fucked himself. He'd ridden the pirate king's massive prick the way he imagined a whore would—wanton and desperate. Shameless.

The memory tightened his bollocks, his nipples tingling, stomach swooping. Curled on the floor, awful blanket kicked aside, he admitted the truth, if only to himself.

I want to do it again. And again. And again.

He'd thought he'd known his body's hunger—the shape and weight of it, its sharp edges and cavernous depth—but he'd only scratched the surface. Now that he'd had a cock inside him, the itch had burrowed deeper than he'd imagined possible. It burned in every inch of him.

Hawk had left to go on deck, and in the dawn light, Nathaniel poked around in nooks and crannies, opening drawers. Yet he found no mirror, the one Hawk used while shaving and trimming his shadow of a beard apparently locked up with the weapons.

Nathaniel laughed at himself for wondering if he'd somehow appear different. Standing by the bed, which was less luxurious than it looked—the mattress had been surprisingly hard beneath his knees—he reached out and ran a hand over the rumpled linens.

His belly swooped once more, skin flushing, even though a

voice piped up to warn that he shouldn't take any satisfaction in what had happened. Especially considering the kind of man Hawk was. Nathaniel's hand faltered, his smile fading, shame creeping in on schedule.

It was folly to feel any kind of hurt at the way he'd been summarily dismissed. After Hawk had ejected him from the bed, he'd returned to his place in the corner sticky with oil and seed. He'd cleaned himself, feeling sick to his stomach.

Yet when he'd woken, he'd wished the seed were still inside him, that he could feel the evidence between his fingertips, even though the swollen rawness of his arse reassured him that not a moment of it had been imagined. Now guilt and silly hope seesawed inside him like the rocking of the ship on the tide.

What had he thought? That fucking would change anything about his circumstances—that Hawk would hold him close like a lover? Kiss him?

This was the man who'd promised to gut him if Nathaniel's father didn't pay his ransom. As much as Nathaniel tried not to dwell on that possible outcome, he couldn't expect the fact that Hawk had fucked him to change his fortunes.

And yet... Hawk had been *inside* him. He'd been gentle and encouraging. He'd watched Nathaniel with something new in his blue eyes, an attentiveness like he'd really *seen* Nathaniel for the first time.

He'd confessed to sharing the same nature, and it still sent a thrill through Nathaniel to know he wasn't alone. He'd felt the throb of Hawk's prick in his very core, had been filled with his seed. He'd given Hawk not only his trust, but his very *self*. Would Hawk still be able to kill him if the time came?

Turning away from the bed, Nathaniel huffed in frustration. He knew he shouldn't make more of fucking than it was. They weren't *lovers*. Hawk had taken his pleasure as most men would when offered it. That he wasn't brutal about it meant nothing.

Desire pulsed through him at the idea of being mastered, and Nathaniel cursed his lust. Yet the thought remained: *I want to do it again.*

If only he could speak to someone about it. He'd finally found a man like him, yet he was still alone. He'd fornicated, and it was *glorious*, and the idea of marrying Elizabeth Davenport was more unthinkable than ever. Should he even survive. Should his father pay the ransom.

Will Hawk really kill me?

He thought of the hours and hours Hawk had read aloud for his sake. The way he'd refuted that Nathaniel was stupid. The fresh fruit he'd brought. Why these kindnesses if Hawk truly was nothing more than a cold-blooded killer?

Hands jiggling, Nathaniel paced around the cabin—back, forth, to, and fro—chest tight, breath short. He needed to *run,* to feel the ground under his feet and wind in his ears, his mind clearing with every step, peace flowing with every inhalation, muscles burning wonderfully.

Warring thoughts slithered through him, too hard to catch: contrition, rebellion, grief, refusal. Trapped in the cursed cabin, he rushed to the windows and shoved one out, opening his mouth and breathing deep of the salty air, spray wetting his face as the ship crested a swell and rolled down it.

The water in the West Indies was a clear blue unlike any he'd ever seen, and he longed to go up on deck and look in all directions. In Nassau, he'd been able to glimpse how the sand was almost white, and he ached to sink his feet into it and run for miles.

Of course he'd been promised that, and Hawk had gone back on his word. Nathaniel shouldn't believe a thing he said, no matter how many books he read aloud. No matter how tender his fingers had felt tracing the spot where their bodies were still joined after coupling.

The cabin door opened, and Nathaniel's foolish, foolish heart leapt. But when he turned, Hawk didn't meet his gaze. In fact, he didn't look at him at all. He simply circled his desk, boots thudding, pulled out his chair, and opened his log.

He pushed up the flowing sleeves of his dark shirt, and soon the quill scratched the page. Nathaniel moved back to stand near his corner. Then he crossed the cabin to the bookshelf and stood there.

Then back again. Then over by the bed, and finally right in front of the desk. There was no response from Hawk. Not even a flicker of his eyes, or hesitation as he dipped his quill in the ink pot. Simply…nothing. As if Nathaniel weren't even present. As if he didn't matter at all.

It shouldn't have bothered him. He shouldn't have permitted the well of pain to open and widen, but to be made invisible again after his desires were finally known—and shared—was unbearable. The words escaped before he could creep back to his corner. "Am I really so beneath you?"

The damned quill finally stilled, and Hawk peered up, not lifting his head. "If you think so."

"What am I supposed to think? How can I feel anything but brought low when you won't even *look* at me?"

Hawk sat back in the chair, brows drawn tight, a sneer on his lips. The carved serpents and bird rose above his head, framing it like a dark crown. "Why the fuck should I care about how you *feel?*"

He pushed back the chair to stand and walked toward the door. "You are a prisoner on a God-damned pirate ship. If you insist on being ashamed of taking pleasure where it can be found, that's your choice. Your fucking problem."

Nathaniel stepped to the center of the cabin, legs trembling but fists clenched. "You *make* me feel ashamed by…dismissing me thus. Pretending you don't even see me. You're a hypocrite."

As if speaking to a small child, condescension dripping, Hawk turned and said, "You're my prisoner, Plum. You're nothing. I fucked your virgin ass so I could take my pleasure and return you to your father defiled. There was no other meaning in it."

"There, you see! 'Defiled.' Is that not designed to shame me? Your messages are mixed, sir."

Jaw clenched, Hawk barked, "I'm not a gentleman. I do not owe you a thing. I am also not your fucking nursemaid, here to soothe your little hurts and rock you to sleep. I am not your beloved tutor. I am not a good man." He took a long-legged stride toward him. Then another.

The edge of the desk jammed into Nathaniel's buttocks as he jerked back. He braced his hands behind him, fingers scrabbling over loose paper as Hawk loomed.

"You said your legendarily kind and proper tutor taught you to wrestle. Tell me, did you yearn for him to bugger you?"

The breath whooshed from Nathaniel's lungs, his head spinning. He opened and closed his mouth mutely, and then Hawk had his wrist, whipping him around and bending him over the desk, right arm twisted up behind him.

The heat of Hawk's big body hovered over him, his breath gusting over Nathaniel's ear. "When he *pinned* you, did you want him to pull down your breeches?"

His hand snaked beneath Nathaniel, tugging at the buttons. Cooler air caressed his skin as his breeches and linen drawers were yanked down to his knees. Nathaniel's heart galloped.

With his other hand, Hawk pressed Nathaniel's head down, the polished wood smooth against his left cheek. "Did you want him to fuck you?"

He gasped, lungs burning. The word escaped, a ragged whisper. "Yes."

Hawk's fingers splayed over the side of Nathaniel's face, thumb invading his mouth. The skin was rough and callused, and

Nathaniel sucked desperately, his cock rock-hard. He whimpered when Hawk withdrew his hand.

"Did you even know what it was you wanted?" Hawk slid his wet thumb between Nathaniel's arse cheeks, pushing the tip into his hole. His right hand was still an iron band around Nathaniel's wrist.

As Hawk stretched him with his thumb, Nathaniel's knees almost gave out. "Yes. I knew how... I saw a stallion mount a mare once, and I knew I wanted that." Hawk groaned and mumbled something he couldn't make out, and Nathaniel went on. "I wasn't quite sure if it worked the same with men, but I..."

"*Wanted?*" He shoved his thick thumb inside.

Swallowing a cry, Nathaniel answered, "Yes." His shoulder burned, twisted arm tingling.

"And now you know exactly what it is you want."

"Yes," he groaned.

When Hawk pulled his thumb free and released his wrist, Nathaniel's cheeks went hot. He was bent and displayed, breeches around his knees. He should push himself up and flee—not that he could go far. But he could tell Hawk to go straight to the devil for manipulating him this way.

Yet he remained motionless, his arm still behind his back, legs spread, flushed cheek against the cool desk. He blinked at the bookcase, the titles on the spines too far away to read even if they didn't confound him.

He wanted this. To hell with his pride. To hell with worrying about his fate or Hawk's role in it. No man truly knew what tomorrow would bring. Today Nathaniel was *alive,* and he would get fucked as many times as he could.

God, he wanted to be mounted and pounded with the power of cannon fire until his teeth rattled, until he was bruised and spent. He whimpered. "Please?"

For an awful, soul-crushing moment, he thought Hawk would

leave him hard and aching. Humiliated. Then the exotic scent of the oil they'd used the night before filled the air and fabric rustled.

Nathaniel exhaled in relief, the thrilling edge of fear returning as Hawk did, his rod thick, slick with oil, pressing against Nathaniel's entrance. Fingers dug into his arse cheeks, spreading him. Nathaniel held his breath as Hawk pushed just inside, prick like steel and too big.

But the knowledge that Hawk was hard for *him* set his head spinning with exhilaration and possibilities. Hawk clearly wanted him, despite his transparent attempts at maintaining distance.

Could Nathaniel make himself valuable enough to be spared if the time came? Could the tenuous, flickering connection between them be stoked into a fire with embers that never grew cold? If he could peel away the Sea Hawk's defenses and reach the man beneath, could there be something *real?*

Nathaniel's hole already burned, sore and raw from the night before. But it mattered not—he wanted Hawk inside him again more than anything. The pain somehow intensified the tight pull of pleasure in his groin.

Hawk took hold of his right hand where it was still folded against his lower back. "Good boy."

As pride swelled in Nathaniel, Hawk straightened his cramped, almost-numb arm, pinning it to the desk by his head, then doing the same with his left arm. Then Hawk's heat returned as he leaned over to speak in Nathaniel's ear.

"Tell me. What is it you want, Plum?"

"Your cock. All of it."

"Hmm." Hawk was barely inside him. He pushed another inch. "What do you want me to do with my cock?"

Nathaniel gritted his teeth. "Fuck me with it, you son of a bitch!"

Laughter booming, Hawk thrust in to the hilt, driving the air out of him like a bellows. Pain flared, but as Hawk fucked him, bollocks slapping Nathaniel's arse, the torment became exquisite. Nathaniel was well and truly pinned, by his wrists and with Hawk's prick filling him.

It still didn't seem possible something so big could fit, and he was undone by it, limbs jelly, everything in the world narrowed to the cock stretching him, the iron grips around his wrists, the warm blasts of Hawk's grunts. Nathaniel moaned, "Oh, yes. I have yearned for this so long."

He realized some of the guttural noises he heard came from his own throat, his lips parted as he was fucked like a dog. He couldn't move even if he wanted to, and the thought only made his balls tighten.

His throbbing, leaking cock was pinned against the desk, rutting against the wood as Hawk slammed into him. "Please," he begged.

"Would your good and proper tutor ever have given you what you needed?" Hawk punctuated his question with an extra-vicious thrust. "Would he fill you with his seed?"

"No! Only you."

Hawk leaned closer, his bulk dwarfing Nathaniel. He pulled out almost all the way, then pushed in again with shallow strokes, angling until he brushed the spot that buckled Nathaniel's knees.

Sparks exploded behind his eyes, white dots appearing as he cried out. With another few strokes Nathaniel spent, spurting and shaking, crying out loudly, pressed to the desk.

Hawk began fucking him powerfully again, their skin slapping in the creaking, swaying cabin. Nathaniel groaned along with him when Hawk spilled inside. Panting in gusts over Nathaniel's neck, Hawk rested his head, lips at the top of Nathaniel's spine.

Almost a kiss.

Nathaniel murmured, "Thank you," and the twin iron grips around his wrists went slack, Hawk's thumbs stroking the reddened skin. For all his insistence that Nathaniel meant nothing—for all his bluster—he had fulfilled Nathaniel's wildest desires twice now.

He knew it was unwise in the extreme to underestimate his captor, to allow himself any complacency or sense of security. Yet with Hawk still inside him, lips soft on the nape of his neck, he wondered anew where the masquerade truly ended and the man began—the man he'd glimpsed, who was capable of kindness.

The man who wouldn't be able to harm him or his innocent sister. Perhaps Nathaniel was hopelessly naïve, but his instincts told him Hawk wasn't the villain he purported to be. The villain he *tried* to be.

He squeezed his arse around Hawk's prick still deep inside him, and Hawk moaned, his hand smoothing over Nathaniel's hair. Was fucking always like this? Nathaniel had no other experiences for comparison, and surely Hawk had many. But did he always stay close afterward? His other hand was still over Nathaniel's on the desk, thumb stroking rhythmically.

Nathaniel gasped when Hawk pulled out, the sudden emptiness shocking, his thighs quivering. But Hawk didn't abandon him this time, and Nathaniel's heart sang with possibility.

Thick, callused fingers gently pushed the seed back inside where it dripped from Nathaniel's tender arse. "Only me," Hawk muttered, still leaning over him, lips by Nathaniel's ear.

A shiver skipped down Nathaniel's spine like a stone over a pond's smooth surface.

Only you.

<h1 style="text-align:center">Chapter Eleven</h1>

"OH! IT'S RAINING."

Hawk glanced up from his chart, which he had been studying uselessly for almost an hour, trying, and fucking failing, not to be distracted by Nathaniel—*Plum*—in the corner to his right. Rain showered the glass, and Hawk grunted.

Naked from the waist up in only his breeches, the fastenings under his knees flapping, Plum rose and climbed onto the window seat. He pushed out the glass and curled his feet under him on the cushion, peering out, raindrops splattering his face.

Hawk had awoken that morning with his prick achingly hard, eager for Plum's tight arse, yearning to hear his moans and soft cries, to give him pleasure. Which was the very reason he'd forced himself up before the change of watch, while Plum slept on.

He'd only returned to his cabin mid-afternoon when Snell had grumbled he was wearing holes in the deck with his agitation. Plum had been exercising his arms, pressing up his weight and balancing on his toes, his bare torso glistening with sweat. His muscles had strained, and he'd grunted as he moved down and up.

Hawk had almost retreated, his prick swelling. But why shouldn't he spend the rest of the day comfortably in his cabin? Why should he be chased away by his prisoner? Or, more specifically, the hunger for him. It was a mistake to have indulged it, and now he would master it.

He'd sworn to himself he would *not* fuck Plum again. Would not allow himself to be baited into it as he had the previous day. He'd been doing so well ignoring him, but then Plum had challenged him—and Hawk could admit to himself he had cause, that Hawk had wielded shame as a weapon.

That spirit fired Hawk's blood, how Plum hadn't cowered and denied his own cravings but had submitted eagerly. Hawk had lost all control and couldn't seem to regret it.

But not today. He would prove he was the master not only of his prisoner but his own urges. He would *not* have him. And so far he hadn't, though his prick stirred at the mere thought.

For fuck's sake.

He'd gone months with nothing but his own hand, yet now he seethed with lust. Tupping Nath—*Plum*, deflowering him, should have satisfied the itch. Banished it. Yet here it remained, insistent as a colony of ants.

The rain came harder now, and he rose to place a bucket on the floor by the port side where it tended to leak. The ship swayed in the waves; nothing alarming, the rain mostly coming straight down, winds manageable.

Back at his desk, he picked up his divider and calculated the distance between Primrose Isle and Nassau, eyes on the chart. Still, for some unfathomable reason, he asked, "Why did the Crown choose Primrose Isle for a new colony? It's quite isolated."

"I don't know," Plum replied. "The desire to add every bit of land to her empire, no matter where it sits?" He sat back and wiped rain from his face.

Hawk huffed out a laugh despite himself. "Sounds accurate."

"If not for the grief it would cause my sister, I'd beg you to declare me dead once you have the ransom, then drop me off on some other island."

He should nip this conversation in the bud. Yet he asked, "What of your father?" He fiddled with the divider.

Plum was silent before sighing. "It's been years since I've seen him. I confess I haven't missed him at all. Primrose Isle would be a much more attractive prospect if he wasn't on it. I could run and swim and climb, and no one would call me a fool. Or if they did, I wouldn't care. I'd assume an alias and learn to make an honest living. Carpentry, perhaps. Working the land, picking fruit. Anything in the open air."

Why am I asking these questions? Why do I want to hear more and more and more? "I see the merit in such a life," he said, the words sneaking out, unsummoned and unwelcome. A mad urge to reassure rose in him. Why should he care about young Bainbridge's discontent with his lot in a privileged life? It was ridiculous.

Enough.

"Why do they call you Hawk?"

"None of your fucking business." Yet his tone didn't possess the bite it should, and N—*Plum* only chuckled.

When he glanced over a minute later, Plum was leaning so far out—shapely backside in the air, knees coming up off the narrow window seat—that Hawk's heart skipped, and he found himself in the corner holding down Plum's feet.

Face drenched, Plum looked back over his shoulder and grinned, a delighted laugh on his lips as he reveled in the downpour. There was no artifice there, his happiness in such a small thing as being rained on shining from him and capturing Hawk in its rays like dust motes dancing in a shaft of sunlight.

He tried to discern the warmth flowing through him, an unfamiliar sensation that wasn't lust or triumphant satisfaction. It was... Good fucking God, he was *charmed.* He wrestled with the peculiar sensation, letting go of Plum and stepping back until he hit the corner of his desk, wood digging into his hip.

You make me feel young again.

Christ, it really was time for him to retire, as his brain had evidently become addled. Yet, in these dangerous waters, he found himself unable to retreat to shore. He wanted to see the world through Plum's eyes. He wanted to be so...*new*.

As Plum leaned back inside, twisting around on the window seat, his smile stuttered. "What?"

"Such a simple pleasure, but it runs deep."

He flushed, skin going red down his firm chest, which Hawk had to stop ogling *immediately*. N—Plum ran his fingers through his curling hair, exuberance disappearing. "Well, I'm a simpleton. It stands to reason."

Hawk frowned. "I've known my share of the slow-witted over the years. You are not among their number. Taking joy in the mundane is nothing if not wise. For what is life if not largely fucking mundane?"

"Says the pirate king." A little smile, tentative like a bud poking through soil in spring, played on Plum's lips.

Hawk turned away to lean over his desk so he wouldn't smile back. "I'm sure you've seen for yourself that the ordinary is well at home here."

"Yes, despite your flimflam. It seems piracy is an act of theater as much as dastardly deeds."

"It is," he admitted, needlessly moving the ink pot and quill on his desk from one side to the other, then back again. "We spread rumors of the Sea Hawk's tyranny in Nassau, Port Royal, Tortuga. It's far easier being a pirate when most ships simply surrender upon spotting our flag."

The bucket was filling with alarming rapidity, and he went to inspect the ceiling, which would have to be fixed. It was a good time for it, while they waited for their ransom. His gaze was drawn back to Plum, and a knot tightened in his gut.

Plum bit his lip, looking hopeful, and Hawk narrowed his gaze before realizing what he wanted. Of course Hawk should deny him, yet he found himself sliding the bucket toward Plum with his boot and replacing it with a bowl.

There were a few cups of water in the bucket, enough to wash with, and from the corner of his eye, he could see Plum strip naked and splash himself before fetching a cloth that had been left in his corner. He hummed softly, standing by the window, pulling the material over his body.

There was absolutely no reason Hawk should cut him a sliver of soap, yet he did, keeping his eyes averted as he tossed it over, grunting in response to Plum's delighted thanks.

After a few minutes had passed and Hawk had thoroughly examined the port side of the cabin for any other leaks and found two, he turned back to find Plum still dragging the damn cloth across his wet skin, his gaze over his shoulder on Hawk.

Heat lashed through him like the rain beating the windows as Plum dipped the cloth between his buttocks, lips parting on a sigh.

The little shit knew exactly what he was doing.

Hawk could imagine his entrance was quite tender after how hard it had been fucked. Surely too tender to be breached once again so soon—not that Hawk was entertaining such an idea, since he'd vowed not to stick his cock in that sweet arse again. Well, certainly not today, at any rate.

What about my tongue?

Visions ran riot through his mind: Plum on his knees, head out the window, backside up. Hawk's face buried between his cheeks, licking into him while Plum moaned and shuddered; Hawk bringing him off without even touching his cock, then jerking himself and spurting all over Plum's back and arse, marking his pale skin, claiming—

Enough!

"Get your clothes back on," he barked.

Plum blinked. "You don't want to...?" In the silence that followed, he dropped his head and lunged for his shirt—Hawk's old white linen—holding it to him, clearly chastened.

"There's work to be done." Hawk slammed around in his desk drawers, gritting his teeth and willing his cock to deflate and the fire in his veins to be doused.

Plum quickly tugged the shirt and his breeches over his wet skin, crossing his arms over his chest and returning to the corner. Hawk found himself adding, "Besides, you don't want to go up on deck naked."

Why he'd said it, he didn't know. He shouldn't want to ease the sting of rejection and offer a gift. But he had, and Nathaniel—*Plum*'s head shot up, anticipation brightening his face. Hawk had to look away, striding to the door. "Come on, then. No talking to the men. No trickery."

Up top, the crew paused in their work to stare at Plum, then each other, then Snell. As Hawk glowered, they all bent to their tasks again. Plum tipped his head back, baring his throat as he opened his mouth and swallowed fresh, cool rainwater. It did nothing to ease Hawk's half-hard prick, but at least if they were on deck, he would not break his vow.

Plum's white shirt clung to him, translucent in the rain, and Hawk made himself no promises about tomorrow.

Chapter Twelve

T**HE DECK WAS** almost dry beneath his feet, the sun having reappeared in all its glory to banish the rain and clouds, and yet *he* hadn't been banished to the cabin once more.

Nathaniel stayed by the port railing, out of the way, not breathing a word. It seemed that Hawk had perhaps forgotten about him, and he was simultaneously grateful and resentful.

He'd felt so bold, taking off all his clothes and washing in front of Hawk. Lingering over it, waiting for Hawk to come to him, to fuck him again.

But he hadn't, and Nathaniel's skin prickled as he shifted uncomfortably, wishing for the hundredth time he could run or swim and clear his head. Perhaps Hawk had had his fill now, and Nathaniel no longer tempted him.

He should be glad of it, but of course he despaired. How would he go without it now? Sin or no, he didn't care. He wanted Hawk inside him again. He didn't care if it hurt—he'd take every bruise and ache to experience the release again, the sensation of *rightness,* that he had finally become himself—*real*—in a way he couldn't explain.

Lord, how he wanted a kiss, to taste Hawk's mouth and share his breath, feel the scratch of his beard, be consumed…

The idea that Hawk was no longer interested left him hollow with want. Which was daft, since, as a logical voice reminded him,

Hawk was a pirate. A pirate who had kidnapped him and threatened his sister most foully.

A thief and killer who brought terror to the seas. Twice his age, if not more. The list of reasons Nathaniel should cringe from his touch was extensive. Yet...

It had become intolerable to believe Hawk would deliver on his promise to murder Nathaniel or Susanna if the ransom was not paid. Nathaniel recognized that he might be deceiving himself in hoping Hawk was a good man beneath his hard shell, but surely his odds of survival only increased the closer they grew.

So what was the harm in believing there was more to Hawk? If he was so cold-blooded that he could still follow through on those threats, Nathaniel tormenting himself with worry would only make his last weeks unbearable and change nothing. Taking pleasure with Hawk could only help his chances—and bring him satisfaction deeper than he'd known possible.

No, Nathaniel would not allow Hawk to keep him at arm's length. He refused.

He spied on Hawk from time to time where the man stood at the helm or at the bow, occasionally conferring with Mr. Snell. The crew went about their tasks, and they really were just...men. Men with hopes and fears, who could be brutal, yes. But the workaday routine on the ship was much the same as it would be on a vessel under any flag.

The crew clearly respected Hawk—and feared him, judging by the nervous glances shot his way after some sort of equipment was dropped and had to be repaired. He glowered, and Mr. Snell went over to give the men a talking-to.

Hawk stood apart from his crew, and Nathaniel supposed it was what men in power typically did. It seemed rather lonely. Pirates boasted of a brotherhood, but Hawk didn't appear truly part of it.

A shriek split the air above, and Nathaniel jerked his head

back to see the lookout dangling from the mainsail rigging, arms flailing, one tangled foot all that stood between him and crashing too far to the deck.

Heart racing, Nathaniel leapt onto the rope ladder, flying up it the way he'd once scaled the towering oak at the edge of Hollington's farthest meadow.

Shouts below blended into an indistinguishable din, fading as Nathaniel focused on the terrified lookout, his screams like shattering glass. Squinting into the merciless sun, Nathaniel climbed, willing the man to hold on just a few moments more…

Hooking his arm through a rung, he stretched to the left. "Grab my hand!"

The lookout reached for him wildly, face beet red beneath his beard, long, dark hair flapping in the breeze. His slick fingers slid past the tips of Nathaniel's, and the poor man's ankle—holding up his entire weight where the line was twisted around it—was surely about to give way.

Nathaniel leaned farther, muscles straining, left foot off the ladder now. His belly swooped and spun, his instincts howling to retreat to safety. Another few inches and he'd lose his grip, dooming them both. But as he met the man's terrified eyes, he couldn't abandon him.

"On three, you swing this way, and I'll lean out. One, two, three!"

Clutching the edge of the ladder with one hand and foot, Nathaniel lunged as the lookout did, and their hands met firmly. Hauling the upside-down man closer, Nathaniel got both his feet back on the ladder. "Now untwist the rope from your ankle. Kick it free. I've got you." *Please let me have him.*

Panting, the man did as he was told. For a sickening thump of Nathaniel's heart, he fell, their hands still clasped. But Nathaniel held fast, ignoring an agonizing grind in his body, the man's entire weight jolting his shoulder—which screamed, although Nathaniel did not, tasting blood where he bit his tongue.

Don't let go! Come on!

It was likely only seconds before the lookout got his feet on the ladder below Nathaniel and let go of his hand to cling to the ropes, but a lifetime rushed by in a tangle of images—Susanna's sunny smile; Mr. Chisholm grasping his shoulder fondly; running across fields and swimming through clear summer lakes; Hawk's blue eyes boring into him, his tattoo covered in Nathaniel's seed.

With a wretched sob, the lookout clambered down, clearly desperate to have solid wood beneath him. Nathaniel followed, eager himself to be off the wavering rope.

On the deck, the lookout had crumpled to his knees, one man patting his shoulder and another handing him a measure of rum. The crew had of course all gathered, and one said, "Are you part fucking monkey, or what?"

Blinking, Nathaniel realized the man was talking to him. He glanced around, finding all eyes looking his way, including Hawk's. Hawk stared at him with such intensity, nostrils flaring, that Nathaniel found he couldn't speak. He shrugged, wincing as his left shoulder flared hot.

"Mr. Pickering!" Hawk shouted. "He's injured."

Nathaniel's throat was dry as a desert, but he croaked, "No, I'm fine."

Hawk still watched him with a thunderous expression, hands fisting and unclenching. "What the hell were you thinking? You have no business up there."

"Saved O'Connell's life. I say he gets a round of rum tonight!" a voice called out, others joining in with their agreement.

Mr. O'Connell pushed to his feet, swaying, his face still alarmingly red, long, curly hair sweat-soaked. He stuck out his hand. "Thank you. God bless you!"

Nathaniel grasped his rough, sweaty palm, and a cry of "Huzzah!" went up among the men. Nathaniel smiled, but it quickly vanished when he caught Hawk's narrowed gaze again.

Through a clenched jaw, Hawk bit out, "Mr. Pickering, take him to my cabin and examine him fully."

More cries of "Huzzah!" echoed after Nathaniel as he climbed down the ladder to the lower deck, the pain in his left shoulder intensifying with each step. The surgeon, an older man with a rounding belly and gray hair, urged him to sit on the side of the bed. Cheeks hot as he remembered the filthy, *wonderful* things he'd done on that surface, Nathaniel did as he was bade.

Hawk marched in, demanding of Mr. Pickering, "Well?"

Ignoring him, the surgeon slipped on round glasses, then poked and prodded. When he rotated Nathaniel's shoulder just so, Nathaniel couldn't bite back a gasp, the joint on fire. Hawk was suddenly right there, grasping the surgeon's arm as if he meant to toss him across the cabin.

"Don't hurt him more!" Hawk shouted.

"I was merely assessing the scope of the injury." Mr. Pickering glanced down at his arm, where Hawk's fingers dug in. "If you please, Captain?"

Hawk released him. "It's only that if he doesn't make it back to his father alive, all this will have been for nothing."

Mr. Pickering turned back to Nathaniel, his expression neutral aside from a tiny quirk to his eyebrow. "Yes, well. It likely came very close to dislocating, but it's only a sprain. Hardly life-threatening, I assure you. I'll prepare a comfrey poultice to help with inflammation. Other than that, just rest it." He gave Nathaniel a kind smile. "No more heroic rescues for a few days, hmm? Back in a tick."

Uncomfortable silence stretched as they waited. Hawk stood at the stern window, facing out, his hands clasped behind his broad back, his long, muscular legs parted slightly, boots planted. A striking, shadowy outline against the sun's rays.

"I'm sorry if I worried you." Nathaniel caught his breath. Had he said the words aloud?

Indeed he had, because Hawk's spine stiffened. He growled, "I worry about you getting yourself killed before I can exchange you for the money I'm owed. Nothing more."

Nathaniel had heard it before, and there was no reason it should hurt now. Yet his chest tightened, throat too thick to reply even if he'd had a retort.

Still… Hawk fidgeted with his hands, and soon started pacing, occasionally glancing at Nathaniel and then jerking his head away and muttering to himself.

It seemed an awful lot like worry from where Nathaniel sat, and he bit back a smile.

Mr. Pickering bustled in carrying a small mortar. He placed it at his feet and reached for the hem of Nathaniel's shirt. "Here, let's get this off."

"That will be all," Hawk barked. "Return to your duties."

"These *are* my duties, Captain. But as you wish." He nodded to the mortar. "Spread it on several times a day. It'll stain the skin a bit brown, but it'll fade soon enough." With that, he left, closing the cabin door behind him.

Nathaniel winced as he tugged at his hem, and a moment later Hawk batted his hands away. He lifted his arms, shoulder protesting, and Hawk peeled off the worn linen.

With one knee on the bed, Hawk scooped up a handful of the poultice, which was a greenish gray and smelled vaguely of dried bread.

Slowly, Hawk tended to Nathaniel's shoulder, massaging the remedy over the sore joint with a light touch. Though it was soothing, Nathaniel's heart skipped, and he realized he wasn't breathing.

He took shallow sips of air, not wanting to betray his… What? Agitation? Excitement? No, that wasn't quite it, as his prick remained unmoved.

"There." Hawk stepped away, and Nathaniel had to bite his lip to refrain from calling him back, eager for more of that calming touch. He jerked his gaze to the floor as Hawk did return with a towel he spread on the mattress.

"Rest," he ordered.

Nathaniel stared up at him. "You mean… Here?"

"Or the floor." He huffed. "I don't damn well care." He stormed from the cabin, and Nathaniel gingerly stretched out on the mattress.

Compared to the floor, the hard, lumpy mattress was a soft, feather embrace. The motion of the ship lulled him to sleep, a voice in his mind whispering that perhaps Hawk *did*, in fact, care.

"Huzzah!"

The men lifted their cups and drank to Nathaniel yet again, and he gamely attempted another sip. The rum burned less now than it had when the evening started, and he was having trouble feeling his lips.

The ship rolled on another great wave, the wind having blown up suddenly as night closed in, rain clouds returning with a vengeance. Saliva flooded Nathaniel's mouth, his stomach roiling.

Mr. Richards poured another round, the men laughing and boisterous, blithely unconcerned with the rough sea. Nearby, someone played a fiddle, and sometimes the men burst into sea shanties, their voices surprisingly tuneful.

Leaning a shoulder against the wall, Hawk stood steady as a rock as they pitched to and fro. He'd had one drink, and one drink only, unless Nathaniel had missed the others. He was certain he hadn't, since he'd kept an eye on the captain throughout the evening.

Hawk watched from the shadows with an unreadable expression. Light from the swinging lanterns hanging from the ceiling caught the gold on Hawk's belt and gleam in his ear.

Then his eyes locked on Nathaniel's, the blue appearing almost black in the dim light of the forecastle. Nathaniel swallowed, his head light, queasy excitement unfurling through him, making him feel like he was floating.

The metal cup was thrust into his hand again, one of the men shouting, "Down the hatch!"

Nathaniel gamely choked it down, enjoying the camaraderie with the crew while he could. He wanted to prove he was man enough to keep pace with them—and that he was someone they liked too much to kill.

When he belched, his stomach gurgling dangerously, they laughed and cheered him. But when his cup was refilled again, he could only take a sip, his head swimming.

He pushed to his feet, shoulder throbbing, barely managing to step over the bench without tripping on his face. The ship rocked, and he held out his arms for balance, saliva rushing in his mouth. He swallowed a few times and belched again. "I think I've had enough."

This garnered a roar of laughter from the men, and a smirk from Hawk. Nathaniel's stomach lurched and so did he, making for the entryway. This time, he would have stumbled flat out, but Hawk was suddenly there, holding him by the arms, thankfully well below his sore shoulder.

Then Nathaniel simply erupted—remnants of stew and what seemed to be an endless stream of liquid that was likely pure rum. Worse than that, it spewed all over Hawk's shirt, trousers, and boots, splattering the polished leather and gold as Nathaniel retched.

Coughing on the last bits of acid bile, he realized there was utter silence aside from the low howl of the wind, the men's mirth vanished. Nathaniel's knees would have given out if not for the steel grip of Hawk holding him up.

Blinking at a chunk of potato clinging to black cloth, Nathaniel's face burned. He couldn't bring himself to raise his head to witness Hawk's fury at the repulsive mess Nathaniel had made all over him.

Light and dark blurred in a swirl of movement as he was spun around and marched out. Nathaniel's feet barely skimmed the planks as Hawk propelled him down the corridor. For a gut-wrenching moment, he feared he might be tossed overboard into the sea's black, endless depths, but then they were inside the cabin, door slamming behind them.

Blinking, Nathaniel focused on the bookcases and swinging lantern. He could barely enjoy the relief of being safe before his guts lurched once more and he gagged, trying to keep it down. Hawk released him, and Nathaniel crumpled to his hands and knees.

Then a bucket—mercifully clean—was in front of him, and he heaved into it. He coughed and spat, his eyes watering, and thought perhaps being thrown overboard to meet his end might be preferable.

"That's it. Get it all out."

Nathaniel tried to obey Hawk's command, although it hadn't been spoken sharply, but in fact gently. After another minute of bringing up nothing more than drops, his empty stomach twisting fruitlessly, Nathaniel sat back on his feet, pushing the bucket away feebly.

Eyes closed, he breathed as deeply as he could, his brain seeming to seesaw along with the ship's rocking. He'd conquered any seasickness after several days on the *Proud William*, but hadn't contended with the demon rum.

He jerked as something pressed to his mouth, then swallowed gratefully when cool water passed his lips. Hawk's voice was a low murmur. "Slowly."

Taking little sips, Nathaniel's heart seized when something passed over his head. Opening his eyes was too monumental a task, but he realized it was Hawk's big, callused hand brushing back his sweat-damp hair. Not angrily or cruelly, but with infinite tenderness.

Then the hand and cup were taken away, and Nathaniel choked back a whimper at the loss. Nathaniel managed to pry his eyes open and crawl to his corner. His clothes had been splashed with vomit too, and he tugged at them hopelessly before giving up.

He had to sleep, and had only just curled into a ball when Hawk tugged on his legs for some unfathomable reason. He tried to kick, but it was no use.

Then he was lifted to his bare feet. The world spun mercilessly, and he glimpsed Hawk's face—still not angry, but soft and patient—before closing his eyes once more. He shivered as cool air flowed over his flesh, his soiled clothing stripped away until he was naked.

Thick bands of warm steel lifted him under his back and knees, and he registered that Hawk was carrying him like a maiden who had swooned. He should protest, but instead buried his face in Hawk's bare neck, realizing Hawk must have stripped off his own ruined clothing as well.

The hard bed was luxury once more, and he sank onto it gratefully. He mumbled about being lucky twice in a day as he settled, sighing as strong, gentle fingers smoothed more of the poultice onto his shoulder.

Though the ship still pitched and rolled, his head along with it, Nathaniel curled on his good side, eager to escape into dreams, instincts telling him he was safe. Hawk's warm, powerful body soon pressed close behind, enveloping, an anchor in the tempestuous night.

Chapter Thirteen

CLOUDS HAD EVIDENTLY made way for the moon and stars, which would soon enough give quarter to the dawn. The blackness was now broken by pale silver that revealed the shape of the desk and carved chair, the bookcase and rolled charts, melted hunks of wax in the candelabra.

Hawk's bed was still in shadow, and he needed to leave soon. He liked to be present for the changes of watch, to be with the men, to guide them if necessary, but usually to stand apart and observe.

He needed to dress and take to the main deck and issue whatever orders were necessary as another day approached. He needed to fulfill his duties as captain of *The Damned Manta*.

Yet for the moment, he found himself utterly content to be a mere man. A man more than satisfied to be cocooned in the darkness with…whom, exactly?

My lover.

The traitorous words rang through him like the clang of the ship's bell, solid and true even as he listed dangerously, his equilibrium gone.

My lover. Nathaniel.

Despite the peril, Hawk found he could no longer think of him another way. Not "Plum," not "the boy," not mere cargo to be ransomed. Oh, he was a prize, but of a very different sort.

Nathaniel snorted and shifted onto his back with a murmur, his hand coming to rest over Hawk's arm across his belly. Even in sleep, Nathaniel beguiled him. The thought occurred once more that if it was all an act to gain Hawk's favor, Nathaniel belonged on London's stages.

Hawk could just make out his parted lips in the dim light, and wondered what it would be like to taste them, to swallow Nathaniel's sweet moans and sighs, plunder his mouth; fuck him with his tongue as surely as he did with his prick.

Said prick swelled at the notion, pressing into Nathaniel's hip. It had been years since Hawk had kissed. There had been a few other men after John, but only rough, quick tumbles, a means to an end. He'd found if he didn't know the man or care a damn about him, he'd rather achieve release without any further bother.

Usually his hand was sufficient, although the first privateer ship he'd served on had had a little closet with a cock-sized hole and eager, nameless, faceless mouths on the other side of the wall. Perfect to find easy release.

Now he thought of Nathaniel on his knees for him, those pink lips stretched over his shaft, swallowing him guilelessly. This did nothing to abate his erection.

He'd sworn to himself that he wouldn't fuck Nathaniel again, but that had been yesterday. He hadn't sworn it today, which had barely begun and stretched out before them tantalizingly.

Closing his eyes, he turned his attention to the slap of waves against the hull and the swaying of the ship, much gentler now than it had been last night. They had dropped the sea anchor and only drifted slowly.

Would he miss being rocked to sleep if he did find a way to retire?

The sea had been his home now for many more years than the land, and he didn't think he could ever leave it entirely. Yes, an island would be perfect. A house within sight of the water, a fishing boat bleaching in the sun where the sand and grass met, out of the tide's reach.

He hadn't fished since he was a boy, and he'd like to learn again. Maybe he'd even climb a tree or two.

Images of Nathaniel hanging from the rigging intruded, Hawk's heart kicking up, abating his hardness. *Fuck,* the terror that had gripped him when Nathaniel had clambered up with no thought to the danger had been…soul-shaking.

He'd climbed amazingly fast, stunning the crew, and even Hawk for crucial moments. When Hawk had leapt to follow, Snell had hauled him back down, shouting rightly that the extra motion would be more of a danger to Nathaniel and O'Connell.

Nathaniel had seemed only a speck in the sky, far beyond reach. The moment when O'Connell had been freed from the frayed footrope and swung onto the rigging ladder was seared in Hawk's memory.

His mind substituted a different outcome wherein O'Connell's weight tore Nathaniel loose and they plummeted to the deck, skulls cracking like eggs, blood and brains splattering the wood while Hawk could only watch uselessly.

To have that light snuffed out, those honey eyes go distant and cold, to not have the opportunity to tell Nathaniel… *What?* Hawk wasn't sure, a tumult of mixed emotions tormenting him.

How could he feel anything but contempt for Walter Bainbridge's son? How could he want to hold him near and keep him safe? He should only care about the ransom, about revenge, yet…

Groaning, Nathaniel stretched his arms overhead. When he winced, it drove all other thoughts from Hawk's mind. Nathaniel's eyes popped open, shining blearily in the hint of moonlight.

Hawk murmured, "Careful. How does your shoulder feel this morning?"

Nathaniel licked his dry lips, voice froggy. "All right. Still sore, but not too bad. The surgeon knows what he's about."

Hawk choked down the irrational stab of resentment directed toward good Mr. Pickering. It was insane to have been *jealous* of him trying to remove Nathaniel's shirt.

But the thought of any other man touching Nathaniel sparked fire in his blood that drew his itchy fingers to his cutlass handle.

What is this madness?

Exhaling out the tension and managing an easy tone, Hawk tapped Nathaniel's head lightly. "And how's this?"

"Mmm. Rather…heavy."

Hawk chuckled. "Have you ever had rum before?"

"No. Wine with late dinners, some scotch or port, but only to sip."

"I thought as much. You handled it manfully. The men were impressed."

Nathaniel grimaced. "Until I spewed all over you. I'm so sorry."

He should feign the expected anger, but only shrugged. "I've suffered worse."

"And now I've gotten that gunk all over you and your bed, haven't I?" He patted Hawk's chest, apparently trying to find traces of the offending poultice. "You should have left me in the corner."

Hawk ignored that. "No more heroics, and no more rum, or at least less of the latter."

Nathaniel's hand still rested on his chest, caressing. Hawk should roll away, find fresh clothes, clean his boots, and get on deck. Eight bells had already rung for the change of watch at four, then one bell half an hour later, then two after another thirty minutes, marking the progression of the watch.

Yet he found himself staring down at Nathaniel, his own hand smoothing rhythmically down Nathaniel's side and over his hip. Soon three bells would chime.

"Do you like the men?" Nathaniel murmured.

Hawk wasn't sure he'd heard the question correctly. "Do I…like them?"

"Mmm. You don't seem to speak to them unless giving orders."

"I… Well, they are a necessity to operate a ship. I care for their futures, such as they may be. As long as they are loyal to me, I shall be to them."

"But not friends. Brothers."

The echo of John's impish smile flitted through his mind and was gone. "Once, perhaps. But as captain, I must hold myself removed." Snell was a friend—of a sort. Hawk trusted him. Depended on him to keep the peace. "As long as our goals are aligned, the men and I are in accord with one another. That's all that matters."

"Sounds lonely."

Nathaniel's fingertips teased the hair on Hawk's chest before tracing up the vulnerable skin of his throat. When Hawk swallowed, Nathaniel's fingers charted the movement of his Adam's apple. His heart drummed so hard he was certain Nathaniel could hear it.

Those clever fingers ghosted over his face—circling his mouth, following the slope of his nose, then seeking something by his temple, exploring until they found the raised skin of the jagged scar, following the old wound back and forth, back and forth.

Nathaniel's bow lips were parted just a fraction, and it would be so easy to lean down and claim them. So easy to lose himself and discover what sweet noises he could coax using only his mouth…

Enough!

Lungs seizing, he caught Nathaniel's wrist, pressing it back to the mattress as Nathaniel watched. Hawk wouldn't kiss him—he'd already gone too far adrift, and time was running out.

He had to find his way back to the shore by the time they reached Primrose Isle; by the time he would return Nathaniel to the life he'd interrupted and collect his ransom. Nathaniel couldn't be anything more to him than a means to an end.

What if Walter Bainbridge doesn't pay up? I've promised the men bloodshed if not. Sworn to murder Nathaniel.

Hawk shoved the worry aside, schooling his wayward mind and taking a long breath to calm the sudden gallop of his heart. Bainbridge would pay, Nathaniel would return to his family unharmed, and that would be the end of it. In the meantime…

No, Hawk wouldn't kiss him, but he'd put his lips to work. What was the harm? Had Nathaniel ever experienced the hot slick of a mouth around his cock? Hawk presumed not, since he'd said his prick was untouched by anything but his own hand.

Hawk shifted on top of him, urging his legs apart to rest between them. Pressing his face to Nathaniel's chest, he wasted no time and latched onto a nipple, pride surging at the shocked gasp. No, Hawk wouldn't kiss him, but he would lay claim to this.

Nathaniel squirmed. "Feels good. Oh, Lord."

Hawk flicked his tongue against the nub of sensitive flesh. "Only devils here." Nathaniel bucked, his swelling cock seeking friction. "Patience," Hawk chided, draping his arm over Nathaniel's hips, just out of reach of his member. "Not too much vigor. You're recuperating, remember?"

"This is good medicine for a headache."

Huffing out a laugh, Hawk felt strangely light as he kissed and sucked, teasing Nathaniel's nipples until any more might be painful. He smiled against Nathaniel's belly, rubbing his beard over the soft skin with hard muscle beneath, dipping his tongue into the indentation where he'd been linked to his mother.

That drew a ticklish giggle from Nathaniel, and Hawk couldn't remember the last time he'd had *fun* when fucking. He explored Nathaniel's navel, hoping to replicate the sound.

Their coupling had been intense and sometimes rough, and Hawk found he relished this chance for soft touches and discovery, finding sensitive, secret places he wanted to caress instead of pummel.

When Hawk swallowed the head of Nathaniel's cock without warning, Nathaniel's cry fairly rattled the windowpanes. The whole ship would hear in the quiet of night, and the thought made Hawk queasy. This was between them. Private.

His arm was long enough that he could slap his hand over Nathaniel's mouth, whispering, "Let the bells wake the men."

As Hawk sucked tightly from root to tip and back again, Nathaniel panted against his palm in humid gusts. It had been years since Hawk had tasted a throbbing prick, and he groaned around it before pulling off for a breath.

He nudged Nathaniel's thighs with his head, and Nathaniel spread them farther, bending his knees up to expose his bollocks, two dark globes against the sheets.

"Such a good boy," Hawk told him, and Nathaniel whimpered against his hand, their eyes locking. Hawk teased the slit of his prick with his tongue, and Nathaniel gasped against his hand, eyes closing, eyelashes fanning over his cheeks.

From this vantage, the tiny divot in his chin was visible, and Hawk shifted his hand to trace it with his thumb. Wiry hair scratched at his face as he suckled Nathaniel's heavy balls, lapping at them and teasing the sensitive skin behind.

Nathaniel's moans and quivers made Hawk's own cock throb against the mattress. He only had the chance to suck Nathaniel's shaft one more time, swirling his tongue around the leaking head, before Nathaniel spent. He flooded Hawk's mouth, and it was salty with a hint of sweet, an earthy musk Hawk swallowed like the finest wine, head spinning as if it were.

When he'd lapped Nathaniel clean, he reached down to jerk his own cock roughly, knowing it wouldn't take long. But

Nathaniel stilled his arm.

"May I? I want to taste your spend."

Hawk couldn't deny him that—or himself the pleasure, not when it was requested so politely, which made him smile against Nathaniel's skin. But when Nathaniel gritted his teeth, sucking in a breath as he tried to shift down into a suitable position, Hawk stilled him.

Taking care not to jostle Nathaniel's shoulder, Hawk straddled his chest and fed him his cock, groaning as he sucked eagerly. His mouth was wet, and he sucked his cheeks in tight, sending shivers over Hawk's skin, raising the hair on his arms.

Bracing himself with one hand on the wall, he rocked gently, and Nathaniel matched his rhythm, a quick learner at this, like all physical things.

It was bright enough now through the stern windows that Hawk could see his cock disappearing between Nathaniel's pink lips. Nathaniel licked and sucked industriously; sweat dampened his hair, curling it. Hawk reached down with his free hand, brushing back the silky strands, smoothing them through his fingers.

Nathaniel looked up at him, his mouth full of Hawk's prick, eyes shining with a tender light, pure and deep. Hawk's climax ripped through him, and he grunted as he spilled, snapping his jaw shut to prevent a shout of pure bliss.

He emptied in long, powerful pulses, and Nathaniel gamely tried to swallow it all until he made a desperate sound in his throat, eyes wide.

Hawk pulled out, the last spurts splashing on Nathaniel's chin and flushed cheeks. Milky seed leaked from the corners of his mouth, and he swiped with his tongue as if determined to reclaim every drop. Hawk's throat went dry, the urge to bend and taste himself on Nathaniel's tongue thrumming through him.

Before he could do anything else foolish, Hawk rolled onto his back, and Nathaniel burrowed close after wiping his face. Of its own accord, Hawk's arm snaked around Nathaniel, careful of his shoulder.

As light pierced the horizon and threw a beam across the ceiling, Hawk thought of his mythical dream island and fishing boat, his simple house and fruit trees to climb. And he thought of Nathaniel racing up the branches with sunshine in his hair and laughter on the breeze, birds soaring overhead.

Heart clenching so powerfully he shuddered, Hawk struggled for air. Nathaniel nuzzled his chest, warm and wonderfully limp. "All right?"

Hawk managed a grunt in the affirmative. He had to push him away. Had to regain control in the perilous current in which he'd allowed himself to be caught. He wanted to shove Nathaniel aside and impose his will and return the world of *The Damned Manta* to its proper order. Instead, he held him close for just another minute or two, waiting for four bells.

Perhaps five.

<h1 style="text-align:center">Chapter Fourteen</h1>

"WHAT THE FUCK do you think you're doing with that?"

Nathaniel looked up from the dagger he turned over in his hands. He sat perched cross-legged on Hawk's too-hard bed, where he was trying to catch the cross breeze through the open stern windows. "Thinking that I don't know how to use it. And I should learn."

Hawk stood on the threshold, key in hand, dark sleeves rolled to his elbows, sweat glistening in the hollow of his exposed throat. The gold-tipped boots were on his feet, even though the day was sticky and hot.

He closed the door with his foot, then looked to the open chest on the floor. Then back again at Nathaniel, his expression hardening. "I didn't leave that unlocked."

"No. I worked out how to pick it." He nodded to the desk as he scratched at his bare chest. He hadn't bothered putting his shirt back on after applying the poultice to his shoulder, which was much improved. "Found a pin in there."

"A pin? From what?"

"No idea. But eventually I poked it in the lock just the right way, and it opened."

Hawk's eyebrows almost disappeared into his hairline. "And you're just...*telling* me all this?" He glanced at the door. "Do I have to set up a barricade?"

"Where would I go? Aside from up on deck for air. Really, I'm freer in this room than I've ever been."

"Is that so?" Hawk set his hands on his hips.

"It is." He shrugged. "You see me as I am. A sodomite. A simpleton."

"You're not—" Hawk pressed his lips into a thin line and strode to the chest to slam the lid, boots thudding. He didn't lock it. "I should punish you for this. Cut off your rations for a day or two."

But you won't. Nathaniel simply said, "Hmm," still weighing the dagger. For the past day and a half, since he'd gotten so spectacularly drunk and sick, Hawk had pestered him to take enough water and eat.

At least the ship had taken on fresh food in Nassau, although the stronger spices hadn't done his recovering stomach any favors. Eventually he'd had some lovely warm, clear broth that he suspected Hawk had requested for him specially.

Nathaniel had also slept in Hawk's bed again, instead of being banished to the corner. More than that, he'd slept nestled in Hawk's arms even though they hadn't sought pleasure.

Part of Nathaniel wanted to confront Hawk and assert his flourishing belief that Hawk wouldn't harm him, no matter what became of the ransom. That he wasn't a monster without feeling, and that he felt for Nathaniel in particular.

But he was leery of rupturing and unraveling the intimacy that grew between them like climbing vines, curling and seeking. He must wait until they were wound too tightly to deny.

"What are you smiling about?"

He said, "Nothing," but didn't try to wipe away his grin. "Will you teach me? How to use this?"

Hawk snorted and opened his log with a sneer. "So you can gut me with it? I think not."

"Surely you don't imagine me *that* quick of a study? Of

course, I did win our bet about the knots. Speaking of wagers, I still haven't received my reward for correctly predicting you'd need stitches to close that wound."

"You'll get your run soon enough," Hawk grumbled, dipping his quill in ink and bending his head to the pages.

"If I don't, will you suck my cock again in recompense?"

Hawk jerked his head up, and then—*there.* Along with an incredulous laugh, Nathaniel spied a true smile, twin creases in his cheeks, the wrinkles around his blue eyes fanning out, teeth gleaming white, but not with a feral edge. No, it was all gentle and genuine, and Nathaniel imagined he was the only one gifted that sight.

Hawk's smile turned sly, one side of his mouth tugging up, his voice dropping. "Did you like it?"

"You know I did." His prick stirred at the memory of the wet, perfect pressure of Hawk's mouth, lips and tongue teasing relentlessly. A torment he'd wanted never to end.

More than that, the sight of his cock disappearing between Hawk's lips, being serviced in such a way—with tenderness and intensity, Hawk's only goal seeming to be Nathaniel's release— had been something he'd never dared dream of.

"Mmm." Hawk watched him, quill still in hand, dripping ink.

Nathaniel contemplated the question, then frowned. "But honestly, who wouldn't?"

There. Another true smile graced Hawk's face, his eyes fairly twinkling. "Indeed." Nathaniel wanted to hold on to the smiles and collect each one like a magpie's baubles. Although these gifts were no mere trinkets.

"Can I suck you, then? Practice makes perfect, as my tutor always said."

But now Hawk's expression darkened. He bit out, "Useless prick should have taught you how to use that dagger." He fiddled with something in his desk, head down. "That's enough talk anyway. I have work to do."

Was that an odd jealousy of Mr. Chisholm? Nathaniel hid his smile. "So… You don't want me on my knees for you? I really would like to taste cock again. If you're not interested, should I find a volunteer amongst the crew?"

Nathaniel fought a victorious grin as Hawk snapped, "I don't fucking think so," and shot him a glare.

How he ached not only to taste Hawk, but undo him. Hawk had been in control, as always, when he'd fucked Nathaniel's mouth, and Nathaniel wanted to have him moaning and at his mercy.

He tried a brazen tone and playful wink. "It would only be for the sake of practice, of course. If you're otherwise engaged."

"I don't think your cock-sucking skills will be much use with your betrothed," Hawk grumbled.

Nathaniel sat up straighter, all mirth vanished. "What?" He opened and closed his mouth. "But… No. I shan't be marrying her now. It would be impossible." He hadn't formulated the thought until that moment, but he recognized its truth.

"No?" Hawk's head was still down as he rummaged around. "Why not?"

"You know why." The notion of marrying Elizabeth Davenport, of retreating once more and hiding not only his reading deficiencies but his very *essence*, sent cold dread down his spine despite the humidity.

Men were said to possess souls, and he had only just discovered his and given it weight and shape.

Hawk frowned. "Surely you understand that there are countless men like us who marry women and hide their nature. Countless women too, for that matter."

Holding the dagger, Nathaniel imagined how it would feel slicing into his flesh. Possibly akin to the idea of living the rest of his life cloistered, his true self secreted away. His voice croaked as he said, "Yes. I shall not be among them. I can't. I would turn to stone."

He drew a drop of blood from the tip of his first finger. It sat there on his skin, a perfect circle. Then he drew the blade down the pad, watching the crimson line blossom.

"What the hell are you doing?" Hawk was across the cabin in what seemed like a solitary bound, snatching the dagger away and taking Nathaniel's wrist in an iron grip. He sucked Nathaniel's finger into his mouth with hard pressure, looming above him where Nathaniel still sat on the bed.

Breath coming short, Nathaniel said, "You see? I need lessons."

Pulling out the finger with a pop, Hawk closed his fist around it. He huffed. "Not cutting yourself shouldn't have to be taught."

"I've always been a slow learner."

Hawk watched him, eyes flashing. "There are no words involved, so that excuse will not fly."

"I was just…making sure I'm still real." *Not stone. He sees me. He sees me as I truly am.*

Hawk's brow furrowed, and he squeezed Nathaniel's finger tighter. "I assure you, this is flesh in my grasp."

What would it be like to taste those lips, to steal a kiss and press close, to drink him in? Would he taste his blood on Hawk's tongue? Hawk was staring, so Nathaniel cast about for something to say. He asked, "Do you think that pirate will attack again? The man with one eye?"

Hawk's expression grew more perplexed. "Perhaps. It's impossible to know."

"Or the British or Spanish. What would happen to me if you and the crew were overrun?"

"We won't be."

"Still. I should know how to defend myself. If not on this ship, in the New World."

"Your father will have men, surely. You'll be quite safe."

"I won't be staying on Primrose Isle. I've decided. I have to invent a new life." He thought of Susanna with a sharp pang. He'd miss her desperately, but she had Bart, and would soon have a child as well. He wondered for the hundredth time if she was safely at the colony and prayed she was.

He cleared his throat. "I won't follow blindly and obediently because the world tells me I must. If being kidnapped by pirates has taught me anything, it's that there is a world beyond my borders."

Sitting beside him with a soft grunt, still holding Nathaniel's finger, Hawk asked, "Then what will you do?"

"I don't know." The knot in his stomach tightened, a hitch or perhaps a figure-eight. "Run away, I suppose. Somewhere else in the colonies. Boston, perhaps? Or Carolina. I hope it will be easier for someone like me in the New World. What will you do? Once you've exchanged me for your ransom?"

Will you let me go? Do I mean anything to you, or is it all in my mind?

The notion that he and Hawk would part clawed deeper at Nathaniel than he would have thought possible. This man had kidnapped him, threatened him, and yet here he sat stanching the flow of Nathaniel's blood even though the cut was nothing of concern.

Nathaniel truly had seen beyond his borders for the first time, and he couldn't go back to his former life. What about Hawk? Was he satisfied with a pirate's uncertain, brutish existence? Nathaniel thought not. He suspected the Sea Hawk wasn't at all the man he purported to be.

Rubbing his bristly chin with his free hand, Hawk stared into the distance through the stern windows. Nathaniel prompted, "Will you continue to haunt the shipping lanes, relieving merchant ships of their cargo? Evading the navy? The noose?"

Hawk exhaled, loosening his tight grip on Nathaniel's finger but still holding on, although the blood had surely stopped. "Perhaps it will be the end of the Sea Hawk once I have my bounty. I could find a quiet island. Build a home strong enough to withstand the summer storms. Fish and farm. Stay close to a safe harbor."

His words seemed the bare truth, and Nathaniel held his breath, afraid to move an inch and shatter the spell.

Blinking after a few moments of silence, Hawk sat up ramrod straight, looking to Nathaniel as if he'd forgotten he was there. Then Hawk stood, his hand going to his lower back as he stretched it. "That's nonsense, of course. Pirates find their fate on the gallows, or in the deep." He handed over the dagger. "Come. On your feet."

Heart leaping, Nathaniel hopped up. Hawk came behind him and said, "First thing to learn is the proper grip." He covered Nathaniel's hand with his own, molding his fingers just so around the dagger's handle before releasing him. "Now, what would you do, if your attacker approached from behind?"

Elbow pinned to his side, Nathaniel tried to bend his arm around, but of course it was useless. With one hand on Nathaniel's hip to still him, Hawk covered his hand on the dagger again. "So here you must change your grip."

Nathaniel watched as Hawk rearranged his fingers, turning the dagger toward Nathaniel's wrist. He leaned back into the wall of Hawk's chest, warmth spreading in his own. Hawk said, "There. Now, as we go, remember what you know from your wrestling lessons."

"That I'm a sodomite who yearns to be fucked by men?"

The huff of Hawk's laughter wafted through Nathaniel's hair, sending a shiver down his spine. Hawk swatted his hip, and Nathaniel found himself grinning.

"Oh, you mean the machinations of the sport. All right then."

He ducked and spun, using the element of surprise to try to send Hawk off balance.

Hawk stumbled, a feral light in his eyes as he righted himself. "Let's begin."

Hawk took him through grips and slicing techniques, and they circled each other, Nathaniel parrying and thrusting, dodging and weaving. Sweat glistened on their skin as time passed, bells chiming on deck, the ship rocking in rougher winds.

Their eyes were only for each other, and Nathaniel listened avidly as Hawk corrected his form. His shoulder throbbed, but he ignored it.

At least an hour had passed when Nathaniel darted in with the blade, using the momentum of Hawk's jerk away from it to hook his ankle and send him crashing to the floor.

On top, his left leg over Hawk's thighs, Nathaniel had the dagger in his right hand to Hawk's throat. Although he knew Hawk had the strength to lift him off and turn the tables in a heartbeat, he couldn't resist a victorious, "A-ha!"

Hawk let him have the win. He stayed put, chest rising and falling, both of them breathing heavily, hair damp. Without thought, Nathaniel cupped his left hand over Hawk's crotch and squeezed, the blade still at his throat.

Hawk laughed. "Have you always been so fucking bold?"

"Lord, no. Not until I met you." He squeezed again, feeling Hawk's prick swell, his own still half-hard from the lesson. A low groan escaped Hawk, and Nathaniel worked him through the rough material of his trousers. "May I suck you now?"

"Is that the prize you desire for your victory?"

He squeezed and rolled his hand over the growing bulge. He licked his lips, and Hawk's hooded gaze followed the movement, cock jumping against Nathaniel's palm, tenting his trousers.

Nathaniel said, "Yes. I want to taste your prick. Get it good and wet, swallow it until it's as deep as it will go, until I can hardly breathe." He rocked his erection against Hawk's hip. "Want to make you spend and drink it all down."

His hand trembled, the dagger's tip against Hawk's skin, yet Hawk didn't flinch. Nathaniel could slit his throat, dig the blade into that vulnerable flesh, but Hawk only watched him, arching his hips into Nathaniel's touch.

The *trust* stole Nathaniel's breath, an answering impulse flowing through him. That this was the fierce, fearsome pirate who had swept aboard the *Proud William* and abducted him was difficult to believe. What a performance Hawk had given.

Now that the shield was lowered, the layers of his disguise peeling away, Nathaniel was determined to burrow deeper.

"Or maybe I won't let you come yet," Nathaniel added, squeezing Hawk's shaft. "Maybe once your cock is good and wet, I'll ride it. Take every inch inside me so deeply I fear I might break."

Hawk bucked his hips. "Like the first time?"

"Yes," he breathed, massaging Hawk's prick, rutting against him. At this rate they were going to spend in their trousers. He leaned down and caught Hawk's gold earring between his teeth, then his lips, sucking the whole earlobe into his mouth, tracing the gold square with his tongue.

Lips wet at Hawk's ear, he whispered, "Perhaps I'll go down on my hands and knees for you or bend over your desk. Or spread my hands on the hull, brace myself and take your cock like I was born for it."

Hawk groaned, and Nathaniel sat up just enough to see his face, Hawk's lips parted and blue eyes dark with desire. Nathaniel leaned closer, thrumming with the need to kiss him—to seal this mysterious power between them that was like the ocean's current, dragging them both under…

The knock preceded the door opening only by a moment, and Nathaniel jerked his head up, staring uncomprehendingly at Mr. Snell, his brain still struck by the idea of kissing Hawk until neither of them had breath, of rubbing his barely stubbled face against Hawk's beard until his skin burned, their tongues entwined, consuming.

But Mr. Snell was drawing his pistol. "You little fuck! Get off him!"

Clutching the warm handle of the forgotten dagger, Nathaniel bolted up and scrambled back as Hawk shouted, "No!" and rolled to his knees in front of him. Pistol outstretched, Mr. Snell stared at them, huffing and shaking his head when realization set in.

"Oh, for fuck's sake, Hawk." He shoved the pistol back in his belt, lips a thin, grim line, his words clipped. "If you can tear yourself away from our prisoner—*Walter Bainbridge's* brat, the rich, spoiled little shit whose only worth to us is a hundred thousand pounds—for a few moments, you're needed on deck. *Captain.*"

Their arousal was obvious, and Nathaniel shifted, panting. Hawk stood and said evenly to Snell, "Lead the way, Mr. Quartermaster."

Nathaniel watched them go, his breath freezing painfully, the need to see Hawk's face again—to be acknowledged—greater than his body's demand for air. Hawk apparently didn't feel that tug, the current between them seeming to vanish easily for him, like the moon behind a bank of storm clouds.

Then Hawk looked over his shoulder and grinned, his eyes crinkling, the creases in his flushed cheeks practically dimples. When the door closed, their footsteps fading, Nathaniel could almost believe he'd imagined it. But no, it had been real, and it had been for his eyes only.

It was folly to chart Hawk's smiles, trying to collect them for his own. Folly to crave Hawk's caresses as much as the pounding of his cock, his soft chuckles as much as his fierce smirks.

Yet he couldn't resist, for in these glimpses Hawk wasn't hard muscle and bone, but shifting sand to be molded between Nathaniel's toes.

Chapter Fifteen

A T THE BOW, Nathaniel stood by the forestay under an ink-blot sky. The swath of stars stretched out beyond him, and from Hawk's perspective at the helm, it was as though Nathaniel was sailing right through them.

There was a looseness in Nathaniel's posture, his feet bare on the wet deck. Hawk's too-big shirt billowed around him, untucked from his breeches, the knee fastenings undone.

When the rain came, Hawk had brought Nathaniel up, ignoring the sidelong glances of the crew, who appeared surprised Nathaniel wasn't beaten black and blue after vomiting on Hawk several days earlier.

Said boots were soaked now, the damp leather chafing his feet. The wind and rain had pelted them, but only for a short time, the clouds clearing as the watch changed.

Hawk had also ignored Snell's pointed glares and attempts to engage him in conversation. It was late now, the deck quiet. Hawk had missed evening mess trying to avoid Snell but made sure Nathaniel ate before he brought him up to the main deck.

It was time to sleep, but he did another round of the ship, ensuring everything was in order. There was no reason it shouldn't be—no sails spotted, the seas and wind calm now, no need to drop their sea anchor.

Although he should have been sleeping himself, Snell approached, trapping Hawk on the port side near the stern. The breeze lifted strands of Snell's thinning hair from his head. "Captain. There's been a vote."

Hawk's heart skipped, and he tensed from head to toes. He managed to keep his tone casual. "I wasn't aware there was an issue." If they voted him out as commander… He didn't know what the fuck he would do, and what of Nathaniel? No. This was Hawk's ship. He couldn't let it happen. *Wouldn't.*

"The issue is the prisoner." Snell cut a glance toward Nathaniel, far out of hearing range at the bow. "O'Connell made his case, and the men think he should be allowed up on deck during the day. Too hot now, being shut down there. He saved one of us, so they reckon he should get a taste of freedom." He grimaced. "Little do they know he's already had a taste of quite a few things in that cabin."

"It's nothing," Hawk insisted.

"Nothing? What do you call that scene I walked in on?"

He squared his shoulders. "I call it none of your damn business. Since when do you barge into my cabin like that?"

"Since you didn't come up for the change of watch like you always do. The men get antsy when there's an alteration in routine. Routine is what keeps us all alive and well and working in concert." He lowered his voice, hissing, "And I had good reason to be concerned, given our prisoner had a fucking blade to your throat!"

Hawk gritted his teeth. "It was a lesson."

"In what, exactly?"

"Knife skills. He should know how to defend himself."

Snell blinked for a few moments, his eyebrows almost meeting the receding line of his thin hair. "You think *our prisoner* should know how to defend himself?"

"Not against us. For the future." *What would that be? Would Nathaniel really strike out on his own?*

"Since when do you care about that little fuck's future beyond the prize he will attain for us?"

Clenching his fists against the urge to grab his friend by the collar and demand respect for Nathaniel, Hawk turned to the rail and gazed out at the horizon where the stars and sea became one.

Rubbing a weary hand over his face, Snell leaned on the rail beside him. "It's one thing to have a bit of sport and bugger him—although I've never known you to care much for that."

It was true, and for a mad moment, Hawk wanted to confess that he felt as though he was under some spell. That he couldn't get enough of Nathaniel's touch, of his breathy moans and sheer delight in fucking. How his innocent passion made Hawk feel young again, his body's aches and pains somehow erased.

The way Nathaniel listened avidly when Hawk read to him. The warmth of him curling near as they slept, Hawk sharing his bed for the first time since John. Why shouldn't he have something good, even if it came from a most unexpected source? Even if it was for a brief flicker of time?

After a few moments, Snell added, "And I'm sure you realize he's only bending over for you to save his skin."

A furious denial whipped through him, and Hawk barely resisted the urge to slam his fist into Snell's face. He clenched his jaw and exhaled. "Perhaps. It matters not. Why shouldn't I take my pleasure?"

"Buggering the brat is one thing. It's another altogether to allow him any sort of advantage. To put yourself in danger. You can't trust him. You know that."

Intellectually, yes. Yet his soul protested. Hawk couldn't explain it and didn't try.

Finally Snell sighed. "Well, as I said—the motion has passed by a wide margin. They see it as only fair that Bainbridge be allowed fresh air. I think I should suggest he take a hammock with us in the forecastle. I'll keep a close watch. It's not safe to have him in your cabin."

Hawk gripped the rail, indignation rising. "I haven't forced him, if that's what—"

"Not safe for *you*, for fuck's sake. The dagger was at *your* throat, and while you may not see the danger, it is increasingly obvious to me."

"He's staying in my cabin until the ransom exchange." As Snell opened his mouth, Hawk bit out, "End of discussion. Do your job and make sure the men don't get too attached. Or it will be harder when the time comes to hand him over."

Snell glared. "Indeed it will. Or when the time comes to kill him if his father doesn't pay."

Stomach knotting, bile in his throat, Hawk eked out a nod, knowing without any doubt that Nathaniel's death was not something he could perpetrate or allow. Still, he did not pretend they could have a future together; that was too fantastical a notion to entertain beyond daydreams. This madness was temporary, and Hawk comforted himself with that.

Snell said, "I'll remind the men. And you'd do damn well to remember yourself."

"The money is what matters," he insisted. In the end, it had to be. That was the way of their world.

"Indeed it is. We could be chasing other prizes, and instead we're twiddling our thumbs. They all want their share of what you promised." He looked to Nathaniel, who had turned and watched them now. Had the wind carried snatches of their conversation? Snell added grimly, "If the men don't get their prize, sentiment will only go so far."

Nodding, Hawk faced the stern, his back to Nathaniel's intent gaze. Snell took his leave belowdecks, and Hawk pulled out his spyglass to survey the horizon and calm his racing heart. His view of the world at a remove was sharp as ever even though his mind was hopelessly muddled.

Snell was right. Hawk should distance himself from Nathaniel immediately. Sever whatever this strange tie between them was. Regain his fucking senses. Fine, so he wouldn't kill Nathaniel. That didn't mean he had to allow himself to sink any deeper into the abyss.

"Captain?" Hawk lowered the glass to find a crewman named Peters a few feet away, a frown on his lined face. "Anything amiss?"

"No."

Peters nodded, still clearly dubious, and went back to the rigging. Hawk supposed it was uncommon for him to be up on deck so late. Usually he paced in the privacy of his cabin unless there was some problem.

It truly was time to go below. He needed sleep. Who knew what could appear on the horizon tomorrow? There was no reason to be hesitant.

What the fuck am I afraid of?

Striding to the bow, he took Nathaniel's arm, pulling him to the ladder without explanation. Because Nathaniel was his prisoner, and Hawk was a *pirate*. No explanation was needed.

A lamp still burned low in the cabin, and after Hawk bolted the door and turned, the yellow light flickered over Nathaniel's bare skin as he stripped off his clothes. Hawk should tell him to stop—tell him to go to the corner.

Yet he said no such thing as Nathaniel sank to his knees, tugging on the laces of Hawk's trousers and freeing his cock, pressing eager, openmouthed kisses to it and muttering, "Finally."

All the blood rushing from his head, Hawk thumped against the door, biting back a groan as Nathaniel swallowed him clumsily.

This. This is what I'm afraid of.

It shouldn't have troubled him—being pleasured by his hostage, Nathaniel submissive and naked at his feet. Why shouldn't he allow himself to enjoy it?

Why indeed.

Because his fingers threaded through Nathaniel's hair, which had curled even more after the rain. Because he didn't pull or plunder, only caressed as Nathaniel sucked him, slurping and breathing hard through his nose, lips stretched, the vibration of his moans shuddering through Hawk, making him painfully hard.

Because he loved the way he could see his prick pressing against the inside of Nathaniel's cheek. Because he reached down to trace the bump of it, feeling unbearably tender.

Because a hook tugged in his chest, the urge to keep Nathaniel safe and happy, away from his cursed father and anyone who would make him feel lesser for his pure and honest desires, for his struggles with words on a page.

What devilry is this?

Nathaniel had eased back the foreskin, and now he sucked at the glistening head of Hawk's shaft, hands sneaking into Hawk's open trousers to caress bare flesh, eager and bold.

"Denied yourself this," Hawk murmured. Nathaniel met his gaze, honey eyes big and dark in the flickering light. He went on, stroking Nathaniel's head. "You love it—having a cock in your mouth. My cock."

Nodding, Nathaniel sucked harder, one hand circling the base where his lips couldn't quite reach without making him cough. He kept trying, seeming desperate to swallow Hawk whole.

Eyes watering, he gagged and had to pull off. Hawk petted his hair, then pulled down his own trousers so they pooled around his knees, the wooden door cool against his bare arse.

Quietly, he said, "Take your finger in your mouth. Yes, that's it. Make it wet." Hawk watched as Nathaniel obediently sucked on his index finger, spitting and letting saliva drip down onto his hand. Nathaniel looked up at him with his finger between his lips, waiting, his chest rising and falling unevenly. So trusting.

Hawk had to touch him, and he traced the shell of Nathaniel's ear, then spread his legs as much as he could with his trousers at his knees. "Now suck me again, and push your finger inside me."

Eyes wide, Nathaniel latched back onto Hawk's prick, reaching his hand between Hawk's legs to find his hole. He didn't hesitate, invading boldly, and Hawk couldn't hold in his moan, his bollocks tightening as he clamped down on Nathaniel's questing finger.

It had been years since he'd been breached by a cock, and he'd never much enjoyed it. But he'd shoved his own finger in his arse on occasion, and the wet suction of that ravenous mouth combined with the welcome pressure had Hawk spurting without even being able to give warning, losing control as if he were a boy again. He held Nathaniel's head as he emptied into him, Nathaniel swallowing convulsively.

When Nathaniel eased out his finger and sat back on his heels, a long, ropey strand of seed stretched between his swollen lips and Hawk's prick. Hawk's knees almost gave out, and he was unable to look away, sure it might be the most beautiful thing he'd ever seen.

Although the lamp was almost out, the colors of Nathaniel's body and face seemed vivid, as if the sun had suddenly beamed through the stern windows.

Breath short, sweat prickling his skin, Hawk caught the strand on his finger and fed it to Nathaniel, who licked thoroughly. Nathaniel's cock strained red and hard, and Hawk whispered, "Bring yourself off."

Almost as if he'd forgotten about it, Nathaniel looked down and took hold of his shaft, moaning and tipping forward to rest his head against Hawk's hip as he jerked himself, his hand a blur. Hawk stroked his hair, and it was no time at all until he spilled, soft cries escaping his red lips.

Breathing hard, Nathaniel sat back on his heels again, peering up. Then Hawk realized his boots were splashed with spend, white drops stark on the black leather, a bit right over the gold tip of his left boot.

He should have been angry at his prisoner for making a mess on his boots like that, but when Nathaniel bit his lip, a saucy light in his eyes, Hawk found he could only smile and brush his knuckles against Nathaniel's heated cheek.

Then Nathaniel bent and licked his boots clean of seed, and Hawk groaned, sparks flaring through him like smoldering ashes in a grate poked back to life. He couldn't possibly get hard again so soon, but his balls twitched at the sweet submission.

Perhaps Nathaniel knew precisely what he was doing and the effect it would have, but it seemed utterly open and sincere. When he sat back up, Hawk brushed his damp hair, and the urge to protect him from those who would shame and belittle him thrummed with every heartbeat.

He pulled up his trousers, leaving them loose around his hips. "Time for sleep." He eased Nathaniel to his feet, still careful of his shoulder, and when Nathaniel turned to the corner, Hawk tugged him to the bed and urged him onto it, trying to ignore how Nathaniel's grateful smile wrapped around his heart and squeezed.

Turning away before he could dig himself any deeper, Hawk ordered, "Sleep," and went to his desk, pulling out the chair, then fiddling with the contents of a drawer. He should shove Nathaniel back into the corner. He needed to collect the ransom and put an end to this.

When the lamp had been extinguished for some time, Hawk stripped off and lowered himself to the bed on his belly, not bothering with the sheet, which Nathaniel hadn't pulled up either in the humid night.

Keeping his head facing away from Nathaniel, Hawk glimpsed the blanket of stars through the stern windows, open to the night air. He listened to the slap of water against the hull as the ship rocked gently, Nathaniel's soft, even breathing seemingly in rhythm with the sea.

A shiver skated down his spine, but it wasn't on account of the breeze. The mattress had shifted, and Nathaniel's fingertips traced the long scars that snaked across Hawk's buttocks. Back and forth, back and forth. Hawk found himself answering the unasked question.

"The lash."

Nathaniel pressed closer, his left leg sliding between Hawk's. There seemed no sense of purpose to it other than closeness; Nathaniel's cock was soft against Hawk's thigh.

Hawk should squirm away and put space between them instead of allowing this entanglement, but his limbs were heavy and warm, and the tickle of Nathaniel's breath across his shoulder soothed as much as the ship's easy rocking.

"When?" Nathaniel asked.

Don't answer. Tell him to go to sleep or you'll put him back in the corner. Heedless of his better judgment, Hawk replied, "I was a few years younger than you. On a Royal Navy frigate."

Nathaniel's hand stilled for a moment before he continued his exploration of the scars. "I can't imagine you my age. Or taking orders from anyone."

Hawk had to smile, keeping his head turned toward the stern. Somehow if he didn't look at Nathaniel, the talking seemed more…permissible. "I didn't emerge from my mother's womb a pirate."

Nathaniel's chuckle ghosted over Hawk's skin. "No, I suppose you didn't." He still traced the scars. "What was her name? Your mother."

"Anne." It had been years since he'd spoken of her, or really since he'd even thought of her. All that remained were fleeting images of dark hair and flour-dusted hands, a short temper, but soothing caresses when Hawk had been trampled by a panicked sheep in the paddock.

Nathaniel seemed to be waiting, and Hawk found himself adding, "She was struck by fever. I barely knew her."

"I'm sorry. Your father? Was he a sailor?"

"A farmer. Sheep. He loathed the sea, and I wished fervently I'd been born to a fisherman."

"And what did you think of sheep farming?"

"Fuck, I hated it." Memories of mud and shit and stinking animals tumbled through his mind. Endless days spent between the boundaries of their land, trapped there while the rest of the world spread out beyond the horizon, out of reach. "The sea was so close I could smell it beyond the cliffs."

"Mmm. Did you live in the West Country?"

Hawk blinked in surprise. "Near Plymouth. Cornwall, close to Devonshire."

"I thought I heard a hint of it in your voice. We once had some minor nobility from Plymouth for dinner. Did you have many brothers and sisters?"

"Seven. Sometimes my brother Richard would lie for me and risk our father's fury when I sneaked out of the pasture to sit on the cliffs. I'd watch the water, fishing boats, and sometimes ships in the distance. I became adept at spotting sails on the horizon. Any flicker of movement, of…promise. It stood me in good stead once I was at sea."

Nathaniel still smoothed his fingers over the scars, back and forth. "And what is your true name?"

It was a name he hadn't spoken aloud in many years, and Hawk's heart thumped. *Perhaps he's hypnotizing me,* he thought as the truth slithered up his tongue. He was only just able to swallow it down deep again.

He wondered what it would mean for his name to be on Nathaniel's lips. Something unfurled in him, a dark knot that had been cinched tight. He wanted to hear it, but couldn't permit it.

Apparently letting that question go, Nathaniel asked, "What did your father say when you decided to become a sailor?"

Hawk briefly closed his eyes to the distant stars, a shiver rippling through him. Perhaps he should close the window after all. Yet he didn't move, the warm weight of Nathaniel's leg hooked over his like an anchor.

"He had no chance to say a thing. I slipped down to the docks to go fishing. There was an old man who was happy to teach me in return for labor. Some nights, I'd climb out the window and steal away. The days on the farm were long, but I was young enough that excitement could fuel me instead of sleep."

"How young?"

"Fifteen. Depending on the tides, the fisherman went out in the darkness sometimes. It was past midnight when we returned to the harbor. I was wet, the reek of cod replacing the stink of sheep. I should have been more careful. Should have paid more heed as I made my way past the tavern. But I was thinking of the thrill of full nets, still tasting salt on my tongue, feeling the rock of the boat beneath me. They came upon me in an instant."

Nathaniel's hand stilled again, now resting on the swell of Hawk's arse. "They?"

"Press gang."

He sucked in a breath. "I've heard the tales."

"There were five of them with clubs." *Rough hands dragging him back to the docks, fetid breath, his bare feet barely touching the cobblestones as they bore him away from home and all he knew. Powerless.* "I tried to tell them I was a farmer, not a seaman, but of course all evidence pointed to the contrary. And I had no money to pay them off."

Nathaniel whispered, "They simply…*took* you?"

"The navy needs men. It's so vast it can't operate without impressment. They said it was my duty to serve king and country. Hauled me aboard the *Leaside*, and soon we were away. I was finally at sea." Hawk laughed derisively. "I learned to be careful of wishes, lest they come true."

A lesson he still hadn't quite learned, it seemed.

"It's awful. Barbaric. You didn't even have a chance to say goodbye?"

The pang of missing his family had long ago faded to a dull echo of another existence. "I would have left one way or another. It wasn't for me, a farmer's life. My father couldn't understand. He was a good man. Fair. Hardworking. But he thought me a fool for wanting anything beyond our fields. Still, I would have liked to give my farewells."

"I'm sorry." Nathaniel pressed his lips to Hawk's shoulder.

Holding his breath, Hawk watched the stars shift as the ship rocked. Then he made his voice hard. "Don't pity me too much. I kidnapped you, after all."

Nathaniel's warm presence didn't waver, his hand still resting on Hawk's backside. "I suppose you did. I learned to be careful of what one wishes for as well." Before Hawk could wonder too much at what he meant, Nathaniel asked, "What was it like? Aboard the frigate?"

"Dank. Crowded. Freezing or sweltering, seemingly never anything in-between. Rations were hard biscuits, sometimes crawling with weevils. Salted meat. The officers ate better, of course."

"Of course."

"I was given the choice to 'volunteer' for service or remain a pressed man and get nothing. Volunteers were given two months' salary in advance to buy slops—clothing—from the ship's purser, and perhaps a hammock. Since I clearly had no choice, I agreed to volunteer. And I was promised more salary, but I barely saw a shilling. I probably should have refused their offer on moral grounds, but it seemed an exercise in futility that would harm me far more than them."

John's voice echoed in his mind. *"I ain't giving them the satis-faction."* He had been stubborn and righteous, beautiful in his rebellion and rage. But he'd smiled so sweetly when Hawk had offered to share his hammock one night, then every night following until…

Nathaniel's hand stroked up and down his spine, and Hawk realized he'd tensed from head to toe. Part of him wanted to shove Nathaniel away and spring from the bed, escape up to the main deck and breathe the night air until he regained his senses and stopped this slow, steady loosening of truths.

Yet he couldn't seem to move, and he exhaled under Nathaniel's caress, still keeping his head turned away as if that was some kind of protection.

Nathaniel said, "I thought they couldn't take you if you were under eighteen."

"That's a fairly new amendment to the law. Then, there was no limit. And the Crown's rules on paper don't often matter a whit in the real world."

"What did you do aboard the ship?"

"Powder monkey at first—carried gunpowder from the magazines to the artillery guns. I was still small, so I could get around well in tight spaces."

"You? Small?"

Hawk found himself smiling. "Again, I didn't emerge from the womb this way. But my father was tall, and it kicked in after a couple of years. I sprouted up and didn't stop."

"What were your duties outside of battle?"

His right arm cramped where it was folded, Nathaniel's weight against it where he pressed all along Hawk's side. Yet Hawk didn't shift to alleviate it.

"Hauled the lines. Manned the bilge pumps. Whatever menial tasks they ordered since they realized I was a landman after all. But I was eager to learn the ways of sailors. It wasn't the way I'd imagined, and the reality was stark compared to my boyhood fantasies of the sea's freedom. But I was determined to make the best of it. Better myself. They soon discovered I had the keen eye to be a lookout. Called me the little sea hawk."

Nathaniel laughed softly. "Ah. So that explains it. And you kept learning as the years passed?"

"One of the officers took an interest in me. A fatherly sort. Saw my potential, he told me. Eventually taught me to read as well." He hadn't allowed himself to think of Lieutenant Wiltshire in years. Now, Hawk closed his eyes to the memory of the man's neck impaled with wood, the deck having exploded with a direct hit, his eyes bugged out.

Nathaniel's feather touch returned to the faded scars across Hawk's arse. "What was your crime to suffer this?"

"Theft of rations."

John had actually been the one to squirrel away the extra food, determined that they should desert as soon as they could and that they'd need their strength. He'd protested when Hawk took the blame, but Hawk couldn't bear the thought of that smooth, pale flesh being marred.

He went on. "I was still young, so I was lucky. I had to kiss the gunner's daughter instead of being lashed to the grate on the main deck and having my back whipped. I was given the reduced cat—five tails instead of nine. But they gave me twenty strikes, to show the severity of my crime."

Nathaniel gasped. Then he asked, "Kiss the gunner's daughter?"

"Bent over a cannon so they could whip my arse. Arms straight out in front of me along the barrel, trousers down. The crew gathered around, especially the other boys, so they learned a lesson. The boatswain administered the punishment. It was humiliating, of course. I couldn't sit for a week. Could barely sleep." Poor John had tried everything to ease his pain, to little avail. "They didn't intend for it to scar, but here we are."

"I wonder..." Nathaniel caressed the ridges.

Hawk waited, gaze sweeping over the arc of Ursa Minor. Finally, he prompted, "What?"

When Nathaniel spoke, it was a whisper. "I wonder what's wrong with me, that I enjoy such treatment."

Jolted by surprise and sudden fury snaking through him, Hawk turned his head and shifted onto his left hip to face Nathaniel, reaching for him. "Was it your father? Did he often cane you?"

Nathaniel blinked. "No. No, I meant...the other day, bent over your desk."

His mouth went dry. "Did I truly hurt you? I thought..." Self-loathing burned a path through him like cheap rum.

"No, no." Nathaniel pressed his hand flat on Hawk's chest. "As I said, I liked it. But it's odd, isn't it? Wrong? I know I'm unnatural, but in this I seem doubly so."

Hawk cupped his face, thumb brushing against the hair that struggled to grow on Nathaniel's cheek. "Would I not be wrong as well? Since I'm the one who restrained you and gained such pleasure from it?"

He curled his fingers in the hair scattered over Hawk's tattoo. "I don't know."

"It wasn't the same as the punishment I received. I took no pleasure from that. No pleasure was offered. What we did isn't the same. My sense was that you wished it. Had yearned for it. To be fucked that way. Mastered, but also...liberated."

Nathaniel nodded. "I did. I wanted it. I want it still." He inched closer, eyes gleaming in the faint moonlight, palm stroking Hawk's chest, their legs tangled. "I can't explain it, but I've craved it. To give myself over like that. You don't think it's wrong?"

"Not if permission is granted. Not if the desire is present in both parties, and I assure you it was."

Nathaniel seemed to ponder that. Then he asked, "When a man falls victim to impressment, how long is his service?"

"As long as they want it to be, I believe. I was on that frigate eight years."

"How did you get away?"

"We had a new captain. He was intolerable. Cruel and impervious to reason, and there are no votes on navy ships. Several of us conspired to desert. We decided that even if we ended up hung from the yardarm, it would be preferable."

"Did you ever go back to Plymouth?"

"Couldn't. As a deserter, it was too risky. Besides, my family would have been strangers. They still would be. I think it would be worse, to see them now and be utterly unknown to each other." He quelled a shudder.

"So then you became a privateer?"

"Yes. I assumed a new identity and made my way to the New World. Found work aboard a privateer ship as a rigger and lookout. Worked my way up to boatswain. At least I had learned much in the navy. Eventually I won my own ship and hired a crew."

"What Christian name did you use as a privateer? Surely you weren't simply Hawk."

His heart clenched. Tonight he was poking at that old wound like he was loosening a tooth, and the name caught in his throat. "John."

It was an exceedingly common name—one he'd seen and uttered many times. Yet this was the first time he'd said it and meant *his* John. And Nathaniel seemed to know somehow.

"Who was he?"

And somehow, Hawk *answered*. "A friend. More than. He was pressed aboard the frigate as well. We were both young. He… He died in battle."

"I'm so sorry. Did you and he…"

"Yes. Strictly forbidden in the navy, but of course it happened. I think for many it was a matter of circumstance. Trapped at sea with other men for months on end, it came down to practicality. Most men needed release."

"But for you, it was more?"

Swallowing hard, he thought of John's breathy whimpers in his ear, his hands urging. "Yes." His time with John was so brief, hardly more than a blink when the hours of Hawk's life would be tallied.

What will Nathaniel amount to?

"And you never felt shame for it?" he asked. "For being a sinner?"

Hawk smirked. "I'm a sinner in many ways. It never bothered me. My father once told me that to fight against nature was a losing battle every time. Of course he was talking about how much bloody rain we got one winter. Still, his words rang true."

Nathaniel frowned. "You don't think it unnatural? What we do together?"

"How can it be? It occurs in animals as well. There were always a number of rams on the farm who wouldn't have anything to do with the ewes. They'd only mount each other."

"Really?" A grin brightened sweet face. "That's wonderful. Perhaps it all makes a curious sort of sense."

He curled a lock of Nathaniel's hair around his finger. "Indeed."

"Tell me more about how John Hawk, legal privateer, became a captain of his own ship. You said there was a wager involved? And later you transformed into not only a mere pirate, but a king amongst them. How exactly?"

He scoffed. "I'm no king. I've managed to cultivate a reputation, but I believe I've told you much of that has to do with planting the right stories in the right gullible ears in the right ports."

Nathaniel murmured, "Answer the questions anyway."

Although he was supposed to be the one giving orders, Hawk obeyed. "I got lucky one night playing at cards in Port Royal. A fool bet this ship. Thus, I became a captain. The Admiralty in Jamaica didn't look too closely into my details. The Crown was in great need of privateers to help battle the Spanish in the West Indies."

"So John Hawk was awarded a letter of marque and reprisal."

"Yes. I was authorized to capture enemy ships and bring them before the Admiralty Court. The Crown took a share of the prizes. It was regulated. Honorable, even. At least it seemed so to me. I was eager to serve my country."

He shook his head, remembering the strange sense of pride it gave him to be valued. "I don't know why, given what she's done to me and others. Kidnapped her own men in the night, and worse than that, built the New World on the backs of slaves. Yet I still wanted to prove myself worthy."

Nathaniel's sleepy smile was rueful. "I certainly understand the sentiment." He slid even closer, nuzzling Hawk's throat. "I take great pride in pleasing you. Proving myself."

Despite being directly compared to England and her depravity, warmth spread through Hawk's chest, and he carded his fingers through Nathaniel's hair. He was on such dangerous ground, supposedly the one in control yet helpless to disentangle himself, Nathaniel safe in his arms as if he belonged there.

"Then my father claimed you'd broken regulations and hadn't treated the Spanish captain properly," Nathaniel murmured. "He could just strip you of your letter of marque without a hearing?"

"Yes. He'd been appointed a judge. He had total power. In an instant, I was declared a pirate. I've heard of other privateers being similarly branded. If treaties are signed while privateers are still at sea, they can return to port having captured a ship of a nation that is no longer an enemy. No quarter is given, and the privateer is suddenly heading to the gallows, considered a pirate."

"It's so unfair. It doesn't make any sense."

"That's government for you. In your father's case, I think he was desperate to get a foothold in the New World. Rumor says he seized my prize to keep it for himself, that he and his cronies only gave a portion to the Crown and lied about the cargo."

Nathaniel sighed. "I can believe it. He has always had a thirst for power, which requires riches. Riches he feels are owed to him. He married my mother for her estate and modest wealth, then squandered it. Doomed her for me so he could have a son for the sake of his pride. His name."

I'm sorry for your mother's fate, but glad of your life.

The words burned on his tongue, but Hawk choked them down. Instead he said, "Fortunately, your father underestimated me and my crew. They freed me, and we made our escape."

"Now revenge is close at hand." Nathaniel burrowed nearer, pressing his lips to Hawk's throat.

Hawk wished he could see Nathaniel's face and ask what he was thinking. Only days remained before the ransom exchange. Hawk's gut seized, acid roiling. He wrapped Nathaniel in his arms, and it seemed neither of them wanted to speak aloud the hard questions they should.

How had they entangled themselves so thoroughly in such a short time? What would happen if Walter Bainbridge didn't pay the ransom? Had they both gone mad to lower their defenses?

As much as Hawk tried to deny it, this fragile, wonderful peace was merely the eye of the storm.

Chapter Sixteen

HAWK'S VOICE CARRIED over the deck from where he stood at the bow, the sun at his back. "We'll be going ashore for two nights."

The men cheered, and Nathaniel grinned where he stood off to the side. He was grateful the men had voted to allow him up on deck, but aside from Mr. O'Connell, the crew largely kept their distance. Nathaniel was still their prisoner, after all. Their chance at a windfall.

As the date of the ransom exchange neared, his worries increased. Taking a deep breath, he scolded himself to focus on each day in turn. Each hour, even each minute. It was all he could do.

He allowed himself another smile. If they were going ashore, he would finally have the chance to run. If Hawk tried to renege on his prize again, Nathaniel would raise holy hell. But he was confident Hawk wouldn't go back on his word this time.

Nathaniel had glimpsed white beaches in the distance and leafy trees far more exotic than those in England. Oh, how he longed to explore. Inhaling the salty air, he focused on how wondrous it would be to finally run for the first time in months.

"Are we going to Nassau?" a hopeful voice called.

Mr. Snell answered, "Do you still not have any fucking sense of where we are, Barney? We're many miles from Nassau, you loggerhead. In fact, the closest port is Primrose Isle, where we'll be heading immediately after this excursion."

Nathaniel's stomach swooped, bumps rising on his skin as Snell's gaze came to rest on him as he added, "The time is almost here to exchange our piece of loot for money in our hands."

Of course all eyes now cut to Nathaniel, although Hawk kept his gaze firmly ahead, his jaw tight and hands clasped behind his back, spine straight. The men closest to where Nathaniel stood by the starboard rail edged away from him, even grateful Mr. O'Connell. Nathaniel kept his gaze on his bare feet, sweat prickling his spine, the attention like needles.

Hawk spoke as if the unfortunate Mr. Barney hadn't interrupted. "We'll spot land any minute now. The island is out of the trade channels, big enough for our needs, and uninhabited. There should be crab, fish, and fruit." He smirked. "Of course we have brought a large store of rum."

After another cheer, he added, "And quick as lightning, we'll be repairing the ship tomorrow. Careening what of her we can now that we've found a suitable beach."

A collective groan filled the air, and Snell held up his hands. "It's no one's favorite task, but we all know it has to be done. Those barnacles on the hull slow us down. Our cargo holds are empty, so it'll be far less work to beach the ship. We made all the repairs we could inside after our skirmish with the *Javelin,* but some work needs to be done on land. And we want every knot of our speed to make off with our ransom from that scum Walter Bainbridge. Just think of the money you're soon to receive. You want to keep it, don't you? After we drop off the little lord, we must make haste and leave Primrose Isle firmly behind us."

Then what becomes of me?

While the men went back to work and Hawk conferred with Snell without glancing Nathaniel's way, Nathaniel remained at the rail and stared at the speck of land growing larger.

Soon the next land they approached would be Primrose Isle,

and the adventure would be over. His gut churned, melancholy thickening his throat and stealing his breath.

Assuming Walter paid the ransom—and he refused to dwell on the idea that he wouldn't, banishing the flare of panic—Nathaniel would have to find a way to leave the colony and build a new life.

Hawk's confession that he wished to retire echoed in Nathaniel's mind. He peered at Hawk surveying the crew, pacing a few steps, then stopping, his hands clasped behind him, coat left in the cabin given the heat, dark sleeves rolled. His black trousers hugged his slim hips and muscular thighs, gold belt and tips of his boots gleaming.

Flushing, Nathaniel remembered the taste when he'd licked those boots—his own salty, musky seed and an oak flavor that reminded him of dark red wine. He could scarcely believe it was all real and not some feverish imagining, that he'd lain with this man, fantasy made flesh.

Hawk gazed out to the horizon, his lined face calm, poised and ready for whatever crossed their path. Would such a powerful man really be satisfied living a simple life by the sea instead of snared in its embrace, miles from anything?

Perhaps he would wish to share a life with Nathaniel, and they could build a house somewhere, live simply and most of all *together…*

No. Stop. Marshaling his wayward mind—treacherous as ever—Nathaniel forced away the vision of early morning fishing and picking fruit under the sun. He couldn't allow himself down such a dangerous path.

Hawk was fucking him and had shown kindness. More than that: compassion and care. He'd told him things perhaps he hadn't shared with any other person. And while Nathaniel truly didn't believe Hawk would harm him, he daren't expect their connection to become more, to last beyond his captivity. That was far too much to hope for, no matter how close they'd grown.

Wasn't it?

Surely they would soon part, and Nathaniel would strike out for…somewhere. He would do…something. In the meantime, he would relish every touch he could coax from Hawk, every confession, every smile. Hour by hour. Minute by minute, leaving the unknowable future in its place, beyond reach.

UNDER THE FAINT light of the sliver of moon amid clouds, the beach stretched out in front of him, waves rolling over the sand. Behind Nathaniel, men went about their work.

Some set up camp, others catching supper, and still others ferrying supplies from the ship, which was as close to shore as it could get, the sloop's shallow draft allowing it to bob in only eight feet of water, a hulking shadow at anchor that would be heaved over in the light of day.

Nathaniel stared at the empty expanse before him, then turned to Hawk, who watched him with a tiny smile before saying, "Go on, then."

He didn't waste a moment, racing along the damp sand near the placid water's edge, delighting at the surf swirling around his ankles from time to time. He pumped his arms, breathing steadily, legs flexing, feet pushing off the sand. His heart thundered in the best way, reminding him he was wonderfully *alive.*

There was nothing but him and the beach, his body working, mind free and clear as if he were racing across a meadow at Hollington. His breath came shorter than usual after weeks cooped up, and his muscles burned more quickly. But he didn't hesitate as he blazed across the sand, determined to enjoy every moment to the fullest, no matter how hard he had to work for it.

He should likely have been more careful in the darkness, slowing to ensure he didn't trip and break his neck on an outcropping of rock, but there was only fine sand beneath his feet.

It was seemingly endless until the beach abruptly gave way to a slew of rocks and boulders at the end of the island. The only direction to go was back the way he came, unless he wanted to veer into the hulking shadow of the tropical forest.

He wasn't sure how far he'd gone, and he stopped at the edge of the nameless island, wonderfully *alone*. Inhaling deeply of the fresh air, sweet with tropical blooms and heavy with impending rain, he caught his breath before trotting back along the beach.

After a time, the moon disappeared, and he could barely make out the white crests of the waves as the wind increased. The crew's bonfire was faintly visible in the distance.

He stopped and tugged at his sweat-drenched shirt, peeling it over his head and tossing it behind him. The water was blissfully cool without being cold, and he waded in to his thighs, breeches clinging.

He was about to dive under when a voice called from the darkness, "Wait!" Splashing into the surf in his boots, Hawk tugged Nathaniel back onto dry sand.

Nathaniel laughed. "Do you think I'm going to swim to Jamaica?"

A huff of breath. "I think you're going to drown. There may not be low and high tides in this particular sea as such, but there are still fucking currents!"

It was too dark to clearly make out Hawk's expression, but his concern was obvious. Hawk's hand was still wrapped around Nathaniel's upper arm, but not in a punishing grip, just a steady one, anchoring him.

What if we could *have a future?*

Nathaniel's head battled with his heart as the skies opened in a blink—fat, warm rain splatting down. He reminded himself: *Minute by minute. Enjoy every moment.*

He laughed, pulling free of Hawk's grasp and spinning with arms wide, head tipped back. He stripped off his breeches and drawers, needing to feel the rain everywhere, rivers over his skin.

It poured down. Dizzy, Nathaniel stumbled to a stop, facing Hawk. "Isn't it glorious? I could die happy in a place like this."

Through the rain, the imagined weight of Hawk's gaze was like a brand on Nathaniel's flesh in the darkness. Naked, soaked to the skin, wild and free, Nathaniel knew absolutely no shame.

Going closer, he glimpsed lust shining from Hawk's eyes, and a wave of power swept through him, sending blood rushing to his cock. It swelled under Hawk's watch, and Nathaniel kept his arms at his sides, not hiding.

In the night, fully dressed in his dark shirt, trousers, and boots, Hawk could have been a wraith, a demon. One of the horsemen of the apocalypse. Forbidding and unyielding.

A stallion.

"Will you fuck me like this?" Nathaniel asked, unable— unwilling—to stop himself. "Here. Right now. You still clothed, and me naked on my hands and knees. Will you mount me and—"

Hawk strode forward, yanking at his belt and laces, and spun Nathaniel around, shoving him to the sand. Nathaniel arched his back, and with a groan, Hawk pressed behind him. In another few moments, Hawk had his hard cock in hand, spitting and pushing it into Nathaniel's hole.

Nathaniel cried out at the rough entry. He was sure he was being split in half, but he moaned, "Don't stop. Harder."

Grunting, Hawk clung to Nathaniel's hips, fucking him in short strokes, not all the way inside yet. Nathaniel spread his fingers in the wet sand, pushing back against Hawk's prick.

The pain was part of it, and he wanted more. *Needed* more. He looked back over his shoulder at Hawk's grimace, his teeth clenched as he fucked him.

"All of it," Nathaniel commanded, and when Hawk's glazed

eyes snapped to his, he implored, "*Please.*"

Hips stuttering, Hawk growled, then pulled out and slammed all the way home. They both cried out, and Nathaniel could only drop his head and take it greedily, the sharp burn laced with pleasure as Hawk fucked him the way he needed.

Hawk's hands curled over Nathaniel's shoulders, digging in as he plowed him, the coarse fabric of his trousers rubbing against Nathaniel's arse. Hawk's hips drove as relentlessly as the rain, open belt slapping Nathaniel's thigh.

His healing shoulder protested the rough treatment, but Nathaniel didn't flinch away from Hawk's grasp, desperate for more. The world narrowed as if seen through a spyglass, nothing else existing but Hawk's prick inside, stretching him with punishing thrusts, their harsh panting echoed in the rain.

No matter how fine the sand had seemed between his toes earlier, it was coarse beneath his knees. When Hawk slammed into just the right spot, Nathaniel shouted, chanting nonsensical noises. "Uh, uh, oh. *Nnngh.*"

He imagined how they must look, the pirate captain all in black, mounting his pale prisoner, giving him every inch of his massive prick. "Harder," he pleaded, although in his hoarse voice it sounded like an order. "Make me spend with your cock."

Grunting with each thrust, Hawk pounded him, shifting his hips for the perfect angle and finding that secret, miraculous little nub inside. Nathaniel cried out, his own cock straining, leaking in the night air. The pressure that had been building in his bollocks burst.

White stars exploded in Nathaniel's vision, bliss so intense sweeping through him as he spent that it left a hollowed-out trail in its wake. He clamped down on Hawk's prick, jerking, tipping his head back, lungs burning. "Fill me. Only you."

With a shout, Hawk did, fingers practically embedding in Nathaniel's shoulders, his seed spilling so deep inside, Nathaniel imagined it reached his very soul. The thought should have frightened him, but his balls drew up and spurted again, another few drops into the sand.

The rain hadn't eased, and Nathaniel turned his head to catch a few drops on his tongue. His arms shook, every muscle in his body burning, and he dropped to his elbows, arse still up, Hawk leaning over him. He knew it would hurt when Hawk withdrew, and he braced himself when the fingers uncurled from his shoulders.

Yet Hawk seemed in no rush, easing out his softening member inch by inch, one rough hand smoothing up and down Nathaniel's spine. In his wake, Nathaniel felt incredibly stretched and unbearably empty.

When Hawk was free, Nathaniel flopped on his belly with legs spread, grains of sand sticking everywhere, too drained to care. He folded his hands under his cheek and closed his eyes, waiting for Hawk to tug him to his feet and back to the ship.

The rain eased slightly, still steady and cool on his fevered skin. Hawk's callused palms caressed Nathaniel's arse, then opened him to the rain, cleaning him with fingertips that were shockingly gentle after the fierceness of their coupling.

Then his tongue was there, textured and *marvelous*, beard bristly against Nathaniel's tender, used hole. He licked and kissed, surely tasting his own seed. The thought made Nathaniel's spent bollocks twitch to life, a gasp on his lips, the wet sand too much against his soft, sensitive cock.

Hawk spread Nathaniel wide, poking into him with his tongue. Nathaniel groaned. "You can't make me release again. It's impossible."

That was how he found himself on his back, wet sand in many crevices, the downpour fortunately washing much of it away. Hawk cupped his hands to the rain, gathering water to rinse Nathaniel's groin of any lingering sand.

He breathed hard between Nathaniel's bent legs, staring down at him with carnal purpose, a devil's smile curving his full lips.

Groaning again, Nathaniel said, "That wasn't a dare. Simply a statement of fact."

Hawk closed one damp fist around Nathaniel's shaft, his other hand reaching down to press just so against the sensitive skin behind his balls.

A lightning bolt of pleasure struck, stealing Nathaniel's breath. His whimper trailed into a laugh. "I bet you'll do anything to prove me wrong, won't you?"

The rain tapered off, stars shedding a little more light as the clouds dissipated. Hawk laughed too, not a derisive bark or triumphant shout, but soft and true. His face was shockingly boyish, creased with his grin, hair plastered to his head and skin soaked.

He tracked his knuckles down Nathaniel's cheek, then brushed them over his lips. Nathaniel's heart hurtled back to a gallop as Hawk leaned down, his expression unmistakably tender, eyes searching as though he could read some answer upon his face.

For a heart-stopping moment, Nathaniel was sure Hawk would kiss him. That he would press their lips together and share breath in an intimacy Nathaniel imagined would be more profound than any of the fucking they'd done.

Then the mask slipped back into place, and Hawk's smile went positively feral.

Before Nathaniel could hope to think of a response, Hawk pulled Nathaniel's arse up onto his thighs. He was splayed under the stars, writhing and utterly wanton for the world to see, Hawk's head buried between his legs, licking and sucking his spent cock and balls mercilessly.

It was one wager Nathaniel was only too happy to lose.

Chapter Seventeen

S O MUCH CURSED sand.

Even though Hawk hadn't taken off his clothes, it had burrowed everywhere. Under the large canvas tent, he shifted on the scattered collection of pillows and blankets that made his bed. A table from the mess and his desk chair stood nearby.

Clad only in a too-big white shirt, Nathaniel slept curled on his side with his back against Hawk's chest, Hawk's arm slung around him. The sides of the tent hung loose, flapping in the morning breeze, sunlight dancing in and making the tip of Nathaniel's ear glow.

Hawk didn't know what sorcery had taken hold of him, but beholding Nathaniel in the rain, naked and beautiful with delight, lean muscles gleaming, he'd wanted to do *anything* Nathaniel asked. Anything to keep him so happy, so free.

Maybe he was a sea nymph, spinning some kind of magic. Although perhaps not, given how he'd splashed out without a thought to the currents, especially with the wind whipping.

Even now, Hawk's heart skipped a beat as he imagined Nathaniel disappearing under those dark waves and never resurfacing.

What the fuck is the matter with me?

The chorus of "Heave!" as most of the crew hauled the ship onto her side filled the air. Hawk glimpsed them as the tent flapped open, ropes taut as lines of men took turns pulling, the

Manta's hull being revealed to the merciless sun, a mess of barnacles evident along with boards that needed replacing and God knew what else.

Hawk should be out there supervising, encouraging, lending a hand himself given their tight turnaround. He had a job to do, and it wasn't to stay secreted away in his tent with their prisoner in his arms.

But God, he just didn't *care* anymore.

Part of him wished the men would take the ship and leave him and Nathaniel be. For so many years, the sea had been his home, and he had no doubt now he'd had his fill. Snell had said he wouldn't be able to leave the pirate life behind, but Hawk knew he must.

Perhaps he would fail miserably. Yet as he listened to the steady song of Nathaniel's breath—felt its rise and fall, wanted to press his lips to the mole on the top of Nathaniel's shoulder—the world seemed full of possibility.

It was madness. He shouldn't care about anything but collecting the ransom in two days.

Tension gripped him, a shiver of fear slithering down his spine. He had to stay on task, especially when some of the men were growing restless. He'd been taking a piss in the trees, dawn not even a hint on the horizon, when he'd heard the voices. Voices not as hushed as they should have been thanks to the barrel of rum.

"If you ask me, this ransom is a fool's errand. Captain's going to get us all killed for nothing."

"No one asked you, Deeks," a voice replied dryly. Sounded like the navigator, Boland, a lettered man who'd deserted the Royal Navy. Hawk hadn't asked why.

"Bainbridge might not even have the money." Hawk strained to hear, trying to place the voice. Ah yes, Tully, the newest, troublesome recruit. Tully went on. "You heard the bitch say it, Deeks. So what

happens if he still don't have it by the deadline? Then we've been sailin' around doing naught but wastin' our time when we could be waylayin' ships."

"She did say it," Deeks confirmed.

Tully added, "We all know the captain's fuckin' that little fop."

"Can't blame him for that. Most of us would take a go at that sweet arse given half the chance."

Boland spoke up again. "Yet when was the last time the captain actually bedded anyone? It's not his usual way." He paused. "It's concerning, I'll grant that. This…playing at courtship."

Hawk stood stock-still in the trees, the men's shadows barely visible on the edge of the beach. He'd finished pissing, but he didn't move, his cock hanging out, heart thudding.

Deeks laughed. "I heard he was dreaming about retiring and becoming a fucking farmer or the like."

A round of raucous laughter, and Hawk stood there in the darkness feeling unbearably small. Who had Snell told? Or had someone overheard them? He supposed it was immaterial, yet it stung nonetheless.

Deeks added, "A man like that? Can you imagine? Who the fuck does he think he's kidding?"

Tully said, "Seems clear t'me the captain's more interested in buggerin' that fancy arse and spinnin' fantasies than doin' what's best for the ship. For us. Is he even going to give the little brat up?"

Someone Hawk couldn't place spoke. "Bainbridge did save O'Connell. He's not so bad."

"Yeah, and we's grateful," Tully said. "Lettin' him up on the deck, not restrained nor nothin.' No offense to O'Connell, but is he worth your share of that ransom? We've been good to the whelp. Left him alone and not laid a finger on him."

Deeks replied, "'Cause you know the captain will have your bollocks for earrings if you even looked at the boy the wrong way."

"Exactly! Proves our point, don't it? Sure, there's keepin' the prize unsullied to make sure we get the ransom. But it's more than that.

Cap'tn's not in his right head about this. You saw how he let Bainbridge run off down the beach. His thinkin's..."

"Compromised?" Boland suggested.

Tully said, "That's it. Compromised and the like. You've all been servin' under him too long. I see it clear."

"So what are you proposing?" Boland asked. "Mutiny?" Hawk's stomach clenched, his breath shallow.

There were low murmurs, then Tully said, "It ain't mutiny if we take a vote, is it? I thought pirate ships were all...what's the word?"

"Democratic," Boland answered, and Hawk could imagine the roll of his eyes. "Yes, but you weren't with us when Walter Bainbridge cheated us. We followed England's rules to the letter, and he lied and declared us pirates. We would have all likely swung for it if we hadn't taken them by surprise. They underestimated us—especially the captain. That is a deep wound. He wants his revenge against Bainbridge, no matter how infatuated he might find himself with the man's pretty son."

Deeks said, "'Tis true. Underestimate Captain Hawk at yer own peril. We got to be smart about this."

Tully insisted, "All I'm sayin' is that we make sure we get what's owed us. If it weren't for me, he might never have known who the little shit was."

The nameless voice said, "There's no way the captain will give up that ransom or spitting in Bainbridge's face. No arse is that sweet. He's getting it while the getting's good, and like we said, who can blame him? But if Bainbridge doesn't have the money, Captain Hawk will cut that boy into pieces and deliver them to his father one by one."

Hawk tasted bile, reaching out to grip the rough bark of a tree as the men went on.

"Probably the ears first. Maybe lips."

"Fingers."

"Then his prick."

Tully said, "But will he? I don't reckon there's as much call to fear him as you think. He's grown weak. Don't have his priorities straight *from where I'm sittin.'"*

Hawk tightened his arm around Nathaniel, who murmured and shifted in his sleep. He'd wanted to stride onto the beach, draw his cutlass and slice *them* to pieces for the birds and insects to swarm. Especially Tully, whose tongue Hawk would take great pleasure in ripping from his big mouth.

But the truth of it was they were right. His thinking was compromised by his prick. No, far worse than that—by soft, tender places within that he hadn't unearthed in years; hadn't known still existed, not since John so long ago.

He'd allowed Nathaniel to dig away at him, shifting sands grain by grain until he was laid bare.

His lips brushed the knots of Nathaniel's spine, heart warming at the whisper of his sleepy sigh. The entrance to the tent flapped up in a gust of wind, and across the beach, Hawk spotted a cluster of men speaking, Tully among them. They glanced back at the tent, and Hawk wasn't sure if it was too bright out there to see in. To see him holding their prisoner in his arms.

Enough.

Time to put a stop to it. Closing his eyes, he thought of Walter Bainbridge and that day at the Admiralty Court when Hawk had stood in disbelief as he was branded a pirate after so many years in faithful service to the Crown.

He pressed at the wound that had festered ever since, calling on his fury. Yes, he would have his revenge and his ransom. If not, he would lose control of his ship. Worse than that, if the men determined he'd been acting against their interests, he could be put to death. He'd seen crews turn, and it could happen in a blink. How had he let himself drift so far off course?

Snell's words echoed through his head. *"Sentiment will only go so far."*

And it had gone more than fucking far enough. Rolling away and grabbing his boots, he tugged one on.

A sleepy voice murmured, "Tell me you aren't really going to wear those boots. We'll be on the beach all day. The men will still respect you, you know." Nathaniel remained curled away on his side, unable to see what Hawk was doing.

Christ. Does he know me so well already? How did I allow this?

Nathaniel was probably right. Hawk likely didn't have to dress the part. But he pulled on the other boot anyway, his feet already protesting in the damp, musty leather that would soon be like two ovens. He couldn't take Nathaniel's counsel. He had to put an end to this unwanted attraction that stirred far too fucking much.

Soon he would exchange Nathaniel for the money and never see him again. That was the plan. That was how it would be. Except Nathaniel insisted he would forge a new life for himself.

Maybe…

Nathaniel laughed softly, and from the corner of his eye, Hawk watched as he pushed himself up and inhaled sharply. Hawk had already asked, "What?" and taken hold of Nathaniel's shoulders before he could think twice. Gasping, Nathaniel shrugged and squirmed away, leaning his hands on the tangled, sandy blanket.

Hawk tugged the collar of Nathaniel's worn shirt to the side, taking in the finger-shaped bruises. Guilt stabbed, razor-sharp and jagged. And never mind his shoulders—Hawk could imagine how tender Nathaniel's arse was after what they'd done without oil and in the sand. Before he could say a thing, Nathaniel did.

"It's not your fault. I asked you to. I wanted it like that."

True, but… Hawk cleared his throat. "Do you need the surgeon?"

Nathaniel glanced over his shoulder, rolling his eyes. "For a few bruises? I'm confident I'll survive."

"Are you sure it's only bruising?"

Nathaniel shifted gingerly, coming around to sit. He smiled softly. "I believe so. If I discover otherwise, I'll tell you."

Frowning, Hawk folded his arms and considered shouting for the surgeon anyway. "If there's tearing—"

"I'm fine." He placed his hand, warm and gentle, on Hawk's bare forearm where the sleeves were rolled up, his thumb stroking. "Don't worry."

And *fuck*, it was too much to take—the easy familiarity, the way Nathaniel scratched his chest absently with his other hand, yawning, as if this were a lazy morning in another place. Another life altogether.

It was a fraud, and a potentially deadly one at that. Hawk shook him off and jumped to his feet in the stupid fucking boots, almost losing his balance on the sand, a blanket caught around his ankle.

He kicked it free. "I'm not *worried*. But I can't return you to your father with too many bruises."

Nathaniel infuriatingly gave him another winsome smile. "Perhaps you don't have to return me at all. We could—"

"Hawk!" Snell stood just outside the tent. "If you're quite ready to start the day, there are a few matters at hand."

Without glancing back at Nathaniel, Hawk strode out and up to the tree line, well out of earshot of the tent. His boots were already too hot, and he hadn't put on his belt. He squared his shoulders and stiffened his spine, swatting at a fly. "What is it, Mr. Quartermaster?"

Snell exhaled a long breath, his lips in a thin line. "Well, *Captain,* I want to make sure your head's in the game. The head atop your shoulders, for the record. Because the crew are starting to wonder."

Hawk kept his tone even, aware of the men's eyes on them across the beach. Had Tully been sowing more seeds of resentment? "If they're so keen to elect a new captain, they should have at it."

"What kind of nonsense is that?"

"Maybe it would be for the best. I could…move on."

Sighing, Snell shook his head, shoulders slumping. "For fuck's sake, Hawk. I know you've been restless. But I tell you I've seen it before, and there's no way you'd be satisfied doing anything else. The only rules we have are our own. Not fucking England's tyranny. Would you really go back to that? Not that they'd have you. You're a wanted man in the New World and old."

"Surely there's another way to make a life out of England's reach. A Spanish island, or French. Or somewhere new entirely. It won't be easy, but… Well, why the fuck shouldn't I try? Why shouldn't I live to be a fat old man with my lover at my side instead of this constant struggle to survive?"

Snell's eyes narrowed. "Don't tell me you're dreaming about that fancy little lord."

It was all Hawk could do to keep from slamming his fist into Snell's pudgy, weathered face, a face he'd always regarded with affection. He vibrated with violence begging to be unleashed.

Hands lifting in surrender, Snell shook his head. He lowered his voice, pleading. "Tell me you don't really think he'd *want* you? Once he's back in civilization, in a grand house, with pretty girls and hot baths at the snap of his fingers, succulent meat on his plate every night? As much as he enjoyed your cock, do you really think Bainbridge's son would give up a life of luxury and riches for *you*?"

Hawk wanted to scream *Yes!* He managed to get out, "He said he didn't want that. He said…" Hawk was flayed apart, bare under the cloudless sky, sweat beading on his forehead.

The sympathy in Snell's eyes was the worst thing. "He said whatever he thought you wanted to hear. He's a clever lad. He's kept himself not only alive, but in comfort. Granted far more freedom than any prisoner I've ever seen. You remember what you told us the night we captured him? Not to be taken in by him. Not to be ensnared. I fear it is too late, but you must heed your own words, Hawk. I'm begging you. And if you actually care for him, let him have his privileged life."

Hawk opened his mouth, then snapped it shut again.

Snell went on. "He's young. He was caught up in adventure, warming a pirate captain's bed. It was a fantasy for you both. Don't do this to yourself. I've seen many a sailor chase after some sweet young thing, and it always ends the same. I don't want that disappointment for you. That lad has his whole life before him. Truly, what can you offer? Think about it. The reality is, we're thieves. Killers."

Denial sparked, and Hawk spat, "Because Bainbridge cheated us and branded us pirates. Criminals." Snell was silent for a few long heartbeats, assessing him with an unreadable expression, until Hawk shifted on his feet, desperation clawing at him. "Well, he did!"

"Aye. And we embraced it. We made the Sea Hawk one of the most feared names in these waters in a few short years. We stole and we killed. Yes, there are other pirates who are worse. We haven't raped or tortured under your watch. But don't fool yourself into thinking you're something other than what you are."

Hawk jerked as Snell gently clasped his arm. "You're too good at this to give it up. You don't know any other way to live. You'll forget him before long, and these doldrums will pass. You'll remember what you love about the sea and hunting our next prize."

Hawk's throat was bone-dry, but he scraped out, "What's wrong with wanting a little peace?"

Snell sighed and gave his arm a final squeeze. "Men like us don't get peace."

Hawk watched the closest thing he had to a friend turn away and rejoin the crew. Snell was right. Hawk didn't deserve a moment of serenity. He didn't deserve a life with a man as bright and beautiful and *good* as Nathaniel. More importantly, Nathaniel deserved better than a scarred, worn-down pirate with too much blood on his hands. Hawk knew this.

Knowing was one thing. His heart's thudding desire, flowing through his veins like the tide—relentless, unforgiving—was another. But it was clear he'd indulged his fantasies far too much and for far too long.

He marched back to the tent, ducking through the flapping entrance. He tucked his shirt into his trousers and snatched up his belt, the urge to rejoin Nathaniel in their makeshift bed tugging at him, fishhooks in his flesh.

Nathaniel rolled to his knees, trying to hide another wince. "Can I help with the barnacles?"

Keeping his gaze anywhere but on Nathaniel as he stalked to his makeshift desk, Hawk snapped, "No. You'll stay here."

"Here? Inside the tent? But—"

"But nothing. You are the prisoner, and you will fucking stay where I tell you to. *I'm* the one in charge." The dagger had to be at Nathaniel's throat, not his own. "I've let you have your way too much. That is at an end. Soon you will be returned to your treacherous father on Primrose Isle, and I'll be rich."

Nathaniel was silent for a few moments, then cleared his throat, his voice shaking. "What did Mr. Snell say to you? What's changed so suddenly?"

"Nothing has changed." Hawk kept his gaze averted. "This has always been the reality of the situation. This will soon be over."

Nathaniel's voice was hoarse. "Yet until then, we can still have this between us."

"There is nothing *between us*."

"But... Last night, we..."

With jerky motions, Hawk strapped on the belt, ruthlessly pushing away the memories of their wild coupling—Nathaniel's cries, the heat of his body, rain soaking their fevered skin, Hawk certain he could hear their hearts beating as one.

He spat, "We fucked. I stuck my cock in your tight little hole. Nothing more. I'm a pirate captain, and you are our prize. I've enjoyed fucking your virgin arse, knowing how much it would horrify your father, but have grown tired of it. You're used up now."

"You don't mean that."

He roared, "Don't tell me what I mean!" and shoved his pistol in his belt, his fucking hand *trembling*. This conversation had to end. He had to hold his resolve.

Casting about for a source of particular cruelty, he found his target. "I must say I eagerly anticipate relaying to your father in great detail all the filthy things you've said and done. How you begged for my cock. What a whore you are. Perhaps I'll draw him a few pictures."

Nathaniel sucked in a breath. "You wouldn't."

He laughed harshly. "Wouldn't I? This is about revenge, N— *Plum*. Nothing more. If I've lulled you into a false sense of complacency, you have no one to blame but yourself. For I'm a pirate, after all. Notoriously untrustworthy."

Don't look at him. Put an end to this now before tumbling any deeper down this chasm.

"I don't understand what changed overnight."

Hawk stopped by the blankets, his legs spread, looking down from his full height, sneer firmly in place. He struck the killing blow. "Then apparently you're an imbecile after all."

With that, he stalked off, already trying to forget the image of Nathaniel's mouth open in surprise, undeniable hurt creasing his beautiful face.

Chapter Eighteen

Nathaniel knew he shouldn't allow the insult to cut so deeply, but it did all the same. He'd welcomed the bruises on his body, but Hawk's sudden reversal left his soul battered, an awful hollow sensation taking up residence. He should have known this was coming, but it had taken him utterly unaware.

As the morning went by and Hawk didn't return, Nathaniel curled on his side to take pressure off his arse—which throbbed dully, a constant reminder. To be caught so off-guard was beyond foolish, given that Hawk *was* a pirate. A killer, a thief, a criminal.

Hadn't Nathaniel initially hated him? Cowered from him, felt the punishing grip of Hawk's hand on his throat? He shouldn't have forgotten for a moment.

Yet they'd taken such pleasure in each other, and he knew Hawk hadn't faked that. And it was more than fucking. They'd *talked.* Confessed truths. Hawk had cradled him in his arms, and none of that had been to aid base desires. Hawk had bestowed on him those beautiful smiles.

Nathaniel's eyes burned now to think of them.

Through the flapping sides of the tent, he spied him marching around in those ridiculous boots while everyone else went the practical route in bare feet. The thunder of Hawk's commands echoed across the sand, the men sharing looks as they scurried to obey.

Midday, Mr. O'Connell brought him water, fresh-cooked fish, and tangy, sweet fruit that should have been a delight. Nathaniel sat up and poked at his plate glumly, thanking him, glad he'd put on his breeches earlier.

Frowning, O'Connell tugged on the loose ends of his long, curling hair, which he'd mostly tied up against the heat. He was perhaps five and thirty, wrinkles starting to line his bearded face, the hair below his chin long enough to bead together into a point. "What happened that's got the captain so furious and you stuck in here?"

Nathaniel shrugged despite his shoulders' protest. He was unable to keep the bitterness from his tone. "I am a prisoner, after all. Just a thing to be bartered. He saw fit to remind me."

O'Connell sighed. "Well, don't fret. It'll be over soon and you'll be home safe." He gave Nathaniel a smile.

Home. Safe. The two words rattled around Nathaniel's mind. He had no home, and the safety he'd felt in Hawk's arms had evaporated. Had he tricked himself to think that Hawk cared, even a little?

God, was he really that stupid? And truly, what *had* he expected? That he and Hawk would sail off into the sunset together? He didn't even know the man's true name.

He jolted when Mr. O'Connell clasped his arm, kneeling beside him. "Truly, I'll do everything I can to see you home safely."

Nathaniel nodded gratefully, then asked, "Where is your home, Mr. O'Connell?"

"Alan." He shrugged, sitting back and crossing his legs. "And it's the ship. Wherever the wind takes us."

"But originally? Was it Ireland?"

He smiled. "I tried to get rid of the accent, but aye. County Clare. My family died when a fever swept through our village. I came across the sea to try my luck in the New World. Never planned on becoming a pirate, but here I am. Life is funny that way."

"How did you end up on *The Damned Manta*?"

"I was on a merchant ship in port in Tortuga. Captain Hawk was recruiting. I knew I might die sooner than I'd like as a pirate, but the conditions on the merchant ship were even more deadly. Scurvy was rampant. We had no freedom. No respect. Captain Hawk offered both. He's a harsh taskmaster, but he's fair."

Nathaniel toyed with his food. "I'm sorry about your parents. How old were you?"

"I was nineteen, but my parents survived. 'Twas my wife, Nuala, and our daughter who perished. She'd only just been born. Aileen." His gaze went distant, and his shoulders lifted with a deep breath in and out. "That was her name. She had a wisp of red hair, just like her mother's. Would have been freckle-faced too, I reckon, if..."

He took another labored breath. "We didn't have a chance to baptize her." Looking down, his Adam's apple bobbed. "But at least I know my Nuala is safe in heaven." He shook his head. "Christ, I don't know what's gotten into me! I suppose they've been on my mind more than usual since that day in the rigging. Facing the sudden end of your life, it..."

"Has an effect."

Another small smile. "That it does."

"I'm so very sorry about Nuala and Aileen." He wished there was something he could say or some gesture to make. He took Alan's shoulder gently.

"What the fuck is this?" Hawk roared, storming into the tent, reaching for his pistol.

Leaping to his feet so quickly he almost toppled over, Alan backed away with hands raised. "Nothing, Captain. I swear. I just brought his rations."

Between gritted teeth, Hawk ordered, "Get the fuck out."

Alan practically leapt for the door, away in an instant. It was Nathaniel's turn to jump up and demand, "What is the matter with you?"

Fisting the loose neck of Nathaniel's shirt, Hawk glowered down, hot, harsh blasts of air skimming over his face. "Did you think you'd work your charms on him? Turn the men against me?"

"Well, I *am* a whore, according to you." Nathaniel leaned in, going up on his toes, their noses close to touching. "But no. I was simply listening to him tell me of his dead wife and child."

"Why should I believe you?" Hawk shoved him back a step, looming over him with his bulk.

Nathaniel unclenched his hands and grabbed Hawk's shirt, digging in his heels, determined not to give another inch. "You know what I think? You're jealous. But most of all, you're afraid."

Hawk shoved him away and made his escape. Nathaniel staggered but stayed upright. He paced around the tent for long minutes, blood rushing in his ears, the urge to punch something nearly overwhelming.

Finally the fight drained away, and he sank back to the nest of blankets. Determined not to weaken himself, he had a bite of fish but almost hurled it back up, his stomach too knotted to eat.

Of course that reminded him of when he'd vomited all over Hawk, and Hawk hadn't been angry at all. He'd tended to Nathaniel so kindly and brought him into his bed for comfort.

Why had he done that if Nathaniel was nothing but a hole to fuck? Why had he taken such care later to bring Nathaniel pleasure with his mouth and hands? Read to him for hours even when his voice became hoarse?

Putting his bowl aside, Nathaniel curled atop the nest of blankets again. Burying his face, he inhaled deeply despite himself. He'd become accustomed to Hawk's smell—a woodsy scent and the salt sea spray that clung to his skin. Accustomed to the sounds he made—low grunts and groans, but also small sighs when he thought Nathaniel was sleeping.

Most of all, he'd become used to the touch of Hawk's callused hands on his body. The wonderful fullness and power of his cock. How his weathered fingertips sometimes skated over Nathaniel's skin with an impossibly soft touch.

Was Hawk now becoming familiar with Nathaniel in the same way? Did he experience a pulse of desire simply from his scent?

But the desires bottled within Nathaniel had grown too big and unwieldy. Oh, how he yearned to peel away more of Hawk's scarred layers and wriggle into the spots where soft smiles and even laughter lived.

He wanted to hold and be held, to share wine and bread and the warmth of a hearth in winter, listening to Hawk read aloud. To create a home together.

"I really am an imbecile," he muttered. He had no home. He couldn't make one on Primrose Isle, no matter how much he'd miss dear Susanna. Lord, what would she think if she knew the things he'd done?

Hawk's threat to expose Nathaniel's true self to Walter echoed harshly in his mind, and now resentment grew. Hadn't Hawk told him there was no dishonor in it, that Nathaniel's desires were natural? And now he threatened to shame him for it.

Nathaniel's skin crawled with humiliation, yet the hypocrisy galled him—infuriated him.

Whore.

He'd felt so at home in his own skin with Hawk, sucking and rutting and fucking unabashedly. When Hawk had held him down, mastered him, an odd sense of power had filled Nathaniel along with that massive cock. And now Hawk said he should feel guilty for it, that it was wrong after all?

Tears pricked his eyes, and he swiped at them angrily. No. He wouldn't allow Hawk to strip him of the fulfillment he'd found in his soul, the harmony he'd finally achieved within himself. The knowledge that he *could* have the things he'd always craved, and it wasn't a sin. It was true and proper and he wouldn't deny himself.

Fists clenching, he sat and reached for his bowl, shoveling the food in, letting rage simmer and fuel him along with the rations. He would keep up his strength; he would not be bowed by Hawk's bluster. He would not submit to this cruelty, no matter how strenuously and absurdly Hawk insisted on it.

"I don't believe him," he whispered.

Staring out at Hawk on the beach, working shoulder to shoulder with his men to clean and repair the hull, Nathaniel vacillated between anger and compassion like a ship rolling on rough seas.

He thought of the boy who'd been snatched by a press gang and forced into the navy, and yet had still wanted to serve his country. Then was branded a pirate. But he'd embraced the role, no matter what—or who—drove him to it.

Nathaniel rooted around for his dagger, which Hawk had allowed him to bring ashore with nary a blink. *He trusts me.*

Yet why should that fill him with warmth and satisfaction? No matter how tender he had been at times, Hawk was his captor. Nathaniel shouldn't care about his thoughts or feelings.

He jumped to his feet and practiced his blade work, feinting and lunging for invisible opponents, sweat slicking his skin. If Hawk said he didn't give a damn, Nathaniel should take him at his word.

Still, each time he tried to convince himself there was nothing between them, that he'd imagined it all, memories of Hawk's gentle hands, genuine smile, or laughter rippled through him.

Gripping the dagger, he slashed at the air, no end in sight to his confusion—especially since Hawk was apparently determined to avoid him like the blackest of plagues.

The crew's work went well beyond sunset, and Nathaniel

paced the tent, dagger still in hand. It seemed there was a worse thing than being demeaned: being ignored. After a day holed up, with trees and water and that glorious beach taunting him—along with Hawk's utter disregard—Nathaniel had had quite enough.

It was late now, many of the men asleep, others still drinking their rum around a fire. Clutching the dagger like a talisman, willing himself strength, he strode from the tent and across the beach with no hesitation.

He was past the fire when he heard the first shouts, and soon Hawk's voice boomed. "Where the fuck do you think you're going? Get back in the tent. *Now.*"

Heart thumping, Nathaniel spun around. Still a distance away, Hawk marched toward him, lips in a thin line, all eyes on them. Nathaniel yelled, "I'm going for a run!"

"You had your run yesterday." In the firelight as he approached, the lines of Hawk's face were granite, fists clenched. "I told you to stay in that tent. I will not allow this."

Nathaniel waited until Hawk was almost in reach. "Bet you can't catch me."

Hawk's curses exploded in the night as Nathaniel sprinted away, followed by his command for the men to stay put and his promise that he would indeed catch the prisoner.

A laugh bubbled up in Nathaniel's throat, manic and wild as he led Hawk on the chase, knowing he could outrun him by far—especially since Hawk insisted on those boots.

Nathaniel reached the end of the island in what seemed like a blink, his feet flying over the sand, heart pumping, dagger in his grip—powerful and alive. Unbroken.

At the end of the island, the sand ended in a huddle of rocks and boulders. Dagger in his mouth, Nathaniel clambered up to wait for Hawk, but determined not to be ignored. He would confront Hawk with the truth. He would—

A man appeared from the corner of his eye, cresting the other side of the rock jumble. Nathaniel's heart stopped as he spun to face him, dagger still between his teeth.

They stared at each other in the starlight, and Nathaniel made out the outline of a ship anchored offshore—three masts, one clearly splintered and damaged. Men in longboats rowing ashore, no uniforms from what he could tell.

Pirates.

The man opened his mouth to shout, and Nathaniel dove, smashing him back against a rock and knocking the air from him in a pained heave. Then they tumbled between two boulders—fortunately onto sand—and Nathaniel's own lungs seized with the impact as he bit painfully into the dagger's wooden handle, refusing to relinquish it.

About Nathaniel's size and wiry, the pirate tried to scramble out of their tangle of limbs in the narrow space between the boulders. On his back, Nathaniel managed to get his dagger in hand as the pirate punched at his head and face, the blows glancing, not enough room for full swings.

Still, blood streamed from Nathaniel's nose as they grappled, squawking and scrabbling and spitting, the man on top of him. When the pirate's blunt fingers closed around Nathaniel's neck, panic took hold.

Dying! No!

Nathaniel kicked madly, striking stone with his bare feet and trying everything to shift off the man's weight and turn the tables, gasping for air, white stars bursting in the blackness.

The man was too strong, his hands impossible to pry free from Nathaniel's throat, not enough space to get a knee up or to twist and use momentum.

This was how he'd end.

Nathaniel flailed out, the dagger blade clanging off rock. He changed his grip and stabbed upward, and the pirate howled as he struck flesh and a shoulder bone.

Then a shriek trailed into a gurgle as Nathaniel jammed the blade into the man's neck. He pulled it out and slashed, warm blood spurting over Nathaniel's face as the pirate choked, hands on his throat now, trying to stem the unrelenting tide.

The pirate was still on top of Nathaniel in the dank, dark space, and Nathaniel shoved at him, climbing over the man he'd just killed, not waiting until the deed was finished, desperate to escape those wheezing last breaths.

Standing on him, Nathaniel hauled himself up, finding hand and footholds on the boulders, blood in his mouth along with the wooden dagger handle, metal and oak.

Sucking in the fresh air, limbs shaking, he stood atop the rocks as Hawk approached, chest heaving, steel in his voice and no weapons on his belt as he said, "I don't know what the hell you think you're doing, but—" He stopped and stared, inhaling so sharply he jolted with it. Bafflement creased his face.

With a glance behind him at the pirates organizing on the island's east side, Nathaniel tucked the dagger into his breeches and scrambled down toward Hawk, who met him halfway, confusion replaced with drive, reaching for him with strong hands, lifting him from the rocks onto his feet, eyes wild as they took him in.

Hawk asked, "How?" as he passed his hands over Nathaniel's head, arms, and chest, then took hold of his stained cheeks. "Where are you hurt?"

Nathaniel reached up to wipe at the blood on his face. "I killed him. Pirates. They're coming."

After sitting Nathaniel down on a low rock, still checking him for injuries, Hawk climbed to peek over the boulders. He quickly returned, hissing, "Fuck us. One-Eye didn't give up after all." On his knees by Nathaniel's feet, he held his face again. "Can you run?"

"Yes." Shock gave way to the horrible thrill of battle that he understood for the first time, and Nathaniel jumped to his feet. "Yes."

Still on his knees and gazing up, Hawk gripped his hands. "Tell Snell to bring everyone. We're helpless with the ship still out of the water. This is all or nothing. We're outnumbered, so we must take them by surprise."

He held Nathaniel's fingers so tightly Nathaniel feared they might snap. "Wait at camp. If we fail, surrender and tell them who you are and what you're worth. Tell them they can't hurt you or there will be no money. Promise you won't fight. Promise you'll stay safe."

"No, I can help! I killed him. He was going to kill me, but I didn't let him. I couldn't. I had to... There are so many of them, I have to—"

On his knees, Hawk implored, "*Please*," and Nathaniel found he couldn't deny him. He nodded, and Hawk rose, giving him a crooked smile. "I bet you can make it back before I reach their ship."

"Their ship? But... There are too many of them."

"Yes, but they're gathering on the beach, which means only a skeleton crew remaining aboard." He bent and tugged off his boots. "Good night for a little swim. Now go."

There were so many things Nathaniel wanted to say—too many things. Instead, he pulled his hands from Hawk's grasp and pressed the bloody dagger into Hawk's palm.

Then he ran.

His mind spun with what Hawk would do in the meantime, praying he'd wait for reinforcements and knowing he wouldn't. Nathaniel flew down the beach, denying himself the lunatic urge to return to Hawk, as if *Nathaniel* could somehow protect him from the hordes of men arriving from the other ship.

He shouted for Mr. Snell as he approached, and the men jumped into action, casting their cups of rum aside and gathering their weapons. They seemed to forget about Nathaniel as they stormed down the beach, Mr. Snell sending contingents into the trees as well. It was simple for Nathaniel to follow, staying close to the foliage, protected by the shadows, sand forgiving under his battered feet.

The explosion rocked the night as he neared the end of the island, almost knocking him back on his arse. Ears ringing, he rushed onward, ducking into the forest, ignoring the rough twigs, roots, and rocks under his soles, nearing the men Mr. Snell had sent into the trees, following their lead.

At the edge of the jungle he stopped, taking in the fire-illuminated scene below. The unprotected *Javelin* burned, orange flames licking up the mainmast they hadn't fully repaired, men screaming as the gun deck was engulfed. The flint of gunpowder was thick in the air even at a distance, thick plumes of black smoke rising.

Hawk! Where was he? Had he been able to swim away fast enough after presumably lighting a fuse? Nathaniel stood on the precipice above the beach, scanning it desperately, calculating the quickest path to the water as the *Manta* crew streamed forward from two sides.

They cornered the pirates of the *Javelin,* who were apparently taken by surprise, fumbling and flustered, stunned to see their ship burning. Then—*there.*

Hawk emerged from the water, outlined by the orange glow behind as he grabbed the closest man and snapped his neck, taking up the man's cutlass as he joined the fight, clashing steel echoing.

The other crew fought with deadly fervor of their own once the shock had subsided, and Nathaniel held his breath in his battered lungs, his ribs aching. The terror that he would see Hawk struck down gripped him, but he was rooted to the spot by his promise to stay safe—and his own fear of joining such a fray.

Shouts and screams of agony filled the night, clawing at him.

He'd killed a man, and now death was everywhere. Metal clashed and gunshots exploded. Nathaniel had never witnessed such brutality; had not been able to fathom it.

He should have been horrified, yet all that mattered was that Hawk survived. Hate for the other pirates boiled in Nathaniel, and he wished them all dead so Hawk could live.

The one-eyed captain ran at Hawk with a battle cry, tumbling him to the sand. They bared their teeth as they grappled. Each turn and shove lasted a lifetime to Nathaniel as he willed the upper hand to Hawk with all of his soul.

Hawk used the dagger to kill the other captain. How strange to think that Mr. Chisholm had gifted it to Nathaniel what seemed like a lifetime ago, and now it was an ocean away in a pirate's grasp. Nathaniel cheered the pouring blood as Hawk carved the man hollow, victorious.

One-Eyed Alfred's men were broken, the remaining crew surrendering, but Nathaniel couldn't draw a full breath until Hawk shouted orders and left the smoldering carnage to climb over the rocks, determination in his stride.

Returning to me.

Nathaniel retreated through the trees, beating him to the other side, waiting farther down the empty beach. In the distance around the tip of the island, shouts echoed in the aftermath of battle.

Yet here, it was only the two of them. When Hawk spotted him, he skidded to a stop, his chest heaving and feet still bare. They stared at each other as a bird shrieked above, waves breaking on the shore, fiery destruction in the distance, and smoke on the wind.

Hawk started toward him, and Nathaniel couldn't stay rooted, racing to meet him. Face streaked in red, Hawk took a breath to speak, but Nathaniel dragged down his head and silenced him, kissing him the way he'd dreamed of for weeks—yet not how he'd imagined it at all.

Crushing their lips together, rubbing against the wet burn of Hawk's beard, Nathaniel drank him in fiercely, plundering with his tongue when Hawk gasped for breath, tasting sweat and gunpowder and metallic blood—their own or that of the men they'd killed, he couldn't say.

He should have been filled with abhorrence. Disgust or despair. None of those emotions came calling. Instead, Nathaniel had never felt so powerful, so free—so *alive.*

Groaning, they clutched each other, all lips and bruising hands, clasping, drowning. Hawk lifted Nathaniel clear off his feet, wrapping him in his arms, their mouths desperate, tongues devouring as they stumbled about.

Nathaniel broke free, lungs burning as he propelled Hawk toward the trees and into the darkness. Hawk grunted as his back hit a wide trunk, the gleam of his eyes just visible under the umbrella of palm trees. Nathaniel bit at his lips, kissing him feverishly, all teeth and spit.

He muttered, "I don't believe anything you said this morning. This is real." He tore open Hawk's wet shirt and spread his hands over his chest, digging his fingers into the tattoo he knew was there. Hair scratched his palms. "We're real."

Inhaling loudly, Hawk pushed him away a step and spun him around against the tree. The bark was surprisingly smooth as Nathaniel's back crashed into it. His head didn't impact at all, cushioned by Hawk's big hand.

Hawk kissed him, moaning into Nathaniel's mouth and rutting against him, all muscle and bone and desperation, lips hot. Nathaniel's cock ached, and he tried to hook his leg up over Hawk's thigh for more friction, the lingering seawater from Hawk's swim dampening Nathaniel's trousers too, the coolness welcome on his fevered flesh.

Hawk's free hand gripped his waist and lifted him like he was weightless, his other hand still behind Nathaniel's head as he pummeled their hips together, groaning and growling.

Between messy, wet, *glorious* kisses, little cries escaped Nathaniel as he wrapped his legs around Hawk's hips, their pricks like rock through the layers of their trousers. He wanted to feel hot flesh but was powerless to stop, the thought of parting even for a few moments impossible to contemplate.

He sucked on Hawk's tongue as they drove against each other. Nothing else existed but their gasping, shameless hunt for release, mouths fused, teeth clashing, slick lips swollen.

The pressure in Nathaniel's groin sparked fire, gunpowder surging through his veins. He wanted to tell Hawk to fuck him, longed to be stretched by his cock again, burned from the inside out.

But he still couldn't bear to break away from their kisses, chasing Hawk's very essence with his tongue, the dam broken, finally tasting his mouth. He clung to Hawk's shoulders but dragged one hand down to his chest, raking his nails over the tattoo, making his own mark.

Hawk tore his mouth away from Nathaniel's with a shout, shuddering and jerking against him, spilling in his wet trousers. He pressed their foreheads together, lips grazing, and Nathaniel tightened his legs around him, lungs tight.

"That's it," Hawk muttered, breath hot on Nathaniel's mouth. "Spend for me." Hawk fucked against him with renewed vigor even though he'd already released, fingers tightening in Nathaniel's curls.

Nathaniel's ecstasy gripped and shook him, a predator with its helpless prey. He could only whimper into Hawk's mouth as he pulsed, the burn of pleasure scouring him, leaving him limp against the tree, Hawk's hand warm in his sweat-slick hair, still protecting his head.

They panted, noses touching, chests heaving. With a groan,

Nathaniel unhooked his legs from Hawk's waist, Hawk helping to ease him to his feet. Neither of them was steady, and they remained leaning against the shelter of the tree.

"Only you," Nathaniel whispered.

Hawk traced Nathaniel's lips with his fingertips, then leaned their foreheads together, stooping to wrap him in his arms. Nathaniel held on, twisting his fingers into the ends of Hawk's damp hair.

When they kissed again, the hint of blood and battle still lingered. But in the embers of the fire that had raged, in the slow, entreating sweep of tongues and now-gentle pressure of lips, in the soft moans and sighs, Nathaniel tasted only love.

Chapter Nineteen

"Heave!"

The coarse line dug into Hawk's palms as they yanked, the ship inching upright. To the east, the sky was finally dark again, the smoldering orange light extinguished, but soon enough the sun would appear.

All hands toiled to bring *The Damned Manta* to rights, the remaining, vanquished men of the *Javelin* knowing they had no choice but to help with their captain dead and ship destroyed, the explosion visible for miles. They were all in equal danger, the Royal Navy always lurking.

Beside him, Nathaniel winced, gritting his teeth, and Hawk knew he'd pull until his hands dripped red. Pride flowed, and he ached to hold him, to lose himself for a few blissful minutes before returning to their toil.

Oh, to kiss Nathaniel again, even though their mouths were both swollen and bruised.

It sent a shiver down his spine although his skin was damp with sweat in the warm night. The way Nathaniel had flung himself into his arms, yanked down his head, and pressed their lips together.

The kiss had been an invasion, Nathaniel demanding entrance, his fingers digging into Hawk's scalp, claiming victory before Hawk could mount a defense.

He'd been utterly conquered in that moment, but it was a glorious surrender. Hawk had happily gone down with the ship, finally tasting Nathaniel—the bitter tang of blood and battle unable to erase a sweetness all his own.

After, their kisses had flowed with a gentle fervor he could only name adoration, neither of them able to get enough, their bodies bruised and battered and entwined as one.

But there was no time as the dawn raced toward them mercilessly, not caring that they'd only careened a portion of the ship, not caring that they must sail the final miles to Primrose Isle and not delay. The possible attention drawn by the explosion was too dangerous to wait another day.

This would be the day he must give up Nathaniel, and Hawk wished the night would never end.

There had been so much blood. In the pale starlight, it had appeared dark and deadly, masking Nathaniel's face like a funeral shroud. In that instant as his heart seized and shattered, Hawk had been certain Nathaniel was doomed—that he'd witness the final moments, hear Nathaniel's final gasp of breath and see those eyes go glassy, feel his body grow cold.

His grief at the thought still haunted Hawk, and he marveled that he ever could have casually—thoughtlessly—threatened to end Nathaniel's life. Now he would protect it with every inch of his being, no matter the cost.

As dawn neared, he yearned to hold Nathaniel close to be sure he wasn't a phantom but still flesh and bone. They all splashed into the water, the crew and prisoners dragging the ship, almost deep enough, their muscles burning, heels digging into the sandy bottom.

Nathaniel groaned, and Hawk wanted to order him to retreat to solid ground and rest his battered body. Selfishly, he kept Nathaniel at his side, knowing Nathaniel would protest anyway.

Knowing his selfishness would soon be at an end.

That Nathaniel still lived was a miracle, and it was one Hawk would not take for granted. He'd glimpsed the scout's body down between the boulders. In his mind's eye, it was Nathaniel crumpled there, his throat torn asunder. Hidden unless one knew where to look.

Hawk might have searched the island in vain for days, only discovering him thanks to the birds circling. He imagined Nathaniel rotting and half-eaten, honey eyes pecked out.

Breath shuddering, an iron band squeezing, Hawk staggered, and might have crashed into the surf if not for Nathaniel holding his arm.

"All right?" Nathaniel asked, breathing hard.

Hawk could only nod, and God, there it was in the distance: the first fingers of dawn reaching over the horizon. He gently took hold of Nathaniel's hand and peeled it away, giving him a little smile that seemed to put Nathaniel's mind at ease as they hauled into deeper water, almost there, almost there…

By the end of the dawning day, Hawk would deliver Nathaniel to the colony—to his family. He would see him leave *The Damned Manta* behind and sleep in a proper bed, eat proper food. Reunite with his sister and make his plans for a new life away from his father.

Away from Hawk. Safe.

Nathaniel deserved a life in a place where he knew no need for a dagger, where he wouldn't be forced to kill and be corrupted any further.

When the ship floated, a cheer rang up, Nathaniel grinning along with the men, even Alfred's crew celebrating. These were the men who hadn't insisted on fighting to the death, the men who cared more for survival than loyalty to a dead captain.

Although Hawk motioned to Snell and ordered them locked in the hold now that the ship was upright, they might make valued replacements for the *Manta* men they'd lost in the battle.

Time would tell.

They had to get under way, and Hawk had to keep his wits about him. He said to Nathaniel, "Can you gather the blankets and whatnot from o—the tent?" As soon as the question was out, he sensed the side glances from nearby crew members, and barked, "Now!"

Nathaniel's lips twitched, but he held back the smile and headed back across the sand. *Fuck.* How had Hawk allowed himself to get this lost in their... God, it was a courtship, wasn't it? He couldn't deny it.

Trying to empty his mind of anything but the task at hand, he conferred with Snell and gave more orders for readying to leave, the stacks of supplies needing to be reloaded onto the ship.

Glancing at the tent, he froze, spotting a blaze of red hair ducking into it in the murky light of dawn. Leaving the men to their duties, Hawk strode across the sand. Tully's rough voice carried beyond the canvas as Hawk neared.

"Don't think we don't know what you've been up to. You'd better not try to fuck things up fer us."

"Duly noted," Nathaniel said.

"Listen, you fancy little fuck. We can all see you's leadin' the captain around by his prick. Wrappin' 'im around your finger. It's pathetic, it is. As if you'd give him the time of day otherwise. I know yer kind. Rich piece of shit. What you been whisperin' in his ear, huh? If you mess with us gettin' what's owed—"

"You'll what, exactly?" Hawk demanded through gritted teeth, storming into the tent. Tully was right in Nathaniel's face, but Nathaniel stood his ground. Hawk still yanked Tully back by the scruff of his neck, digging in his fingers.

Tully struggled, flopping like a fish on a hook. "We just want to make sure yer not goin' soft. Any fool can see the way you look at 'im. You'd better go through with this! Or we need a new captain who will."

"A new captain. Is that so?"

"I think it is!" Tully lifted his chin, indignant. "And I ain't the only one who don't trust you!"

"Well, then let's find out if the men agree." Still with a punishing grip on Tully's neck, Hawk propelled him out of the tent. Time to put a fucking end to the mutinous rumblings.

He turned back, and sure enough, Nathaniel was following. Hawk shook his head. "Back inside until this is over. I mean it."

Jaw clenched, Nathaniel obeyed. Hawk drove Tully down near the water, the murmur of work ceasing, all eyes on them as he let go of the man with a last shove.

Hawk made sure his voice carried. "Mr. Tully has informed me that there is question about my ability as captain. About my loyalty to you. My brothers."

It was one thing to whisper in the night about the captain after a few cups of rum. In the harsh light of day, after they'd fought together for their lives, it was quite another.

Hawk surveyed the crew, looking each man in the eye, sizing them up unblinkingly. They were silent, some scuffing their feet in the sand, heads low.

"If you wish to vote on a new captain, that is your right. I would never stand in your way except in battle, when my word is law. We are equals. I told you we would exchange our prisoner for a large ransom, and that time draws very near. Bainbridge has proven himself brave. He saved Mr. O'Connell in the rigging, and just last night he ran back here to sound the alarm. We are thankful, and he's enjoyed certain liberties. That much is true."

The men waited, some with furrowed brows.

Hawk let them wait another few moments. "Yet he is a means to an end." He allowed a suggestive smirk to paint his face. "In more ways than one, I confess." This garnered a chuckle from the crew, as he'd hoped. "But make no mistake. He has not bewitched me. The money is what matters. Revenge is what matters. Your futures."

At his side, Snell cleared his throat, hands on his thick waist. "And in case any of you have memories shorter than my Great-Aunt Bertha, let me remind you that our captain swam out to the *Javelin* just last fucking night and blew it sky-high. Eliminated the threat of it sailing around the shore and blowing us all to kingdom come with its many, many guns. We lost some of our brothers in that battle, and I wish there was time to give them proper burials. The ceremony will have to wait. But the only reason we're here to remember the fallen is because of Captain Hawk. Because of his brass balls and leadership, which has never steered us wrong. Has it?"

"No!" came a chorus of shouts.

Snell eyed the men. "Because *he* has never steered us wrong, has he?"

"No!" the crew agreed.

"And he won't now, my brothers. We can depend on Captain Hawk, just as we always have."

O'Connell called out, "Tully's been trouble since he joined us."

"That he surely fucking has," Snell said, rounding on Tully, who vibrated with fury. "And you mean to stir the pot now? When we are so close to our prize? This is the time for unity. We are brothers."

Tully's face was beet red, and he balled his hands into fists, peering around at the crew. "Yer all idiots. You know he won't give up that snivelin' brat! He's lyin' to you! I bet he won't let us get our revenge on that colony neither, or on Bainbridge's cunt of a sister. I thought pirates were supposed to be fearless men who take what they want. Who don't follow orders! All I've done on this ship is mop up shit and clean fuckin' dishes!"

Snell stepped closer to Tully, his voice low but menacing. "I'm sorry we're a disappointment. That, yes, we actually have work to do, just like on your merchant ship. The difference is, our crew is treated fairly. Equally. We kill when we must, but we are not animals. And right now, with the Royal Navy possibly appearing on the horizon any minute, we don't have fucking time for a weak, whining would-be mutineer. Especially not one who's been whispering to One-Eye's crew while we've worked. Maybe you're hatching a plot against us."

Hawk didn't know if it was true or not, but it certainly garnered a reaction, the men buzzing with murmurs, resentment and anger simmering hotter.

Tully gazed around, his face going even redder. "I have not! You're a fuckin' liar!" he spat at Snell.

It was a grave miscalculation.

"Ah, so it's not just Captain Hawk who is a liar. It's me as well. Your quartermaster. Well, men, if you believe this true, perhaps we should have two votes here this morning, Royal Navy heading for us or not."

Of course they had no idea if the navy had seen the explosion, but it mattered not. Hawk watched with satisfaction and appreciation for Snell's skills at handling the crew as the men clamored to defend Snell, sentiment toward Tully turning dark.

Deeks, who had been one of the men talking mutiny with Tully the other night, shouted, "I say we leave 'im here! Don't want no rats aboard."

In the din of agreement, someone shouted, "Let's vote!"

Tully snarled, stamping his foot like a child having a tantrum. "Fuck you all! I don't need you!"

"No?" Snell asked, lowering his voice even further to a deadly quiet. "Then you can stay here. Blissfully free of us."

Tully paled. "What?"

"All in favor?" Snell asked, and the ayes had it resoundingly. "Mr. Jones, Mr. Grady. Restrain him by the trees. We'll cut him free before we go. I'm sure you'll be very happy here, Mr. Tully."

As Tully began a barrage of abuse, Snell added, "Gag him too," then watched dispassionately as he was hauled away, kicking and screaming.

How he would survive alone, Hawk had no idea and didn't give a damn. He spoke calmly to the crew although his heart thumped. "That's settled. Soon we will exchange our prisoner for the ransom. If there is no ransom to be had, there will be blood." Since he didn't specify whose, it wasn't exactly a lie.

"Now let's get the fuck back to work," Snell commanded.

Hawk turned on his heel and headed back to the tent, where he knew Nathaniel had surely heard every heated word. What Hawk would say to him now, he had no idea.

Snell caught up. "Been looking for a way to get rid of that annoying little prick since he came aboard."

Hawk murmured, "Thank you."

Snell nodded but captured Hawk's arm tightly. "Don't make a liar of me."

"I won't," he rasped.

"You go to the ship. I'll bring Bainbridge aboard."

Hawk wanted to argue but couldn't, not after what Snell had just done for him. Perhaps it would give him time to figure out what he wanted to say to Nathaniel.

Or what he *could* say.

They ferried supplies on board, including anything salvaged from the east beach, and as the sun rose in the sky, merciless as ever, Hawk once again stood on the deck of his ship, hands clasped behind his back, Nathaniel at his side, tantalizingly close.

Nathaniel stared toward the wisps of black smoke still rising in the distance, quiet as he'd been when they'd leaned into each other and that tree, gathering their strength between kisses.

"I killed a man," Nathaniel murmured after a long silence, breath warm on Hawk's neck. "I'm... I..."

"It's normal. This guilt. Of course you're sorry you took a life."

Nathaniel raised his head, eyes clear. "That's just it. I'm not. He would have taken mine. He almost did. And I'm not sorry I stopped him."

Hawk traced the blossoming bruises on Nathaniel's throat with his fingertips, trying to quell the simmering rage and terror and fucking helplessness.

He swallowed thickly. "Nor am I. It's the way of this world. You had no choice." He tried to imagine what was going through Nathaniel's head, behind his furrowed brow. "Even if you could have outrun him—"

"I wouldn't have tried. I probably could have. But he'd have sounded the alarm. Couldn't risk it. I had to stop him. I couldn't risk you."

Hawk had been powerless to do anything but kiss him.

The livid bruises on Nathaniel's throat were purple now, and Hawk remembered how he'd left his own marks on that pale flesh when Nathaniel had first come aboard. Shame flooded him, becoming a deluge as he thought of the insults he'd spat yesterday. All lies, lies, lies.

Nathaniel deserved so much better.

He deserved the quiet existence Hawk knew he could never have for himself, his pathetic dreams of leaving the sea and sword laughable in the face of all the fresh death he'd wrought—fire and blood and wringing the life from men with his bare hands.

He'd blamed Walter Bainbridge, but the truth was undoubtedly laid bare now. He was a monster, and he'd chosen it. It was he who was clutched in the Sea Hawk's talons. He'd allowed bitterness and anger to reshape him, and now he must accept the consequences.

The sails were unfurled, the wind easing *The Damned Manta* away from the beach where Tully ranted and raved, his curses echoing across the water. Hawk smiled sharply. Perhaps it would have been more merciful to kill the man quickly, but Hawk had never pretended he wasn't vindictive.

He called out, "Mr. Boland." Boland turned, all eyes on Hawk, ready for his command. "Set the course for Primrose Isle."

"Aye, Captain!"

Before Nathaniel could say a thing, Hawk took hold of his arm and propelled him down the ladder and into the cabin, where books were stacked on the floor, his paltry belongings needing to be put back to rights, the massive desk still chained down for the careening.

This little room was his home, and it was foolish to think he could find another. Snell was right. Men like them didn't get to leave the mayhem and bloodshed behind. He wouldn't permit Nathaniel to follow the same path.

No matter how badly he wanted to keep him close—to say to hell with the ransom and face those consequences as well—the image of Nathaniel bathed in blood would not release him. Even though Nathaniel reached for him now as Hawk backed out the door.

"Wait. You must know my feelings are genuine. Don't tell me you're listening to what Tully said! Yes, perhaps when we began, I thought I could improve my odds. Surely you know now—"

"Our time is at an end. I will secure the ransom for my crew. I must. And you must stay safe." He kept Nathaniel at arm's length with a firm hand and gripped the door handle with the other. "I'm sorry for the things I said. You're not a whore. Nor an imbecile. The farthest thing from it."

He closed the door and turned the key decisively, ignoring Nathaniel's pounding and plea that they speak. Hawk hadn't earned peace, but if it was the last thing he did, he would see Nathaniel have his chance at it.

"IT'S TIME." HAWK stood inside the cabin door, Nathaniel already hurtling toward him from where he'd been pacing by the dark windows, a force of nature as he barreled straight into Hawk's arms, reaching around to shove the door closed.

"No. Not like this. You've left me in here all bloody day, and we must speak. I don't want to go. I can't live on Primrose Isle and marry Elizabeth Davenport. Can't do my father's bidding. I won't." He shook his head, desperation shining in wild eyes. "But it's more than that." He leaned in closer, fingers digging into Hawk's flesh. "I want to be with you. I *must* be with you."

Hawk's chest constricted painfully, allowing the dream of a future bright with Nathaniel's smile to take hold for a moment, allowing the idea of peace and *joy* to flicker through him before he snuffed it out. "No. This isn't…"

"What? Is this the part where you hurl more cruel taunts you don't mean? I don't care how mad it is, I want to be with you. And I *know* you want to be with me."

With effort, he pried Nathaniel's fingers loose and stepped back, keeping him at a distance with hands firm on his shoulders. "And you'll what? Join me in a life of piracy? You don't want that."

"No, I don't." But before Hawk could say that settled it, Nathaniel surged forward, wrapping his arms around Hawk's waist, peering up so earnestly that Hawk couldn't push him away.

Nathaniel said, "You don't want to be a pirate either. You never did." He sucked in a breath. "But I would do it if it meant being at your side. I want to stir in your arms at dawn and yield to you at night. I want the freedom to spend our days as we wish, without judgment. In as much peace as we can muster, wherever that may be."

Hawk's heart thumped. It was too good to be possible. "You don't mean that. Not really."

"You truly think I'm lying? Wrapping you around my finger,

like Tully said? After all this?" He squeezed his arms around Hawk's waist, gaze imploring. "I admit that when I first lay with you, it crossed my mind. How could it not? You'd threatened to kill me. My sister. I thought it might be more difficult for you if we grew closer. But I always wanted you. That was always true. It always will be."

Through the door, Snell shouted, "Captain! We're ready for the exchange! Bring the prisoner to the deck!" He burst in and stumbled to a stop, blinking at them. He huffed, exasperation clear. "Enough of this!"

Enough.

But Nathaniel held fast, gaze steady—challenging. "Will you still gut me like a fish if he doesn't pay?"

Part of Hawk wanted to retreat and roar a false threat like a pirate captain should, to not give a fuck about this young man from another world, whom he never should have touched. Whom he never should have allowed to touch him.

"I know you won't," Nathaniel whispered. "I've known it for weeks. This is real between us. You can get the ransom from my father, and we can meet somewhere in a few weeks' time. We can be together. You can leave this life."

"Captain!" Snell shouted as he took hold of Nathaniel and jerked him out of Hawk's arms as a red flare of rage boiled through Hawk.

Snell's eyes widened, and he stumbled back, letting go of Nathaniel and lifting his palms. "I'm trying to stop you from being swept up in this nonsense. As sincere as young Mr. Bainbridge might be in this moment, it is a fantasy. The gentry don't run away with pirates."

Nathaniel sputtered. "You don't know a thing about me! You don't know—"

"What I know is that we need the ransom!" Snell glared at Nathaniel, then took a step toward Hawk, beseeching. "I have supported you in this as far as I can. I helped quell that mutiny, but my first duty must be to the men. They have been promised for a month. They are owed. It is *time.* Enough of this balderdash."

When Hawk looked to Nathaniel, a vision of him covered in blood took hold, flooding his gut with acid. Hawk would only drag him into the abyss. He had to do everything he could to keep Nathaniel safe.

Nathaniel shook his head. "Don't listen to him!"

Gathering his strength with a deep inhalation, Hawk turned and took his coat off the hook on the hull wall, shrugging the hot leather over his shoulders. He tied the red sash around his waist, then strapped on his belt and weapons, the heat of Nathaniel's angry gaze a horrible itch on his skin.

He opened the desk drawer and plucked out his rings, pushing them over his knuckles. Up on the main deck, a voice called, "Launch approaching!"

Hawk faced Nathaniel, who watched him with jaw clenched, nostrils flaring. Hawk asked, "Don't you want to dress properly? Your waistcoat? Shoes and stockings?"

He gritted out, "No. Let's get on with it." He turned, then whirled back. "You're many things, but I never imagined coward was one of them."

"All right, up you fucking go, brat!" Snell hauled him out of the cabin, and Hawk followed, his boots thudding on the deck, blood rushing in his ears. He must withstand this. Nathaniel would thank him once he was back on solid ground, warm and coddled, safe and sound.

Hawk narrowed his gaze on Primrose Isle beyond the harbor, where ships of varying sizes bobbed, none big enough to carry many guns. In the black night, firelight dotted the hillside, fanning out, but not nearly as much as he'd expected. Under the sun it would be easier to judge, but the colony did appear quite lacking.

From the approaching launch, a man called, "Captain Hawk?"

Hawk stood at the bow. "Aye."

"We must see Nathaniel Bainbridge, alive and unharmed."

Hawk reached back for Nathaniel's arm, but Nathaniel jerked free and strode to stand beside him. "I'm here. Unharmed."

Squinting into the wooden boat, which was rowed by two men, the speaker perched in the bow, Hawk asked, "Where the fuck is the governor? My demand was that he meet us. Alone."

"Governor Bainbridge is taken ill with worry. He has been abed for days." The messenger's voice cracked. "I am here as his representative."

Hawk snorted. "Yes, I'm sure he's *quite* ill. Get up here." While he'd looked forward to seeing the whoreson again, to lording his revenge, all that truly mattered was the sack this sweating, quivering emissary held, and whether it contained the ransom. That was all that *could* matter.

Our time is up. This was always where we would end. He deserves far better than me. He'll thank me for this before long.

Yet Nathaniel's plea echoed in this mind. Was it possible to have the money *and* Nathaniel? Right that minute, could he have both?

It would be a battle, but it would likely be a battle regardless, even though they could spy no soldiers in wait and they were out of range of any cannons on land. Excited apprehension vibrated through him.

They could try.

The messenger wore a ridiculously puffy wig and was dressed in fine silks that were too big for his frame. He climbed up the rope ladder they unfurled, trembling as he threw a leg over the rail and boarded on the port side. He held out the sack, and Snell took it, opening it and snapping his fingers for a lantern.

Hawk couldn't breathe. He reached for Nathaniel, taking his

shoulder. Nathaniel panted softly, his eyes imploring in the spray of lantern light. Hawk could keep him safe, couldn't he? In a life away from the sea's turmoil, he could. He *would!*

They had the money—if he kept Nathaniel too, or if they ran, or arranged to meet—

A pistol exploded in the night, and Hawk whipped his head around, reaching for his cutlass, then gritting his teeth at the followed curse and one of the men shouting, "'Twas only a misfire!"

As Hawk opened his mouth to order calm, the emissary lunged toward him with wild, spooked eyes, and Nathaniel was suddenly in front of him, knocking Hawk back.

Hawk stumbled and tried to make sense of it all, Nathaniel's weight sagging in his arms, the emissary shrieking on the end of Snell's cutlass as it ran him through.

"Captain! Sails!"

Another voice shouted, "Brigantine from the west! Must have been hiding around the other side." A pause, then, "Looks like eighteen guns!"

Snell had the sack open and a lantern in his hand. "Money's here. Captain! We must away!"

But Nathaniel couldn't seem to get his feet under him, leaning heavily against Hawk. There was something in the dying emissary's outstretched hand…

A dagger. Its blade dark with blood in the flickering lantern light.

Hawk's cry was distant and hoarse, as if it came from another throat. "No!" He lowered Nathaniel to the deck and tore at his shirt, red staining the linen in a widening circle. Pressing at the stab wound in Nathaniel's gut, he screamed, "Pickering!"

Hawk peered down into that dear face, already frighteningly pale. "Stay with me. Nathaniel!" Nathaniel gazed up at him, moaning, eyes wide.

Pickering dropped to his knees before them, leaning over to inspect the wound, too much blood flowing from it. He shook his head. "He'll die if he stays aboard."

Hawk took Nathaniel's hand, threading their fingers together, keeping his eyes locked on him for fear he would be gone the next time he looked down. "There must be something you can do!"

"He needs better surgeons and a safe, clean place, not to bleed to death on a stinking pirate ship—especially one about to do battle!" Pickering grabbed Hawk's coat and leaned close, lifting Hawk's chin roughly, hissing, "If you care for him, let him go. Or he'll be dead before morning."

"No… I…stay," Nathaniel gasped, twitching.

With one last, lingering look into those rich honey eyes, Hawk ripped his fingers from Nathaniel's desperate grasp. He somehow pushed to his feet without his knees giving way.

Down toward the launch, he shouted, "Bainbridge is coming!" To the crew, he ordered, "Lower him carefully, Mr. O'Connell, Mr. Lee. Everyone else, ready to make sail!" The approaching brigantine would be the death of them all otherwise.

Nathaniel coughed and gasped, fingers grasping at Hawk's ankle, fingers sliding on the leather. Hawk needed to tear himself free, but he stood rooted, even once O'Connell and Lee scooped up Nathaniel, who wailed in agony as they lowered him in the canvas hammock used for cargo.

Hawk couldn't move to look over the rail, standing frozen as Snell shouted, "They've got him! Now get us the fuck out of here, men! Don't let them get their broadsides around, or that's the end."

Nathaniel's screams echoed across the water even as the sails caught the wind, the brig gaining. Hawk finally turned away from Primrose Isle, a ragged hole in his chest as if the blade had found its target.

At the helm, he shouted orders and kept his gaze forward on

the midnight horizon, fingernails gouging the wheel so deep the wood slivered his flesh. Nathaniel had to live, and *The Damned Manta* had to outrun the brig, which flew the Union Jack with the white crest denoting privateers.

No other options existed.

As the first round of cannon fire exploded in the night, he prayed to a Godless universe that at least Nathaniel would survive.

Chapter Twenty

I F HE WAS dead, he was apparently in heaven, since Susanna was there. Nathaniel couldn't seem to open his eyes for more than a heartbeat, but he'd spotted his sister's clear hazel eyes and dark curls, felt her tender ministrations, and heard her soft lullabies and a babe's cry.

Was he imagining it all? Perhaps they were dead, and Nathaniel had joined them. But if he'd met his maker, surely he'd have been doomed to the underworld for his many sins.

Nathaniel knew he should likely regret said sins and repent, but couldn't seem to muster the will, even though death had him in its sights. It seemed he was alive, considering the torment searing his gut every time he breathed in—or out, for that matter.

So, all the time. The dagger that had breached him felt as though it was still there, digging in mercilessly, its steel viciously cold yet scorching all the same.

The heat built, and he imagined flames licking at his face and chest, and of course his belly, which was only agony. The fire grew into a hungry inferno, and he barely made out Susanna's voice after a time, his eyes far too heavy. There was another voice too, a young woman he didn't recognize who spoke with a calming rhythm.

But the voice he heard loudest was one he knew must be only in his mind. Hawk cried his name so fervently, a heartrending plea. *"Nathaniel!"*

Moaning and delirious, soaked with sweat yet shivering, racked with chills, Nathaniel reached for Hawk's damn boots, the gold tips slipping away beneath his fingers as he grasped over and over.

He was unable to do anything else as he huddled there on the deck, trapped and alone, Hawk cruelly out of reach.

"NATHANIEL? PLEASE, PLEASE. Come back to me."

Groaning, he tried to open his lead-weighted eyes. It was Susanna who called for him now, and the thought that she might be in need tugged him from the roiling depths. Blinking, he glimpsed her pale, pinched face.

"Yes, that's it! Open your eyes."

Where were they? He tried to remember the last time he'd been with Susanna—the merchant ship, pirates boarding—*Hawk.* No, they weren't there. It hadn't all been a dream; that was impossible. What he'd shared with Hawk had been real; it had to have been.

So how… The ransom. Primrose Isle. The messenger lunging for Hawk, dagger suddenly in his grasp, the blade sinking to the hilt in Nathaniel's belly, pain burning white-hot and then terrifyingly cold.

The world was a blur. A white ceiling with a pattern etched into it, swirls and loops. Turning his head felt monumental, but it was worth it to behold Susanna's tearful smile. He'd always hated to see her cry. He tried to reach over and wipe her tears, but his hand wouldn't cooperate.

"Susie?" His throat was a desert, nothing but stones and sand.

"Yes. Shh, it's all right. You're safe. Here, drink. You must drink." She held a glass to his lips, lifting his head for him. The tepid water burned going down.

"Where?" He was in a bed softer than any he could remember, but likely his memory was short at the moment. Beyond Susanna, sunlight streamed through an open window, the pale curtains hardly moving in the sticky air.

"We're on Primrose Isle. You're safe at home with us." Her smile faltered, but she lifted her chin.

"What is it?"

"Nothing, nothing. It can wait. Oh, Nathaniel. We thought we'd lost you again. I'm not sure how much you remember. That despicable pirate returned you with a grievous wound, but don't worry—justice will be served."

His heart seized. "What do you mean? Where is he?" Nathaniel tried to sit up, his body trembling, traitorous limbs too weak.

"Don't try to move! Please, darling. The stab wound was bad enough. Just when we thought you were returning to us, infection set in. It's been two weeks, and the surgeon didn't hold out much hope at all. But I did, and Elizabeth did."

"Who?"

Susanna laughed, tired lines creasing her face. "Your betrothed, of course. It will all come back to you soon. You've been mired in this fever, but it's broken now. Elizabeth will be overjoyed when she returns this morning."

It took too much effort to speak, so he didn't bother addressing the issue of Elizabeth Davenport. Darkness had begun to close in at the edges of his vision, but he croaked, "Hawk? Where is he?"

Pressing a cool cloth to his forehead, she soothed, "It's all right. That vile man can't hurt you now."

A scream tore at Nathaniel's raw throat, but he was falling under the surface, dark waves closing over him.

CANDLES FLICKERED AS Nathaniel focused on the bundle cradled in Susanna's arms. He vaguely recalled hearing a babe's cries at some point and realized Susanna's belly had been flat when he'd woken before.

He was able to lift his hand this time, and Susanna jerked her head up, exclaiming. The baby wailed. A young blonde woman hurried in and took the child while Susanna helped Nathaniel drink more water.

Resting back against the downy pillows, Nathaniel tried to recall what they'd discussed earlier, his heart plummeting as it hit him. "Where is he?"

"Who? Father? He was in earlier with the surgeon. Of course he's been worried sick. We all have."

His gaze returned to the young woman, who lingered, jiggling the baby and cooing to it. "Elizabeth?"

The woman replied, "The babe's name is Grace, m'lord."

Susanna laughed awkwardly. "This is Cecily. The wet nurse. Elizabeth returned earlier, but you slept for hours. She'll be back in the morning, don't fret."

She rose and spoke to Cecily in low tones Nathaniel didn't try to decipher, his mind turning over the possibilities of Hawk's fate. Cecily left with the baby, and Susanna retook her seat. She wore a blue dress that had seen better days, although jewels sparkled in her ears.

He wanted to demand more information but remembered his manners in time. "You're both doing well? She's beautiful. Grace."

Susanna beamed. "She is, isn't she? And yes, we're wonderful. Bart and I couldn't be happier." Her smile dimmed. "Father would have preferred a grandson, of course, but next time, we hope."

"Father can go fuck himself."

She gasped, a hand flying up to cover her mouth. Then she craned her head to peer out the open doorway. Apparently seeing no one, she leaned in, trying to hide her mirth. "You have been on a pirate ship indeed."

Worry gnawed. "Where is he? Captain Hawk. I must know."

Susanna brushed back his damp hair. "I told you, that monster will never trouble you again. You needn't be frightened. Oh, Nathaniel. Was it awful? Of course it was, why am I asking that? Forgive me." She took a shuddery breath. "I can't tell you how relieved I am to have you home. I thought I'd never see you again."

"I'm fine, Susie." He rubbed his face, which had been shaved smooth. Probably at his father's order, since a gentlemen must always be respectable even when at death's door gripped in a fever.

A dark-skinned woman with graying hair knocked at the open door and entered with a steaming bowl of broth. Too weak to feed himself, Nathaniel had no choice but to submit as Susanna lifted the spoon to his lips.

After they coddled him like *he* was the infant—and despite his resentment, he couldn't deny his helplessness—his eyes grew heavy again, but his heart raced, the ache in his wounded belly throbbing.

"Susie. What happened to the pirate?"

"Father had hired a privateer ship to battle the pirates, since we have no redcoats here. He'd hoped to sink them right there in the harbor, but they led the privateers on a merry chase. All for naught—Captain Hawk is soon to face the gallows. So, you see? Nothing to worry about. You needn't ever think on that abominable creature again."

He was certain the dagger had returned, twisting into him, stealing his breath. Susanna sat straighter, her eyes widening. "Nathaniel? No, lie back. Don't thrash, or you'll reopen the wound." She turned her head, calling, "Judith!"

The older woman returned, and Nathaniel's mind was buzzing too much to make out what she and Susanna were saying as they held him down. Soon they were administering bitter drops of medicine, and he gagged, gasping.

"There, there." Susanna pressed another cold cloth to his head. "Sleep again, darling. You need your rest."

What he needed was to save Hawk, to see him safe and happy and whole, but the black claimed him once more.

Chapter Twenty-One

THUNDER RUMBLED, AND Nathaniel wasn't sure of the hour. The light beyond the windows was muted. He focused on the young woman sitting beside his bed, running a needle and colorful thread through material with nimble fingers, a candle beside her in the dimness, her ruffled silk dress a dusky rose.

She had fair hair but wasn't the wet nurse, whose name he couldn't recall. She certainly wasn't Susanna. He stared at the needlepoint, the design some kind of flower.

"Elizabeth?"

Her head shot up, and a wide, slightly horsey smile broke out over her face. "Nathaniel! How do you feel? Let me fetch Susanna and send a messenger for the surgeon. He was here earlier, but you were sleeping very soundly. We must call him back before the storm hits. Are you thirsty?" At his nod, she helped him drink. Her forehead was high, hair on the ashy side, brown eyes bright and kind.

He felt as though he'd been sleeping for weeks, which he supposed he had. At least his head was clearer, and when he tried to lift his hands, they cooperated. Although the stab wound ached like it was open and bleeding, his boost in energy was an encouraging sign.

Before she could call anyone, he asked, "When is the trial? For Captain Hawk?"

Elizabeth opened her mouth but then closed it again, glancing to the door, which stood open. She whispered, "I don't think they want you troubled with it. At least not until you give your testimony."

"Testimony?"

"At the upcoming trial, such as it will be with our…limited resources. The pirate is being transported back here."

His heart hammered dully. "From where?"

"I'm not sure. But apparently he and his men led the privateers on a chase all the way to Hispaniola. The pirate ship was damaged and listing badly, but some of the crew escaped ashore, to a peninsula. Apparently the captain created a diversion, allowing his men to flee. I suppose there is some honor amongst thieves after all."

Nathaniel could only nod, the faces of the crew running through his mind. Who had survived? Dour Mr. Snell? Alan O'Connell? "When is he arriving?"

"I don't know. A hurricane might be brewing."

He registered that she'd mentioned a storm earlier. Indeed, a gust rattled the windowpanes. "Is he injured?"

Elizabeth had glanced at the windows, her lip between her teeth. "The pirate?" She shrugged. "He'll be dead soon anyway."

The words were a punch to his wounded stomach. He wanted to lash out but restrained himself. It certainly wasn't this girl's fault. None of it. "Is the courthouse nearby?"

She grimaced. "They will merely build a platform in the town square. An actual courthouse is still to be constructed and now never will be, like most things on this wretched island." Elizabeth seemed to catch herself, and she painted on a smile. "Don't trouble yourself with any of it, my dear." Tentatively, she took his hand, and he stared down at their linked fingers with puzzlement.

How strange it was that this pleasant-enough girl he'd woken to was his betrothed. He burned to tell her immediately that they'd never marry, but he only listened as she said, "I can't tell you how happy I am that you're alive. We'll be able to build a good life back in Jamaica once you're well enough to travel. Or England, even."

"What of this place?"

Elizabeth's cheeks flushed. "Don't worry yourself about it. My father will see us set up nicely elsewhere. No matter how stubborn your father is. As I said, nothing to worry about! Susanna is lovely, and she's told me so much about you. I feel I know you already."

"Uh…" This was the part where he should say something kind in return, but he could only blink at her, his mind blank.

Susanna appeared, thank goodness. "Oh! You're awake again. Mr. Taggart is here."

The tall, balding man had much to say about how lucky Nathaniel was and how the wound nearly killed him outright, never mind the infection. Elizabeth and Susanna stood back, giving the surgeon room, but Walter strode right in and practically elbowed him aside.

"Are you finally in your right mind?" he demanded.

Nathaniel blinked up at his father, seeing him again for the first time in years. The curls of his white wig were perfectly powdered, and his pale shirt, waistcoat, jacket, and breeches weren't creased despite the syrupy heat.

Nathaniel had remembered him as an old man but saw now that he was still relatively young. His face was lined as he neared fifty years, but his spine was straight, a sharp vibrancy about him that called to mind a knife's edge.

"Yes, Father."

Walter seemed slightly mollified. "Well, good. Since you were almost murdered by that pirate, we've been eager for you to recover."

"I… Thank you. But H—he didn't stab me. Captain Hawk. It was your emissary."

Walter laughed like the crack of a whip. "Nonsense. Your mind is clearly still muddled. Surgeon?"

"Oh yes, some confusion is quite natural. Don't trouble yourself, m'lord."

"But I'm telling you, it wasn't the captain or any of his men who injured me."

Mr. Taggart leaned over Nathaniel. "Now, now. Don't agitate yourself. Too much laudanum will slow your recovery."

Nathaniel cringed at the thought of the bitter medicine and the powerless, long sleep it brought. He needed his rest, but also required his wits about him. "I simply want the truth to be known."

His father stared at him imperiously. "The truth is that one of the most dreaded pirates in the New World kidnapped you and almost killed you once he had his ransom. They are a scourge that must be destroyed. All those devils care for is money." He glanced around the room. "Of course I would have paid any sum to see my son returned."

As the surgeon and Elizabeth nodded in agreement, Susanna piped up with, "I thought Bart said it was mostly counterfeit anyway."

Walter gritted his teeth. "Regardless, the Sea Hawk shall hang. That is all that matters." Belatedly, he added, "And that Nathaniel is safe." Sighing, he seemed to soften, coming closer to the bed to rest his hand on Nathaniel's arm. "We were greatly concerned for your welfare."

Despite everything, Nathaniel still wanted to believe his father cared, cringing at the childish longing welling up.

A bewigged man appeared in the doorway. "I'm sorry to interrupt. Governor, we have a problem."

"What is it?" Walter snapped. "Can't you see I'm tending to my son, who was nearly murdered by pirates?"

"More wood is needed to board up windows on the main

street as the storm approaches."

"Then get more bloody wood! Why should I be concerned with such trivial matters?"

"There aren't enough men left to cut it. As it transpires, several transports left yesterday for Jamaica in advance of the storm. More citizens fleeing."

Clearly all was not well in the least on Primrose Isle. Nathaniel wanted to ask for the details, but didn't wish to anger Walter any further at the moment.

"We'll need to board up our windows as well, won't we?" Susanna asked.

With a tight smile, Walter said, "Everything is in hand. Don't worry, my dear. Rest up, Nathaniel. When the storm has passed, the pirate will arrive and his trial will begin. Your ordeal will soon be at an official end."

Walter strode out before Nathaniel could argue, and the surgeon banished the ladies to examine Nathaniel's wound thoroughly, poking and prodding, humming to himself from time to time.

Finally, he said, "It's healing well, now that the infection has passed. You'll be up and about soon enough." He glanced at the darkening sky through the closest window. "Rest up, and by the time the sun returns, you'll be out of bed."

If his sluggish mind understood it all correctly, the storm's passing would herald Hawk's arrival. Nathaniel nodded. "Yes. I'll certainly be on my feet by then."

BART NEARLY CARRIED him down to a small, windowless chamber on the ground floor that night, but Nathaniel had taken a few steps, at least. Granted, the pain threatened to bring up the broth and small amount of bread he'd eaten, but he'd kept his food down. While it might have been a tiny victory, he'd take it.

After Bart had gone and Susanna fretted over Nathaniel, he asked, "How about some *Don Quixote*? I haven't heard that in years."

Susanna winced as glass shattered in the distance, the upper floor of the house in particular taking a lashing from the storm. The wind howled, and Nathaniel wondered for the hundredth time where Hawk was and if he suffered.

Would the privateers treat him fairly? He had once been one of them, and if their letter of marque was revoked for any reason, they would suddenly be deemed pirates too. Perhaps Hawk could appeal to their reason. Nathaniel didn't hold out much hope, but it was all he could cling to.

"Yes, a good choice. I'll fetch it from the library." Susanna left the door ajar, and Nathaniel listened to the household staff bustle about.

Walter was holed up in his study, the baby and wet nurse in the sitting room, where Susanna would sleep as well. The upper floor had been deemed unsafe, even with boards hastily nailed over the windows.

Earlier, Susanna had insisted she wasn't tired in the least, and Nathaniel was happy to hear her read to him again while the baby slept for a few hours. He needed something—anything—to keep his mind from fixating on Hawk.

Have they hurt him? Is he angry with me? Does he love me as I love him? I do love him, more than anything. Is he afraid? Does he despair?

Nathaniel had last beheld him much as he had the very first time: Hawk wearing his costume—his armor—that announced him a fearsome pirate king. The rings on his fingers and slash of red around his waist, the steel of his cutlass winking on his hip; the coat that acted almost as a cape.

Yet he would remember Hawk not as the myth, but the

man—scarred and tired, passionate and tender. The raw terror on his face as he'd uttered Nathaniel's name aloud, leaning over him, shielding him, holding his fingers so tightly before tearing himself away.

"All right, here we are." Susanna jumped as a gust of wind shrieked, rain battering the house. From what little Nathaniel had seen of the two-story building, it was solidly constructed, with at least a dozen rooms.

How would the rest of the colony fare? From the sound of it, there was little left. Susanna pulled her winged chair close to the narrow bed, which was more of a cot. She cleared her throat and began.

Her familiar voice and cadence soothed Nathaniel's raw edges enough that he could unclench his fists and breathe evenly. Susanna read into the night as Mother Nature railed, threatening at times, it seemed, to tear the house from its foundations.

Nathaniel closed his eyes and tried to focus only on Susanna's warm, familiar voice. As she read, the wind and rain keened. He shivered, the earlier heat chased away.

Soaked to the skin, Bart stuck his head in, water dripping into his eyes from his floppy curls. He had an appearance not unlike a massive shaggy dog. Susanna waved him in, assuring him the baby was sleeping comfortably, at least until the next time she woke wailing, as babies inevitably would.

"You must promise not to go out again!" Susanna said. "Please stay here until this passes."

Bart sighed, wiping water from his face. "The remaining people are in need, and there aren't enough hands. It feels cowardly to hole up here with the women and children." He looked guiltily to Nathaniel. "What I mean to say is—"

"I know," Nathaniel assured him. "I take no offense. I possess the strength of a kitten at the moment."

"Father is here, and he's not infirm," Susanna said.

Bart raised his eyebrows. "Regretfully, your father is not a man I aspire to emulate." He took her hand. "Forgive me for speaking so frankly."

She sighed and plopped back into her chair. "No apology necessary. We all know Father's…limitations. Which have become all too clear."

Nathaniel asked, "Bart, what do you mean, the remaining people? What is happening on this island? There's something going on that no one wants to explain. I know the colony was struggling, but it sounds as if it has collapsed. I assure you I can withstand the cold truth."

Sharing a look with Susanna, Bart said, "Let me get another chair." When he was settled, the door pulled halfway shut, he nodded to Susanna, who leaned toward the bed, her voice low.

"Oh, Nathaniel. It's a *disaster*. They say the terrain is all wrong. Too sandy in some places, too rocky in others. Far too hilly. The men who initially proposed this colony to England were fools. Overconfident that no matter the landscape, it could be molded and tamed to do our bidding."

Bart added, "To be fair to your father, that was not his doing. The rest, however…"

Susanna sighed. "Father wasted untold amounts of money insisting on planting crops that wouldn't take. The colonists have left in droves, and the rumor from Whitehall is that the Crown is abandoning this place and cutting its losses. Father has failed in every conceivable way. He hasn't admitted it yet, but we're going back to England. Or perhaps somewhere else in the New World. There's simply no alternative."

"He and Mr. Davenport are on shaky ground," Bart said, unbuttoning his wet jacket. "Davenport gave up a successful venture in Jamaica, expecting more power here than he had in Kingston. If not for your engagement to Elizabeth, I fear their partnership would dissolve completely. Walter would have had you married when you were barely conscious if Susanna hadn't spoken out so strongly against it."

Nathaniel's heart skipped. "You don't think I should marry her, Susie?"

She blinked. "Oh, of course you should. She's an absolute treasure. Isn't she, Bart?"

"Yes. Very levelheaded, and a kind soul. She'd make a fine wife for any man."

Any but me.

Susanna added, "She deserves a proper wedding in a church, wearing her fine dress. And surely you'll want to be awake and in your right mind on your wedding day."

"I… Yes," he had to agree.

"There's no telling now when this pirate will arrive for his trial," Bart said. "Your father had already ordered the gallows constructed, which was a complete waste of time. Not to mention lumber." He shook his head. "These winds are like nothing I've ever seen. I fear there will be very little left when the dust settles, as it were. They should have just tried him in Kingston, but your father insisted he preside, as if it will somehow legitimize this place and save it. His pride will be the death of us all if we're not careful."

Susanna sighed. "Yes. He was determined that his colony would be the most like England, no matter how impractical that might be. All show and no substance."

"One wonders why he ever wanted to leave England in the first place." Bart grimaced. "Of course, as a fifth son of an earl myself, I understand wanting to strike out in the New World. There should be more opportunities here." He glanced at Susanna and lowered his voice further. "In fact, Mr. Davenport and I have had some discussions. He still has many connections in Jamaica and a respected name in shipping. There could be opportunities for us there. You, me, Nathaniel, and Elizabeth."

Susanna stared at him. "But... But what of Father? We couldn't just..."

"Why not?" Nathaniel asked. "Why should our fates be controlled by his whims? Haven't they already been long enough?"

"Yes," Bart hissed. "Quite long enough." He took Susanna's hand again, holding it between his own. "My dear, your loyalty is one of your best qualities. But the time has come when we must remove ourselves from your father's shadow. With haste."

"He's right, Susie. You know he is."

Tears glistened in her eyes. "Yes." She swallowed hard. "I must check on Grace. Please excuse me."

When she was gone, Bart rubbed his face. "You agree, then? That we shall leave Primrose Isle as soon as this storm and trial are over." He looked up as another shriek of wind battered the windows. "Whatever unfolds, I feel strongly that we must try our fortunes away from your father's influence."

Nathaniel said a quick prayer for Hawk and nodded. "I couldn't agree more."

HE'D SLEPT FITFULLY for a time, and Susanna had returned in the night, the storm still raging, dark circles under her eyes. They didn't speak of their father or Bart's nascent plan. Susanna had always been practical, and while she sometimes needed to brood on an idea for a time, she would accept good sense.

They had simply shared a tired smile, and she'd briefly clasped his hand before again opening *Don Quixote*. Sometime later, the candle guttering, she read:

"I was born free, and that I might live in freedom I chose the solitude of the fields; in the trees of the mountains I find society, the clear waters of the brooks are my mirrors, and to the trees and waters I make known my thoughts and charms. I am a fire afar off, a sword

laid aside."

He couldn't catch his breath. Was this what Hawk wanted, despite his protestations? *A sword laid aside.* If Nathaniel could somehow free him, would Hawk leave piracy behind and build a life with him?

Despite the storm's fury, reminding him that there was no easy path, Nathaniel yearned for fields and trees, clear waters and freedom. And Hawk had confessed it once as well.

"I could find a quiet island. Build a home strong enough to with-stand the summer storms. Fish and farm. Stay close to safe harbor."

"Darling?" Susanna asked. "Are you feeling unwell?"

"No. Fine." *Is he safe now?*

She pressed her hand to his forehead. "Are you certain? You were trembling."

"I'm sure. I… I was thinking of the future."

Susanna squeezed his shoulder. "There's no reason to worry. Father always lands on his feet, and…" She sighed. "Well, you heard Bart. It seems we very well might have another avenue open to us. We shall make the best of it. Mr. Davenport will see you and Elizabeth well settled." She frowned at his silence. "What is it?"

"Elizabeth. I can't marry her."

Susanna stared in clear shock. "Surely you don't find her lack-ing? She has been so steadfast. I know I'm getting ahead of myself, since you've only just met her, really. But when you spend more time with her, I'm certain—"

"It won't matter. I cannot marry her. Susie, I don't love her."

She shook her head with affectionate exasperation. "Well, not *yet.* You've had no time together. Love will come, I'm sure of it."

Nathaniel's throat tightened, along with his chest. "It's impos-sible."

"Why on Earth is that?" Glancing to the door, she went and closed it firmly before returning to her chair and folding her hands. "She is a wonderful match. Practical, to be sure, what with her dowry, but I've grown to love her as a sister already. Truly, she is good and kind. And she possesses a certain…understated beauty." Susanna's brows drew together, her mouth turning down. "You've never struck me as a man whose head is turned overmuch by fancy faces. I hope you don't mean to reject her on superficial grounds without taking the care to really know her."

"It's not that. She is quite pretty enough. I don't care about that."

"Then what is the issue? This has been planned for months. You are promised to each other. Our fathers have agreed." She laughed. "It's not as if you're in love with someone else."

His throat closed completely, and he had to turn his head away from Susanna's sharp gaze.

Her fingers were firm on his chin. "Nathaniel!" She hissed, "What is this? Don't tell me all those times you scampered away to fields and forest it was because you were meeting someone?" A gasp escaped her lips and she pressed a hand to her chest. "Are you pining? Do you have a secret sweetheart?"

"Please," he whispered, barely holding the agony at bay. "I can't tell you." Hawk had left him, yet he couldn't stop hearing his name finally tumble from Hawk's lips. The way Hawk had clung to his fingers, the wild fear in his eyes, all artifice stripped before he allowed Nathaniel to be torn away.

"But you can. Of course you can. Anything, my dear. Tell me. Who is the lady?"

In whom could he confide if not Susanna? His breath stuttered. Without warning, he stood at the precipice. Outside, torrents of rain streamed down, and in the little windowless room they were as alone as they could be—perhaps as alone as they ever would be again.

His sister watched him with concern, her eyes imploring. Before he could talk himself out of it, he stripped away the last vestiges of the disguise he'd worn since they were children.

"There is no lady. I'm a sodomite."

The words hung there as the wind keened. For a terrible moment, as Susanna stared with wide eyes, Nathaniel thought she would abandon him and pretend he'd never spoken at all. Then she sat back, her gaze going distant.

He could barely get her name out. "Susanna?"

"I should have known. I should have seen this. Perhaps I did." She spoke absently, as if to herself.

He had to ask, although his stomach churned, fearing the answer. "I know it's unnatural. A sin. Do you hate me?"

Her gaze snapped to his, and she bolted up straight. "What? Oh heavens. Never." She gripped his hand. "*Never.* You are my brother." Blinking back tears, she said, "More than that. We were always such good chums, weren't we?"

Nathaniel could only nod, his throat too thick for words. He squeezed her fingers.

She swiped at her eyes with her free hand. "All right." She nodded to herself, mind clearly working, digesting this revelation. "Yes. All right." Her face creased. "Do *you* think it a sin? Does it feel like one? To…be the way you are?"

"Perhaps it should, but no. I don't think it a sin anymore. I've accepted it now. I've been this way for almost as long as I can remember, and I wanted to tell you so many times."

"Oh, Nathaniel. Surely you know I would never turn my back on you? Never."

He clung to her hand. "I prayed you would not."

"Certainly not. No, you are my brother, and well… This is a shock. But you are not an evildoer."

"Still, it's not only my mind that's lacking. I'm not a normal man. I never shall be."

"When you were born—" She broke off with a sudden sob, tears overflowing. "I watched Mother die, and I promised God I would look after you. Did I fail you?"

"No! This is no fault of yours, I promise." He couldn't fight his own tears. "No one could have cared for me better, Susie. Thank you." He pushed up, ignoring the scream of pain in his gut, and pulled her into an embrace as they wept.

They were all sniffles and gulping breaths, and when Susanna eased back to the chair, she wiped her cheeks. "All right. Now. Is there someone you…care for?"

Fresh tears threatened as he whispered, "Yes."

"Yes. All right." She laughed, slightly giddy, eyes still wet. "I keep saying that, don't I? I'm sorry. So, this… Well, who is he? Someone from Worthingside? You often spent time in the woods nearest to that estate. Mr. Stanford, perhaps? He was still unmarried last I heard."

"No, it's no one from home. It's… On the ship…"

Her brows shot up. "The merchant ship? I don't recall that you spent time with anyone in particular…" Eyes widening, she whispered, "You don't mean… My God, the pirate ship?"

He nodded. "Captain Hawk."

"The… The captain? The man who took you?" She waited for his reply, mouth agape.

"Yes. I know what you must be thinking—"

"I don't understand. What are you saying? That you… That you and he… With a *pirate*? With that nefarious man?" She gasped. "When you arrived, you were quite bruised. Tell me truthfully. Did he…*ravish* you? Force you to submit to his cruel desires?"

"No, I swear. I wanted it. I lay with him willingly."

"But it's unthinkable! Nathaniel, it's…" Susanna pressed her hand to her chest, lowering her voice conspiratorially. "It's terribly *thrilling*."

His heart skipped, hope blooming amid the dark muck of misery. He waited for her to continue, watching her breathe fast and shallow.

She gave a little gasp, covering her mouth again, as if shocked by herself. She lowered her hand and whispered, "Did you truly…with that pirate captain?"

His throat felt like he'd swallowed gravel, and he sounded like it too. "I did. I was his prisoner, granted, but I chose it of my own free will. He was… I began to know him—the real man behind the myth. I…" Emotion choked Nathaniel. "I began to love him."

"Love?" she murmured, eyes like saucers. "I didn't think… So it's more than simply…" She waved her hand.

"Yes. Much more. There was tenderness and sharing. I'm not sure how to describe it."

"But he stabbed you! You almost died."

"It wasn't him, nor any of the crew. It was Father's messenger. He tried to kill Hawk, and I jumped between them. I couldn't bear to see him hurt."

"My goodness." She fanned her face with her hand. "I feel like one of those terribly fragile women who are prone to the vapors."

He sat with difficulty. "Should I call for someone?" He threw back the blanket, groaning as he tried to swing his legs around.

"No, hush." She urged him back to the mattress and tucked the blanket around him. "I've never suffered from delirium a day in my life. I shan't start now." Exhaling a long breath, she nodded. "All right. You love this man. Does he love you?"

Nathaniel's stomach swooped. *Does he? Am I fooling myself most cruelly?* "I think he might. I want to find out. I must. I want to be with him. Wake by his side, live our days like… Well, like anyone else, I suppose."

She took this in. "I confess it's difficult to imagine. He was so fearsome!"

"It's an act. Most of it, at least. Father forced him into that life by revoking his letter of marque unfairly years ago. And yes, he's committed many crimes. But there is more to him, I swear.

Kindness and longing. He's a man like any other. Everyone sees him as a pirate—"

"Because that's what he is! A killer."

So am I. But Nathaniel could not utter it aloud. If he exposed this truth as well, he'd never be able to look Susanna in the face again for fear of what he'd see there.

"Yes. Without question. Yet I accept it. If that exposes a deficiency in my character, I have to accept that as well. I can't marry Elizabeth. I could never be a proper husband. It wouldn't be fair to her. As unnatural as it may be to desire other men, it *is* my nature. I have made peace with it. I must find a way to have a life where I am not in misery all of my days. Hiding. Alone, even if surrounded by a family."

Her face crumpled. "Oh, Nathaniel. It would break my heart. No, I would never wish that for you. You should have love and comfort and happiness." She sat back and was silent, wiping her eyes.

She was quiet for so long that Nathaniel grew sleepy. He was so easily drained, and he closed his eyes, listening to her steady breathing, her familiar presence a balm. He'd revealed his core and she hadn't turned away.

After a time, she spoke again. "They say it's only about base desires. Two men being together. Venal and depraved. But as I think about it, I remember a case of two men in Guildford who shared a cottage. An accusation was made, and soon it was a scandal. One went to prison, the other the gallows. If I recall, there had been suspicion of them for years. *Years.* I didn't consider it at the time, but why would they have lived together for so long if there was no affection? Granted, plenty of marriages sorely lack it, but they had *chosen* their companionship."

He opened his eyes and found Susanna's full of tears again. She shook her head. "That pirate. Father will see him hanged. And my God, you would be in such danger if the truth were discovered. They could *kill* you for this love."

"I must stop the trial. With him, I was…whole. A worthy man. Powerful in my own way, not stupid and useless. With him, I felt I could do anything. That the world has new possibilities to be unearthed, as sea shells are by the retreating tide. That there is so much more. Unseen, but ever-present under the surface."

He remembered the roughness of Hawk's beard against his face countered with the softness of his lips, the wet slide of his tongue, and how Nathaniel had wished they could kiss forever under the palm trees. How he'd felt utterly protected and cherished in the aftermath of death and destruction.

"But how on Earth will you stop the trial?"

It was a fine question, and Nathaniel fervently wished he had the answer.

Chapter Twenty-Two

NEVER AGAIN.

Those two words echoed, taunting Hawk endlessly in the black belly of the privateers' brigantine. The air was dank in the small hold serving as his cell, and he was almost certain a storm brewed.

Sweat clung to his skin. His leather coat was musty and damp, the chains on his wrists pulled tight, wearing away at his festering skin where he'd uselessly attempted to pry himself loose. His feet had swelled in his boots, and he couldn't have yanked them off if he tried.

He supposed his one consolation was that he wasn't trapped in the bowels of a Royal Navy ship. From what he'd overheard before being locked away, Walter Bainbridge had hired privateers to thwart him. The navy could not be negotiated with, but privateers? Perhaps.

He had no notion of time in the blackness but for the distant bells and occasional delivery of brackish water and scraps of food. Nathaniel's screams of agony echoed in his mind.

Why the devil had he wasted so much time keeping Nathaniel at bay? He should have kissed him every moment he could. Now he never would again, and it tore at him with razor teeth.

Did Nathaniel live? Hawk prayed uselessly to any god listening that he'd survived. That he hadn't died to save Hawk's sorry life.

It played out again and again in his memory: Nathaniel hurling himself in front of that blade, accepting its grievous wound without a second thought.

Hawk hadn't believed he could love again, and in that moment he'd known how wrong he'd been. How deeply love could truly gash, crippling him. He offered bargain after bargain to the universe, promising up anything—*everything*—in return for Nathaniel's safety.

To not know Nathaniel's fate was torture, the misery waking him from fitful bouts of sleep, his heart seizing, lungs frozen. Of course he'd asked for news, and of course he was denied. He hadn't even been told where he was being taken for trial.

And what of the men? He'd drawn the attention of the privateers with explosions and mayhem so Snell and the others who'd survived the battle could escape. He'd stayed with his ship as long as he could, and would have remained to the end if he hadn't been beaten into submission by too many men to fight. *The Damned Manta* might sail again, but without the Sea Hawk.

He laughed harshly, rats scurrying at the burst of sound. The Sea Hawk was dead, at least in spirit, with his body soon to follow. His ending had been inevitable, and Hawk only wished it had not come at Nathaniel's expense. All that for a ransom that meant nothing now.

He should have left Nathaniel aboard that merchant ship with his sister, should have left him to his safe, comfortable future. Stifling and unfulfilling as it might have been.

One night—or day—he awoke hard, craving Nathaniel. In his dream, Nathaniel had reached for him, entreating him to come to bed. Yet Hawk had been unable to move. Now he ached, and not merely to fuck.

He yearned to hear Nathaniel's cries of pleasure. To bring him bliss with mouth and hands and cock. Then to hold him as they slept, breathe him in, close and safe and warm.

God, to kiss him.

The loss should have been like an arm or leg destroyed in battle and then excised. Over the years, several of Hawk's men had suffered this fate, the mangled, useless limb sawed off before it could cause any more damage. An infection could spread to the bloodstream.

That ruined flesh and bone was tossed overboard, abandoned in the ship's wake to be devoured by the creatures of the deep.

Yet Nathaniel refused to be left behind. The loss of him was more than a phantom ache or a hollowed-out chasm. No, it filled Hawk to his very limits, unyielding pressure against his skin, expanding with every breath, choking him.

Hawk wished his own soft, useless flesh would dissolve and leave him made of only pitiless bone.

To love could only be madness.

He'd been so certain he'd learned that lesson after John, but locked away with only rats for company, it was clear he was a glutton for punishment. That Nathaniel had thrown himself into harm's way for Hawk's sake clawed at him, the guilt a living, pulsing creature. He would give anything to change it, to take the pain away and keep Nathaniel unharmed.

Hawk clenched his empty hands. It was foolishness to yearn for a memento he could touch, some token or scrap of cloth or jewelry, Nathaniel's plain-handled dagger, even. Hawk had tucked it in his boot, but it had been confiscated, lost to him now.

There was nothing tangible left of Nathaniel. Even the scratches on his chest—the marks Nathaniel had made when he'd insisted their relationship was real—were gone, his traitorous flesh mending.

Real.

As the days passed in perpetual darkness, Hawk did wonder if it had all been a feverish dream. He knew distantly that his captivity could have been worse. He wasn't tortured, and they shoved in enough water and hard biscuits to keep him alive.

Torment wasn't being trapped in the stinking bowels of the brig, knowing he would soon die. That he could accept. That fate he'd expected for years. It was the idea of living the rest of his miserable life without Nathaniel that was utterly loathsome.

True hell was to love.

WHEN THE STORM hit he wasn't surprised, the portent thick even in the scant air that reached the filth of his cell. He hated not being at the helm, and could only hope the men in charge were able. He had no reason to think they weren't, but as he was tossed from side to side like a child's plaything, he wasn't so sure.

The shackles around his wrists were attached to the wall, and his shoulders burned as he was thrown about. He feared they might be wrenched from their sockets, which of course conjured memories of Nathaniel racing up into the rigging to rescue O'Connell. Fearless and brave and beautiful.

The yearning would have brought Hawk to his knees if he hadn't already been sprawled, powerless in the heaving waves. Squeezing his eyes shut even though he was in darkness, he allowed himself the luxury of pretending he was back in the cabin that had been his only home for so long.

Returned to his bed, Nathaniel sweet and sighing in his arms, their lips meeting endlessly, no words needed.

THEY'D SURVIVED.

And judging by the ship's speed and telltale noises echoing along the hull, they were nearing a harbor and making to drop anchor. Sure enough, sailors came soon to drag him from his cell, pulling and shoving him like an animal. Wrists still shackled, he was barely able to get his feet under him.

The captain, a tall, older man named Taylor who'd styled his graying hair as if it were a wig with curls over his ears, approached belowdecks, scowling. He buttoned his waistcoat. "This is your final port of call, scum. I can't decide which is the worse offense— the piracy or desertion. Suppose it doesn't much matter, given you'll hang regardless. Shame you won't have a bigger audience."

To the crew nearby, he announced, "I'm taking him ashore with the vanguard. As soon as we have our money, we're leaving this godforsaken place."

Blinking in the harsh glare, refusing to bow his head, Hawk shuffled onto the main deck and saw Primrose Isle by the light of day. "Where the fuck's the rest of it?"

Chapter Twenty-Three

THE CRASH REVERBERATED so violently the windows in the drawing room—which were still covered by slapdash boards—rattled. The storm had raged for days, but the sun had finally reappeared.

Nathaniel pushed back his chair at the empty breakfast table, wincing as he stood. He followed the rumble of his father's indistinct shouting, meeting Susanna in the hall.

She drew up short. "Why aren't you in bed? I was about to bring your tray."

"Because I've been in bed quite long enough. I shall go mad if I don't *move*, even if it's only shuffling to the table. And why would *you* be bringing my breakfast?"

She tucked back a loose brown curl, her hair tied in a hasty knot, flour sprinkling her blue silk skirt. "The servants have fled. They waited until the storm abated just enough, and they're gone. Either by sea or into the interior. It doesn't matter which. Not Cecily, thank God. But the others."

"You mean the slaves?"

Susanna's face flushed. "Yes."

"Good."

She smiled. "Yes, I think it jolly well is good. Now we need to abandon ship as well. Bart is talking to Father about Mr. Davenport's plans to return to Jamaica and the opportunities he could provide us." She whispered, "I haven't told Bart that you'll be breaking your engagement. Best to let that…unfold."

He nodded as Father roared at the end of the hall, and Bart stormed from the study to stalk down the corridor, his face an alarming shade of scarlet, breeches and waistcoat splattered with mud.

Bart hissed, "He is being entirely unreasonable! I swear he has gone quite mad. He's still acting as if there's a colony left to govern. He won't go down to see the destruction. Perhaps things would be different if the buildings had been erected with the care necessary, but barely anything is left standing." He rubbed his face, dark circles under his eyes. "On that note, I must return to see what further assistance I can give." He kissed Susanna's cheek and nodded to Nathaniel.

They watched him go, and Nathaniel squared his shoulders. "I'm going to speak with Father."

"Dressed like that? Father will…" She shook her head. "Listen to me. What nonsense. Yes, go speak with him. I'll see about breakfast." She gave his arm a squeeze.

His feet were bare and his white shirt loose, but he'd pulled on clean breeches. When Nathaniel opened the study door, he found his father dressed fully, although one stocking sagged at the ankle and his ridiculous wig was askew.

A bookcase had been toppled in his rage, a casualty that slumped across the far corner, gouging the polished floor. The boards had been torn from the study's windows, likely by Bart, since Father's buckled shoes still shone, not a speck of mud evident.

"What?" Father barked.

There were many things to say, and Nathaniel didn't know how to begin any, so he decided to jump directly into the fray. "Captain Hawk wasn't the first honest privateer you cheated, was he? How many men did you and your corrupt partners unfairly doom to the gallows as pirates so you could seize their ships and cargos for your own gain, lying to England about their worth?"

Walter stared at him for a long moment, stunned, as if the gilt-framed oil painting of some ancestor hunting with a dog at his feet had come to life. Finally he said, "After all I've done to see you home safely, you would interrogate me? I shouldn't be surprised. As ungrateful as ever."

"Answer the question. How many privateers did you cheat?"

Walter waved a dismissive hand. "Privateers, pirates. There's hardly a difference."

"The difference is that privateers are endorsed by the Crown! Given letters of marque to legitimize them. They aid England against her enemies. If you want men to follow England's rules, then you must abide by them as well!"

"These men are savages, as you should well know." He scowled. "Look at the state of you. This is civilization, and you will dress and act accordingly!"

Nathaniel ignored that. "Some men are beasts, yes. But many have been left with no options to make a living. To have any sort of freedom from horrendous conditions, to get paid fairly. Or paid at all!"

Scoffing, Walter said, "Worthless dregs of men. Besides, your argument, if one can call it that, has a fatal flaw: Captain Hawk is a deserter from the Royal Navy." Behind his desk, he snatched up a sheaf of paper and thrust it at Nathaniel. Then his face twisted cruelly. "But you can't, being utterly feeble-minded. Leave this business to the men who understand it. Men with all their wits."

Despite Nathaniel's best efforts to steel himself, the blows landed. He opened his mouth, then shut it again, and Walter sensed blood in the water.

"Shall I read it to you? I'll use small words." He cleared his throat. "Michael Biddle incited a mutiny aboard the *HMS Leaside,* then deserted on the twelfth day of…"

Nathaniel stopped listening to his father, instead rolling the name around in his mind with care, as if the words might break. *Michael Biddle. Michael.*

An angel's name, and if Hawk heard that, he'd snort and say there were only devils here. The pang of longing rocked Nathaniel, and he had to reach out for the edge of Walter's desk.

Lord, to hear Hawk's voice again and feel the rough warmth of his touch. Simply to talk to him, to just *be*, to do anything as long as they were together. Nathaniel would rescue him, no matter the cost.

"And as such, Michael Biddle—" Walter sneered disdainfully, "now known as the notorious pirate the Sea Hawk—should receive no quarter."

Standing straight again, ignoring the dull throbbing of his wound, Nathaniel clenched his fists, thinking of the scars on Hawk's flesh. "A deserter of a navy that enslaved him. You talk of savages—how is our government any better? They stole him from his home and impressed him against his will. Yes, he eventually deserted under a cruel tyrant of a captain after years of service. And despite this, he *still* wanted to aid his country. You destroyed that. He wasn't the first, was he? You lied and stole. You cheated for your own gain."

"Oh, for God's sake." Walter's face reddened and creased. "Enough of this nonsense. What does it matter? This pirate almost killed you, and you argue for his welfare? You truly are a simpleton."

"You forget that I was there. I know it was your man who attacked, waiting for his opening to kill H—Captain Hawk. I foiled his assassination attempt. He had to have known it was suicide. I wonder how you convinced him to do your bidding; what threat you employed. And why you tried to have Captain Hawk killed like that and not in a public spectacle."

"If that bumbling fool Taylor had been on time with the brigantine—" Walter broke off, nostrils flaring. "I had to have a secondary plan in place. The pirate had to die one way or another. I could not be bested by that *nothing* of a man. I had to prove that pirates will fall if they dare cross Governor Bainbridge. I had to be the one responsible for the Sea Hawk's demise." He slammed his fist onto the desk, an inkpot rattling. "I am to be respected!"

"And what of me? If your assassin had hit his target, do you think the pirates would still have released me? Or if they'd realized the ransom was largely counterfeit?"

Walter's cheek twitched, a nervous tic. "It would have been…regrettable. But in war, some losses must be borne."

Nathaniel stared at his father, this stranger in a crooked wig who had loomed so large over his life even from across the ocean. His voice was hoarse as he said, "You're the criminal."

Narrowing his eyes, Walter hissed, "We both know you haven't the wits to understand how the world works. You are my greatest disappointment. To think I was so determined to have a son—" He broke off, swallowing thickly. "I might still have my Margaret if not for you."

Guilt slashed through Nathaniel, anger eager on its heels. "I didn't ask to be born so you could prove yourself a man with a proper heir. Not that there's anything to inherit. You are bankrupt, morally and otherwise."

Ignoring the jab, Walter shrugged. "Temporarily. There is a fortune up for grabs, and you will marry the Davenport girl and acquire it. Her brother is dead, and her father has willed everything to her. Even if the fool returns to Jamaica, as long as you marry the girl, we will eventually have enough to rebuild here. I'll make the Crown see that Primrose Isle is not dead. Davenport's an old man. His heart is failing. God willing, it won't be long until the girl inherits."

"I won't marry her. I don't love her, Father."

Walter gaped. "*Love?* What does that have to do with anything? I know you are an imbecile, so I will explain the situation slowly. Marriage—"

"Fuck you."

Walter jerked, more blood rushing to his face. "My boy, you are treading on thin ground."

Nathaniel shook his head, saying it louder this time. "*Fuck. You.* I won't give up my life for your delusion. You've destroyed this place with your greed. Almost everyone has fled. Susanna and Bart are going to Jamaica with Mr. Davenport. The Crown pulled out the militia weeks ago, Bart told me. There's nothing left. He said the buildings are almost all flattened but for this one and several others. It's over, Father."

The bell at the front door rang distantly, and in the silence following it, they stared at each other. The paper in Walter's hands shook, and he smoothed out the pages on his desk. "I will not accept defeat. Primrose Isle will thrive. So help me, I shall be respected." The bell rang again, and he snapped, "For God's sake, why isn't anyone answering that?"

"Because they've all gone, Father. It is the worst wickedness to enslave people, and I pray they are never returned to you."

A voiced called, "Er… Hello?"

"In here!" Walter barked. "What do you want?"

The messenger appeared in the doorway, a boy of about twelve with a shock of blond curls and mud caking his shoes and trousers almost to the knees. "The pirate has been delivered."

As Nathaniel tried not to sag in relief, Walter clapped his hands once. "Ah! Some good news this morning. Excellent."

"Captain Taylor is demanding his fee, sir. He's taken the pirate back aboard until you deliver it."

Nathaniel eyed his father's pinched face. *My God, he doesn't have it.* His mind whirled. If the messenger relayed that to Taylor, there was no telling what would become of Hawk.

Nathaniel spoke to the messenger. "Please tell Captain Taylor he will be paid in full tomorrow morning. In the wake of the storm's devastation, the governor is occupied assisting his citizens."

With a dubious glance at Walter, the boy nodded and scurried away.

A vein pulsed in Walter's temple. "I do not require your assistance. I am the governor, and my word is law. When I demand the prisoner be handed over, Taylor will do as instructed, or regret it."

You'll revoke his letter of marque too? Without a single redcoat to help enforce your rule? Nathaniel bit his tongue. Let Walter entertain his delusions for the moment.

Walter spoke almost to himself. "Yes, let Taylor keep him tonight, and tomorrow at noon, Captain Hawk shall swing. It will be a historic day for Primrose Isle. We have withstood the hurricane, and we will see the fearsome pirate who has terrorized these seas brought to justice. They said it couldn't be done, that he was some kind of sorcerer. Now the New World will see he is only flesh and blood. Thanks to me."

Nathaniel's feet itched to run to the harbor, but he had to be patient. There was only one thing to do, and he would have to wait for the cover of darkness.

"NATHANIEL?"

"Hmm?" He tried to smile.

Susanna's brow creased, and she swiped at a stray curl, her skin flushed. "You're staring. What's the matter?"

I'm memorizing your dear face because I shall never see it again. "Nothing."

Grace fussed in her arms, but Susanna waved off Cecily. Elizabeth smiled wanly and said to Nathaniel, "Your sister's such a dedicated mother. I hope it comes as naturally to me." She worried a pleat on her full skirt between her fingers, the tight bodice of her yellow dress thrusting up her bosoms. Traces of dirt clung stubbornly to the dress's hem, although she'd tried to clean her slippers. She had to be unbearably hot.

"Mmm," he answered. He belatedly added, "I'm sure you'll make a fine mother," and Elizabeth beamed. Guilt simmered in his gut.

Even in the shade of the house, which had lost most of the tiles from the roof and several windows, the afternoon heat blistered. Still, they dutifully sat at a round table. Bart had brought it out from one of the drawing rooms, since the previous garden set had been snapped into kindling.

The governor's house was inland and on a rise, a view of the sea from the ruined garden stretching out in the distance to the east, away from the commotion of the harbor. From this vantage point, there was only twisted, tangled foliage, a sea of green giving way to blue.

They drank tea and ate day-old biscuits, pretending the island didn't lie in waste around them, that felled trees with gnarled roots didn't litter the property. That the remaining inhabitants of Primrose Isle weren't fleeing, too many buildings blown asunder, the failing colony now clearly irrecoverable.

From a distance, the strident voices of Mr. Davenport and Walter reached them, the words too faint to make out. Elizabeth swallowed thickly and stirred another cube of sugar into her tea with rapid clanks of her spoon. Susanna gave her a sympathetic smile, then raised her eyebrows at Nathaniel.

Yet he couldn't muster any soothing words. Not when they were still pretending that Elizabeth and Nathaniel would marry. The truth seethed on his tongue, eager to fly into the still air amid the cicadas' droning chorus.

I'm a sodomite, and the pirate king fucked me every way you could imagine—and some you likely can't even fathom. I'm going to rescue him and cleave to him if he'll have me. I want to live out my days at his side, because even if they are severely numbered, it will be truly living.

"Is it ever this hot in England?" Elizabeth asked, her voice trembling as another echo of their fathers' fury reached what was left of the garden, even the grass beneath their feet churned to bits.

Susanna and Nathaniel looked to each other, and Susanna leaned over to give Elizabeth's hand a kind squeeze. "No. Summers are very pleasant there."

"We left when I was so young that I can't recall. I should like to visit one day. Although most of all I'd like to go home to Jamaica."

Nathaniel said, "I think you soon shall." *I hope you do, with all my heart.*

Walter's voice rang out. "If there will be no gallows built in time, then we'll hang him from a God-damned tree!"

Susanna's mouth tightened, her sympathetic gaze too much to bear. Nathaniel imagined Hawk aboard the brig for the hundredth time, so close and still out of reach until nightfall. Was he injured? Fed? Had the privateers treated him fairly?

Bile surged into his throat at the thought of Hawk suffering, and he gripped his teacup so tightly he might have shattered it if Susanna hadn't covered his quivering hand with her own, guiding the cup back to its saucer.

"Are you well?" Elizabeth asked, leaning toward him, then shaking her head. "But of course you aren't. It must distress you terribly, knowing that monster is so close at hand."

"It does," he agreed, struggling to keep his tone even.

Elizabeth sighed. "I can't wait to leave this place."

"Nor can I," Nathaniel added truthfully. "I think soon we shall let nature reclaim Primrose Isle."

On his feet, grimacing through a wave of pain in his belly, he gave Elizabeth a stiff bow, then leaned over Susanna to kiss Grace's plump cheek, clenching his fingers to keep from trembling. Susanna watched him intently, and hot tears pricked his eyes.

He kissed her forehead and tore himself away, counting the minutes as the day ticked away more slowly than any he could recall.

There were preparations to be made.

IN THE END, he wore his funeral suit.

It was somehow fitting. Buttoning the black coat over his dark shirt, forgoing the waistcoat, he regarded himself in the tall mirror in the corner of his chamber.

His hair was longer than when he'd left England, curling over his ears now, face dotted with a few new freckles. Any tan he'd acquired had faded during his convalescence, but the freckles remained.

Somehow he appeared older, although he wasn't sure when he'd be able to grow a proper beard. He was too thin, and his weakened, soft muscles cried out for activity. They'd soon have it.

He wished he had trousers instead of breeches, and boots rather than the silly black stockings and buckled shoes, but they would have to do. The most important thing he did have was his father's pistol, liberated from his study when Walter had been busy in the drawing room shouting at Bart to see to the hasty construction of a gallows. Walter was determined to have his spectacle for the few dozen people left on Primrose Isle. For his lunatic pride.

Carefully tucking the pistol into the back of his breeches, Nathaniel reached for his long dark cloak and wrapped it around his shoulders. It made him think of Hawk's coat. The burning to see Hawk again, to smell and taste and hold him, set his head spinning.

He hadn't wanted food at all, his stomach knotted with the wound and nerves, but he'd forced himself to eat bread and a cold chicken leg. He'd need every ounce of strength he could muster.

Staring at himself critically in the flickering candlelight, he weighed whether he was at all capable of appearing intimidating. The cloak helped, but he needed… Ah! He knew just the thing and went in search of a sewing kit.

A short time later, Nathaniel held the needle to the hiss of the candle's flame. Leaning close to the mirror, he tugged down his right earlobe and winced as he carefully impaled it. A spot of blood appeared, and he squeezed the pierced flesh for a minute, then sucked the blood from his fingertips.

The metallic tang tasted of his first kiss, and he closed his eyes, remembering their desperate coupling against the palm tree; how they'd almost devoured each other when their mouths had finally met.

As night fell, he forced himself to stretch out and rest. Waiting. He had a satchel prepared with clothing, medicine, silver candlesticks and cutlery, and a golden snuffbox. He wasn't sure how much Walter had promised Captain Taylor, but surely some gold and silver was better than nothing.

It was near midnight when Nathaniel slipped into Susanna's dressing room with a letter, his candle cutting a swath through the shadows. He placed the letter carefully on the table and opened her jewelry box.

While she hadn't had any jewels of worth left when they'd traveled to the New World, she'd mentioned Walter had insisted that on Primrose Isle, his daughter's ears and throat would gleam with gems and pearls. Lord knew how he'd acquired them.

Nathaniel's heart skipped as her chamber door creaked open. Glancing over her shoulder, she crept in and closed the door behind her. "I've been waiting," she whispered, looking between him and the dresser, face creasing. "You were only intending to leave a note?"

"I thought it might be easier." The ache in his belly from the wound pulsed, and his chest and throat tightened, threatening to choke him. "How did you know?"

"That you would attempt to rescue your…pirate? I know you, Nathaniel. You have always been brave and pure of heart." She frowned. "Yet… Are you…*stealing* from me?"

"No! Well… Yes." He nodded to the letter. "I explained it. I need an earring. And a few of your jewels as payment to the privateer."

Her hair was loose, nightgown slipping off one shoulder. Barefoot, she trod quietly toward him. "An earring? What on Earth are you talking about? You know this is madness. What if you get yourself killed?" She glanced behind her, then to Nathaniel, and back again.

"Please, Susie. If you alert Bart, it will put him in an untenable position. He must remain blameless so you can start anew in Jamaica. I'm leaving, one way or another. I'm embarking on a new life. I must look the part. It's silly, I know. An earring. It feels symbolic, though."

"A new life as a *pirate*?"

"I don't know. All I know is that I must save him. And even if…" The idea that Hawk wouldn't want him after everything was a lead ball in his gut, and he tasted bile, the uncertainty of it all gnawing at his nerves. "Even if it doesn't turn out the way I want, Nathaniel Bainbridge will be dead. I must forge a new path, and you must go to Jamaica with Bart and get out from under Father's thumb. He doesn't care about any of us. Only his own glory. He's gone mad."

"I know. Oh, Nathaniel. But I only just got you back." Her eyes glistened in the candlelight.

He whispered, "Tell me you understand."

Lips trembling, she gave another look over her shoulder at the closed door to her chambers, where Bart snored faintly. Then she took the candle and bent over the jewelry box, putting on a brave face, voice quavering. "Silver or gold?"

His throat was so thick he could barely answer, "Gold."

After several moments, she straightened up and set down the candle on the polished wood dresser. He turned his pierced ear toward her, and she gently inserted a small, simple hoop. "There. You look quite the swashbuckler now."

"Thank you." He barely managed to get the words out.

She inspected her jewelry box. "Here. You must take all of these. I have pearls, and these earrings are ruby. Oh, this necklace as well. And these. None should have been mine in the first place. Father likely cheated them from someone."

"No, I couldn't."

She gave him a sharp look. "Open your pockets. You certainly can. And you will."

He nodded, not speaking for fear he'd sob. They embraced fiercely, and he inhaled her lavender scent, resting his cheek against her soft, wild curls.

Nathaniel told himself it was a luxury most people were never afforded—to know beyond doubt it was the last time he'd see her. They would never meet again in this life barring a miracle, but as he tore himself away and picked up the candle, he said a quick prayer for a merciful reunion in the next.

"I shall think of you always and wish you only happiness." Susanna took a shuddering, wet breath as he opened the door to the hall.

Nathaniel couldn't resist turning for a last look, hating that he could see the tears so clearly on her cheeks even though she stood half in shadow beyond the candle's reach. "And I you. Always." Tears streamed down his own face.

He plunged into the corridor with his satchel, carefully slinging it over his shoulder, wincing as pain lanced through his stomach. Downstairs, light shone from beneath the door of Walter's study, and Nathaniel realized the rumble he heard was his father's drunken muttering.

Part of him wanted to fling open the door and savor the look on Walter's face when he discovered his only son was running away for a life of sodomy with an enemy, and that the Sea Hawk would escape his noose if Nathaniel had his way.

But of course Walter wasn't worth it—not even a little bit—and Nathaniel slipped into the night without a word. Hawk was waiting, and he was all that mattered.

Nathaniel was barely out of the crumbling house's shadow when a figure appeared out of the foliage, hissing, "Mr. Bainbridge! It's me, Alan O'Connell." He had a pistol in hand, and the blade of his sword gleamed in the moonlight.

"Mr. O'Connell?" Nathaniel stared at him, not quite believing his eyes.

Alan grinned. "I'm no phantom, I assure you. I'm relieved to see you alive, let alone up and about." He held out his hand, and Nathaniel clasped it.

His wound already tugged, but he ignored it. "I'm glad to see you too. You've come to rescue the captain?"

"Aye. Mr. Snell and some of the others are waiting in the hills west of the harbor while a few of us get the lay of the land. We stole a little sloop in Hispaniola. Left her on the windward side. Have two dozen crew, barely enough men to sail her, but we had to try and save Captain Hawk. He gave himself up so we could escape those privateers."

Nathaniel's pulse raced, but he breathed easier. "I was just going to attempt a rescue of my own, and I'm extremely glad to hear I won't be doing it alone. Hawk is aboard the privateer ship anchored in the harbor."

"All right, you leave it to us. The captain would never forgive us if you were hurt again. We'll swim out and board them before they know what's happening."

"But surely you'll be vastly outnumbered?"

Alan grimaced. "Aye, but we'll have surprise on our side. It will have to be enough."

"But if it's not?" The idea of Hawk being so close at hand and then killed in some bloody brawl was unbearable. "I have another idea. A better one, I wager. Less violent."

"It'll be up to Mr. Snell."

"I'm sure I can convince him. Perhaps with your help?"

"Aye, if it saves the captain and our own skins, I'm all for it." Alan glanced at the house. "Are you planning on coming back?"

Imagining Susanna and her babe inside, Nathaniel swallowed hard over the lump in his throat. He shook his head and plunged into the night.

Chapter Twenty-Four

As if he'd never left, Hawk huddled in the dank hold in total darkness. His leather coat and boots would possibly never dry, but it seemed fitting Captain Hawk would wear his costume to the end.

Damp, with rats scurrying, it was a foretaste of the grave save for the lack of earth and wriggling insects. The ship creaked at anchor, the quiet indicating it was likely still night. He wondered again if Nathaniel was safe and well, or even alive.

Please live. Please.

It seemed Walter Bainbridge didn't have the privateer's fee, so the noose would wait for another day. Hawk slept fitfully, no longer sure of when he woke or dreamt.

When there were shouts and splashes and the thudding footsteps of multiple men, he wasn't sure if he'd slept again and now it was morning, his execution at hand—assuming Bainbridge had satisfied Captain Taylor.

But when he was hauled up to the main deck once more, stars blanketed the heavens. He peered around, discerning two tense groups at odds. Some of the privateer crew were scattered around the deck, weapons outs. Captain Taylor stood in the center, eyeing a cluster of men by the starboard rail.

In the silvery light, Hawk immediately recognized the slope of Snell's shoulders and his barrel silhouette. His heart soared. And yes, there were some other crewmen he knew alongside Snell, and—

Knees almost giving out, Hawk knew joy more powerful than he'd dreamed possible. He opened his mouth to call out to Nathaniel, then snapped it shut lest he put him in more danger.

His heart was a war drum, steady and true, ready to shake off the hands gripping him, ready to gnaw through their fingers with his teeth if it meant getting to Nathaniel, who *lived*.

Nathaniel stood dressed in black, a cloak concealing his body. His curls were tousled, and something glinted in his ear. His face seemed pale, but Hawk wasn't sure if it was the moonlight or the effects of the stabbing. He itched to hold him and feel for himself that Nathaniel was whole.

"All right," Captain Taylor said. "I'm listening." His hand rested on the hilt of his sword. One of the gray curls over his ears sagged, and he'd shrugged on his jacket without a waistcoat, likely hastily woken in his cabin.

Instead of Snell speaking, Nathaniel did, and Hawk could only gape as he said, "I'm Nathaniel Bainbridge. I understand my father owes you a considerable sum."

"That he does. Twenty-five thousand pounds, a quarter of your ransom. Told him I wouldn't take less to go after the Sea Hawk." Taylor glanced over. "Although he isn't quite so fearsome now." Some of the privateer crew sneered and laughed.

Hawk ignored them, willing Nathaniel to look his way. Yet Nathaniel remained focused on Taylor, who asked disbelievingly, "Are you in league with these pirates now, Bainbridge?"

"I am. I've had quite fucking enough of my father and his lies." He spoke with such conviction—and profanity. Pride washed through Hawk with a wave of *want*.

Nathaniel went on, shoulders squared and head high. "We have your twenty-five thousand pounds, as well as some gold and silver from my father's house as a bonus. All we ask is Captain

Hawk's return, and safe passage away from this cursed place."

If this was a dream, Hawk would gladly sleep forever. He held his breath as Taylor pondered it. Nathaniel added, "My father doesn't have two shillings to rub together. If you throw in your lot with him, you will end up with nothing." He motioned toward land. "You can see for yourself the colony has collapsed."

Taylor grimaced. "Indeed."

"My father will cheat you, just as he did Captain Hawk, who was once a privateer like yourself until his letter of marque was revoked without warning for a fabricated offense. To avoid his debt, my father will not hesitate to do the same to you."

Taylor shifted from foot to foot, his face pinched.

Nathaniel added, "Surely there has been enough blood spilled thanks to my father? And surely you do not think our numbers are this small?" He indicated Snell and their little party, O'Connell and Grady and a few others.

Taylor's crew shuffled uneasily, peering out at the water and squinting toward land. Taylor's lips thinned. Then he said, "Let me see the money. And this silver and gold."

It was done quickly after that, a sack handed over and inspected, and Hawk unshackled and shoved toward his men at the rail. Toward his lover. He cupped Nathaniel's face all too briefly, thrilling at the feel of him warm and whole and *alive.*

He ached to kiss and hold him and say a hundred other things he didn't have words for, but they weren't safe yet. "Thank you," he murmured. It would have to suffice as he turned his attention back to Captain Taylor, who motioned dismissively.

"All right, off with you!"

Snell said, "Our ship is a small sloop. *Essa's Fate.* If you think to engage us once we are aboard her—"

"I think to get the hell away from this place and back to chasing Spanish treasure ships." Taylor sneered. "Begone."

Soon they were over the rail and down into a small launch,

rowing back to shore. Nathaniel sat in the bow with too many men squeezed between them for Hawk to reach him. Hawk grabbed an oar and rowed vigorously.

After splashing ashore, Hawk and Nathaniel fell into step together, and Hawk took his hand, squeezing his fingers, aching to kiss him and feel for himself that he truly was healed and alive and not a ghost.

Nathaniel bumped their shoulders together and whispered, "We must stay on our guard."

Indeed they must, and Hawk forced his attention to navigating the debris-laden path past the eerily quiet harbor where only a few small ships remained.

The colony's buildings had largely been flattened, water still flooding ditches, trees uprooted. Whatever citizens remained likely huddled in the church, which had been made of stone and withstood the storm, or several other larger buildings visible in the distance at the edge of the jungle forest.

Hawk kept a careful watch, ready to tear out the throat of anyone who would dare stand in their way.

Then there appeared such a man indeed.

Walter did not come upon them by surprise, instead announcing his presence with a tumult of footsteps and cursing, practically frothing at the mouth as he shouted, "So it is true! You are in league with these villains!"

Hawk gripped Nathaniel's hand, and with his other, reached to O'Connell, who passed over his sword wordlessly. A large, curly-haired man who had yanked on breeches under his nightshirt followed after Walter, slip-sliding down the slope in bare feet.

Nathaniel called, "Bart, I'm all right. Please stay back." To Hawk, he added, "He is my sister's husband. A good man. Please don't harm him."

Hawk nodded and regarded Walter Bainbridge, meeting him

face-to-face for the first time since that fateful day in the Admiralty Court. Although he wanted to lunge and strangle the man with his bare hands, he nodded and calmly said, "Good evening, Governor."

Bainbridge's wig had come off, and his dark hair stood up at all angles. He was fully dressed, his shoes and stockings splattered with mud, eyes wild. "I thought the messenger had gone mad when he said my son had been spotted down here. My son, who has barely been out of bed, my son—" He broke off, mouth dropping open as his gaze fell to where Hawk and Nathaniel held hands, their fingers entwined.

Nathaniel said, "Your son, who is a sodomite. Your son, who is in love with Captain Hawk, and who is leaving to make a life with him."

All the soft places in Hawk that had festered when he and Nathaniel had been parted now healed in an instant, his heart singing as it hadn't in decades. He squeezed Nathaniel's hand, which trembled slightly.

Walter stared agog, and Bart did too. Then Walter snapped his jaw shut, growling and baring his teeth in a grimace. "You little imbecile. You have always been weak and useless. I should have seen that you were an abomination as well!"

The words still echoed as Hawk let go of Nathaniel and surged forward, toppling Walter to the ground, his boot on Walter's chest and sword at his throat.

Walter screamed, "Bart! Do something, you coward!"

Hawk glanced at Bart, who shook his head, backing up. To Nathaniel, he said, "Take good care, brother."

"I will. You as well. Susanna and Grace."

Bart nodded, then gazed down at Walter, squirming in the mud. "As you sow, so shall you reap." With that, he turned and marched back up the slope, disappearing into the torn foliage.

It would be so easy—to skewer Bainbridge with his blade, to

slice open his throat, or even cleave off his head and display it on a pike for all to see, a reminder that the Sea Hawk should never be crossed.

Yet as he watched the man whimper and curse in the mud, at turns defiant and petrified, his fury faded. This man who had changed the course of Hawk's life, whom he'd hated with such passion for so long, had destroyed himself.

"You're not worth another moment of my time." He lifted his blade, and Bainbridge sputtered, perhaps at the affront to his pride.

Hawk wanted to spit on Walter's face, but he only stepped back and reached blindly for Nathaniel's hand, breathing deeply when Nathaniel's warm fingers grasped his.

At Hawk's side, Nathaniel peered down at Walter. "Goodbye, Father."

In their wake, Walter screamed curses, left behind in the muck and utterly ignored.

IF ANY FURTHER alarm had been sounded, it didn't echo across the water as *Essa's Fate* headed west, what was left of the colony fading from view. The sails of Captain Taylor's ship could be seen in the distance, and they kept a wide berth.

"Can it really be over?" Nathaniel whispered, standing at the stern. He held Hawk's hand, his thumb rubbing idly, gaze on their wake and the ripples soon swallowed by the sea. He'd already stripped off his stockings, shoes, and cloak.

"We are due some winds of fortune, wouldn't you say?"

Nathaniel's eyes met his, a tentative smile on his lips. "I would say yes."

Content to let Snell issue orders, Hawk struggled for the right words. "I... I feared you dead. On account of saving my sorry hide. It was…" His chest tightened. "Never do anything that foolhardy again. Promise me."

Nathaniel shrugged. "No. It would be a lie. Because I'd risk anything for you."

Hawk swore softly, yet he couldn't deny the warmth flowing through him. "Clearly, since you did it again tonight."

"I knew you might turn me away—may still. But I had to try. I couldn't live with the regret. At least this way I'll be certain."

"Turn you away? From rescuing me from execution? Surely you don't think me daft in my old age."

Nathaniel's gaze skittered away. "No. I mean from…this. Us. You said…"

Hawk gripped his fingers. "A great many things." With his free hand, he lifted Nathaniel's chin, brushing his knuckle over the little divot, not needing to see it to know exactly where it was. "Lies for what I believed to be your benefit. On that island, when I saw you soaked in blood… I only wanted to protect you. Now here you are, safeguarding me once again. Why? After everything I've done."

"I meant what I said. I love you." Nathaniel gazed at him and hitched his shoulders. "Maybe it's dunderheaded, but I've never been that bright."

Hawk let go of his hand to cup Nathaniel's cheek. "You are no man's lesser. Least of all mine. And the love I have for you is like no other."

He was filthy and had to smell foul, but Nathaniel kissed him deeply, sighing into his mouth, tugging him close, eager and precious and perfect. The salt tang in the air filled Hawk's nose, coupled with a scent that was all Nathaniel—musky sweetness.

Then Nathaniel stiffened with a gasp. Before Hawk could ask, he assured him, "It's nothing. The wound is just a bit sore." With a rueful smile, he ran his fingers over Hawk's cheek. "Don't look so guilty. As I said, it's nothing. You must keep kissing me."

Although Hawk didn't think his regret and shame over the stabbing would ever abate—even now, he had a vision of Nathaniel throwing himself into the blade's path—he could only acquiesce, bringing their lips together once more, tongues softly exploring.

"Ahem."

Hawk and Nathaniel turned to find Snell a few feet away, wearing an expression that comprised exasperation, fondness, and resignation. He asked, "Where would you like to be delivered?"

Hawk raised an eyebrow. "You aren't going to try and convince me to stay on as captain?"

Snell snorted. "I know a lost bloody cause when I see it."

Hawk smiled. "Should we say Port Royal? Nathaniel and I can gather supplies and plot our course. What is left of the ransom?"

Snell huffed. "Well, we'd already suspected most of it was counterfeit, with the true thing on top for good measure. Mr. Bainbridge here confirmed it."

"Ah," Hawk said. "And the payment to Captain Taylor?"

"Mostly counterfeit, with the true thing on top for good measure."

They all laughed, and Hawk reached out his hand. "Thank you, my friend. For everything. And for letting me go."

Snell clasped his palm. "Well, if you insist on this nonsense, who am I to stand in your way?" He yanked him into a rough embrace, and Hawk gripped him, throat too tight to speak.

Clearing his own throat, Snell stepped back and eyed Nathaniel. "I suppose the young lord has proven himself." He offered his hand, and Nathaniel took it, grinning. Then Snell spun away, grumbling and returning to the helm to bark more orders.

God, Hawk would miss him.

When Hawk and Nathaniel turned back to the rail, the waxing moon caught the gleam in Nathaniel's ear. Hawk ran his finger over the golden hoop as Nathaniel huffed out a laugh and said, "I thought I should look like a proper pirate to rescue you."

Hawk followed his gaze over the ship's wake, their only pursuers a flock of birds swooping across the night sky as one. "And rescue me you have."

Gently, Hawk eased the earring open and removed it from Nathaniel's ear. Nathaniel laughed again. "Does it look that foolish on me?"

Wordlessly, for none could do justice to his affection, Hawk removed his own earring and fit it into the fresh hole in Nathaniel's ear. Mirth vanished, Nathaniel watched intently as Hawk then slid the gold hoop into his own ear.

Nathaniel was silent for so long Hawk thought perhaps his meaning wasn't clear—that he wanted no other by his side for the rest of his days. But then Nathaniel leaned in and captured Hawk's mouth in a breathless, fervent kiss that said everything.

Chapter Twenty-Five

Hawk would never harm Nathaniel again, but in that moment, he missed the days when Nathaniel would quiver in his presence. It was useful in getting his way. He tried again, barking, "When did it start bleeding?"

From where he stretched out on the pallet in the captain's cabin, Nathaniel shrugged in the faint light. "Sometime during our escape."

"Sometime," Hawk echoed, cold, clammy sweat trickling down his spine in the humid dawn.

Once he'd been certain they were far enough from Primrose Isle and weren't being chased, Hawk had tugged Nathaniel belowdecks with a smile, eager to get cleaned up and lock themselves away. His visions of fucking until they reached Port Royal had vanished when he'd felt the dampness on Nathaniel's dark shirt, his hand coming away a terrifying red.

"Why didn't you tell me the wound had reopened?" he demanded.

"There was nothing you could have done about it. I didn't want to trouble you with it."

"Mr. Pickering! Get the fuck down here!" Hawk marched to the door to go drag down the surgeon, whom he'd seen amongst the remaining crew. "You will stay here. In bed. Yes?"

Nathaniel made a show of contemplating it, and if Hawk's

heart wasn't in his throat, he'd have been charmed. Nathaniel said, "I wouldn't really call this a *bed*. More a hard hammock, the way it's suspended by ropes."

Hawk pressed his lips together and did his most fearsome *loom* over the small cabin's pallet. "I will throttle you if you so much as sit up."

"Well, then I *will* need the surgeon." Nathaniel had the nerve to smile. "It's really nothing."

"'Nothing' apparently does not have the same meaning for you as it does me." He narrowed his eyes at the blood that had soaked through the bandage on Nathaniel's stomach. "This is not nothing! It's because of me you were injured in the first place."

Nathaniel lifted his hand, and Hawk took it, sinking to his knees. Nathaniel said, "Because of my father. Not you." He squeezed Hawk's fingers. "I'll rest now. I promise. Go get the surgeon, and I'm sure he'll agree that all is well."

Hawk kissed him quickly and stood, or else he'd dally too long against those lips, the novelty of their mouths meeting still too fresh. He couldn't imagine tiring of tasting Nathaniel or hearing his sighs.

"Would you give me a real smile?" Nathaniel asked.

"What?"

"There is a vast difference between that hollow grimace and a true, joyful smile. I have charted them."

Warmth bloomed despite his worry. "Have you?"

"Mmm. I've become an expert."

"Well, I'll be sure to smile genuinely as soon as the bloody surgeon tells me there's nothing to fear."

Fortunately, O'Connell arrived with Mr. Pickering, who clucked his tongue as he examined Nathaniel while Hawk paced the tiny cabin, contemplating ripping out said tongue with his bare hands. O'Connell shot him nervous glances.

"He should recover nicely," Pickering pronounced. "I'll restitch the wound, and as long as you rest and eat to keep up your strength, you'll be good as new."

"Oh, he'll rest." Hawk glowered. "Trust me."

"Thank you, Mr. Pickering," Nathaniel said, rolling his eyes.

"Any rum on hand?" Pickering asked. "This will hurt."

After Hawk rummaged through the cabin, Nathaniel had several slugs and nodded. "Ready. Any more and I might puke it up." He caught Hawk's eye and gave him a secret smile.

Sinking to Nathaniel's side, Hawk took his hand and told Pickering to be fucking careful. As the surgeon worked, Nathaniel squeezed tightly, his lips pressed together, nostrils flaring. But he withstood it, as he did everything, and Hawk bent to kiss his forehead, not caring what Pickering or O'Connell might think.

When Pickering had finished and left, Hawk sat on the pallet with Nathaniel's head pillowed in his lap. He twisted a curl around his finger, listening as O'Connell recounted what he knew of the rest of the surviving crew, who had splintered in their desperation to escape. O'Connell leaned against the nearby desk, clearly weary.

Hawk said, "They'll probably show up in Port Royal or Nassau before too long."

"Perhaps you could gather them together again." Nathaniel slurred his words a bit. "Form another crew with another captain."

"I suppose. Mr. Snell is capable but reluctant. The captain is a hard act to follow. How do you top the Sea Hawk?"

Nathaniel shrugged against Hawk's knee. "Maybe you don't. Maybe you re—re—resurrect him."

"I think that's enough rum for you." Hawk laughed. "And no, I'm quite finished with piracy."

"Not you. Someone else. It's the name that matters, isn't it? The repudiation? No. Reputation? I mean, most people don't know what Hawk actually looks like."

O'Connell swigged from the bottle of rum. "Aye. Some men

in the New World have seen him, but plenty haven't. Wouldn't that be something? The Sea Hawk flying again."

Hawk found himself smiling, and he thought Nathaniel would deem it a real, proper smile. "He escaped from Primrose Isle before its demise. Who can say where he ended up? Who can say what he truly looks like?" He raised an eyebrow at O'Connell. "Perhaps he grew his hair."

O'Connell blinked. "You mean…" He looked over his shoulder and back again. "*Me?*"

"The thing that would identify him beyond a doubt would of course be the tattoo across his chest. A sea hawk in flight." Hawk gently eased out from under Nathaniel's head so he could shrug off his leather coat. He nodded to O'Connell, holding it out.

O'Connell watched him with wonder, unmistakable excitement lighting his eyes. Hawk swung the coat over O'Connell's slimmer shoulders. He was a little shorter as well, but still a big enough man. Besides, it didn't matter. He would do quite nicely as long as he held himself proud and aloof. Powerful.

"Me?" O'Connell asked. "A legendary pirate? Oh, I'm not sure."

Hawk eyed him critically. "Well, you'll have to work on your attitude to pull it off. It's all in the performance. Be confident. Be certain in every single thing. Betray no doubt or fear."

"Alan, just think of what Hawk would say in a given situation, then sneer and growl. Should do the trick," Nathaniel said. "I've determined that three-quarters of piracy boils down to theater."

O'Connell's smile faltered. "I wonder what my Nuala would think if she could see me now."

Hawk didn't particularly care who Nuala was and what she might think on any given subject, but Nathaniel gave O'Connell a kind smile. "She'd be smitten all over again. And you know, there's one more thing Captain Hawk is famous for."

"Of course, the flag," Hawk answered. "Reproduced easily

enough."

A sly smile tugged at Nathaniel's lips. "Yes, that. But also his boots. The golden tips announce his arrival without his having to say a word."

"I suppose they do." After a deep breath, Hawk could only smile as he bent and pulled his feet free of the warm, worn leather once and for all, handing them to O'Connell, who took them dubiously.

"Not sure they'll be a good fit on me. In more ways than one."

Hawk shrugged. "Then you and Mr. Snell find someone they fit like a glove. The Sea Hawk shall rise again like a phoenix."

Later, as Nathaniel slept, Hawk went to the desk and purloined the previous captain's log, smiling at the creak of the battered spine. There were books on a shelf, and he squinted at the titles.

Nathaniel had mentioned his sister had begun reading him *Don Quixote*, and perhaps Hawk would pick up where she'd left off in the morning.

How he'd missed his books and the sturdy captain's log, its hefty feel in his hands, as if his life had meaning and worth through its pages. He went through the earlier entries from the former commander of *Essa's Fate,* a Captain Rosewater.

The scribblings were nothing of note, but he read through them all dutifully, then left a blank page and dipped the quill. On the next fresh slate of white, he began a list.

First item: *New boots.*

"So there's no one left on Primrose Isle?"

"Don't think so. Perhaps some of the slaves who made a run for it. Navy sent a ship to take anyone else left to Kingston. And that crazy fucker of a governor burned his own house down in a fit of anger. They had to shoot him in the end."

"Yes, I heard he tried to attack the officers who came to fetch him. Went into a frenzy and had to be put down."

"Aye, he's dead."

Good.

Over his cup of beer, Hawk watched Nathaniel in the murky lantern light. Their table was tucked away in the corner, and Hawk sat with his back to the narrow room and one hand on his new cutlass. Nathaniel kept his eyes intently on the men, who were two tables away with an empty one in between.

"Oy, Smitty!" one of the men called, drawling after what was likely quite a bit of ale or rum, "You was there, wasn't you? Primrose Isle?"

"Aye," Smitty answered in a low rumble. "Good riddance to it. Even before the hurricane, it was destroyed by fucking incompetence."

The serving girl came to take Hawk and Nathaniel's plates—empty now but for chicken bones—and refill their cups. Hawk took a gulp and wiped his mouth free of any froth, still surprised to find his face clean-shaven. His hair was getting longer, and no one had recognized him. Of course he kept his head down when they ventured out in Port Royal.

"Did the governor really burn down 'is own house?"

Smitty laughed harshly. "He did. With his daughter and her babe inside and all. Fortunately her husband got them out."

Nathaniel's knuckles were white on the handle of his cup, and he let out a shaky breath. Would this Smitty recognize Nathaniel if he happened to look over? Few people on Primrose Isle would have seen him, since he'd been recovering in bed.

Hawk debated whether it would be better to stay put or to leave and possibly draw attention to themselves. Nathaniel took a sip of his beer, Adam's apple bobbing, and Hawk did as well. They'd stay for the moment.

"Wasn't there some business with his son and the Sea Hawk? A kidnapping and ransom?"

Hawk's breath stuttered. One of the men answered, "Heard Captain Hawk killed the whelp."

"No, no." This was Smitty. "The boy was injured, but he helped the pirate escape from the island before Bainbridge could execute him. That's what led to the fire. The governor was so enraged he lost his faculties completely. He knew the end of the colony was upon him, and I suppose he decided to destroy what was left rather than accept defeat."

"So where's the Sea Hawk now? His ship was sunk, wasn't it?"

"I heard they were able to salvage it. *The Damned Manta* just might sail again. Talk of taking it up the coast toward the Cape."

"So he's alive?"

"Oh yes. You know Jones, from the *Madeline?* He saw Captain Hawk in Nassau gathering a crew."

"I wonder if the boy's still with him?"

"Well, I heard…"

Another few men stumbled over to the next table, and the chatter became an impenetrable din. Hawk sipped from his cup and watched Nathaniel. "I'm sorry."

Nathaniel sighed and sipped his beer. "I suppose I should be, but as long as Susanna and Grace are safe with Bart to care for them, that's all that matters. Bart may be penniless, but he's strong and brave. A good man. I can only assume Elizabeth and her father also escaped. I hope so."

"Ah, your betrothed. You haven't spoken of her." Ridiculously, a kernel of jealousy expanded in Hawk's gut. "What was she like?"

A smile tugged at Nathaniel's lips, as if he could see right into him. "Very pleasant. Steadfast. Would have made an excellent wife and mother. I'm sure her future will be bright with a husband more suited for her. And away from that doomed colony. It's a shame my father bungled it so completely. Tried to bend it to his will instead of using its natural strengths."

"I'm sure there's some biblical parable about a river's flow advising against that very thing."

He laughed softly. "I'm sure there is."

"Any regrets?"

Nathaniel met his eyes directly, steady and clear and honest. "The life I've chosen isn't designed for regret. Even if it were—no." Beneath the table, he hooked his foot behind Hawk's calf, the leather of their new, unadorned boots rubbing together.

"Shall we retire to our chamber?" Hawk asked.

The inn was on the outskirts of town. Port Royal had been decimated by an earthquake some fifteen or twenty years earlier, and more recently, by fire. But it remained a pirate haven, a squalid sprawl of commerce and vice, huts and tents by the water and some buildings crowding narrow streets.

Their room was barely bigger than the bed, but the door locked and they'd been left alone for weeks. It was heaven.

"A swim first," Nathaniel said.

He frowned. "It's getting late. You've had a long day and—"

"And I'm ready for a swim. You know the surgeon said I'm healed." On his feet, he shimmied out from the table. "I'll make you a concession and walk to the stream instead of running. Unless you want to race?"

Grumbling, Hawk pushed back his chair. "We'll walk."

The stream in the swath of forest outside Port Royal was just deep enough that Hawk had to tread water instead of stand. Their clothes were left in a pile on shore. In the night breeze with stars standing guard, the cool water was wonderful.

Nathaniel swam literal circles around Hawk, his strokes long and smooth, clearly delighting in flexing his muscles. "I shall never take being whole and healthy for granted again," he proclaimed, kicking water into Hawk's face, apparently by accident since he didn't laugh or gloat.

Hawk didn't answer as he wiped the water from his eyes, and another wave of it broke over him as Nathaniel surged in close, his hand on Hawk's shoulder as he asked, "What's the matter?"

Hawk blinked at him. "I'm not fucking crying. You keep splashing me!"

"Oh! Sorry." Of course, he took that opportunity to scoop water directly into Hawk's face, then darted out of reach with a laugh that turned into a shriek as Hawk caught his foot.

It devolved from there.

When they returned to shore, out of breath and still tussling half-heartedly, Nathaniel wrapped his arms around Hawk's neck. "Fuck me. I know you want to."

"Of course I want to. But—"

"No buts." He took Hawk's hand and pressed it over his belly. "See? Still intact. Doesn't hurt at all, I promise. Come on." On tiptoes, he whispered in Hawk's ear, "It's been so long since I had your cock."

Hawk traced the two-inch scar with his fingers. In the light of day it was pink now instead of red, and it would continue to fade until it was a silvery-white band. It was hard to believe such a small mark could be all that was left of so much damage.

He took a deep breath, releasing the knot of fear in his chest. "You tire of my hands? My mouth?" he teased.

"Never." Nathaniel took Hawk's prick in hand and stroked, blood rushing to it. "But I miss this. Don't you long to bury it inside me? So very deep, where no other man has been?"

Grunting, Hawk cupped Nathaniel's arse with his other hand. "Where no other man shall ever be."

"Ah, but if you don't fuck me for fear of hurting me, perhaps I'll have to get someone who will." Nathaniel bit his lip, a teasing light in his honey eyes. "Do you think I'll find a volunteer?"

With a growl, Hawk crushed their mouths together. He was

about to tumble Nathaniel to the grassy bank when children's voices rang out, approaching along the stream.

He and Nathaniel groaned and parted, tugging on their clothes and boots over wet skin. Hawk grumbled, "Shouldn't they be in fucking bed?"

"As should we." Nathaniel's eyes twinkled. "I'll see you there."

Before Hawk could stop him, Nathaniel raced off into the night, and all he could do was follow.

Some fifteen minutes later, panting after taking the stairs up to their room two at a time, Hawk found their door unlocked. He didn't release the new knot of worry until he beheld Nathaniel on the bed, waiting by candlelight.

Naked, curls still damp. Legs spread, slowly jerking himself, the pot of oil open on the battered bedside table, his cock gleaming.

After turning the lock, Hawk stripped off and crawled between Nathaniel's legs, leaning over to kiss his scar, then the oily tip of his cock. Nathaniel trembled and moaned, "Please."

Bending Nathaniel's legs and pushing up his knees, exposing his pretty little arse, Hawk spread him and buried his face between his cheeks, licking into him, reveling in the musky taste and scent, a hint of the fresh stream water remaining.

He wriggled and poked with his tongue, taking moments to suck at Nathaniel's rim and spit into him as Nathaniel's cries echoed in the small room, drifting out the open window.

"Oh, please. I can't... It's too much. My darling, I want to come with you inside me."

How could Hawk resist such a plea? He oiled his cock and eased in, both of them groaning, Nathaniel's head tipped back, arse clenching around Hawk. So tight and beautiful. "Oh fuck," Hawk muttered.

Nathaniel's heels dug into Hawk's buttocks. "I can take it. Give it all to me."

Powerless to refuse him anything, Hawk shifted more weight to his arms, planted on the lumpy mattress beside Nathaniel's shoulders, and pushed the rest of the way home. "I never want to stop fucking you."

With a glorious little laugh, Nathaniel lifted his head and pulled Hawk down for a wet, filthy kiss. His breath was hot on Hawk's lips. "You shan't. I won't allow it. You feel so wonderful inside me. You'll just have to fuck me until the end of time."

"I bear a charmed life." He eased back and thrust deeply.

On a moan, Nathaniel laughed. "Let us hope it turns out better for you than poor Macbeth."

Kissing him between smiles, Hawk fucked Nathaniel slowly, pleasure building with each stroke, fire licking through his veins until words were lost and only grunts and gasps remained. Sweat beaded on their skin, the slap of flesh filling the still air, a building crescendo.

Nathaniel clutched at Hawk's shoulder, neck, then his cheek. Their eyes locked, he whispered, "Michael."

Hawk could only cry out as he spilled, the sensation sweeping through him something beyond pleasure or physical completion. It was soul-quaking, leaving him stripped utterly bare—seen, *known,* and vulnerable, trembling as he filled Nathaniel with his seed.

He was scraped raw, and a distant part of him shouted to retreat and fortify. But Nathaniel kept hold of his face. "Stay with me," he commanded.

Hawk kissed him, enclosed by his warmth and light, shaking with another pulse deep inside him, a willing prisoner. As the shudders trailed away, he squeezed a hand between them and took hold of Nathaniel's shaft.

Only three strokes were needed before Nathaniel spent, sticky and wet on their skin, pretty cries escaping his lips. He grasped at Hawk, quivering through his release before exhaling, a perfect curl dipping over his damp brow.

Pressing kisses to that fevered skin, Hawk stayed inside him, loath to break their connection even though he must be heavy and Nathaniel was almost folded in half, ankles in the air. Nathaniel wrapped his legs around him, giving no quarter.

When their sweat cooled, Hawk withdrew so they could rest on their sides, legs tangled and facing each other. It was strange how the bed didn't rock, no constant creaking of wood and splash of water. He supposed he'd grow used to it.

Quietly, he asked, "How did you know?"

"Sorcery, of course."

"Ah. I thought as much. A sea nymph after all." He traced his finger over the tip of Nathaniel's nose.

"I like it. Michael. An angel's name."

Heart skipping to hear it again after so many years, Hawk waggled his eyebrows. "Only devils here."

Nathaniel's peal of laughter brightened his face. "I knew you'd say that! I knew it."

He had to huff. "Am I so predictable?"

"Only to me." Nathaniel kissed him, tongue sliding inside deep and slow, and Hawk surrendered with a sigh.

"I don't deserve you," Hawk whispered when their lips parted. "These past years, some of the things I've done…"

"I forgive you."

He had to smile. "I don't think England would be so swift."

"England kidnapped you." Nathaniel reached to sweep his hand over the scars on Hawk's buttocks. "Imprisoned you in her navy. Treated you most foully. And then my father tried to strip you of your freedom once again. I'm glad he's dead."

They kissed fiercely then, bodies entwined, and Hawk knew that no matter what he deserved, he would keep hold of Nathaniel and never let him go.

They eventually slept, although some time later, Nathaniel

began fidgeting so much Hawk groaned and cracked an eye open. "What? Are you uncomfortable?" A thought occurred, and he was suddenly wide awake, pushing up on his elbow. "Are you in pain?"

"No, no. Just thinking." On his back, Nathaniel took Hawk's hand and pressed it to his belly, the scar still intact.

He exhaled and flopped back down, shifting onto his stomach so he could keep his hand anchored on Nathaniel. "Thinking can wait for morning."

"Mmm. Go back to sleep."

Closing his eyes, Hawk tried for at least thirty seconds. Then he asked, "What are you thinking about?" He wished he could read Nathaniel's thoughts as well as Nathaniel seemed to discern his.

"Where we'll settle. We have Susanna's jewels to ease our way, but where shall we go?"

"Mmm. We need to find a safe place where England has no sway and will never come knocking."

"Is that all? Should be easy."

He chuckled, kissing Nathaniel's shoulder. "Undoubtedly."

As Hawk started to drift back to sleep, Nathaniel bolted up, knocking his hand loose and nearly stopping his damn heart. "Of course! I know the perfect place."

Wide awake again, Hawk rolled onto his back. "All right. Where?"

"It will take a great deal of work, but we have nothing to lose and everything to gain."

"Sounds promising. Care to enlighten me further?"

A grin lit Nathaniel's face. "Yes. After we fuck again. There's so much lost time to capture."

Smoothing his thumb over the divot in Nathaniel's chin, Hawk laughed. "I've created a monster."

"Indeed you have, Michael." He straddled Hawk's hips and pressed kisses to his chest, tongue teasing his nipples and making his cock stir, hands roaming.

His heart soared. "Still can't figure out what the fuck you'd want with an old pirate like me."

Nathaniel raised his head. "I want…" He seemed to ponder it, a little furrow between his brows. Then he shrugged. "Everything."

"Is that all?" He drew Nathaniel's face up for a slow, fathomless kiss. By God, Hawk—or perhaps even Michael Biddle, resurrected—would give it to him.

Epilogue

P ERHAPS THE DAY would come when Nathaniel tired of racing along the windward beach each morning as the sun rose, then again in the evening as it swooped back to Earth and beyond. But after three years, that day wasn't even a flicker on the horizon.

Clad only in his worn, comfortable trousers, he dug his feet into the wet sand. Sweat trickled down his bare chest, his skin now a tanned color he hadn't imagined possible so long ago in England.

He brushed a stray curl from his eyes and waved to their neighbor Juan, who was emptying crab traps by the shore before night fell. The haul appeared excellent, and Nathaniel looked forward to the soup he and Michael would make with their share.

Juan called, "I'm going to Hispaniola for supplies. Shall I check for a letter at the post office?"

Nathaniel slowed, answering, "Yes, please!"

Juan was originally from Spain and was one of the trusted few who had joined Michael and Nathaniel's endeavor at creating a peaceful enclave. Some in their motley community were escaped slaves, others colonists disillusioned with England—not to mention France and Spain. Their island accepted newcomers rarely, and only through strict referral.

Nathaniel wondered if Juan would also bring back rumors of the Sea Hawk's latest exploits liberating rich English ships of their cargo. Whether it was Alan O'Connell or another successor, Nathaniel wasn't sure, but it comforted him in a way he couldn't explain.

Giving Juan another wave and running on, Nathaniel thought of Susanna's careful script. Although words still bedeviled him, he liked to look at them and smell the faint whiff of lavender on the pages.

Her happy letters were addressed to a Mr. Nathan, with instructions to be held until pickup at the post office. Michael would read them aloud as many times as Nathaniel asked, without complaint.

Nathaniel had first written her two years ago with only the general address of her name and the city of Kingston, Jamaica, but the missive he'd dictated to Michael had found its way to her.

Juan and his son only went for supplies every four or five months, but Nathaniel cherished the glimpses into Susanna's prosperous life, with two children now and Bart excelling at Mr. Davenport's shipping company. Elizabeth had married and was with child, and Nathaniel was glad of it.

Toes digging into the warm sand, legs burning pleasantly and arms pumping, Nathaniel breathed the briny air deeply. He turned onto a path past explosions of flowers, vibrant orange, red, purple, pink, and white. Like sunsets captured in leafy form, appearing delicate, yet in truth hardy and uncompromising.

Soon he neared the house he and Michael had built. It was constructed of the island's toughest trees, the ones that bent but didn't break during storms, roots remaining strong and sure, burrowed deep into the ground.

There was a carpenter named Dejen amongst their collective, everyone working together for a quiet, peaceful life. Dejen had taught Nathaniel so much, and he learned more each day.

He and Michael hadn't been able to resist building the house on a hill so they could wake to the vista of the sea's endless embrace each morning. The house sat on a plateau, and was constructed of only two rooms: one for their bed with windows that opened to the salty air, and the main room with a hearth, table, and kitchen.

It was all they needed, the privy tucked away in the shade a bit downhill by the forest's edge—but out of range of falling coconuts.

The hilltop was a good vantage point for Michael and his spyglass as he surveyed the horizon every few hours, all directions visible from the hill's crest farther up from the house.

There were other lookouts on the island as well, and a weapons store. If the time came, they would be ready. But forgotten as they were, Nathaniel didn't worry overmuch.

There Michael stood, at the top of the hill, and Nathaniel slowed to a walk up the grassy slope. Feet bare, Michael too wore only his trousers. He kept his hair cut to his chin and pulled back into a little knot, and a trimmed beard shadowed his dear face again.

Nathaniel didn't know how he could stand it in the heat, choosing to keep his own cheeks smooth in summer even though he was finally able to grow a proper beard. In winter, although it was rarely *cold,* he'd let it fill in again.

Passing their house and garden, Nathaniel made a note to pick the tomatoes, which thrived in the sun. He glanced at the coconut trees in the shady grove on the edge of the forest. Yes, the new fruit would be ready soon.

The island wasn't well suited for commercial agriculture, but their family gardens thrived. Chickens clucked in a pen, and the dairy cow eyed Nathaniel dispassionately as he passed, flicking her tail.

Nathaniel knew Michael charted his approach, although he still surveyed the sea. With a contented sigh, Nathaniel wrapped his arms around Michael's waist from behind, their bare skin sticking together.

He went up on tiptoes and kissed the shell of Michael's ear above Susanna's gold hoop. The legendary Sea Hawk's golden earring remained at home in Nathaniel's ear. "Horizon still empty?"

"Blissfully so."

"Mmm."

"How was your run? Seemed like you enjoyed it."

"Michael, you're supposed to be looking out there, not spying on me." Nathaniel pressed his cheek to Michael's warm shoulder.

"It was only for a minute. Or two. Perhaps five." He lowered the spyglass and pushed the top half into the bottom. "You can't blame me. I was thinking about how I'll fuck you tonight."

A coil of desire unfurled in Nathaniel, and he rubbed his still-soft cock against Michael's arse. "Were you indeed?" He lightly raked his nails over Michael's hairy chest, blindly tracing the edges of the sea hawk's wings.

With all the pleasure they'd shared, he hadn't imagined it could remain so vital as time passed. Michael's prick was thick and unyielding, yet his kisses were often gentle with affection and tenderness. Hard and soft at once, he plundered and worshipped Nathaniel's body in the same breath night after night. Day after day.

Nathaniel said, "We'd better get to it. I want to hear more of how Mr. Milton's Adam and Eve are getting on. You must be up before the sun to catch those fish, and I'll have a long day building the new room on Maria's house. We're almost done. The children will love having the extra space."

Michael snorted. "Maria will too, undoubtedly."

"Yes," he laughed, spinning Michael around and pressing close. "Well, you certainly *have* been thinking about fucking me."

Michael dug into his pocket and pulled out two globes of yellowish fruit. "Sanaa discovered a little grove on the other side of the island. It seems a type of plum." He held them out, trying not to smile too much.

Heart skipping, Nathaniel took one. "A plum? Is that so?" The first bite was a little bitter, but the second had a burst of sugar. The third was mixed with the tang of Michael's kisses, and Nathaniel sighed into him, all thoughts of fishing and carpentry and anything else at all floating away on the sticky-honey breeze.

With sweat and steady toil, their little community thrived amid the wildflowers and rocky outcroppings, the sandy coves and climbing vines. It was no longer known as Primrose Isle, or by any name at all. They simply called it home.

THE END

About the Author

Keira aims for the perfect mix of character, plot, and heat in her M/M romances. She writes everything from swashbuckling pirates to heartwarming holiday escapism. Her fave tropes are enemies to lovers, age gaps, forced proximity, and passionate virgins. Although she loves delicious angst along the way, Keira guarantees happy endings!

Discover more at:
keiraandrews.com